Rita Bradshaw was born in Northamptonshire, where she still lives today. At the age of sixteen she met her husband – whom she considers her soulmate – and they have two daughters and a son and two young grandsons. Much to her delight, Rita's first attempt at a novel was accepted for publication, and she went on to write many more successful novels under a pseudonym before writing for Headline using her own name.

As a commited Christian and passionate animal-lover Rita has a full and busy life, but her writing continues to be a consuming pleasure that she never tires of. In any spare moments she loves reading, walking her beloved, elderly dog, eating out and visiting the cinema and theatre, as well as being involved in her local church and animal welfare.

Rita Bradshaw's earlier sagas, ALONE BENEATH THE HEAVEN, REACH FOR TOMORROW, RAGAMUFFIN ANGEL, THE STONY PATH, THE URCHIN'S SONG, CANDLES IN THE STORM and THE MOST PRECIOUS THING, are also available from Headline.

Always I'll Remember

Rita Bradshaw

headline

First published in 2005
by HEADLINE BOOK PUBLISHING

First published in paperback in 2005
by HEADLINE BOOK PUBLISHING

8

ISBN 978 0 7553 0623 7

Typset in Bodoni by
Palimpsest Book Production Limited,
Polmont, Stirlingshire

Printed and bound in Great Britain by
CPI Antony Rowe, Chippenham, Wiltshire

Headline's policy is to use papers that are natural, renewable and
recyclable products and made from wood grown in sustainable forests.
The logging and manufacturing processes are expected to conform to
the environmental regulations of the country of origin.

HEADLINE BOOK PUBLISHING
A division of Hodder Headline
338 Euston Road
London NW1 3BH

www.headline.co.uk
www.hodderheadline.com

This book is dedicated to my precious little furry baby, Jessie-Peg, who was so much more than a dog and who won the hearts of everyone who knew her.

Peg, your amazing understanding, love, quirky little ways and utter devotion have left a void which can never be filled. You were so very brave at the end and fought so hard to get better, but it wasn't to be.

You had my heart in your little paw from the minute you came into my life, and I know I had yours.

Always, *always* I'll remember.

Acknowledgements

I draw on so many sources I can't name them all, but special thanks for some of the background to this book which features the magnificent work of the Women's Land Army must go to *War in the Countryside* by Sadie Ward, *The Wartime Kitchen and Garden* by Jennifer Davies, *Wartime Women* edited by Dorothy Sheridan, and *The World at War 1939–45*, Readers Digest.

Prologue
1921

The tall, golden-haired woman standing at the kitchen window eased the collar of her blouse as she stared out into the mean little backyard. The February day was a raw one and a thin coating of ice covered the thick snow outside, but inside the kitchen the range was glowing, the smell of fresh bread pervaded the air and it was as warm as toast.

'Let him come.' The words were breathed on the air and trembled in the silence broken only by the regular ticking of the wooden clock on the mantelpiece. He had to come now the coast was clear.

It was ten minutes later when she heard the backyard gate creak and her heart began to race. She put the loaf of bread she'd just fetched out of the oven onto the kitchen table and turned to face the scullery, smoothing down her apron as she did so.

The big man who entered the kitchen through the scullery door a moment or two later was good-looking in a rough-hewn way, and as his eyes went to the woman he didn't smile. She stared at him for a second before saying, 'Hello, Ivor.'

He nodded, rubbing his hand across his mouth. 'I told Raymond I'd make sure I brought the coal in and check if there's anything you want while he's on this trip, you just having had the babbie an' all.'

'Did you? That was kind of you.' Her voice was soft, almost teasing, and the thickly lashed blue eyes were laughing at him. 'Well, there is something I want. Can you guess what it is?'

'Don't start that.' It was said on a groan. 'We can't go back to that, we agreed—'

'I didn't agree to anything. You were the one who said we couldn't when I was expecting, but I'm not expecting any more, am I?' She glanced over at the small wicker basket in front of the range which held a tiny occupant who was sleeping soundly. 'She's over six weeks old now and I've missed you. Haven't you missed me?'

'We can't,' he repeated, but more weakly now. 'We never should have in the first place. Damn it, I don't know how it all came about. She's your sister, for crying out loud. Don't you feel any guilt or shame?'

'Do you?'

'Aye, I do. By, I do. It keeps me awake half the night, if you want to know.'

'Poor love.' She reached up and undid the bun at the back of her head, releasing the golden cascade of silky hair which fell about her shoulders, enhancing the deep blue of her eyes and the pearly tint to her skin. Holding out her arms, she said, 'Let me make it all better. I guarantee you'll forget all about it in a little while.'

He swallowed, shaking his head. 'I promised meself it wouldn't happen again.'

'Promises are like piecrust, made to be broken.' As she spoke she walked past him and into the scullery, returning a moment later after she had slipped the bolt on the back door. He was standing exactly where she had left him and he hadn't objected to her locking the door. She smiled. 'I love you,' she said softly, 'and we're not hurting anyone, are we? No one knows. No one will ever know. And you *have* missed me, I know it. She's never done any of the things we did, has she? I could tell. I bet she never even lets you keep the light on.' Her smile widened, showing small white teeth. 'There's fresh sheets on the bed.'

'What about the babbie?'

'She's not been long fed, she'll sleep for a couple of hours or more.' Her voice was triumphant.

He made no reply but stood looking at her. It had started to snow again outside, fat white flakes blowing against the kitchen window and sliding down the glass to collect on the ledge. 'Why?' he asked quietly. 'Why me?'

She looked straight at him, the blue of her eyes very clear and bright. 'I've told you,' she said. 'I love you.'

'But Raymond's a good man.'

'Perhaps I don't want a good man, perhaps I want a bad one.' She was laughing at him again.

'You've got to take this seriously.'

'Oh I do, Ivor. I promise you I do.' She wasn't smiling any more. 'I love you and I can't live without you. Is that serious enough?' She undid the top two buttons of her blouse and as his eyes went to the soft swell of her breasts, she said, 'Tell me you love me.'

'What?'

'Say you love me more than her.'

He said nothing, staring at her as though in bewilderment and after a second she walked over to him and put her arms round his neck. Standing on tiptoe she pressed her lips against his. His arms tightened after a few moments as she'd known they would, and when she drew back to look into his face, she whispered, 'You will, one day. You will say it.'

And then she led him out of the room, into the hall and up the stairs . . .

PART ONE

Abby
1937

Chapter One

'So tonight's the night you're going to tell her, eh? You couldn't see your way clear to wait till I'm away on the high seas and out of reach of her temper?'

He didn't mean it. Abby Vickers grinned at her father and pushed him with her elbow as they walked down the hot dusty street, one of many hot dusty streets which made up the hub of the north-east town of Bishopwearmouth. Her da knew how her mam was with her when he wasn't around. She couldn't remember how old she had been when he'd warned her mam he'd do for her one day if the beatings didn't stop, but it had been after her mam had sent her flying across the room and she'd caught her head against the fender. She touched the small scar on her brow just below her hairline, a memento of that incident. Since then her mother hadn't laid into her when her da was home from sea, but he was away an awful lot.

'I only heard I'd got on the course today, Da, and it starts this Thursday. It's been oversubscribed, the letter said, that's why there was a delay.' Abby's voice held the lilt of excitement. 'But I got in, Da!'

'Course you got in, me bairn. I wouldn't have expected anything else. Even them airy-fairy types at the technical college recognise a little gem when they see one.'

'Oh, Da.' Again she pushed at him, her smile widening. 'You just put all your details on an application form and send it in.'

'Aye, but you said there was a bit where you had to tell them all about yourself and why you wanted to go on the course.'

'Aye, there was, and like I said, I put down I'd been saving for ages and that I didn't want to work in a factory all of my life.'

'There you are then, that'll have clinched it. Shows a bit of backbone, you see.' And his eldest bairn had plenty of that. Raymond glanced at his daughter who, at the age of sixteen, was already showing signs of a beauty that would take a man's breath away in a few years. The last remnants of puppy fat were fast disappearing from the still slightly childish face and body, and the thick wheat-coloured hair and large, heavily lashed brown eyes were an unusual contrast. She'd shot up since her birthday in January too; he reckoned she must be at least two or three inches taller.

This last thought caused Raymond to tweak the long plait falling to below his daughter's shoulder blades as he said, 'You'll soon be taller than your mam, lass, the rate you're growing. I thought you was going to take after my side but I could be wrong.'

She grinned at him again, her round face alight. From her first day at school when two older girls had pointed out she was small and fat like a beer barrel and had made her life a misery for months, she'd become acutely aware of her shape. Even after she had gone for them one day and in the ensuing fracas ensured they didn't pick on her again, she had remained sensitive to the fact that she was tubby and the smallest one in her class. But that was changing at last. It was almost as if reaching sixteen had triggered some magical change and she couldn't be more grateful.

'So . . .' As the two of them turned off Silksworth Row, continuing past the bottom of the tramway depot and into

8

Rose Street, Raymond said, 'How you going to put it to her then, lass? You know she'll kick up blue murder.'

Abby nodded, her bright smile fading. Her mother had raised the roof two and a half years ago when she had said she wanted to stay on at school rather than leaving at fourteen, and she had found herself installed in the pickle factory in the heart of town before she could blink.

She was lucky she had the chance of a decent job, her mother had ranted. Any other girl would give her eye teeth to be set on somewhere, with unemployment so widespread, and what did she want with learning anyway? It was no good to a lass. She ought to be down on her bended knees giving thanks to a mother who would take the trouble to go and see an old acquaintance – who also happened to be forewoman at the factory – to ask for work for such an ungrateful little chit of a daughter.

Abby hadn't gone down on her bended knees. Instead she had argued in vain for her point of view to be heard, and the result had shown itself in a bruise across one cheekbone which had still been faintly visible when her father returned from sea some two weeks later. But it had all been too late by then. She had been forced into the noisy, hot, smelly confines of the pickle factory, where the days were long and exhausting and most of the time you couldn't hear yourself think. The stench of onions was ingrained in hair, skin, nails – a stench which no amount of scrubbing in the old tin bath in front of the fire would remove – and her eyes were constantly irritated, causing them to weep and feel raw. But it was the mind-deadening quality of the job which was the biggest cross to bear.

Abby looked at her father's profile. 'I'm not staying on at the factory a day longer than I need to, but I won't leave until I've finished the shorthand and typing course and got another job. She'll have to be content with that.'

'Hinny, the day I witness your mam being content about anything'll be the day Father Finlay says hello and God bless you.'

Abby giggled, her hand going over her mouth. Her da was awful the way he was about the priest, but then the Father wasn't very nice to her da, saying he'd burn in hell's flames and always going on at him to repent and join the one true faith.

She supposed the priest had to try and convert her da. It was his job in a way – if you could look at it as a job, which you probably couldn't. But Father Finlay didn't have to be so – the word which sprung to mind was nasty but she didn't dare use it about the priest – so dogmatic, did he?

As a child the priest's visits to her mother had made her feel physically sick, worrying herself silly about her da not being a Catholic and taking Father Finlay's dire warnings about the state of her da's immortal soul to heart. It was only when she started work at the pickle factory and heard the chit-chat among the workers at lunchtime that she had begun to think differently, and question – if only in her heart – whether the priest was always right. There were all the missionaries and people like that who weren't Catholics for a start, she just couldn't imagine the same God who sent His Son to die for the sins of the world consigning them to hell's flames along with ordinary men and women who just happened to be Protestants or Hallelujahs or whatever.

'If I were you I'd tell her when we're having a cup of tea after the meal. That way the others can skedaddle with full bellies if they need to.' Raymond had stopped a couple of houses short of their front door, his voice low, and as Abby stopped too she nodded her reply.

The grim terraced street was full of bairns making the

most of the dying sunshine, playing hopscotch, swinging on a rope secured to the iron lamp post or playing marbles in the gutters. Abby knew full well her sister, Clara, wouldn't be outside. In spite of being only four years old, Clara would be inside doing chores their mother had set for her. And Wilbert, a year younger than herself but who'd been working a forty-seven-hour week at Austin's shipyard for the last twelve months, would be expected to do his quota when he got in from work. She didn't know what their mam did all day given the amount of chores that awaited them all when they got home of an evening. Her da was the luckiest one, he was away out of it on the sea for most of the year.

This last thought prompted Abby to say, 'It was nice of you to meet me out today, Da. You been to the shipping office?'

'Aye. You know me, lass, a week on dry land and I've just about had me fill.'

Abby knew it was her mam he'd had enough of but she didn't comment on this, merely saying, 'When do you sail?'

'First thing Thursday morning.'

'How long will you be gone?'

'Two or three months.'

Her heart sank but the training of years prevented it from showing in either her face or voice, and she reminded herself for the umpteenth time that it could be worse – Wilbert could have chosen to follow their da onto the ships and then it would have been only herself and Clara at home with their mam. She had felt pleased but guilty when Wilbert's childish dislike of the sea had grown the older he'd become; her da would have loved his only son to work with him, but for herself she felt only overwhelming relief that Wilbert was staying put. It wasn't just that the pair of them had some good cracks together, or that it was nice

11

to have a man around for some of the heavier jobs like bringing in the sacks of coal or taties, more that Wilbert, with his sunny, relaxed nature, kept an uneasy peace in the house some of the time. Mind, even her brother wouldn't be able to pour oil on troubled waters this night.

Her shoulders instinctively straightened at the thought as though she was already doing battle with her mother, and a battle it would be. She knew it. Her mam was as determined to keep her working in the pickle factory as she was to escape it. It would be seen as a personal insult that her daughter had had the temerity to save what she could from the two shillings doled back to her from her weekly wage of ten and ninepence, solely in order to produce the fee needed for the shorthand and typing evening course at the technical college.

'Well, lass, the fish'll be biting at the dead man's finger if we stay out here much longer. The sooner we're in, the sooner dinner'll be on the table and the sooner you can get what needs to be said off your chest. Ready?'

'Aye, I'm ready, Da.' As ready as she would ever be when a confrontation with her mother was looming. No one, not Wilbert or even her da, knew how her stomach knotted and how bad she felt when her mam was on her high horse about something or other. But she couldn't say nothing and let her mother gallop roughshod over her like the rest of them did. It was just not in her somehow. Her mam said she was an awkward little madam and too big for her boots, and maybe she was, but she couldn't help it.

As always, Abby's spirits dropped as she approached the house. Heavy starched lace curtains hung at the windows, the front door knocker was shining and the front step had the smart cream-edged finish which said the occupant was diligent with the scouring stone. She hated that

12

step. She sometimes spent half an hour or more stoning the surface before her mother was satisfied it was done, and then the next minute someone trod on it with muddy boots or the grime and dust of the street settled again. It was pointless. She didn't intend to ever stone her step when she was married and she didn't care what the neighbours said.

For some reason the thought strengthened her, enabling her voice to sound quite perky as she opened the front door and called, 'We're back, Mam.'

There was no reply but she hadn't really expected one. Quietly now, she and her father hung their coats on the brown pegs along one wall of the hall and walked past the front room door which, as always, was closed, and into the kitchen at the back of the house.

Number 12 Rose Street comprised four rooms and a scullery, being a two-up, two-down terrace with a privy in the backyard. The brick-built lavatory was their own but they shared a wash house and a yard tap with number fourteen. Her mother's sister lived in this house with her husband and four children and Granda Dodds, who had been bedridden for years due to an accident at the shipyard just after the influenza had taken his wife in the winter of 1928. Abby loved her mother's father and she knew the irascible old man loved her; she'd also known from a child without a word being said that this was not the case between her granda and her mother.

'You're ten minutes late.'

Nora Vickers did not look at her husband and eldest child as she spoke. She lifted a large casserole dish out of the oven and placed it on the steel shelf at one side of the range, then began to slice a large loaf of new bread into thick slices. Clara was busy setting the table with cutlery and dinner plates, and the sisters exchanged a swift smile

13

before Abby said, 'Da met me out of work and we got talking.'

'Got talking! Nice to have the time to waste to talk.' It was said with contempt.

Abby's father shook his head in warning and Abby bit back the hot words hovering on her tongue and followed him through into the scullery. A tin dish half full of water and a tablet of carbolic soap were standing on a small table under the narrow window, next to which hung a towel from a nail driven into the brick wall. As they were drying their hands they heard Wilbert's voice, and a moment later the tall, gangly figure joined them in the scullery. Smiles were exchanged but not a word was spoken as Abby and her father went into the kitchen and took their places at the table. Wilbert followed a moment later, rubbing his damp hands on his trousers.

As her mother ladled out the first plate of meaty stew and dumplings from the dish beside the range, Abby said, 'Shall I help you with those, Mam?' and rose from her seat.

'Bit late for any help.' It was sharp. 'You stay where you are.'

It wasn't until they had all begun to eat, helping themselves to shives of bread from the plate in the centre of the table, that Nora broke the silence. 'Did you get a ship?' she asked, without looking directly at her husband.

'Aye.' Raymond ate a large piece of dumpling, chewing slowly and swallowing before he added, 'We sail Thursday.'

If anyone had been looking at Nora they would have seen her stiff frame relax slightly, but no trace of this came through in her voice when she said, 'How long will you be gone this time?'

'Couple of months, maybe three.'

Let it be three. Three months free of the irritant of having to look at him, to feed him, to lie with him. How could she ever have thought herself in love with this useless windbag of a man? It was a question she had asked herself numerous times over the years, and the answer was always the same: I was young and silly and swept off my feet by his looks and manner. He'd been so charming and handsome then – he still was handsome, but his attractiveness had long since failed to hold any appeal.

All her pals had been mad on the small but personable sailor. When he had singled her out, her head had been turned, it was as simple as that. But she had paid for her vanity a thousandfold and would continue to do so – unless the sea claimed him. This thought made her uncomfortable – not the idea itself because it was by no means a new one, but the fact that it carried an ever increasing yearning with it.

Nora glanced round the well-stocked table, her gaze moving to the shining range a moment later. She worked her fingers to the bone keeping them all fed and the house like a new pin, and not a word of appreciation, she thought bitterly, yet her fat lump of a sister was like a pig in muck and everyone thought she was wonderful. Her next words followed on from this train of thought. 'Did you know next door have just got a new wireless?' She looked straight at her husband for the first time since he had entered the house.

'What? A wireless? No, I didn't.'

'Strikes me Audrey would have been better spent putting the money into the house. Her curtains are a disgrace and there's holes in the lino and dirt an inch thick on the mats. Filthy hole.'

Raymond's hand moved stealthily under the tablecloth and tapped Abby's knee in silent warning. His daughter was sitting bolt upright, her face flushed with indignant colour. 'Ivor made their old set donkey's years ago,' he said mildly. 'Likely it gave up the ghost.'

15

'What's that got to do with anything?'

'It's their choice how they spend what comes in. I don't suppose they're doing too badly with Ivor and the three lads back in work now all this talk of war is making the powers that be windy. You can't fight a war without ship-yards.'

'War. Huh.' Nora tossed her head. 'Ten to one nothing will come of it and they'll be back on short time or the dole before you can say Jack Robinson. And what good will a new wireless do them then, eh?'

He'd known something had got her goat from the minute he had walked in but he'd thought it was him and the lass coming in together – she never had liked it that Abby thought a bit of him. But it was her sister and this damn wireless. By, she was a bitter pill, was Nora. He bent his head to his meal without saying anything more, pushing his plate from him when he was finished.

This was the signal for Abby to rise to her feet and gather the dirty plates and dishes together. She took them through to the scullery where she placed them on the table next to the tin dish ready for scouring later. She returned to the kitchen, took the kettle off the hob and swilled the big brown teapot with a little hot water to warm it before thrusting the kettle into the heart of the flames to bring the water to the boil. Once the tea was mashing she busied herself bringing the milk jug, sugar bowl and cups and saucers to the table, her heart thumping a tattoo all the while. It was only when she had poured everyone a cup of tea, Clara's being mostly milk with a little sugar to sweeten it, that she took a deep breath and said, 'I've some news, Mam.'

'You? You've got news, you say?'

Her mother's tone made Abby's heart beat still faster. 'Aye. Good news.' Just say it. Don't make a big thing of it, just spit it out. 'I applied for an evening course at the technical college, shorthand and typing, and I heard today I got in.'

Her mother's eyes were unblinking as she stared at her.

Wilbert smiled. 'Well done, Abby. When did—'

Abby cut across him, the look on her mother's face causing her to gabble. 'They had to turn some people away because they had too many for the one course but I got in, so that's good, isn't it? Thursday and Monday nights I've got to go, every week till Christmas, then if I pass the exams I can go on to the next stage and—'

'How long have you been planning this?'

'What?' Her mother's voice had been so quiet it took a moment for the words to register, and then Abby said, 'For-for months,' hating the fact she had stuttered. 'Ever since I left school, I suppose,' she added more strongly.

'And where do you think the money's coming from to pay for it? Thin air?'

'No. I—'

'It's out of the question. There's an end to it.'

A swift rise of anger suffused Abby but she forced herself to say calmly, 'It's all paid for. You have to give the money when you apply and then they return it if you don't get in. That's what the lady in the office said.'

'You gave her the money?' Nora rounded on Raymond so quickly she took everyone by surprise. 'How dare you put her up to this!'

'It wasn't Da,' Abby protested, her tone vehement. 'I saved up.'

'Saved up? Oh, of course you did.' Nora nodded her head, her tone vicious. 'It must have been easy with all them pounds and pounds you're earning. Do you think I was born yesterday, girl?' And then, as a thought hit, she said, 'You had a raise you haven't told me about?'

'You know I haven't. You have my wage packet each week with the slip still in it. Like I said, I've been saving, right from when I first started at the factory. It's taken me a long time but—'

'Then it's a pity the money's been wasted because you're not going.'

Abby was stumped for words for a second; there had been a grim finality to her mother's voice.

Raymond had been quietly sipping his tea but now he inclined his head towards Wilbert and Clara who made themselves scarce. Then he faced his wife.

'No need to get on your high horse, Nora,' he said. 'There's no reason why the bairn can't do this if she wants to. She'll still be working at the factory in the day, after all.'

'Oh you, I might have known you'd take her side, encouraging her to think she can go behind my back like this. Well, I won't have it, I tell you. It's all right for you, you're not here for the best part of the year and it's me who has to do everything.'

'Don't start that tack. Through the worst of the Depression you were damn glad I wasn't in the mines or the shipyards like them lot next door, now then. You still collected me wage from the shipping office each week and you wanted for nowt, so think on. Trouble with you, Nora, is that you've got a short memory when it suits you. Half of Sunderland were starving and your own sister among 'em. And while we're on the subject, if them poor blighters next door want to buy a wireless after the misery they've been through for years I, for one, don't begrudge 'em it.'

'No, well, you wouldn't, would you! You've never been able to see further than the end of your nose.'

It was with visible effort that Raymond controlled his

18

temper. He took a deep breath before he said, 'This isn't about you an' me, it's about the bairn and this notion she's got to try her hand at something different.'

'And I've said I'm not going to have her gallivanting off here, there and everywhere. I need her here helping me in the evenings.'

'I've paid for it and I'm going, Mam.' Abby looked straight into her mother's eyes. 'I'll still help in the house but I'm doing the shorthand and typing two evenings a week.'

'You are not, madam, so think on.'

The brown gaze did not falter. 'I am.'

Nora now rose from her seat, coming to stand in front of her daughter. Her voice low, she said, 'You'll defy me then? Is that what you are saying?'

Her mother's eyes were cornflower blue and her face heart-shaped. All Abby's friends at school had thought she was lucky to have such a pretty mam. Why this thought came into her head at that precise moment she was not sure, unless it was the way her mother's face had pulled tight so she didn't look pretty at all. Abby jerked to her feet, pushing back the kitchen chair with her legs. She had seen the look in her mother's eyes, the look that always accompanied a ringing slap across the face, and in spite of her father being home she knew her mother was incensed enough to go for her. For the first time in her life it made her angry rather than afraid. She hated her mam. It might be wicked and against everything Father Finlay preached, but she did.

She took a deep breath. 'Fanny Kirby at the factory, her lodger's just done a moonlight flit and he only paid three bob a week for his room,' she said loudly, as though her mother was in the scullery rather than right in front of her. 'And she likes me, Fanny does.'

She saw her mother's eyes widen for a split second. 'You threatening me, girl?'

'No.' Normally by now she would be backing away from the intent in her mother's face but tonight there was fire in her belly. Her dream, her lovely dream of getting out of the factory and working somewhere where the air was clean and sweet, of doing something she liked, was not going to die. She wouldn't let it. And her mam needed her at home. Only the two of them knew just how much she needed her – all the ironing, cleaning the range from top to bottom every week, scouring out the privy every other day and doing the kitchen from top to bottom every second Saturday, besides the everyday cleaning and washing and seeing to Clara. All that on top of giving her mam most of her wage each week. Her mam would be a fool to let her go and, whatever else she was, she wasn't that. 'I'm not threatening you, I'm saying I'm going on the course whatever happens.'

Abby saw the indecision in her mother's face and knew her hand was fairly twitching, but Nora didn't lash out and send her flying. They stared at each other for what seemed like a long time to Abby's overstretched nerves, and then Nora said, her words slow and flat, 'You're an upstart, girl. You know that, don't you? From the minute you were born you've been trouble. But just remember this, there's none that get so high that they can't be brought down, and that's what'll happen to you one day.' And she turned on her heel and left the room.

Abby was still biting hard on her bottom lip to prevent it trembling; it didn't register for a moment that she had won.

'That might have been hard, lass,' her father said, 'but if I'd stood up to her years ago instead of taking the easy road, things'd be different now.'

Only then did Abby relax. But she felt no flood of joy that she had got her own way. The look on her father's face and the way he had just spoken had taken care of that. He didn't like her mam any more than she did and she wondered why the seriousness of that had never fully dawned on her before.

Chapter Two

When Abby walked into her aunt's backyard the next morning she could smell bacon frying. She opened the scullery door and called, 'Anyone at home?'

Her aunt's voice came back at her from the kitchen. 'Abby? Is that you?'

'Hello, Aunty.' As always Abby felt a sense of coming home as she took in the cluttered kitchen and the plump figure of her aunt standing at the range. This kitchen and more especially the woman in it spelled comfort and warmth and belonging, and what was a layer of dust or battered, tatty furniture anyway? Her aunty's house wasn't dirty like her mam said, it was just that everything was old and worn but that didn't matter a jot.

'This is a turn-up for the book, your mam letting you come round here at this time in the morning,' Audrey Hammond commented wryly.

Abby grinned at her aunt. 'She doesn't know. She's gone to first Mass and she's made Wilbert and Clara go with her.'

Audrey's eyebrows lifted. 'And not you?'

'She's not speaking to me.' Abby's nose wrinkled. 'We've had a row, a big one.'

'You'll have another if she finds you in here.'

'I don't care.' Abby settled herself down at the big wooden table, the top of which was marked with a hundred indentations and scratches. 'I wanted to talk to you before I go to work.'

'And it couldn't wait until tonight?'

'Everyone'll be here then.'

Audrey nodded. Another ten minutes and Ivor and the lads would be down and then it would be bedlam until they'd eaten and she'd packed Ivor and the oldest three off to work, and little Jed, the baby of the family at five years old, to school. And the evenings were worse. But she wouldn't swap a minute of her days for all the tea in China. The good Lord had blessed her when He'd seen fit to send Ivor her way, and none knew that better than she did. Daft as it might be, and she'd certainly never voice it to a living soul, but he still made her feel weak at the knees when she looked at him. She flapped her hand at her niece. 'There's still some tea in the pot, hinny, and I'll be making a fresh brew for that lot upstairs in a minute so help yourself. You want a bacon butty with it?'

'No thanks, Aunty, just the tea. I'm supposed to have breakfast ready for when Mam gets back. Da's still in bed.'

Audrey nodded, turning the bacon which sizzled madly in protest before she began cooking the first batch of griddle cakes. 'So, let's have it,' she said, her broad back to Abby. 'What's upset the apple cart this time?'

'I got in for the college and so I told her about the lessons.'

The effect of this statement was to spin Audrey round with a lightness which belied her bulk, and the next moment Abby was enfolded in her aunt's embrace. 'I knew you'd get in, lass. Didn't I say you would? Oh, hinny, I'm right pleased for you. When did you hear?'

Once she could breathe again, Abby said, 'Yesterday morning. At least I won't have to wait at the top of the street for the postie any more. I think he was beginning to believe I was soft on him.'

Audrey chuckled and returned to the range. 'He should

23

be so lucky! And your man played up, did she? Well, lass, if nothing else it confirms you were right to say nowt until you knew for sure.'

'She was horrible.' Abby looked down at the mug in her hand. 'And when Da stuck up for me she went for him an' all.'

'When does your da sail again?'

'Tomorrow.'

Abby's voice was flat. After turning the griddle cakes Audrey surveyed her niece whom she loved every bit as much as her own lads. Nora was mental the way she was with this bairn, but then her sister had never known which side her bread was buttered. Right from when Abby could toddle she'd made her way into this kitchen, and was it surprising the way her mam was? She had lost count of the times Nora had knocked Abby into next weekend for some little thing no one else would have bothered about. And Nora had had the cheek to come round here accusing her of stealing the bairn's affections when there'd been all that carry-on about the lass being forced into the pickle factory. Anyone with eyes in their head could have seen Nora had lost her daughter long before that. She seemed incapable of love, did her sister. In fact she didn't think Nora had ever really loved anyone, including Raymond, in the whole of her life.

Audrey turned her gaze to the ceiling, giving mental thanks for her own husband, before transferring the griddle cakes to a big tin dish standing on the hot steel shelf to one side of the hob. As she began the second batch, she said quietly, 'For what it's worth, I think you're doing the right thing, lass. That factory is sending you round the bend and you won't get free of it by just wishing. At least now you can go back knowing an end is in sight and it'll make all the difference.'

24

Abby nodded. 'I know.'

'You going to nip in and tell your granda the news before you go back? He's had another bad night an' likely it'll cheer him up.'

'Aye, all right.' Abby slid off the chair. 'Shall I take him a cup of tea?'

'Do that, hinny. He's only had the one this morning so his tongue will be hanging out if I know anything about it.'

The last of the tea was black and strong which was just how her grandfather liked it. Abby had often heard her aunt remark it was only the countless cups of tea he consumed a day which kept the old man going, and maybe it was.

In the hall she knocked on the front room door which was half open. She had always done this and she didn't know why – her grandfather said she was the only one who accorded him such a privilege – but it seemed the right thing to do somehow.

'Hello, me bairn.'

Her grandfather's gaunt face lit up at the sight of her. Abby walked across to the double bed set under the sash window so the old man could see the happenings in the street beyond, bent down and kissed him before saying softly, 'Aunty thought you might like another cup of tea, Granda.'

'An' she's not wrong.' He took the cup from her, patting the side of the bed as he said, 'Take the weight off, lass.'

'I can't stop long, Granda. I'm supposed to be seeing to breakfast right now. Mam's gone to first Mass.'

'Oh aye?' He blinked at her, his rheumy eyes sharp with understanding despite their cloudiness. 'An' what's sent her off to Father Finlay so early then? Got a gripe with your da, has she?'

Abby shook her head. 'It's me. I told her last night I was going to have shorthand and typing lessons at the tech. I've paid for them myself but she still created. You know what she's like.'

Aye, he knew what Nora was like all right. Silas Dodds looked at his favourite grandchild understandingly. Six bairns he and his Elsie had had and the good Lord had seen fit to take the lads, all four of 'em, and each before they had barely drawn breath, and leave the two lasses, Nora and Audrey. And it had been touch and go with Audrey for the first couple of years; sickly little thing she'd been although you'd never think it to look at her now. But Nora . . . Strong as an ox from the day she was born. Funny that the first babbie and the last had been the ones to survive, and eight years between them. Never were two sisters more different. And he thanked God daily they were. As sure as eggs were eggs, he'd have been packed off to the workhouse double quick if it had been left to his eldest.

Silas drew in a careful breath – anything too deep these days and the pain shot through him like a knife – and took a long pull at the black tea.

Did anyone else see what he saw when they looked at Nora? No, of course they didn't, else something would have been said before now. Audrey might be an easy-going lass with a heart of gold but she worshipped the ground her Ivor walked on. If she thought for a minute . . .

'Da's sailing again tomorrow morning.'

This statement was telling in its brevity. Silas nodded slowly. 'What did he say about all this then?'

'He's for me.'

Which would mean Raymond was in the doghouse too. Like Elsie, he'd been against Nora marrying a sailor and one not of the Church to boot, but he'd long since come round to the opinion it was Raymond who'd got the rough end of the deal.

Silas took his granddaughter's hand. 'Don't you let your mam change your mind once your da's gone.'

'Oh, I wouldn't, Granda.'

It was too definite not to be believed, and a slow grin spread over Silas's thin face. Nora had met her match with this one, but wasn't it strange that alike as his daughter and granddaughter were in strength of will and determination, Abby was all softness and her mother as hard as nails? He handed the empty cup over. 'You'd better get back, hinny, but I'm right pleased for you, I am that. You're worth more than that bloomin' pickle factory and haven't I always said so?'

'Thanks, Granda.'

Again the warm lips pressed against his face, and when Abby touched the parchment-like skin of his cheek with her fingers in a parting endearment which had begun in childhood, Silas swallowed hard. One in a million, this bairn was. A little ray of sunshine his Elsie had called their granddaughter, and she'd been right an' all.

As he watched the young figure leave the room the feeling of apprehension which had come on him more and more of late was strong. If he was right in his suspicions about Nora and Ivor – and his gut had never let him down yet – a cartload of trouble was being stored up. Folk thought they could bury such things but they never stayed buried, certainly not when someone was as discontented with her lot as his eldest daughter anyway.

He adjusted his position on the pillows; his crushed legs, which had withered away to mere sticks over the years, pained him.

How far had the pair of them gone? A bit of making on and teasing, or something more? He brought his lips one

27

over the other a few times. Whatever had happened, he'd bet his eye teeth it was Ivor who had called a halt. His son-in-law couldn't get out of the room quick enough if Nora came in, and he was positively sheepish if forced to be in her company, like at Christmas for example. He just thanked the Lord Nora didn't pop round as much as she used to since her and Audrey had had the set to when Abby had started at the pickle factory. But if he knew Nora, she wouldn't take Ivor's rejection lying down. She was biding her time, and sooner or later she'd strike back.

Should he tackle Ivor about it? Would it do any good? He couldn't see it somehow. Aw, he wished Elsie was here. The blue lips worked again. She would have known what to do, would his Elsie. Grand lass and a bonny wife, she'd been. He sighed deeply, his eyes shutting as his tired mind took refuge in sleep.

In the hall, Audrey was at the foot of the stairs, rubbing her hands on her pinny. 'Come on, you lot!' she bellowed. 'This is the last time of calling! I haven't been slaving over a hot stove for breakfast to get clart cold. And bring Jed down with you.'

'I'm off, Aunty,' Abby said.

'All right, hinny.' Audrey followed her niece into the kitchen, shaking her head as she said, 'Trouble with their backs again, can't get 'em off the bed of a morning. Now . . .' A plump hand was placed on Abby's arm. 'If it gets too bad with your da gone, don't forget we're next door and Ivor will always have a word with her. She's more likely to listen to reason from him. If I say anything it'll be the wrong thing.'

Abby nodded but said nothing to this. The Pope himself could have a word with her mother but if she was in one of her moods he'd get short shrift.

'Hello, what's this then? Taking me name in vain again?'

28

The tall, broad man who appeared in the kitchen doorway was grinning as he spoke, and as Audrey turned and flapped her hand at him, she said, 'Ears like a cuddy, you've got. You should know by now you never hear anything good if you flap 'em where they're not wanted.'

'Hark at her.' Ivor raised his hands to his ears, pulling at the lobes as he said, 'There's many as admire these, I'll have you know. "You're a fine man, Ivor," they say, "and with a grand pair of lugholes an' all".'

'Half sharp, you are.' But Audrey was laughing as she spoke, and her husband gave her bottom a playful slap. 'If you must know,' she continued, turning back to the griddle cakes, 'Nora's in a tear with the lass again and I said with Raymond going tomorrow you'd speak to her if things get too bad.'

Ivor didn't comment on this but the smile left his face. 'What's the trouble this time, lass?'

Abby told him quickly, adding, 'But don't say anything, Uncle Ivor, there's no need.' She knew he didn't want to, she'd seen it in his face as her aunt spoke. 'I'm going to go and nothing she can do or say will stop me.'

He nodded, seating himself at the kitchen table. 'That's all right then, isn't it?' he said flatly, reaching for the teapot.

Abby said goodbye and walked through to the scullery and out of the back door, but after closing the rickety gate to her aunt's backyard she stood in the narrow lane and looked up into the sky. The lane could be a sea of mud in the winter but it hadn't rained to speak of in weeks and the ground beneath her feet was cracked and dusty, the sky above clear and vividly blue. The air was fresh, at least where she was standing although she knew at the far end of the path where the Craggs and McArthurs lived the privies would be stinking to high heaven.

A blackbird flew right past her ear, settling on the yard wall a couple of houses down, where it proceeded to sing its little heart out. It was a lovely morning. Abby frowned to herself. She'd felt fine in spite of her mam until her Uncle Ivor had put a damper on things. Not that he'd meant to, she thought, trying to be fair, but he would never say anything about her mam or indicate he cared about how things were at home.

She shrugged the disgruntlement away, drawing the bright summer morning into her lungs. She wouldn't let anyone spoil things. She'd made her stand and this was a new beginning. Why, this time next year she might even have left the factory and be working in an office!

When Abby got home from work the next day and stepped into the hall, her gaze went immediately to the front room door which was ajar. Even before she heard the voices within she stifled a groan. Father Finlay. It had to be Father Finlay ensconced with her mother because no one else who called, except maybe Dr Jefferson, would be shown into the front room. And everyone was well at the moment. Added to which, her father had sailed that morning so her mother would have felt the coast was clear to call in the priest.

Abby slipped off her coat and hung it on a peg. As she did so Clara appeared from the kitchen at the far end of the hall, her eyes red and puffy, but before she could reach her sister her mother's voice called, 'Abigail? Is that you? Come into the parlour please.'

The parlour! Ever since her mother had read in *Home and Country* that well-bred women referred to their front room as the parlour she'd adopted the word, affording the rest of the household some private amusement, although Abby didn't feel like smiling right now. She pushed the door wide open but did not enter the room. She stood on the threshold and surveyed the two occupants for a moment, before she said, 'Good afternoon, Father Finlay.'

The priest took a moment to raise his eyes from their contemplation of the cup of tea in his hands, and then his cold stare was on her. He inclined his head slowly.

'Come and sit down, the Father has something to say to you. And not on that chair,' her mother added sharply as Abby went to seat herself. 'Your sister's had an . . . accident.'

Oh dear, poor Clara. The little girl was absolutely terrified of the priest but to wet herself on the dark green embossed suite which was their mother's pride and joy! This was a major disaster.

Because Father Finlay was sitting in the middle of the three-seater settee and her mother on the other chair, Abby pulled one of the two intricately carved hard-backed chairs which stood either side of the fireplace into the middle of the room and sat down. Her mother insisted these were valuable, but whether they were or not, Abby thought they were hideous and bone-bruisingly uncomfortable.

The priest had not taken his eyes from her and Abby's stomach was turning over. Nevertheless, she forced herself to sit quietly without fidgeting, her hands in her lap as she met his gaze again. There was a long pause during which Father Finlay and Abby stared at each other, and Abby knew the priest was willing her to speak first. For that reason she kept silent.

After finishing his tea, the Father cleared his throat. '"For God commanded, saying, honour thy father and mother: and, he that curseth father or mother, let him die the death." Do you know your Bible, child?'

'I read the Bible, Father.'

'So you know this scripture? Where can it be found?'

31

When Abby didn't reply, he said slowly, 'Matthew fifteen, verse four. Read it, meditate on it and ask the Lord's forgiveness.'

'For what, Father?'

'For what?' Her mother's voice was shrill. 'How dare you sit there and ask for what? You see, Father? You see what she's like? Insolent and defiant to the last.'

'Do you deny that you have brought grief and worry into your mother's life by your refusal to be guided by her loving hand?' Father Finlay said softly, without looking at Nora.

'If you mean because I want to take an evening course at the technical college, I don't see why that should worry her,' Abby answered with more courage than she felt. 'And my da is happy for me to go.'

Too late she realised it was the wrong thing to say. Any mention of her father was like a red rag to a bull as far as the priest was concerned. Abby watched him stiffen and his voice was no longer soft when he said, 'You know as well as I do that your father is not of the Faith but walking the road to eternal damnation. It grieves me deeply to say it but your poor mother has had to battle alone to raise you in truth and holiness.'

Abby stared at Father Finlay, colour hot in her cheeks. 'My da might not be a Catholic but he's a good man, a fine man,' she said, her voice rising. 'He's better than some of the men who go to Mass on a Sunday and then get drunk and behave exactly how they want the rest of the week. My da's not like that.'

She heard the intake of breath from her mother and knew she had gone way too far, but she didn't regret what she had said. The thought must have been there for some time but only now had it emerged from the recesses of her mind. It was true and Father Finlay must know that.

'Temptation will always present itself to mortal man. That is why our souls need to be cleansed by the blood of Christ,' he said coldly.

It wasn't temptation, not for men like Shane Mullen three doors down who drank most of his wage every Friday night and then came home and knocked three bells out of his wife and bairns. It was a way of life. And Father Finlay would give him absolution come Sunday, even with his wife sitting there black and blue. Mrs Mullen had lost two babies because of the beatings when she was expecting, it was a known fact round the streets. Abby's chin rose a fraction higher. 'I'm sorry, Father, but I don't see it like that. I know there are lots of good Catholics but—'

'It is not for you to judge others.' The priest's eyes were gimlet hard now, black orbs with a piercing quality which was unnerving. 'I will be hearing confession until eight tonight, Abigail, and in view of our conversation I shall expect you to be there.'

He knew she was supposed to be going for her first lesson tonight. Abby's mind was racing. And her mam had planned this. Oh why couldn't they have gone to St Peter's and had Father McGuigan as their priest? Everyone loved Father McGuigan. Her stomach turned over. 'I'm sorry, Father, but I have to be at the college for half past six.'

'You are putting the things of the flesh before the things of God?'

'I don't see it that way, Father,' she said again.

The priest rose to his feet and his voice was deep when he said, '"For the Lord sayeth, rebellion is as the sin of witchcraft, and stubbornness is as iniquity and idolatry".' He held her with his eyes for one more moment before turning to Nora who had also risen. 'May God bless and uphold you in your trial, Mrs Vickers.'

'Thank you, Father.'

Her mother didn't seem overjoyed at the priest's bene-diction. Abby replaced the chair in its rightful place as her mother saw Father Finlay out, then walked through to the kitchen where Clara was sitting with her little arms wrapped round her middle, tears still rolling down her cheeks. She didn't have a chance to speak to her sister before her mother's voice said, 'Well, madam! I hope you're satisfied with yourself, answering the Father back like that. I've never heard anything like it in my life.'

Abby turned and looked steadily at her mother. 'He shouldn't have spoken about Da like that.'

'Your da!' Nora gave a short, bitter laugh. Wouldn't she love to shout the truth at this hoity-toity little madam who thought herself the cat's whiskers. To tell her that her precious da had no claim to her at all, that there wasn't a drop of his blood running through her veins, that he was a useless lump of nowt who couldn't father a kitten. She took hold of her temper, turning her venom on her youngest daughter who was watching her with wide, unblinking eyes. 'Come here,' she said grimly.

Clara's face was white with terror and although she knew she would get an even worse hiding if she didn't obey her mother at once, she found herself glued to her seat. The sin she had committed, the awful huge enormity of it was paralysing. Her mam's suite – a crumb wasn't allowed to fall on it or a speck of dust touch its surface, and she had . . . She couldn't bear to think what she'd done, and in front of Father Finlay too. But when he had said to her mam that all children were born wicked and that the devil had to be purged from them, and then swung round to fix his eyes on her, she hadn't known what was happening until she'd felt the warmth trickle between her legs.

It was obvious to Abby that the small girl was frozen with fright, so when their mother repeated herself with a

34

certain formidable satisfaction that indicated she was fully aware of Clara's state of mind, she said, 'Clara didn't mean to do it, you know that, but she's scared to death of Father Finlay. I don't know why you always make her sit in with you when he visits.'

'This is nothing to do with you so keep out of it.'

'I'll see to the chair if that's what's worrying you. It will clean up as good as new.'

'I said keep out of it.'

It was the little whimper Clara made, which could have come from an animal, that made up Abby's mind. She was nearer to her sister than her mother was, and she reached out and lifted the stiff little body into her arms. Cradling the cold flesh against the warmth of hers, she said, 'You're not braying her for something she couldn't help, Mam. Anyway, she's been punished enough already. Look at her.'

For a second it was as though Nora couldn't believe her ears. Clara put her arms round her sister's neck, burrowing into her, her face pushed deep into Abby's shoulder. The child's trembling made Abby's temper rise. Clara was a skinny little thing, she didn't even have the meat on her bones she'd had when she was little to protect her a fraction from her mother's fury. The mood her mam was in she'd do the bairn a serious injury.

A quiver passed over Nora's face and her hands tightened into fists. 'What did you say to me?'

'I said you're not beating her. Sitting in here and waiting for you has been punishment enough.'

'You're telling me how to deal with your sister now? I think not, madam. And you're not too big to get the same as her, I'm telling you. Give her over.'

'I won't.'

The two women faced each other and Clara found herself swallowing hard to stop the sickness rising out of her stomach.

'And I'll tell you something else, Mam, while I'm at it. You lay a finger on me and you'll get as good back, I'm warning you.'

'*You're* warning *me*?'

'Aye, I am! And you can get Father Finlay here or the Pope himself but it'll be the same. I've had enough, Mam. You're not hitting me again.'

Her mother's face contorted with fury. Abby held her ground and clasped Clara tighter to her, but she knew she couldn't carry this through, her mam would see it was all bluff. What would she do if her mam lashed out at her? Would she really hit her back? She couldn't, she couldn't hit her mam. And then as mother and daughter continued to glare at each other, they heard the front door open followed by Wilbert's voice calling, 'I just saw Father Finlay at the corner and he was in a right tear about something or other. Face like thunder, he'd got. I pity the poor devil who gets the end of his tongue the night.'

What would have happened between herself and her mam if Wilbert hadn't come home when he did? Abby's stomach was still churning as she hurried along South Johnson Street towards Green Terrace where the technical college was situated; she had visited the privy three times before she left the house.

Her brother had taken in the situation at a glance when he'd entered the kitchen, and in his mild way he had managed to coax their mam to sit down whilst he'd made her a cup of tea. Always the peacemaker, he'd excelled himself this time, Abby thought wryly.

While Wilbert sat with their mother, she washed Clara down in the scullery before putting her to bed. Worn out with all her crying, the child was asleep within a minute or two, which gave Abby the time to clean the chair in the front room, wash her sister's clothes and put them through the mangle before hanging them on the line which ran the length of the yard. It was the day she was supposed to scour the privy so she saw to that chore as well and one or two others before quickly washing her hands and face and smoothing her hair with her damp hands. She didn't have time to eat – her stomach felt too upset anyway – and she said goodbye to her mother and Wilbert as they sat eating their evening meal. Wilbert answered her but her mother ignored her.

It was only a short walk to the college. As Abby turned the corner into Green Terrace, the imposing building of the technical college was in front of her, its domed tower seeming to reach the sky. Abruptly she halted. What was she doing? She ran a clammy hand over her face, the rumbling of her stomach reminding her she hadn't eaten since lunchtime. She would never keep up with the other girls, she knew she wouldn't. And she'd never find her way round this building, it was so huge.

'Hello there.' The tap on her shoulder almost made her jump out of her skin, and she swung round to see a big girl with a pretty face smiling at her. 'I saw you when we had to enrol, didn't I? You down for the shorthand and typing course?'

'Aye, yes I am.' Abby swallowed hard. 'It's a bit overwhelming, isn't it?' she said, nodding at the building.

'What, this place?' The other girl grinned at her. 'Me da calls it the Whisky Palace 'cos it was built by the council with money they got from Customs and Excise. Me da don't hold nowt in awe, or no one for that matter. Me mam says if King George himself were to knock on our door, me da'd just invite him in to look at his pigeons and bend his ear on the government making such a mess of the country the last fifteen odd years. Me da's a big union man,' she added by way of explanation.

37

'Does he work in the shipyards?'

The other girl shook her head, causing her short, glossy brown hair to swing with the movement. 'No, he's a miner, like his da afore him and his da afore him. Well,' she inclined her head towards the building, her voice suddenly brisk, 'we'd better go in and see what's what. We won't get nowhere standing out here like lemons.'

Abby nodded, her nervousness changing to anticipation as her new friend linked arms with her.

'Me name's Winnie, by the way, Winnie Todd. What's yours?'

'Abby Vickers.'

'Pleased to meet you.' Winnie grinned at her. 'We'll pair up, shall we, if they ask us to? Though likely it's not like school,' she added as an afterthought. 'Least, I hope not. I hated school. Our headmaster was the spitting image of this German bloke, Adolf Hitler, who's causing all the trouble, an' he was a nasty bit of work an' all. And our teacher,' she raised her eyes heavenwards, 'by, she could pack a wallop with the cane. You'd feel it for weeks when she let fly. I've never known anyone wield a bit of wood like Miss Ramsbottom.'

'Ramsbottom?' Abby giggled as they mounted the steps to the front door of the college. 'That wasn't really her name, was it?'

'Straight up. She looked like one an' all. Mind, she'd been walking out with old Adolf for years an' years so that'd be enough to give anyone the hump. Well, here we go then. Time to shake a leg and knock 'em dead, as the actress said to the bishop.'

The corners of Abby's mouth lifted as she pushed open the door and the pair of them stepped into the building. She was going to enjoy Monday and Thursday evenings. With or without the shorthand and typing lessons.

Chapter Three

Twelve months! She could hardly believe a full twelve months had passed since that first night when she had stood in fear and trepidation outside the college. And now here she was feeling pretty much the same at the thought of the forthcoming interview. With a mental shake of her head at her nervousness Abby tweaked her smart Sunday frock further over her knees and breathed out deeply, catching the eye of one of the other girls sitting in the small waiting room as she did so. She returned the weak smile the girl gave but didn't instigate a conversation, it didn't seem the time or the place somehow.

When the door opened and the woman who had previously called out two other applicants – with a twenty-minute break between them – said her name in a somewhat bored tone, the butterflies in Abby's stomach did an Irish jig. This was it then, her first ever interview. Mrs Travis, their teacher at the college, had gone through the procedure time and time again until they were all well versed in how to deal with the possible pitfalls, but suddenly that didn't seem as encouraging as it had been.

Abby didn't glance at the other two girls in the room as she left, concentrating on the woman in front of her who, once they were in the corridor outside, said in a more friendly tone, 'You'll have a shorthand and typing test first and then Mr Wynford, the Accounts Manager, will see you. All right?'

'Yes, thank you.' She was being whisked through doors and along corridors so fast it was making her head spin. She'd never find her way out of here. Price and Osborne, Engineers, had looked pretty impressive from the outside but it was even bigger inside. Winnie had said she was daft to even apply for the post of secretary to the Accounts Manager when they had seen it advertised in the *Echo*. Most girls fresh out of college were happy to find work as a shorthand typist. Price and Osborne were situated at the end of Alfred Street, only a short walk away from home, but this wasn't what had made Abby decide to try for the job, or even the fact that a secretary's wage would be much more than a shorthand typist's. The reason was her mother's dismissive sneering attitude about her future prospects all the time she had been attending the course at the college. Abby wanted something better than the lowest rung of the ladder, just to show her. She hadn't felt able to discuss this with her friend or anyone else for that matter, so she'd just said to Winnie that the interview would be good experience, if nothing else. Winnie had given her a look that said better than words she thought Abby was mad.

Abby had taken to shorthand like a duck to water, much to Winnie's envy, for she wouldn't have completed the course but for Abby's help. Abby had galloped ahead of the other students, eager to master each stage in Mr Pitman's book. She found it fascinating, like another language, which in a way it was, she supposed. The typing hadn't held her interest in the same way but her speeds were good nevertheless, and she found great satisfaction in translating the squiggles and dots in her notebook into neatly set out letters and documents.

The woman who had collected her from the waiting room conducted the shorthand and typing test in a small office

40

with just one chair, one desk and several filing cabinets in it. The test proved to be remarkably easy and when Abby had finished, the woman held out her hand for the letter she'd dictated, making no comment except to say, 'If you'll just wait here a moment I'll see if Mr Wynford is free.'

She was back within a minute or so, and took Abby further down the corridor and into a large main office which was fairly buzzing with activity. At the far end of the room was a door with a brass nameplate which read, 'Miss Boyce, Mr Wynford's secretary'. Once again Abby had to wait while her guide disappeared inside.

This was all so different to anything she'd experienced before. Everyone was busy doing something or other and no one took any notice of her at all. Winnie had started work in a typing pool at Pallion shipbuilding yard a few days ago and there was another vacancy there; perhaps she should have gone for that rather than trying for this just to prove something to her mother. Abby was beginning to feel awkward standing about like a spare part when at last the door opened and she was beckoned into the secretary's office and then through to the one beyond. This room was spacious, with wall to wall carpeting which made it seem bigger still and very luxurious to Abby, though the furniture was plain and functional.

A man was sitting at the far end of the room at a large, polished desk. Daylight from the window behind him streamed over his shoulders. He stood up at Abby's approach, bent forward and held out his hand. 'Good afternoon, Miss Vickers,' he said evenly. He did not smile. 'Please be seated.'

'Thank you.' Abby sat down, staring into steely blue eyes and willing herself not to glance away. Mr Wynford was middle-aged, possessed of a military bearing and as neat as a new pin.

The unnerving gaze held for a moment more, and then he glanced down at the papers in front of him. 'Mrs Travis has given you a glowing testimonial both to your character and qualifications, but the fact remains you are still only seventeen years of age, Miss Vickers, with no practical experience. My present secretary,' he waved his hand towards the door, by which Abby assumed he meant the woman who had conducted the test and shown her in, 'had already worked for two other employers when she came here eighteen months ago.'

There was nothing she could say to this and so she merely continued to look at him.

'She's leaving, incidentally, because she's getting married and the fellow in question has been offered a very lucrative job down south.'

After a moment's hesitation she said, 'Yes, I see, sir.'

'Bernice, my secretary, was impressed with your shorthand speed. I am not the most patient of men and I dictate as I speak and don't like to repeat myself. Neither do I respond well when files go missing or papers can't be found. In effect I run a tight ship, Miss Vickers. Excuses aren't tolerated.'

It was almost as if he was accusing her of something and now Abby sat up straighter, her cheeks burning.

'Are you a clock watcher?'

She almost said, 'What?' but just in time changed it to, 'I beg your pardon?'

'Are you the type who makes sure they're out of the door at five o'clock come hell or high water?'

What a horrible man. It wasn't so much what he said as the tone of his voice, and she'd bet his face would crack if he ever smiled. 'As you have already pointed out I haven't worked in an office before, sir,' she said crisply, 'so my reply to that question would be rhetorical at best.' She

42

hoped she'd used the right word there. 'But I have never thought of myself as a *type*, and certainly if there was work which needed to be seen to on any particular day, it would be dealt with.'

'Would it now.' He settled further back in his big leather chair. 'Why did you apply for this particular post?' he asked suddenly. 'Why not something more suited to your limited knowledge of office work? You must realise that however successful you were at the college it is not like being in a real work environment. Most girls in your position go into a typing pool or something of that nature, I believe.'

And she could understand why now. Aware she was glaring, she tried to smooth her face clear of expression and moderate her voice as she threw caution to the wind and, with some bravado, said, 'I am not most girls.'

'So why did you apply? Was it the money?'

Wonderful! Not only had he got her down as inadequate to the task and flighty, but now she was grasping too. She drew in a long breath before she said truthfully, 'No, it was not the money.' But she could hardly tell him the real reason. 'I felt I wanted something more interesting and demanding than a typing pool, and whatever I might lack in experience I'm determined I can make up for with hard work.'

'You've worked in a factory for three and a half years since leaving school.' He narrowed his eyes at her. 'It took you a while to decide what you really wanted to do, didn't it?'

Again his tone caught her on the raw. She stared at him, lost for words. But only for a second or two; then she said, rising to her feet, 'You don't know me, Mr Wynford, and I resent that remark. From the day I started work I put money aside for the time when I would be able to pay for

43

a shorthand and typing course. It took me a while but I did it. We're not all born with silver spoons in our mouths—' She stopped abruptly. She shouldn't have said that last bit, she'd gone too far. She would have known it even if the look on his face hadn't told her so.

Expecting a sharp reprimand she stood staring at him, wanting to turn tail and leave the room with every fibre of her being but feeling that would be to admit total defeat. Some ten seconds ticked by, and then he said flatly, 'Sit down, lass.'

It was the 'lass' that seated her. It was so unexpected after everything that had gone before. She sank down more out of surprise than anything else.

'You're eighteen in,' he consulted the papers in front of him, 'six months' time. Is that right?'

She nodded. 'In January, yes.'

'You appear older, in your manner, that is.'

He didn't seem so nasty now but she wasn't sure how to take him so she said nothing.

He pulled his chin into his neck, looking at her over the top of his horn-rimmed glasses. 'This is the second batch of applicants I've seen today and there were some yesterday too. It was difficult enough finding Bernice eighteen months ago. Why the damn fool woman has to marry a man who's determined to take himself off down south I don't know.' He stretched slightly, taking off the glasses, and again the sharp blue eyes bored into her. 'Are you looking to up and skedaddle in the near future with some young man or other? Not that you'd tell me if you were, I suppose.'

Abby felt herself redden as she said, 'I'm not and I would not have applied for the post if I were.'

It wasn't very grammatical but he didn't comment on this, continuing to stare at her for a moment or two before he said, 'Hmph!' which could have meant anything. 'So

44

. . .' He stood up and turned to look out of the window towards the river. With his back towards her he said, 'Would you want the job if it was offered to you?'

From being absolutely sure minutes before that she didn't want it, she now found herself saying, 'Yes, I would, sir.' Which probably made Winnie right when she'd called her daft, Abby thought wryly.

He swung round to face her. 'Got something to prove to them all, have you?'

His perception took her aback. She could have said, 'Not all of them, no, just one person actually,' but what she did say was, 'I'm not sure I know what you mean, sir.'

The 'Hmph!' came again but he did not pursue the matter, contenting himself with, 'Well, there's worse motives for taking a job than being determined to succeed come what may, certainly from where I'm standing as the one likely to benefit. Now Bernice is not getting wed for another two months and she's staying on to instruct her replacement on how I like things done and so on. That means you'd have a few weeks before you're thrown in the deep end.'

Her eyes opened wider. Was he saying she had the job? Was he actually prepared to take her on?

'Well?' The irritation was back. 'What do you say? You didn't seem to have too much trouble speaking your mind a minute or two ago.'

'Are you offering me the post of secretary, sir?'

'Well, I'm not about to give you my job, am I?' He smiled at her and she smiled politely back at his little joke, noticing the difference the smile made to his face. Her heart raced with excitement.

'Thank you, thank you very much,' she managed a trifle breathlessly. 'When would you like me to start?'

'Soon as possible, I suppose, but sort that out with

Bernice.' His tone made it plain he hadn't the time or the inclination for such minor details, and this was further emphasised when he pressed a buzzer on his desk, saying, 'I take it your next question is how much you can expect to be paid, eh?' in the irritable voice.

She'd been so surprised and thrilled to be offered the position she'd forgotten to ask about her wage! Too late, Abby realised all Mrs Travis's instructions on interview technique had flown out of the window.

Mr Wynford obviously didn't expect a reply. Before the door opened to reveal his secretary, he said, 'As you would expect, remuneration is in line with experience, age, qualifications and so on, added to which you'll be working with Bernice for some weeks to see if you like the job and are suited. A trial run, so to speak. All right?'

She nodded.

'You starting wage will be reviewed in two months' time if and when you take on full responsibility, but if we say twenty-one shillings per week for the present, does that seem fair to you?'

Abby stared at him. Her last rise at the pickle factory had taken her up to twelve shillings – although lads of her age doing the same job earned more, which had always been a bone of contention with her – and here he was saying she would *start* at twenty-one shillings with a review once Bernice was gone and she was the secretary properly. If she was suited, that was. But she would be. She'd work twenty-four hours a day if necessary to make sure of it.

'Thank you,' she said again. 'Thank you very much, sir.'

Whether it was the tone of her voice or the look on her face Abby didn't know, but Mr Wynford smiled again, a real smile this time, which crinkled the skin around his eyes.

'You'll do, lass,' he said, and she realised he was not as grim as he made out. 'Now you wait in the main office while I have a word with Bernice and then she'll see you out, all right?'

Back in the main office Abby stood just outside the secretary's door, trying to calm her racing heart. She glanced round the large room. There were not as many people in it as she had first thought. Apart from two fairly young girls who had their heads down typing away in the far corners of the office, the rest of the personnel comprised one elderly man with white hair, two middle-aged men and three youngish men, one of whom was looking straight at her. She didn't know whether to glance away or say hello – the former seemed rude and the latter forward – so in the end she just smiled and then looked down at the new white gloves she had bought specially for the interview.

A moment or two later she was aware of him standing at her elbow. His smile was wide as he said, 'That's a good sign, you being asked to wait like this. All the others have just been shown straight out.'

He was very good-looking. She stared into deep blue eyes set under a shock of light brown hair and found herself tongue-tied.

'My name's James Benson by the way.' He held out his hand and she was aware that her smaller one was lost in his. 'I'm Mr Wynford's junior accountant, but don't let the grand title fool you – general dogsbody, more like,' he added with another smile.

'Abby Vickers,' she said a little breathlessly as her hand became her own again. 'I'm . . .' She hesitated, not knowing how to put it. 'Mr Wynford has just offered me the job as secretary, on a temporary basis to see if I suit,' she added quickly.

'Has he? Good for him.'

The tone was frankly appreciative and Abby knew she had gone as red as a beetroot. When Bernice appeared in the next instant the older woman took in the situation at a glance. Her voice was indulgent but carried a slight warning as she said, 'Hasn't taken you long to make Miss Vickers's acquaintance then, Mr Benson? I suggest you return to your work before Mr Hardcastle accuses you of slacking.'

'I was just going.' His grin took in the secretary but lingered a mite longer on Abby's pink face. 'See you again soon, Miss Vickers.'

As he turned away, Bernice said quietly, 'I won't introduce you to everyone now because you won't remember their names anyway, but Mr Hardcastle,' she inclined her head towards the elderly man who had the biggest desk in the room and a leather chair like Mr Wynford's, 'is Mr Wynford's chief clerk and in charge of the office any time Mr Wynford isn't here. If you get on the right side of him from the word go it'll pay dividends, believe me. And Miss Cook and Miss Turner,' she nodded to the two far corners of the room, 'are your juniors, don't forget that. It doesn't do to get familiar with them, not when you have to give them orders and keep them up to scratch when necessary, all right?'

Abby nodded, totally out of her depth.

'Come on.' Bernice took her arm and ushered her out of the office. 'You'll get used to everything much quicker than you think,' she said softly, 'but right from the first day you need to remember what I've just told you. Start as you mean to carry on.'

Bernice took her on a short tour of the factory and sheds and the rest of the plant, all of which were situated at the rear of the office building. Abby was overwhelmed by the

48

sheer size of Price and Osborne, not to mention the noise and general clamour once they had left the offices.

But it was exciting. And she was going to be someone's secretary! Not a general typist in a pool, not even a short-hand typist attached to a secretary, but a secretary in her own right. What was her mam going to say to that?

This thought stayed at the forefront of her mind on the short walk home, so it was something of an anti-climax to find her mother out. After taking off her hat and coat Abby climbed the stairs to the bedroom she shared with Clara – Wilbert had been sleeping on a desk bed in the kitchen for the last few years. Abby pulled off her gloves and changed out of her Sunday dress and into one of her two weekday frocks before walking across to the narrow sash window and staring into the street below.

She had the rest of the afternoon free; she had told the forewoman at the factory she wouldn't be back that day. Clara and Jed wouldn't be home from school for a while, so she decided to pop round and tell Aunty Audrey her news. No doubt her mam would play up if she found out she'd been next door before telling her, but it wasn't her fault her mam wasn't in. And she had to tell someone. She was bursting. Her Uncle Ivor would likely be in too; he had hurt his back at the shipyard the day before and the doctor had told him to take the week off unless he wanted to end up unable to move.

Decision made, Abby ran lightly down the stairs and through the house into the backyard, taking just a moment to breathe in the warm sunshine in the lane beyond before she made her way into the yard next door. It was a beau-tiful day, a beautiful, *beautiful* day! Twenty-one shillings! *Twenty-one shillings*.

As she entered her aunt's scullery, Abby called her normal greeting, 'Anyone at home?' before pushing open the kitchen door which, unusually for her aunt, had been shut. And then she paused on the threshold to the room, staring in surprise at her mother who had just got to her feet from where she'd been sitting or kneeling by the side of Ivor's armchair to the left of the range.

Her mother stared at her with what Abby could only describe to herself as a strange look on her face, but it was her uncle who spoke, drawing her gaze. 'Hello, lass,' he said, his voice natural but his face strained. 'You're back early the day.'

'I've been for an interview.' Her uncle's back must be giving him gyp, he looked awful.

'Oh aye? Where was that then?'

'Price and Osborne. The Accounts Manager wanted a secretary and I thought I'd try for it.'

The lilt in her voice was a giveaway, and her uncle smiled as he said, 'Don't tell me you got it?'

'Aye, I did.'

'Well, I'll be blowed. You're a canny lass an' no mistake.'

It was noticeable her mother hadn't said a word, and now Abby's eyes turned to her. 'I'll be giving in my notice at the factory tomorrow, Mam,' she said. 'All right?'

'Why ask me if it's all right? You'll do exactly as you please as usual.' Then her mother turned and seated herself at the kitchen table.

As Abby looked at her, such a bewildering mix of feelings washed over her she couldn't have told anyone how she felt. Her voice flat, she turned to her uncle and said, 'Is Aunty Audrey in?'

'She's gone to the shops, lass. Your mam just missed her by a minute or two.'

Abby watched her uncle as he carefully adjusted his position in the battered old chair, wincing as he did so,

50

and his voice was irritable when he continued, 'Damn nuisance being stuck here like a sitting duck,' and his eyes moved to her mother.

A sitting duck? That was a funny thing to say, wasn't it? And she had never seen her uncle in such a bad mood. She didn't know what to say for a moment and then she proffered, 'I'm sorry about your back, Uncle Ivor.'

He nodded. 'Thanks, lass. To tell you the truth I'm counting my blessings the day. A twenty-foot plank fell from the deck above and caught me a glancing blow on the back but it could've easily sent me off the platform I was working on. There was a thirty-foot drop beneath and I've seen a bloke killed like that in the past. It's not pretty.'

If he had a face like that when he was counting his blessings she didn't know what he'd be like when he was annoyed about something. But everyone knew how dangerous the shipyards were and she'd worried about Wilbert when he first started working with his uncle and cousins. He hadn't been able to sleep the first week for the awful ringing in his ears due to the noise from the squads of riveters, caulkers and drillers, and the second week he had come home and vomited after seeing a shipwright crushed by a falling rudder. There wasn't a week went by when Wilbert didn't relate some horror story, and he was always covered in cuts and bruises and had already lost the tip of one finger when he had caught his hand between two metal plates.

'Sit yourself down, lass,' her uncle said now. 'There's a fresh brew and a piece of your aunty's sly cake if you've a mind for a bite. She'll be back soon.'

Abby looked at her mother but she didn't raise her head from her cup or offer to pour the tea. Still, at least her mam had come round to see her aunty, which was a good thing, Abby told herself. Likely it had been to enquire how

51

Uncle Ivor was, but that didn't matter. She just wished her mam would come down off her high horse and be nice to her aunty now and then.

'Has Granda had a cup?' Abby asked her uncle, and when he shook his head, she said, 'I'll take him one through then. No doubt he'll be gasping.' Her uncle smiled at this but her mother's face remained straight, and after a mental shrug Abby poured the tea and left the room.

Nora stood up and closed the door into the hall after her daughter before reseating herself, and when Ivor said, 'You shouldn't have done that, it'll look queer,' her only response was to shrug her shoulders.

After a couple of moments had ticked by she raised her head, staring at the man who had become an obsession with her. Her voice low, she said, 'I meant what I said a minute ago before she marched in, I'm at the end of my tether. I'd run away with you tomorrow if you'd give the word.'

Dear gussy. Ivor ran his hand across his brow. When would she ever let up? Apart from that one time five or six years ago when he'd been blind drunk on New Year's Eve and she'd caught him outside in the privy and damn near helped herself, he hadn't touched her since she'd been pregnant with Wilbert. She knew how he stood, he'd spelled it out plain that it was over and that he regretted every sordid minute. What more could he do, for crying out loud? 'There's no question of us running anywhere,' he said flatly.

'Because of her. You feel a responsibility to her.'

'I love her, Nora. I've told you times.'

'I don't believe you. You love me, I know it.'

'Look, Raymond's a good man—'

'*Don't.*' Her voice came sharp as a razor and silenced him. 'Don't say he's a good man because I can't stand hearing it again. Do you understand me? I can't stand it.'

52

Why couldn't he face up to things and accept that nothing was more important than their being together? Admittedly she might have started the affair with him to pay her sister back for the way Audrey had gloated and preened when she'd had Donald, Leonard and Bruce one after the other in the first three years of marriage, but that had soon changed. And no one could have blamed her for how she'd felt then. Her and Raymond had been married for umpteen years and no sign of a bairn and then Audrey had wed Ivor and the bairns had come thick and fast. But things always went smoothly for her sister. Their mam and da had had no time for her once Audrey was born, in spite of her sister being a plain little thing with nothing to commend her. And look at her now, with her great wobbling breasts and fat belly.

Ivor turned his head away from her and stared into the glowing coals of the fire. As Nora took in his grim profile, hatred for her sister gave way to panic and despair.

Some days each individual nerve in her body seemed to be raw, needing only the slightest provocation for her to become someone she barely recognised any more. But all that would change if Ivor would come away with her. She knew she couldn't threaten him. She'd tried that once years before, and it was the only time she'd ever seen him really angry. He'd warned her he'd deny everything and take Audrey and his bairns and disappear for good if she followed through on her threat to tell her sister the truth, and she'd known he meant it. And of course Audrey, silly gullible Audrey, would believe him. The sun rose and set with her Ivor. But the thought of them lying together, laughing, sharing the day-to-day happenings of life was more than she could stand at times. It should be her. Oh, it should be *her*. Nora dug her thumb and finger into the corners of her closed eyes, pressing until it hurt.

'You all right, Mam? You got a headache?'

The sound of her daughter's voice brought Nora's teeth clenching. She didn't allow herself to acknowledge that the irritation she'd always felt when confronted with her eldest child's strong will had grown into deep, bitter resentment in latter years. Neither did she concede that the main reason she could hardly bear to look at Abby was because the girl was determined to make something of herself and had her whole life before her still. Abby wouldn't make the mistakes she had and find herself trapped in a loveless marriage with a man who made her flesh creep. And the girl was growing more beautiful every day . . .

Nora raised her head, forcing herself to gaze at the youthful loveliness in front of her. Her hands itched to mark and spoil it. It reminded her that her own looks were fading fast; the mirror told her so more and more often of late even if she hadn't already noticed that men's eyes didn't follow her any more when she walked down the street or stood waiting for a tram. And it frightened her.

She swallowed hard, tearing her eyes away from the bane of her life. She told herself she hated the little upstart, she hated the whole lot of them, barring Ivor. Oh Ivor, *Ivor.*

'Mam? You feeling bad?'

As her daughter's hand went to touch her, Nora brushed it away and got to her feet. 'There's a pile of ironing a foot high waiting for you so I suggest you get your backside home where it belongs.'

'Granda wants another cup of tea first.' It was flat.

'I'll take it.'

This brought Ivor's head turning in surprise. It was rare Nora ventured into Silas's room; the last time had been at Christmas and only then because the rest of them had had a sing-song in the evening round the old man's bed and

54

Nora hadn't been able to avoid joining in. He and Abby exchanged a glance as Nora filled the cup Abby had placed on the table but neither of them spoke. Ivor returned to his contemplation of the fire and Abby said a subdued goodbye and left the house by the back door.

Nora braced herself before she walked into her father's room. She was never able to look at him without remembering what had occurred when she was eleven and Audrey three years old, an incident which was still as crystal clear in every detail as on the evening it had happened. Earlier that day Audrey had tumbled out of a dilapidated go-cart some of the lads had made and bumped her head badly, resulting in a visit from Dr Jefferson and a pronouncement that Audrey had been fortunate to get away with a case of mild concussion and not a fractured skull. It must have been nearly midnight when Nora had woken to the sound of Audrey being sick for the umpteenth time that day. She had gone to find her mother, but her parents' bedroom was empty. She heard the sound of voices from the kitchen below and had almost been at the kitchen door when she heard her name spoken. Curious to hear what her parents talked about when they were alone, she paused outside.

'Aye, well, I'm not saying it's right but it's the way I feel an' I can't help it, lass,' her father muttered.

'The way you feel is one thing, Silas.' Her mother's voice was so low Nora had to strain her ears. 'But to admit to praying a prayer like that is quite another. Asking the Lord to take one bairn at the cost of the other – you ought to be ashamed of yourself. It was a prayer to the devil, more like.'

'Aw, lass, don't take on. I've told you I'm not proud of it, haven't I? But when I thought our little lassie might be taken . . .' There was silence for a moment, and then her father went on, 'She's as different to the other as chalk to cheese, now you have to admit that. Our Nora is a cuckoo in the nest, she always has been.'

The shock had been like having a bucket of cold water poured over her. The rest of the conversation she had overheard suddenly became clear. Her da had prayed that Audrey would live and she would die. He had prayed that, her da.

How long she stood there she didn't know, but eventually she turned and climbed to the top of the stairs and it was from there that she had shouted for her mother to come and see to Audrey's bed. She had cried the whole night through, and when in the morning her mother had found her hot and swollen-eyed, the doctor had come again and diagnosed a fever. But it hadn't been that. And nothing had ever been the same again.

'Hello, Da.' She pushed the door wide and walked into the room, looking at the emaciated old man in the bed without a trace of pity in her voice or in her heart. She placed the cup of tea on the small table at the side of the bed, just far enough away to guarantee he would have to struggle for it, and then stood looking down at him for a second more before leaving the room as abruptly as she had entered it.

Chapter Four

Abby had been working for Mr Wynford for one month when James Benson asked her to go to the cinema with him. And she didn't have to think about her reply.

Two weeks after she had started at Price and Osborne, he had suggested walking her home to Rose Street. His home in Felstead Crescent off West Moor Road was in quite the opposite direction to Rose Street; so she knew he must like her a lot to go so far out of his way to see her alone. And she liked him back, that had never been in doubt, but with his father being a doctor and the family living in a select area on the outskirts of town, she had felt shy and a little awkward with him at first. He was so different to the lads she'd grown up with, that was the thing. But after two weeks of chatting about this and that on the way home she had learned a lot about him and her misgivings faded.

So when he finally suggested the cinema, taking her arm as they stood in their normal spot at the bottom of the street, Abby looked into his beautiful violet-blue eyes and said, primly enough but with her heart beating a tattoo, 'That would be very nice.'

'My thoughts exactly.' His hand on her arm relaxed slightly, a slow smile covering his face. 'It will be very, very nice, Miss Vickers.'

'You're laughing at me.'

'Not at all.' His hand lifted to her face, his smile dying and his eyes taking on a depth that suddenly made her hot all over. 'I would never do that, Abby. I guess I'm just relieved, that's all. I was worried you'd say no.'

No? This perfect being had thought she might say no? She could hardly believe it.

'I'll come and pick you up at seven o'clock, shall I? If I can sweet-talk my father I might be able to borrow the car.'

In one sentence he had highlighted the gulf between their backgrounds although Abby knew he hadn't meant to. She could just imagine the talk over the backyards the next morning if an automobile drew up outside their house. But she didn't want James to call at her home, she didn't want him to meet her mother yet. Her mam would try to spoil things, she felt it in her bones. She hesitated for a moment before saying quietly, 'Could I meet you at the corner of the tramway depot instead? My mam . . . Well, I know she wouldn't take kindly to my having a lad.'

The minute it was out she blushed crimson. How could she have said that? It sounded as if she had assumed they were courting now. He'd think she was taking a lot on herself.

He didn't appear to notice her confusion. He nodded and said, 'Yes, that's fine. The tramway depot it is then. See you at seven.'

She was too mortified at her blunder to do more than incline her head and hurry away, but when she reached her front door she looked back for a moment and saw he was still standing watching her. She raised her hand in a little nervous gesture of farewell before stepping inside the house and closing the door. She leaned against it for a moment, her eyes shut tight and her fingers pressed to her burning cheeks. Mr Wynford had told her only this morning that he was very satisfied with how she was shaping up, both in her work for him and the way she handled the staff in the outer office. What would her boss say if he could see her now? But Mr Wynford and her work were one thing, James Benson was quite another.

Well, it was too late now. She straightened, unbuttoned her light summer coat and hung it on one of the pegs in the hall. She'd said it and she couldn't take it back. She just dreaded to imagine what he was thinking right now though.

As it happened, James was thinking more about what Abby hadn't said than what she had as he walked home. Over the last couple of weeks they'd had some right good cracks on the way to Rose Street, their footsteps becoming slower each night, but in all their heart-to-hearts Abby had rarely mentioned her mother. He almost felt he knew the rest of the family, especially little Clara for whom Abby had an attachment which bordered on the maternal, but her mother . . .

James frowned, tilting his bowler hat further over his forehead as he walked on. It was obviously the mother who had prevented Abby having a gentleman friend before. Abby's evenings and weekends seemed to be spent mostly working in the home, from what he could gather. Mind you, he had to admit the mother had unwittingly done him a favour there. With looks like Abby's, she'd have been snapped up by some enterprising lad long before this otherwise.

He paused, glancing about him. This street was just like the ones surrounding it, depressing and claustrophobic. He'd love to take her out of this. Had she guessed how hard he'd fallen for her? Probably not, he answered himself. She was a complete innocent, after all. In the six years since his seventeenth birthday he'd been out with more than a few girls and some had been generous with their favours, but he'd always known he'd recognise the right one as soon as he saw her. And he had. It was just his luck that it had happened at a time when war with Germany was looking inevitable, not that he was going to let that put him off. Oh no. With or without her mother's blessing, he intended to start courting Miss Abigail Vickers without delay.

When Abby left the house later that evening to keep the rendezvous at the tram depot, her face was paler than normal, but otherwise she showed no outward sign of the row she'd had with her mother. It was not just about going to the pictures with a friend from work, Abby had also thrown in for good measure that she would no longer give her mother her unopened wage packet every week and receive pocket money back. From this very Friday, Abby had declared, she would pay fifteen shillings for board – five shillings more than if she'd still been at the pickle factory – but the rest of her money was her own. She needed new smart clothes to dress as she should as Mr Wynford's secretary, and she intended to buy a good sewing machine and quality material and make what she needed. She'd always been good at needlework and found patterns easy to follow. Mr Wynford had today confirmed that she'd be kept on in the post when Bernice left; it was high time for things to change.

The uproar had sent Wilbert and Clara diving for cover, but at the end of the commotion it was Nora who had conceded defeat. She knew only too well that her daughter could get lodgings anywhere for a great deal less than fifteen shillings, and she was not about to cut off her nose to spite her face.

When Abby turned the corner of Trimdon Street, she saw James waiting for her. Her heart leaped but she continued walking steadily towards him without a change of expression. She'd already made a fool of herself by all but declaring she thought she was his lass; she had to be circumspect this evening, however she was feeling inside.

'Hello.' He came striding to meet her, his face one big smile, and in spite of all Abby had told herself she found the blood was singing through her veins. She couldn't prevent her voice from trembling a little as she greeted him, but she hoped he hadn't noticed.

He looked so handsome but he seemed almost a stranger. The formal business suit he wore for the office had been replaced by a fine tweed jacket and beautifully cut Oxford bags and suede shoes.

'Father's partner is on call tonight so I've got the car,' he said happily. 'How about we try the Regal in Holmeside? I understand they're showing *The Lady Vanishes*. Do you like Alfred Hitchcock?'

Abby wasn't about to admit the only time she had been to a picture palace since the penny matinees as a child was when her father had taken her and Wilbert to see *The Bride of Frankenstein* three years before, on her brother's birthday. And then it hadn't been anywhere so grand as the Regal, the most luxurious cinema in Sunderland. She simply nodded, saying, 'Aye, yes I do,' her cheeks pink.

'Good.' He smiled at her. And then, his voice faintly throaty, he said, 'I'm glad you haven't had your hair cut in one of those bob things all the girls seem to go for these days.' His eyes moved to the thick shining coil of hair at the back of her head. 'It would be a crime to spoil it.'

'Thank you.' She was even pinker.

He cleared his throat and took her elbow as they began walking to where he had parked his father's Austin 7. 'I've wanted to ask you to come out with me one evening from the day you came for the interview but I didn't dare hope you felt the same as me.'

Abby found herself too taken aback – more from the look on his face than the words themselves – to reply for

61

a moment. And then, reminding herself he might just be being kind after her remark about him being her lad, she said, 'Well, you did in the end – ask me out, I mean.'

They reached the car but James did not immediately open the passenger door. Instead he drew her gently round to face him, looking down into the velvet brown of her eyes. 'I'd promised myself I wouldn't rush things, Abby, but I want you to know – well, what I mean is, I really like you.' And then he shook his head, his voice wry as he said, 'I'm making a right mess of this, aren't I?' He took a deep breath. 'I think I'm trying to say that even if your mother isn't too happy about you walking out with someone, I hope that won't stop you seeing me.'

She stared at him, and the silence stretched. He fiddled with the collar of his shirt, looking uncomfortable. It was enough for Abby to pull herself together. 'No, it won't.' She smiled widely.

'Good.' He grinned at her. 'For a minute there I thought I'd said the wrong thing.' He squeezed her hand, his eyes still on her face even as he opened the car door and settled her inside the vehicle.

Abby looked at James as he walked round the bonnet of the car and he was still grinning like a Cheshire cat. She bit hard on her bottom lip to stop herself doing the same. Here she was sitting in an automobile for the first time in her life and James Benson wanted her to be his lass! This was going to be a *lovely* evening.

It was a wonderful evening. From the first moment they walked into the extravagant foyer, Abby was in awe of her surroundings, even before James purchased tickets for the royal circle at two whole shillings each. A large box of chocolates tied with an enormous pink bow followed, and when they were shown to their seats she felt like pinching herself to make sure it wasn't all a fantastic dream.

The cinema's band, the Eagles, played before the programme commenced, and again between the main film, the newsreel, the magician doing his tricks and the short cartoon, and in the interval the Regal's mighty Compton organ came up and the organist entertained everyone while they ate their ice creams. By the time they re-emerged into the warm darkness of the late July evening, Abby knew James must have guessed she hadn't been to the Regal before, but by then it didn't matter.

'I don't want the evening to end.' In the car, James turned to her, his blue eyes glittering in the shadows.

Neither did Abby. She had noticed more than one pair of female eyes turn in his direction for a second look, and although she'd felt proud he had chosen to be with her above any other lass, she'd been surprised at how jealous she'd felt too.

'Do you fancy coming dancing on Saturday at the Empire? Lew Stone was there a few weeks ago and I think Billy Cotton's on for Saturday. Anyway, it'll be a good band at the Empire whoever it is, it always is.' Added to which he'd get to hold her as close as he wanted, for some of the evening at least.

She didn't have a dance dress or shoes but she had Saturday to find what she needed. Abby nodded. 'Yes, please.'

'Great.' He smiled at her. 'My pals are going to be pea-green with envy that I've got the most beautiful girl in the world on my arm.'

She giggled, and then, as his face came nearer, she knew he was going to kiss her and she became very still. His mouth was warm and firm, the kiss was everything she'd dreamed her first kiss from a lad would be and now he was so close she could smell a faint spicy perfume coming from his skin and it was intoxicating.

As for James, he couldn't believe what the feel of her lips, even tightly closed as they were, was doing to him. He had sown quite a few wild oats during his university years; the sudden freedom from the tight restrictions of being an only child and the apple of his mother's eye, not to mention the willingness of some of the liberated young ladies with whom he had associated, had gone to his head. But not even with Mary, his first lover who had taken great delight in initiating him into the pleasures of the flesh – she was studying to be a doctor and needed to be conversant with the male anatomy, she'd teased – had he felt like this. But then he hadn't loved Mary, nor she him for that matter, and therein lay the difference. He might have known her only a few weeks but Abby had taken over his mind and his heart.

'I'd better get you home.' Reluctantly he forced himself to draw away and start the engine, his body as hard as a rock beneath the wide trousers he was wearing. Glancing at the box of chocolates Abby was clutching, he added, 'What are you going to do with that? Your mother will guess you've seen a lad if you walk in with it.'

Abby looked down at the box. It was beautiful, a picture on the lid of a thatched cottage with roses round the door, and it still contained half the chocolates even though she and James had eaten loads. She would keep this box for ever and ever as a reminder of this magical night. 'I don't care.' And suddenly she didn't. 'I'm nearly eighteen, for goodness sake, it's not as if I've just left school or something. I shall tell her about you if she says anything.'

'You will?' He suddenly felt ten feet tall. If she was going to brave her mother's wrath, it had to mean she was serious about him, didn't it? 'You will?' he repeated, his voice low now and soft as he touched the silky skin of her face with the tip of one finger. And as she nodded, blushing rosy pink but holding his gaze, he kissed her again.

64

PART TWO

Goodbyes
1939

Chapter Five

'I am speaking to you from the Cabinet Room of Ten Downing Street. This morning the British Ambassador in Berlin handed the German government a final note stating that unless we had heard from them by eleven o'clock that they were prepared to withdraw their troops from Poland, a state of war would exist between us. I have to tell you now that no such undertaking has been received, and that consequently this nation is at war with Germany.'

'Oh, Da.' Abby was clutching her father so tightly her knuckles were showing white. 'It's happened.'

Wilbert switched off the wireless and looked at his sister, his voice verging on the scornful as he said, 'You're not surprised, are you? What do you think all the preparations have been about the last year or so, with the air raid wardens and the shelters and everything? You said yourself your firm's organised their switchboard so it can be used by other companies and the ARP.'

'Aye, that's all very well, lad, but it's still a shock when the unimaginable happens. And that's what this war will be, make no mistake.' Raymond's voice was grim. 'He's a maniac, that Hitler, and he's got to be stopped, there's no doubt about that, but the cost'll be high.'

'That's right, frighten everyone to death.' Nora glared at her husband. Like the majority of the housewives round about she had refused to believe there would be another war, regarding the ARP service and especially

67

the wardens with some contempt. The only time she had shown a spark of interest was when it had been suggested they might like to share one of the brick surface shelters with her sister's household. This had come to nothing, however, when Ivor had insisted the backyards weren't big enough what with the wash house and privies, even though several families in their street and the ones surrounding it had installed brick shelters. The upshot of Ivor's refusal was that both families had taken an indoor Morrison shelter instead.

Abby glanced across to the steel oblong box which normally served as a table. Her father had insisted that blankets, cushions and a torch be put inside some weeks ago, and that they all got used to climbing inside and pulling the meshed panels at the sides and ends into place. Now it looked as though they would be using the shelter for real.

Abby had no sooner thought this than the wail of air raid sirens sounded, causing them all to freeze and stare at each other for a moment. 'Quick!' Raymond was shouting as though the rest of them were in the next room. 'Into the shelter, all of you. Move!'

By the time it became clear that there was no immediate threat of aerial onslaught, Clara had bumped her head and was crying loudly, Wilbert had knelt on the torch and had a lump the size of a ha'penny gobstopper on his knee, and Nora had split the seam of her Sunday dress and was blaming her husband.

'I don't want to go in there again.' Clara was hiccuping her tears now. 'And I don't want to put that on either,' she added, pointing to the row of gas masks sitting on the kitchen window sill. 'They're smelly and horrible.'

'Come on, pet.' Abby lifted her sister into her arms. 'I tell you what, if you're a good lass you can come for a little ride in James's car this afternoon. Just round the streets for a few minutes so Betty Skelton and Hilda Wright can see you. You'd like that, wouldn't you?'

Clara grinned at Abby and nodded. Betty and Hilda were her two best friends but when she had told them that her sister had a lad with a big car and that they had taken her for a ride in it, they'd said she was telling fibs. But Abby had shown them, Clara thought complacently. The very next Sunday after she had come home in tears because they had fallen out with her for telling lies, Abby and James had taken her for a ride and stopped right outside Betty's house. Betty's eyes had been like saucers. Clara wriggled with ecstasy as she remembered. And the next day at school Betty had given her a whole bag of bullets and Hilda had let her play with her new skipping rope without taking turns, and they'd never called her a liar again.

Hugging Abby's neck she planted a wet kiss on her sister's cheek. She loved Abby the best in all the world.

'Excuse me but isn't it his *father's* car?' Nora sniffed pointedly. 'Good as James's fancy job might be, I don't think it would run to buying and running a car.'

Abby looked at her mother over Clara's blonde head. Her mam never let up, not even on this day when war had been declared. She was like a dog with a bone as far as James was concerned and yet he had never put a foot wrong in all the time they had been seeing each other. But he'd never please her mam, Abby was reconciled to that now.

Right from that first magical night when she had walked into the kitchen with the enormous box of chocolates clutched in her arms and declared to her mother she had a lad, the atmosphere within the house had been such you could cut it with a knife. She could have understood it if she'd decided to walk out with someone like Jack McHaffie or Rory Fallow, who were no strangers to the local constable and the prison cells, but James? Her Aunty

Audrey had declared James was the perfect suitor for any daughter. But when her mother had found out James was a doctor's son and had been to university, and that he was training to be an accountant, you would have thought he was Jack the Ripper from the way she had reacted. Father Finlay had made another appearance, but the fact that James's parents were Catholics, albeit nominal ones, had taken the wind out of the good Father's sails to some extent.

Father Finlay had demanded – and demanded was the right word for his imperious manner – to have a meeting with James, and it was then that Abby realised just how much she had changed. She had looked steadily at the man she had been terrified of all her life and for the first time she saw him for what he was – a man like any other. She refused Father Finlay's demand – what right had he to subject James to what at best would be an interrogation? – and the priest had left the house in a huff, with her mother flapping at his coat-tails.

Her father's voice brought her back to the present. 'You going for a run in the country again, lass?' he asked, and she knew he was trying to pour oil on troubled waters.

She nodded, but before she could speak her mother said with some satisfaction, 'According to the postmistress it won't be long before they'll stop such jaunts. Petrol will be needed for better things than waltzing about in fancy cars on a Sunday afternoon.'

Abby was on the point of firing back when the gravity of the day swept over her anew. Instead of responding to her mother's sniping she remained quiet and walked out into the backyard with Clara. It was a perfect September day. The sky was blue and cloudless and somewhere high in the thermals a lark was singing.

Abby sighed. It seemed incredible war could have been declared on such a beautiful Sunday morning but already things were different. Normally the back lane would be ringing with the shouts of bairns playing their games in the ridges of dried mud and dust, but today there was an ominous silence. Everyone had been glued to their wirelesses since early morning, and the only life she could see was a solitary black cat stalking along a wall some distance away.

Oh James, James. She wished he was here right this minute. She hugged Clara to her. Although he'd said little about his intentions should war be declared, she knew from comments he'd made to some of his friends that he would enlist. They all would. Which was probably why she'd taken a leaf out of her mam's book and buried her head in the sand. Even in the last couple of days, when the country had been under blackout regulations and the town hall clock light extinguished and its chimes silenced, she'd told herself Hitler would back down at the last moment.

'Am I going to get any help with the vegetables or not? And put her down, for goodness sake. She's not a baby.'

Her mother's voice from the doorway behind her caused Abby's mouth to tighten, but again she bit back the sharp rejoinder which came to mind. One half of the world seemed intent on invading and destroying the other half, and all her mam cared about was the Sunday dinner.

The toot of a car horn outside announced James was early. Abby jumped up from the kitchen table, only for Nora to snap, 'You, sit down and finish your dinner. He can wait.'

Abby did not answer her mother but glanced towards her father, and when he gave an almost imperceptible nod, saying, 'Let her go. No one wants to eat the day,' she fairly flew into the hall.

Clara had been sick just before dinner and was now asleep in bed, so when Abby shot out of the house it was only she who climbed into the car.

'That was quick.' James bent forward and kissed her but did not prolong the embrace, being only too aware of staring eyes and flapping ears up and down the street. Now the shock of Chamberlain's speech had diminished and Sunday dinner was over, most people had gathered on their doorsteps to discuss the war. Since courting Abby he had come to understand that although Felstead Crescent was only a mile or so from Rose Street, it could have been another country. There were two doctors, a solicitor and several businessmen of high standing living in the Crescent, and everyone – at least outwardly – minded their own business. But in the last twelve months he'd learned enough to know that any gossip right on their own doorstep would hold more appeal for Abby's neighbours than Hitler's possible strategies.

'Da's home for a few days.'

It was explanation enough and James nodded. He had tried his best to win Abby's mother over in the early days of his relationship with her daughter, but had eventually admitted defeat, coming to the conclusion it was less traumatic for all concerned if he didn't come into the house. Sometimes Nora managed to delay Abby for fifteen minutes or more before she was able to join him, but he did not mind this. He would wait all day for Abby. 'How do you feel?' he asked, starting the engine. 'About the war, I mean.'

'Awful.' She waited until they were clear of Rose Street before she said, 'How about you?'

'The same, I suppose.'

No, he didn't. Abby glanced at him. There had been a bubble of excitement he couldn't quite hide in his voice. Fear for him turned her stomach over but her voice was calm enough when she said, 'I suppose you'll join up now.'

'Would you mind?'

Of course she'd mind. She'd mind more than she could ever say. She smoothed the skirt of her pale pink georgette dress over her knees. She had made it from a pattern she'd found in one of the latest magazines and had been dying for James to see her in it all week. Now it didn't matter.

He glanced at her, one hand going out to cover hers briefly before he brought it back to the steering wheel. 'Look, we'll discuss it over a pot of tea a bit later, all right? At our place.'

'Our place' was a sixteenth-century-style inn they'd found early on in their courting days, tastefully furnished with antiques and serving afternoon teas. The two of them were a favourite with the landlady and she always found them a table, however busy it was.

That afternoon James put himself out to be even more entertaining than usual and Abby's mood lifted. But later, when they were sitting at a table overlooking the inn's pretty Victorian garden, all her fears flooded back. The gleaming silver teapot, lovely crockery, crisp damask table-cloth and the black and white uniforms of the maids failed to hold their normal appeal; even the buttered teacakes kept hot in silver dishes and delicious cream and jam cakes tasted like sawdust. James, however, tucked in with as much gusto as usual so she waited until he had finished his fifth teacake before she said flatly, 'You're going to join up, aren't you?'

'Sweetheart, don't look like that.' He reached across the table and took her hands in his. 'We've got to face facts here. The call-up for men of my age is probably going to come in a month or so and I'd rather not wait till then. Call it pride or whatever, but I'd rather enlist before I'm forced to. I can't explain it any better than that. But I don't want to leave you. Of course I don't want to leave you.'

73

His hands were warm and strong. Abby looked down at their entwined fingers and found it hard to imagine his would soon be holding a gun. Nevertheless, in spite of how she was feeling, she could see he had a point even if she did think male pride was the most stupid thing on earth. James wasn't in a reserved occupation or a member of the clergy, and he was twenty-four years old. It would be expected he would fight.

'What if they find something wrong with you?' she asked in a small voice. 'Nothing serious,' she added quickly, aware she was tempting fate. 'Just something that prevents you being accepted.'

'Oh, sweetheart, come on.' He smiled slowly. 'I don't think that's at all likely, do you?'

No, she didn't. She stared at him forlornly. Her James fighting people, hurting people, *killing* them? It was madness. He'd never hurt a fly. The only time she had ever seen another side to him, a darker side, had been when he'd taken her to meet his parents and his mother had been somewhat offhand with her. He had been angry that day and hadn't tried to brush over the incident but had faced his mother head on, much to Abby's embarrassment. But his mother was a snob, Abby had known that as soon as she'd set eyes on Mrs Benson, just as she'd known James's father was lovely with no side to him at all. Mind, to give his mother her due, Mrs Benson had made an effort over the last months. It was probably partly for James's sake and partly because Dr Benson made her so welcome, rather than that the older woman had begun to warm to her, but that didn't matter if it made for an easy atmosphere.

They said little on the way home, but when James parked the car in one of the secluded leafy lanes they had discovered, Abby found their lovemaking bitter-sweet.

She returned his kisses and caresses as passionately as

ever, but this time there was a desperation to their petting which had never been there before, removing all restraints. Her need of him was spiralling up through her body in shuddering gasps and she clung to him, shutting out all thoughts of what the future might hold. James was telling her she was the most beautiful girl in the world, that he loved her more than life itself – and he was going away to war. He could be injured or worse, and she wouldn't be able to bear it. She knew she wouldn't. What would she do if she lost him? How would she get through the rest of her life?

It was James, more experienced and fearful of what the consequences might be for the woman he loved, who prevented their coming together, but he did it tenderly, making sure she realised how much she meant to him. 'I love you more than I imagined it was possible to love someone, you know that, don't you? And nothing will separate us, my darling. You have to believe that.'

She wanted to. Oh, how she wanted to. Abby continued to cling to him as they sat quietly now in the car, the last birdsong poignant in the scented twilight. She stroked the fine blond hairs on the back of his hand, telling herself she must not cry. Then, sitting up straighter, she pressed his fingers. 'When you go, you will write to me?'

'Every single day.' He smiled, stroking her face gently. 'And don't forget, I'll be home on leave now and again. It might not be so bad, darling.'

It would be horrible. She nodded slowly. 'No, I know. And . . . and I do understand how you feel, James. I suppose it's just that I've been spoiled, seeing you at the office every day and in the evenings too. It's been nice.'

'Wonderful,' he agreed softly, grinning as he added, 'But they do say absence makes the heart grow even fonder.'

'That would be impossible.' She felt she was drowning in the deep blue of his eyes as her own misted. 'I love you so much already.' He would never be able to understand how he had changed her life. Having someone there who was totally for her, who listened and understood and loved her. Her da had always loved her, of course, but being away as much as he had been all through her life she had never been able to rely on him being there when she needed him. It was as if James was the other part of her, that was the only way she could describe the closeness she felt with him.

'Sweetheart, one day when we're old and grey we'll look back at this evening and wonder why we felt so miserable,' he assured her tenderly. 'We'll look at our grandchildren playing about our feet and marvel at the years we've had together. I promise you.'

But he couldn't really promise her. She stared into the dear face in front of her and tried to smile. Because no one knew how this war was going to end and what would happen to the men and women involved in it.

By the time the car drew up outside 12 Rose Street, Abby felt so emotionally drained she just gave James a quick kiss and got out of the car. She waved as he drove off. Although the day had been warm, the night was cool, and she shivered as the car turned the corner and disappeared from view.

Suddenly the one person in all the world she wanted to speak to was Winnie, but she wouldn't be seeing her until Tuesday evening when they had planned to go to the cinema as a foursome, for Winnie now had a steady lad too. He was a bit of a rough diamond, was Lonnie Johnson, being a docker whose family lived in a less than salubrious part of the East End, but as James had said after he first met Lonnie, he was pure salt of the earth.

76

Abby glanced at the dainty silver wristwatch James had bought her for Christmas. Ten o'clock. Too late to do anything other than go to bed but sleep had never seemed so far away.

Chapter Six

It was nearly eleven o'clock before James walked into the office the next morning and the moment Abby looked at his face she knew what he had done. He didn't immediately make his way to Mr Hardcastle to offer his excuses for being late as would normally be expected, instead he glanced over to where she was engaged in giving Felicity Cook some work and inclined his head.

'When do you go?' She spoke as soon as she reached him; there was no point in pretending.

'We leave for training within three days. I'm going to tell them all in a minute but I wanted to talk to you first.'

They stared at each other.

'There was no point in dragging it out, Abby. Mother fairly hit the roof last night when I told her what I wanted to do, and I made up my mind then it had to be done immediately. She came up with a whole host of reasons why it was better to wait until I was called up.'

For once she was entirely with his mother.

'It was pandemonium down there this morning. I saw half a dozen blokes I knew.'

The same bubble of excitement was present in his voice again and Abby found she wanted to hit him. How could he feel anything but the utmost dread at the prospect of going away to war?

'Anyway,' he drew in a sharp, short breath, 'it's done

now and that's that. You'll come and see me off Wednesday afternoon?'

'Wednesday afternoon? That soon?' Abby was silent for a moment. It was taking all her control not to burst into tears.

'Please?'

'Of course I'll come and see you off.' From somewhere she found the strength to smile and added, 'I'd like to see anyone try and stop me.'

'That's my girl.'

His own smile carried a thread of relief and in that moment Abby knew he had planned to tell her in a place where she was unable to give way to her feelings. She didn't know if this made her angry or grateful.

Her eyes were dry and bright as she watched him walk over to Mr Hardcastle but she didn't return to Felicity; instead she made her way to her office which she entered without looking back into the main office. She sat down at her desk and was surprised to find her hands were trembling when she tried to insert a piece of paper into the typewriter. She'd never been more thankful for her little cubbyhole away from prying eyes.

Five minutes later when James popped his head round the door and asked if he could have a word with Mr Wynford, she was perfectly composed, and this state of affairs continued for the rest of the day.

James walked her home but in view of all the preparations he had to make they agreed not to see each other that night. Abby said she would get in touch with Winnie and cancel their arrangement for the cinema the following night so she and James could be alone on their last evening together. All the cinemas had closed at the announcement of war anyway, and schoolchildren had had their summer holiday break extended, much to their delight. Shops were advised to close at six o'clock and even the churches had cancelled their evening services.

Abby stood on her doorstep until James had turned the corner and when he stopped and looked back at her, raising his hand to his lips and blowing her a kiss, the sunlight slanted across his hair and turned it golden. It was in that moment she realised she was angry with him for choosing to leave her a day before he had to, and she stood in the street for a good minute or so more, giving herself a silent dressing-down. She was being silly and weak and unpatriotic and she must never let him guess she'd had such a feeling for a moment, she told herself firmly. He was brave, so brave – like all the other men who were leaving wives and mothers and sweethearts. She ought to be thoroughly ashamed of herself.

When she entered the house, it was to find Clara, her face tear-stained, attempting to sew a name tag onto a pair of her thick woollen stockings. The kitchen table was strewn with clothes.

'Look at that.' Her mother barely raised her head from the scullery sink where she was busy scrubbing an old haversack of her husband's, which carried an odour all of its own. 'That list on the table. Everything has to have a name tag but did Miss Forget-her-own-name remember to tell me that? I've enough to do mending the holes she makes in her things as it is and now they're insisting they want a holder for the gas mask, with shoulder straps.'

Abby picked up the piece of paper. It advised parents of children wishing to be evacuated that suitable clothing had to accompany each child. For boys: one vest, one shirt with collar, one pair of underpants, one jersey or pullover, one pair of trousers, handkerchiefs and two pairs of socks. For girls: one vest or combination, one pair of knickers, one bodice, one petticoat, two pairs of stockings, handkerchiefs, gym slip, blouse, hat and cardigan. Nightclothes, comb and brush, toothbrush, slippers, towel, soap and face cloth had to be carried by the same child separately.

Abby raised her head. Newcastle and Gateshead had already evacuated the mothers, infants and schoolchildren who wanted to leave the towns for the relative safety of the countryside of North and East Yorkshire; Sunderland was due to follow suit on 10 September. Her mother had had this list for weeks but had done nothing about it, refusing to accept there would be a war, and now she was blaming Clara because nothing was ready.

'I'll see to the name tags,' Abby said flatly, 'and I've got a piece of thick linen which will do for the holder for the gas mask. There's still plenty of time.'

'Says you! Sure sign you don't work your fingers to the bone from dawn to dusk like me, that's all I can say.'

Clara had risen from her seat while their mother had been speaking. She went across to Abby and tugged on her sister's dress. 'I don't want to go. Not everyone's going and I don't want to. I want to stay here.' She didn't add 'with you', but she didn't have to. Abby knew what her sister meant.

She bent down and put her arms round Clara, saying softly, 'Jed's going, isn't he, so it's not as if you'll be all by yourself. And Aunty Audrey is going with you and Jed to settle you in. She'll stay for a week or two until you're used to everything. It will be exciting, Clara. Like a holiday.'

'I want to stay here. Jed does too, he told me.'

'You're both going with Aunty Audrey and that's that.' Nora's voice could have cut granite. 'And don't you encourage Jed to play up about leaving or I'll take my hand to you again. Your aunt's said she'll stay for a while so be grateful to her.'

Abby glanced at her mother in surprise. It wasn't often Aunty Audrey got a commendation in this kitchen. 'Where's Da?' she asked, aiming to take her mother's mind off Clara who was now crying again but silently.

'Shipping Office,' said Nora briefly.

'Shouldn't he wait to see what happens, with the war and everything?'

'And what do we do for money in the meantime? Don't talk daft, girl. Life goes on in spite of Hitler.'

Clara, her face working and her lips trembling, stared at her mother who continued to pound at the stained canvas, and then her eyes moved to her sister's face. She had been longing for Abby to come home. Abby wasn't frightened of their mam like everyone else, and whatever Wilbert said, he *was* scared. He certainly never stuck up for her like Abby did.

Abby's voice was low as she said, 'I'll do the rest of the name tags, hinny.' Clara's small fingers were bloodstained with the number of times she'd pricked herself with the needle. 'It won't take long. And you'll like it with Jed on a farm or something in the country. Honestly.'

Blinking, sniffing and wiping her nose on the sleeve of her cardigan, all in one movement, Clara whispered, 'I don't want to go.'

'I know, I know.' Abby's hand cupped her cheek. 'But you'll have Jed and you'll soon make friends.'

Jed. Clara wasn't sure right at this moment if she still liked Jed. Her mam had brayed her something rotten just because she'd said she and Jed didn't want to go away, blaming it all on her, when really it was Jed who had shouted and played up because he didn't want to leave Aunty Audrey. She wouldn't mind leaving *her* mam. Her eyes moved back to Nora's face. Everything would be perfect if Abby could come with her. But she couldn't, she was too old. Jed had said so and that was when she had agreed with him that they should play up a bit.

Just to make sure, she whispered, 'Couldn't you come, Abby? Like Aunty Audrey is with Jed?'

'I can't. It's not allowed, pet. It has to be your mam.'

Clara swallowed hard. She couldn't think of anything worse than being stuck with her mam in a strange place, and when the teacher at school had first explained about evacuation and what it meant, she'd prayed her mother wouldn't want to go. Not that she had admitted that in confession, not with Father Finlay, even though everyone knew God emptied a priest's mind of everything he'd heard in the confessional box. It might be wicked but she felt if any priest would remember, it was bound to be Father Finlay and most definitely about something she'd admitted. Anyway, her mam didn't want to leave Sunderland and it seemed she'd made her mind up about that as soon as evacuation was mentioned, so perhaps it wasn't her prayers that had affected things.

And as though Abby had read her mind – which Clara was quite sure was possible because her big sister could do anything in the world – she said very softly, 'Just be glad Mam doesn't want to go and settle you in, Clara. Aunty Audrey will look after you. You'll like it when you've got used to it, I know you will.'

Not without Abby she wouldn't.

'And if you're a good lass and don't cry any more I'll give you a present when you go. A surprise.'

'What surprise?'

'It wouldn't be a surprise if I told you what it was, now would it?' Abby pushed her slightly with her elbow, making a funny face. 'But you have to be good, all right?'

Clara thought for a moment. She was going to have to go anyway – her mam had said so, so that was the end of the matter – and at least this way she'd have something special from Abby to take with her. She nodded. 'All right.'

Oh, to be that age again, when anything could be made better by the promise of a present. Abby smiled at her sister before gathering up all Clara's clothes and putting them to one side. She began to lay the kitchen table for dinner, trying to ignore the lump in her throat as she worked. She did so want to talk to Winnie, she just hoped she was in when she visited.

Winnie was in and she answered the door herself. Abby had been to the house in Liddell Terrace on the north side of the river several times, and she liked Winnie's family although she wasn't too sure about Mr Todd. Winnie's five older brothers were miners like their father and as the only girl Winnie was constantly chaffed and teased by them, but it was clear they loved their baby sister. And Mrs Todd, although always harassed and tired, obviously doted on Winnie too, but Mr Todd was difficult to fathom and not what Abby had expected, being somewhat dour and sarcastic. But Winnie worshipped the ground he walked on; her conversation was always peppered with 'my da this' and 'my da that' even though he rarely gave her the time of day.

'Ee, lass, I was just about to put me coat on and come and see you,' Winnie said as she waved Abby into the house. 'You'll never guess what Lonnie's done. He's only joined up, daft blighter.'

'So has James.'

'Never! By, I thought he'd got more sense, him being white collar and with a university education and everything. I'd expect Lonnie to do something stupid, daft as a brush he is most of the time, but your James? Never.'

'Never or not, that's what he's done.'

There was a pause during which the two girls stared at each other, and then Winnie said softly, 'I'll tell them we're going to have a chat private like upstairs, all right? Go on up, lass. That's if you can stop a while?' she added.

Abby nodded. 'I can stay,' she said flatly.

The house was a two-up, two-down terrace, with Winnie's five brothers packed like sardines in one bedroom and Winnie in splendid isolation in the other. Her parents had the front room as their bedroom. Winnie's room was the normal higgledy-piggledy mess it always was, clothes strewn everywhere, bed unmade and piles of this and that littering every available surface. Abby picked her way to the narrow iron bed and cleared a space before sitting down. She loved her friend dearly but she could never understand how she could choose to live in such a muddle when she had a whole room to herself. Abby and Wilbert had shared a bedroom with a piece of curtain separating their space before Clara had come along, when Wilbert was despatched to the desk bed in the kitchen and her baby sister's cot took the place of his bed. It had remained propped against the wall until Clara had been old enough to use it.

When Winnie came into the room a few moments later she was carrying a tray on which were two cups of steaming tea and a plate of her mother's gingerbread. 'Me mam thinks you want feeding up,' she said, nodding to the gingerbread, before adding ruefully, 'If you're not going on fifteen stone you're fading away as far as me mam's concerned. Hence my shape.'

'You're all right.' Abby smiled at her even though she felt like crying at Mrs Todd's kindness. But that was because she was all upset about James, she told herself silently, and she couldn't give way here. Winnie was a good friend but she wouldn't understand, she didn't feel that way about Lonnie.

85

And then Winnie proved her both right and wrong when she plumped down beside her on the bed and said, 'He's mad, your James, to join up before he has to, the way you two feel about each other. Have a flippin' good bawl if you want to, lass. Let it all out. It's different for me. I like Lonnie, I like him a lot but, well, we're not like you two. I don't fool myself he won't go with other women if he gets the chance, not Lonnie.'

'Oh, Winnie.' Abby was shocked. 'Surely not.'

Winnie passed her a cup of tea and offered the plate of gingerbread to which Abby shook her head.

'Lass, look at me,' Winnie said. 'I've always known that the only way I got Lonnie was because I was on for a bit of slap and tickle. He likes his bit of carry-on a couple of times a week and if he couldn't get it from me he'd find someone else. And, well, he was the first lad for a while to look the side I was on.'

'You're selling yourself short, Winnie. You always do.'

'No, I just look in the mirror, lass, that's all.'

Abby didn't know what to say. Winnie had a thing about her size and had tried to cut down on her food time and time again, but she could never keep it up. 'Winnie, you're so pretty. You are.'

'It's all right.' Winnie grinned at her. 'It's not that I don't like a bit of carry-on meself mind, so I'm not complaining. And Lonnie's been good to me, kind and all that. It's just that I know he'll have a roving eye, and with him likely to go abroad an' all, I'm not going to fool myself and sit at home twiddling my thumbs thinking he'll come back to me. I'm realistic, lass. I always have been. We've agreed we'll part as pals and no hard feelings on either side.'

She popped her third piece of gingerbread into her mouth, chewed and swallowed, then said, 'With any luck there'll soon be plenty of blokes in uniform at the Empire on a Saturday night to choose from. I *love* a uniform. It sets me knicker elastic trembling the minute I set eyes on one.'

Abby giggled and Winnie, who always loved an audience, set out to play the jester for the rest of the evening.

But when the two girls were standing waiting for the tram which would take Abby over the bridge to Bishopwearmouth, Winnie's tomfoolery fell from her like a cloak. Turning to Abby, she said, 'If me an' Lonnie'd had what you and James have got, I'd wait for him, you know. It'll be all right, lass. We can go out sometimes, just the two of us, without looking at any lads. You can sit and bore the pants off me by talking about James and I'll tell you what I've been up to.'

It was Winnie's way of saying she would be there for her in the weeks and months ahead, and Abby was touched. 'Thanks,' she said softly.

'Mind, regarding the pants, with a bit of luck they might be off more than they're on anyway,' Winnie said with one of her cheeky grins which widened as Abby pushed at her with her elbow and glanced nervously at the couple behind them.

On the tram, its interior lights dimmed as low as possible and its windows half covered with blue paint in accordance with blackout regulations, Abby sank back on the seat. She had laughed more than she would have thought possible in the circumstances this evening; what would she do without Winnie? But it was funny how everyone said it would be all right at times like this. Hadn't she said the selfsame thing to Clara when she'd tried to comfort her about leaving home? Empty words really, meaningless, because how did any of them know if everything was going to work out?

Abby gazed out of the window as the tram rattled and shook its way over the bridge. The dark expanse of the river below was full of tugboats, colliers, salvage ships and trawlers, all jostling for mooring space in the black water as they had done every night for decades. It was a normal sight, safe, and she hugged the familiarity to her, needing its reassurance.

And then she sat up straighter, momentarily angry with herself for the nature of her musing. She had thought her path was all mapped out and that she knew exactly where she was going, but now she had to take a side road. Well, all right, so had thousands, millions of other folk and it wouldn't help anyone, least of all James, if she looked on the black side in all of this. What would be, would be. When she saw James off he'd carry the memory of a smiling face and the knowledge that she was proud of him, or her name wasn't Abigail Vickers!

'You'll write me? I want to know every detail.'

'I'll write, how could I not? It'll bring you closer to me for one thing. I shall imagine I'm talking to you, that you're right in front of me.' James gripped her hands even tighter, his blue eyes locked on her face. 'And this is only training camp, sweetheart. Remember that.'

'I know.' Mindful of the promise she had made herself, Abby smiled at him. Central Station was crowded and busy, people jostling here and there, but they had said their proper goodbyes in private the night before. The memory of this brought an inward glow for a moment and she reached up and touched his face, her voice soft as she said, 'I'll wait for you for as long as it takes. You know that, don't you? Oh, I love you so much.'

'And I you.' He drew her into his arms and she clung to him, willing herself not to break down. He had said that he expected they would be allowed home on leave for a couple of days once the training was completed, but he didn't know for sure. Suddenly the possibility they might not hold each other again for a long time was all too real.

'You'll be careful, won't you?'

It was a silly thing to say and he smiled at her. 'I dare say I will survive the dangers of training camp,' he said wryly, 'but it's you who should be careful with the blackout restrictions making the roads so lethal.' He stared into the velvet brown of her eyes, his gaze moving for a moment to the little silvery line at the top of her brow. He had felt like doing murder when Abby had first explained how she'd got it and the way her mother had regularly whipped her when she was younger. On the few occasions he had met Mrs Vickers he had felt that there was something missing in her, some basic human emotion, but when Abby had opened up to him a couple of months after they had started going out together, he had realised it was more an acute selfishness he had sensed. He wanted to give Abby a wonderful life. He raised his hand and touched the scar tenderly. He wanted to make up for everything she had ever suffered at her mother's hands, to tell her every day she was loved more than she would ever know. 'You're so beautiful,' he said softly. 'Inside and out.' And then, turning his head, he groaned, saying, 'Here's the train, I have to go.'

He gathered her into his arms and pressed her so close to his hard male body she could scarcely breathe. Their lips clung and clung, neither wanting to break contact. It was a minute or more before he reluctantly released her, his voice thick as he murmured, 'I love you, my sweet, always remember that till we meet again and I can tell you in person. Tell me you love me.'

'I do, I do so much.'

They had been moving towards the train and now James opened the carriage door and climbed in, their hands still clasped. Then he had to let go. The train was late and it moved off immediately everyone was on board. Abby stood staring after it for some time, unable to take in the fact that he was gone.

'Always remember that I love you too,' she whispered as even the plume of steam from the engine disappeared. She stood for some moments more and then slowly made her way out of the station.

Chapter Seven

'This is good of you, Audrey, you taking Clara along-side of Jed. I appreciate it.'

Abby glanced at her mother, unaware she had put her head forward slightly as though she hadn't heard clearly, but the tone of her mother's voice was amazing in its warmth.

Audrey looked a little surprised too but she put out her hand and patted her sister's arm, saying, 'Glad to help. Jed wasn't going nowhere unless I went with him and settled him in, that much was clear, so it's no skin off my nose to see to Clara too. At least this way we'll know exactly where they are and who they're with from the word go, eh?'

'Aye, that's right.'

The three women and Ivor, Jed and Clara were in Central Station waiting for the train which would take the two youngsters to Yorkshire. It was a Sunday and the plat-form was packed with men and women come to see their families off to the safety of the countryside. It was so noisy you couldn't hear yourself think.

'It won't do Ivor and the lads any harm to fend for themselves for a few days either. Make 'em appreciate me more when I get back. Isn't that right, Ivor?' Audrey dug her husband in the ribs and he smiled weakly.

'If you say so, love.'

Abby could see her uncle was on edge but then it wasn't surprising; they'd all been affected by the sight of the train station full of children carefully labelled, each clutching a small bag of belongings and a gas mask. News was already filtering through that the best dressed or most mannerly children were likely to be snapped up by the good homes, leaving bairns who were unattractive, lousy, sickly or too tearful to be slotted in where they could. Ivor had called it the devil's sweepstake and he'd hit the nail on the head in Abby's opinion.

Clara was clinging hold of her hand with all her might, the beautifully dressed doll which had been Abby's present to her tucked under one arm. Now, as the train wheezed and belched its way into the station, she said tearfully, 'Abby, I don't want to go. I want to stay here with you.'

'What did you promise me?' Abby crouched down, putting her arms round her sister and swallowing against the lump in her own throat. Clara was such a baby still and so timid, mainly, Abby felt, because of their mother's treatment of the child. Much as she tried to protect Clara, she couldn't be there all the time, and twice in the last week their mam had leathered her for next to nothing.

'That I'd be good.'

'And Aunty Audrey and Jed will look after you. You won't be by yourself.'

'But I want to be with *you*.'

'You can't, hinny.' Abby straightened, adjusting Clara's hat and pulling the collar of her sister's coat more closely round the scrawny little neck. It was a cold day and rainy; the summer was well and truly over. 'Now be a good girl for me, all right?'

Nora gritted her teeth, an impotent rage filling her. Look at her; as if spoiling the brat with that expensive doll wasn't enough, Abby was now aiming to show her up by taking her place in the proceedings. Quite the little mother, that's what she wanted them all to think – oh, she knew her daughter all right. Cunning as a cartload of monkeys, she was, when it came to putting herself in a good light. Just like Audrey. The two of them were like peas in a pod in that respect.

She watched as Abby tucked the gas mask over Clara's shoulder before handing her the haversack containing her clothes, the bag with her nightclothes tucked in the top of it.

But what did it matter? She took a deep breath, willing the frustration and anger which had come to the fore when she'd seen Audrey clinging hold of Ivor earlier – for all the world as though they were a courting couple – under control. Audrey would be gone a while. And Ivor would be alone. She didn't regard the presence of her nephews in the house as an impediment to her plans – didn't the three of them spend more time in the Black Swan or Ship Isis or the local dance halls than they ever did at home? To her father she gave no thought at all.

Her eyes focused on Ivor's grim face. She was well aware he hadn't looked directly at her in all the time they had been standing on the platform, but she knew him well enough to know he was conscious of every little movement she made, as she was of him. She felt the thrill of desire, desire made all the more strong by the nonfulfilment and resentment which underlined it. How could he prefer her hulk of a sister who had a face like a battered pluck to her? But he didn't, she knew he didn't. That was what kept her going. Funny, but when she'd first realised Ivor had impregnated her and she was going to have the thing she'd wanted most on earth, a bairn, she'd imagined that would satisfy her. Instead she'd found her children an intense irritation from day one, all of them. They'd removed the stigma associated with being barren but that was all that could be said for them.

'Bye then, lass.'

As Audrey brushed her cheek with her lips Nora wanted to scrub the contact away. Instead she made herself smile and say, 'Bye and thanks again. I shan't forget it.' And neither would Audrey if she had her way. She had to get Ivor to make the break and leave while her sister was gone; it was now or never with the war and everything changing. She felt it in her bones.

So wrapped up was Nora in her thoughts that it didn't dawn on her she hadn't said goodbye to her youngest daughter until Clara positioned herself in front of her. Her voice was small as she said dutifully, 'Ta-ta, Mam.'

Nora inclined her head. 'You do what you're told, mind,' she said flatly. Then, conscious of watching eyes, she bent and gave Clara a cursory kiss. 'Get yourself away now and have a nice time.' She spoke for all the world as though the occasion was nothing more than a Sunday school picnic.

As the train chugged out of the station, Abby stood watching it with a heavy heart. She hoped she'd done the right thing in encouraging Clara to leave. Her sister had kept her promise and hadn't caused a fuss like some of the bairns, but the misery in the little face had been plain to see. Abby glanced at her uncle who was standing close to the platform edge, waving frantically to Audrey who was hanging halfway out of the train window. Abby's gaze moved to her mother. Her face showed little expression but then she was a cold fish, her mam.

When the guard's van had disappeared, the quiet in the station seemed overpowering, and little was said among those left on the platform. Ivor stood for a few moments more staring down the track and then he turned, making his way over to where Abby and her mother were waiting. 'Damn war,' he muttered. 'Hitler wants stringing up by his toes.'

Nora made no comment to this. What she did say was, 'I've got a nice piece of topside and I've done some extra taties. Why don't you and the lads come round and have Sunday dinner with us?'

'I can't speak for the lads but I don't feel much like eating the day. Thanks all the same.'

'You'll have to have something.'

'Aye, well, Audrey's left some cold brisket and chitterlings. Likely I'll have some of that later.'

'You'll need something hot,' Nora persisted, her hands twisting together over her stomach. 'I'll take a plate in to Da if you're worried about him.'

Ivor made no answer; his face was set as he stood looking at her. Abby realised that her uncle rarely looked at her mother and then never directly like he was doing now. It made her uncomfortable, uneasy, but she didn't feel she could break the silence which had fallen on the three of them, although she didn't know why.

Nora was staring at Ivor, anger and supplication fighting each other in her face. After what seemed like an age, she said, 'Tomorrow then. I'll have something hot ready tomorrow when you come home from the yard.'

'Not for me. I shan't be around the next few days although I dare say the lads'll be grateful for a bite.'

'Not . . . not around?'

'I'm going to see me brother in Consett, him that's been middling the last year. I had word from his wife the doctor's told her on the quiet he's not long for the top and of all of us, me and Art were the closest as bairns. I'd like to see him again afore he goes.'

'Audrey didn't say.'

He shrugged. 'I didn't see the need to mention it to her. She's had enough on her plate the last little while, the way Jed's played up about being sent away.'

'But do you have to go now? Can't it wait a couple of days at least? What . . . what if they don't like where they end up, Audrey and the bairns, an' come home? What then?'

Ivor shrugged again. 'It seems the obvious time to go an' Audrey won't bring the bairns back. Mrs Appleby next door is going to look in on your da throughout the day and see to his meal at midday. It's all arranged so you needn't fret about him.'

'I see,' said Nora, her face white but for two vivid patches of colour on her high cheekbones. 'You've made up your mind you're going then?'

'Aye, I have.'

The three of them left the station without further conversation, but as they stepped into the drizzling rain in Union Street Abby found herself in the peculiar position of feeling sorry for her mother. Her mam had only been trying to be nice in asking Uncle Ivor and the lads round for a bite; he could have sounded a bit more grateful even if he did have to go and see his brother. And her mam had made an effort to be nice to her Aunty Audrey as well – her uncle must have noticed that. Now her mam had gone all stiff and prickly and she'd likely be in a tear for days, making life unbearable at home. At least Clara was out of it. Abby stared ahead, matching her pace to Nora's brisk strides. That was one thing less she had to worry about.

In fact, her mother was very quiet for the rest of the day rather than ranting and raving as she was apt to do when annoyed. The two of them didn't exchange more than half a dozen words, which was fine by Abby, and when she said goodnight to her mother who was sitting staring blankly at the glow of the fire in the kitchen range, she received no more than a cursory nod of acknowledgement in response.

Wilbert was staying overnight with a pal, and Abby lay awake for some time expecting to hear her mother come up. The feeling she'd experienced in the train station of sympathy for her mother was on her again and it was unsettling, that and the ever constant concern for James. She tossed and turned for some time and was just thinking about going downstairs to see if her mother was all right and to get a drink of water, when sleep overcame her.

Nora sat in the kitchen until the clock chimed midnight. She had known all day, ever since the conversation with Ivor in the train station, exactly what she was going to do. After checking Abby was fast asleep she brought her nightie and dressing gown down to the kitchen where she had water boiling on the range. It took her some time to fill the tin bath which she'd brought in from the scullery and placed in front of the warm range, but she did not hurry over it. There was no need. In fact the later the better for what she proposed to do.

Once the bath was ready she stripped off her clothes and stepped into the warm water. She had a bar of scented soap which had been a Christmas present from Wilbert and which she had been keeping for a special occasion. Now she lathered herself all over, luxuriating in the unfamiliar smell of the rich soft perfume. After some minutes she took the pins out of her hair and washed that too, lying in the water until it began to get cool, whereupon she climbed out and dried herself before padding through to the scullery and filling a jug with cold water. She brought this to the bath and, bending over, rinsed her hair free from the last of the suds.

Her skin smelt like apple blossom and peaches, and she held her arm to her nose for a moment, taking deep breaths, before pulling on her nightie. Then she sat drying her hair with a big rough towel until it was only faintly damp, its shine brought out by the washing.

Half past one. As the clock chimed the half hour Nora stood up, pulling on her dressing gown and sliding her feet into her slippers. Very quietly she let herself out of the back door and walked round to her sister's scullery, trying the handle of the door gently. It was locked. Audrey had always had a thing about locking the doors although most folk round these parts didn't bother. Nora reached up and felt for the loose brick at the side of the door. She removed the brick and her fingers closed over hard metal. The spare key.

Still without making a sound she opened the back door and slipped inside, closing it carefully behind her. Her heart was pounding now, and she flitted through the kitchen, into the hall and up the stairs like an ethereal spirit in the pitch blackness.

She could hear snoring from the lads' room but there had been no sound from her father's room. Snores were coming from the room Ivor and Audrey shared too. Good. He was asleep. She opened the door which creaked loudly and caused her to freeze, but no voice met her ears and the snores continued unabated.

When she climbed into bed beside him she was completely naked. She snuggled into his back, wrapping her body round him and kissing and licking the back of his neck. She wanted him so badly it consumed her. She knew when they made love again he would admit it was her he loved. He stayed with Audrey out of duty, she knew that, but the time for duty was past. They were at war, anything could happen. They had to make the most of every minute now. He had to run away with her. It was the only way.

'Mmmm.' He groaned as he began to surface out of sleep, and she slid her arms round him to hold his penis. It was already erect and she stroked and smoothed the hot silk-iness, sure of her power over him now she was here, pressing herself against his back so he could feel her breasts. He murmured her sister's name as he turned to face her in the darkness, but when she whispered, 'It's me, darling, Nora,' he froze.

The next moment his hands caught hers and his voice was a furious hiss as he said, '*What the hell?* I don't believe this. What are you doing here? You've actually come here in the middle of the night? Are you insane, woman?'

'For you, yes.' He was still holding her wrists but she arched her body against him in the darkness. 'I love you, Ivor, and you love me, you know you do. We're meant to be together.'

'Don't move. Do you hear me? Don't move a muscle or so help me I'll throttle you.' He flung her from him as he swung his legs out of bed, and the next moment she was sitting blinking against the light. He was standing with his hand still on the switch, staring at her. 'Get out of here before I do for you. For you to come here, *here*.' His voice was low but she couldn't mistake the ferocity in it. 'You're mad, you know that, don't you? Stark staring mad.'

'Ivor, please. Please listen to me.'

'*Listen* to you? You come here, into my home, and you say listen to you? I could kill you, Nora.'

'Kill me then.' She knelt up, letting her breasts swing, their fullness tipped by hard peaks. 'But only after we've made love. Kill me then.'

'You really don't get it, do you?' He grabbed his dressing gown, pulled it on and yanked the belt tight before walking over to where she was watching him, her hair cascading about her shoulders. 'You disgust me, Nora. You've disgusted me for years. Just looking at you makes me feel sick to the pit of my stomach.'

The colour had drained from her face but she didn't move or make any effort to cover herself.

'I'll live the rest of my life and eternity too regretting I ever so much as laid a finger on you. Is that plain enough for you? Now get out.'

She stared at him a moment more before slowly sliding off the bed. She walked across to where her nightie and dressing gown were lying on the floor. She picked them up and pulled the nightie over her head before she faced him again. She hadn't said a word.

'Get out,' he said again.

'You think you're such a big man.' Her voice was as quiet as his had been but full of enmity, her face burning with humiliation and rage. 'But you're nowt, a big bag of wind.'

'Aye, that's right, that's what I am. Now you've had your say, get out.'

'You'll live to regret this, Ivor Hammond. I'll see you rot in hell, you see if I don't.'

'No doubt I'll be in good company.'

Nora stared at him. For the first time she knew it was really over. He'd chosen Audrey. He'd chosen *Audrey* over her. She had humiliated herself for nothing.

Along with the rising tide of fury there was a pain as though she'd been disembowelled. For a moment she considered screaming to bring the lads running. How would he explain her presence in his bedroom then?

But no, she cautioned herself in the next moment. She must think this through. If Raymond threw her out, where would she go now that Ivor didn't want her?

She walked past him, making her way down the dark stairs and out of the house. She heard him lock the door again as she reached the end of the backyard and the sound of bolts sliding at the top and the bottom. Her lip curled.

Thought she'd return at some point, did he? She'd rather slit her own throat. She continued into her own house, her progress hindered by the scalding salt tears washing her face.

Chapter Eight

To Abby's delight, Clara was home again before Christmas. An excessively wet October and November which had made staying indoors a necessity had added to the strain for both evacuees and those billeting them, and as no bombs had fallen and the newspapers talked scathingly of the 'bore war', people concluded the danger had been grossly overstated.

True, the war was inconvenient and even dangerous for those in the forces, but as Christmas approached, the conflict had not impinged much on the life of the average civilian, except for the dramatic increase in accidents on the roads due to the blackout restrictions.

And so Audrey went off again in the second week of December, returning with an ecstatic pair of children who declared the country was boring, boring, boring! There were no fish and chip shops and no hot pie shops, no picture houses or parks, no port with great big ships and no Winter Garden with plants and birds and a pond full of goldfish. 'There are just cows,' Clara reported solemnly to Abby when she was home again. 'And sheep. Lots and lots of sheep. And muck.' She wrinkled her nose and rested her chin on Milly, the doll Abby had bought her.

'Oh dear.' Abby hugged her sister to her, her eyes brimming with laughter. 'I don't think it was all that bad, Clara. It looked all right to me.' She and Wilbert had made use of the special 'Visit to Evacuees' cheap day returns at the end of October and gone to see Clara and Jed at the farm where they had been billeted, but the short visit had only made her miss the child more. The house had seemed horribly empty without Clara. Of course it didn't help that since the Sunday when her sister had gone, their mother had been even worse than ever. She'd hardly spoken to anyone, even Wilbert, and had taken to slamming doors in their faces and refusing to be civil. The evenings had seemed to stretch into eternity. Abby had spent an increasing amount of time closeted with her grandfather in her aunt's front room, reading to the old man and playing cards and telling him stories about her day, but it was her outings with Winnie which had kept her sane – that and the joy of James's letters. Oh, James's letters . . . He wrote nearly every day, wonderful outpourings of love interspersed with reports of training camp which he kept amusing in the main. And the best thing of all was that he'd be home for Christmas – only a four-day leave, but it was better, a thousand times better, than nothing.

Blizzards and snow made the days leading up to Christmas anxious ones for Abby, even though James assured her in his letters that he would walk the whole way home, and through six-foot drifts too, if it meant seeing her. But then it was Christmas Eve and she was standing on the platform in Central Station again, but this time with her face aglow and her heart bursting. He jumped from the train before it had stopped, striding towards her with his blue eyes sparkling and then they were in each other's arms, murmuring incoherent words of love.

Even her mother's refusal to have a Christmas tree or any decorations in the house didn't dim the wonder of this particular Christmas for Abby. She had bought lots of presents for Clara and after wrapping them in gaily coloured paper put them in a bulging pillowcase at the end of her sister's bed, and the two of them opened them together on Christmas Day. But most of Christmas Day and Boxing Day were spent at James's house, and his parents – unusually tactful – made sure the young couple were left alone as much as possible.

But all too soon they were once again on the platform in Central Station. It had never looked bleaker to Abby, and this time she couldn't prevent the tears from falling.

'Hey.' James's voice was soft as he dried her eyes with his handkerchief before taking her face in his hands. 'It won't be long and I'll be home on leave again with a bit of luck.'

Luck. He'd need luck if he was sent abroad now that his training was over.

'You know the brooch I gave you for Christmas?' he whispered, his thumbs stroking the silky skin of her neck. 'Well, that wasn't your real Christmas present.'

'It wasn't?' She stared at him in surprise, one hand involuntarily touching the gold brooch pinned on her lapel.

'No. I saved it till now, for this moment.' He let go of her, stepped back a pace and then went down on one knee. Out of the breast pocket of his uniform he drew a tiny hinged leather box. 'Will you marry me, Abby? Soon? I'd planned to ask you once I was fully qualified and in a position to give you everything you'd ever dreamed of, but now all that doesn't seem so important.'

She stared at him, taking the box with trembling hands and opening it to find the most exquisite ruby and diamond engagement ring nestling in a bed of velvet. 'Oh James, it's beautiful, beautiful, and yes, I'll marry you,' she whispered. He rose to his feet and kissed her mouth, her eyes, her brow as their bodies endeavoured to merge. They were oblivious to the smiles and nods of other passengers waiting on the platform who had witnessed the proposal, until a voice at their elbow said, 'An' I'll be your bridesmaid, all right, as long as you don't want me in pink satin. I'd look like a blancmange in pink satin.'

'Winnie!' As James released her, Abby stared into the face of her friend. 'What are you doing here?'

'Same as you, seeing someone off.' Winnie inclined her head to a thin lanky individual who was standing some distance away, looking extremely embarrassed. Winnie had been seeing this lad for a few weeks. 'He's just got called up. I saw you as soon as we came but you seemed a bit . . . busy.' She grinned at them both, quite unabashed. 'Congratulations,' she added, before giggling, 'I take it you *did* say yes?'

'Course she said yes.' James smiled. 'You don't think she's hard-hearted enough to send me away with a broken heart, do you? Now you've said your congratulations, and I dare say you're a sure bet for the bridesmaid bit, how about you leave us alone to say goodbye properly?'

'Here?' Winnie pulled a face. 'You're going to say goodbye *properly* here? And I thought *I* was a brazen huzzy.'

They were laughing as she moved off after a lewd wink. Then James reached for the box and slipped the ring onto the third finger of Abby's left hand. 'I love you, Abby. There'll never be anyone but you all my life. Tell me you feel the same. Say it.'

'There'll never be anyone but you.' She touched his face, her hand trembling. 'Never. Oh James, I don't want you to go.'

They were still entwined when the train came but then in minutes he was gone. Winnie joined Abby, slipping her arm through hers. 'Come on, lass. Don't take on. Look, how about we go for a coffee and cream cake at Binns, my treat? We can talk weddings and bridesmaids if you like.'

'Oh you.' Through her tears Abby was laughing. Then she held up her hand, the finger with the ring on it feeling heavy and strangely alien.

'Isn't it the most beautiful ring you've ever seen?' she said huskily.

'It's a corker, lass, and no mistake. You've got a good 'un with your James, I have to say that, and there's not too many of 'em around from what I can make out. You're a lucky girl.'

She knew she was. Abby wiped her eyes and blew her nose before settling her hat more firmly on her head. She was so, so lucky, and in spite of the fact that she didn't know if she believed in the rigmarole which seemed to accompany every procedure in the Church, she'd go and light a candle for James every single night if it wasn't for Father Finlay. She couldn't stand the lectures he'd undoubtedly give her; and he'd be wanting to know the ins and outs of when they were going to get married and everything else if she knew anything about it. But she would go to confession and Communion tonight and pray for James, but maybe at St Peter's with Father McGuigan.

'So, coming for a coffee then?' Winnie asked as they began to walk.

'I can't. I promised I'd get straight back to work once I'd seen James off,' Abby said apologetically, pulling a face.

'Later then. I could meet you out of work if you like.'

'Oh, I'm sorry, lass, but I need to get home. You know how Mam is.' She didn't add that it was less the fact that her mother might throw a tantrum if she was late, more the thought of leaving Clara alone with their mother for a minute longer than she had to which made her want to get home as soon as she could. She knew full well that from the minute her sister got back from school their mother made the child's life a misery, and now Clara was at home

106

all day for the Christmas holidays, Abby didn't like to think about what went on. As Winnie's face fell, she added, 'There's nothing to stop us going to the pictures after tea though if you want.' She could make sure Clara was settled in bed before she left the house.

'Aye, all right.' Winnie was all smiles again. 'With you just having got engaged and me just having given another bloke the old heave-ho due to this blessed war, I think we could both do with a night out.'

'This one wasn't worth waiting for either then?'

'Who, Bernard?' Winnie shook her head. 'He was a long way from being the love of me life, lass. Too besotted with football for one thing. I'm sure if I was small and round and made of leather he'd have declared undying love from day one, but as it was . . .' She shrugged, grinning. 'I'm keeping me eyes peeled again.'

The love of my life. The phrase stayed with Abby long after she had left Winnie. That was what James was, the love of her life, and unless this war finished pretty quickly, he was going to be sent into danger and there was nothing she could do about it except light candles and pray for him. She hoped God wouldn't hold it against her that it didn't seem enough. She crossed herself and made up her mind to have a special Mass said just for him, even though it cost a bit.

But she had to remain positive and believe everything was going to work out. Some people were saying the war would be over before it had really begun, and although she wasn't too sure about this herself, she wanted to believe it. It couldn't possibly go on as long as the First World War anyway, *everyone* was saying that.

James home with her in time for Easter was what she'd wish for on New Year's Eve this year. If she wished hard enough it just might come true.

* * *

Rationing began in the second week of January and this, combined with frost and heavy snow followed by a bitterly cold February which ruined the farmers' crops of winter wheat, and had even the hardy northerners only venturing outside when necessity demanded it, all added to the frustrations of the 'phoney' war. Thick white lines were painted on kerbs and lamp posts but still cars continued to crash in the blackout, and the wardens who enforced the restrictions were roundly disliked. Ivor, who had volunteered to patrol an area encompassing Rose Street and several around it, was bitterly vocal in his objections to this unfairness, and when the *Daily Express* began a campaign against what it called the 'darts and playing cards army', he threatened to call it a day.

'I've a good mind to chuck it all in,' he said to Audrey after one particular incident when a neighbour had threatened to stick his torch up a certain part of Ivor's anatomy where the sun didn't shine. 'If there had been any air raids we'd all be public heroes. As it is we're called wasters and slackers.'

He stamped over to the range, throwing himself down in the dilapidated armchair in front of the fire and proceeding to unlace his boots before the lack of response from his wife registered. 'What's the matter?' He glanced at Audrey who was sitting at the kitchen table with a pile of mending in front of her. 'You bad or something?'

Audrey raised her head. 'Don and Len have had their papers,' she said flatly.

Ivor's hands stilled and he sat staring at her for a moment, one boot on and one boot off. His two eldest called up? His guts twisted. And Bruce's twentieth was in a few weeks' time. The blighters could nail him too.

He rose swiftly and went to his wife, taking Audrey's hands and drawing her gently to her feet. She put her head on his chest and began to cry as his arms went tightly round her. 'Lass, you knew it was coming,' he murmured into her hair. 'Two million or more they said in January and there'll be more after this lot an' all.'

'I know.' She clung to him a minute or so more before sniffing and wiping her face with her pinny. 'Go and put your slippers on, your feet are soaked through, and I've a plate of stew and dumplings in the oven.' Ivor had gone on duty straight from the shipyard that night and had missed the evening meal.

He didn't immediately do what she said. Instead he reached out his hand and cupped her chin, lifting her swimming eyes to his as he said, 'I love you, lass, and there's not a better wife and mother in the whole of the country. I mean that. I'm a very lucky man.' From the minute they'd been married she'd devoted herself to him and then the bairns, that's what crucified him at times like this when the enormity of how he'd let her down with that she-devil next door swept over him anew. By, if ever a man had been a damn fool, he had.

Audrey let herself rest against the solid bulk of him for one more moment before she pulled away, pushing him towards the armchair again as she went to see to his dinner. She mustn't tell him that, terrified as she was for her sons, it was the fear that they might extend the call-up for military service to a wider age band that had really gripped her. But Ivor was nearly forty-eight; surely that made him safe from conscription. It had to, she'd go mad otherwise.

Ivor had changed into dry socks and his slippers by the time Audrey brought two plates to the table. He didn't comment on the fact that his wife hadn't eaten her own meal with the lads and her father but had waited for him because it was something she'd always done, but again he felt the heat of burning coals on his head.

'You told your da about Don and Len?' he asked as he finished washing his hands in the scullery and walked through to the kitchen.

Audrey shook her head. 'I didn't know whether to or not, what with him being so poorly lately. What do you think?'

'He's going to have to know sooner or later, lass.' Ivor paused. 'Do you want me to tell him?'

'Would you?' said Audrey, her relief evident.

'Aye, once I've had me tea. I'll take him a cuppa and break it gently like.'

Silas was aware there was something wrong with his younger daughter and he had been worrying about it all day. Twice he'd asked her if she was all right and twice she'd said yes, but he knew there was something seriously amiss and his mind had immediately flown to his suspicions about Ivor and Nora. He had whittled his way through a hundred or so different scenarios through the long hours and by the time his son-in-law went in to him the old man was feeling exhausted.

Ivor's first words confirmed that he looked like he felt. 'You need one of your pills, Da?'

'I've had one of me pills.' He was irritable. 'They don't do much good.'

Ivor passed him the cup of tea without comment before sitting down on the hard-backed chair at the side of the bed. 'I've got something to tell you.'

'Oh aye?'

'Don and Len have been called up.'

When there was no immediate reaction from his father-in-law, Ivor waited for a few moments before saying, 'Called up to war. You know what I mean?'

'Course I know what you mean. I ain't lost me marbles

yet whatever you might think, and I knew there was something wrong with Audrey today. A blind man would have seen it.'

'Right.' Ivor stared at his wife's father and his tone was slightly aggrieved when he said, 'Well, that's what she's upset about. We're both upset.'

Silas's small round eyes were tight on his son-in-law's face. 'I'm sorry for the lads,' he said quietly, 'but I thought it might be something else.'

'Something else?' Ivor's brow wrinkled.

'Shut the door.'

It was a command and issued in such a way to cause Ivor's mouth to tighten but he did as Silas demanded, shutting the front room door and then coming to the side of the bed again – but this time he did not sit down. 'Well?'

'Like your brother, I'm not long for the top.' And as his son-in-law went to object, Silas waved his hand irritably. 'I'm not daft, man, and it's not that I want to talk about, but because things are speeding up I need to ask you something.' He looked at Ivor long and hard. 'The other one. You're not still messing around with her?'

Ivor was struck dumb.

'I don't want to know what went on, lad. I just need to be sure it's finished with and that you've got your head screwed on straight now before I go.'

The blood had drained from Ivor's face. As if in a trance he sank down onto the seat beside the old man's bed. His father-in-law had given him the biggest shock of his life and for a moment his brain felt scrambled. His hands hung limply between his knees and it was a full thirty seconds before he could say, 'How long have you known?'

'Does it matter?' And then as his son-in-law slowly raised his head, Silas said, 'Oh, I don't know. Years perhaps.' His mouth twisted. 'Ever since you an' Audrey took me in, I suppose, or shortly after. You notice things more when your world stops.'

'Why . . . why didn't you say anything before?'

'For one thing I wasn't completely sure until a few moments ago.' And then Silas wagged his head. 'No, that's not the truth of it. Basically I've always been a believer in never coming between a man and his wife; you're liable to put your oar in and get it in the neck from both sides. An' I don't want to interfere now, lad, not in that sense. But Audrey . . . Well, me lass has always been a mite special, like the little 'un, Abby, and I think I'm asking for me mind to be put at rest.'

'It can be.' Ivor stared at the man he had liked and respected from the first day of meeting him. 'I was a fool, Silas, but you know that. But Nora . . .' He shook his head. 'I can't explain it. It was like she put a spell on me. But there's been nowt the last umpteen years.' He refused to acknowledge the brief interlude in the privy which had been over almost before it had begun. 'And there'll be nowt in the future, I swear it.'

'That's all I wanted to know.' No. No, it wasn't. His voice rasping, Silas said, 'How could you look the side she was on, man, when you had someone like our Audrey at home? I tell you straight, I don't understand you.'

'I don't understand myself.' Ivor felt sick to his stomach.

Silas stared at the younger man for a moment or two more. What was done was done, and Ivor had been like a son to him, he couldn't deny that. Taking him in, and never in word or deed making him feel like a burden. And then he spoke the thing which had given him many a sleepless night. 'What'll you do if the other one tells her? And she's capable of it; don't underestimate Nora, Ivor. There's a nasty streak in her that's got worse over the years.'

'She won't say nowt.'

'How can you be sure?'

'It's been donkey's years since we – you know. Nora would've said something before if she was going to. And I'd deny it anyway, I've told her that. If she said anything, I'd deny it and take Audrey and move if I had to, lock, stock and barrel. I've made it clear I want nowt to do with her again.'

Silas hitched himself up on his pillows, his wince of pain ignored by both of them. 'You do that, lad – deny it, I mean, if it ever came to it because I tell you one thing, our Audrey's not the type to turn a blind eye an' pretend it don't matter. There's only ever been you for her from the day she set eyes on you, that's the way she is. Like her mam, God rest her soul.'

'I know.'

The two men looked at each other and they didn't speak again before Ivor left the room, but once he was alone again Silas lay staring at the stained ceiling which appeared to have the muzzy outline of a horse's head among other things. So Ivor *had* been the one to end it. He chewed on his lower lip, his rheumy gaze moving to what could have passed for an open umbrella where the brown discoloration was particularly severe. Nora wouldn't have liked being cast aside, that was for sure. 'Hell hath no fury like a woman scorned' was true enough in his experience, but doubly so where his eldest was concerned. From a bairn Nora had been like old Nick himself when she was thwarted, and she'd grown into a cold, calculating woman who had determinedly set out to take her own sister's husband, by the sound of it. By, what a dog's ear of a mess.

As a fusillade of hail hit the window with enough force to rattle it, Silas shuddered. But the chill was from within rather than without. Forget old Hitler's bombs, there was

113

one ticking within the heart of this family that would blow them all to kingdom come sooner or later. It was just a matter of time.

As winter passed and the first signs of spring began to show themselves, it could be said that only Silas was living in trepidation.

At the end of February Abby had heard from James that he was part of the British Expeditionary Force sent to the Franco-Belgian border where they had built pill-boxes and dug trenches but not encountered so much as a whiff of a German. From panicking at first, by April Abby's feelings reflected those of the whole British population who had decided the Germans had no intention of attacking France or England. The brave lads of the RAF were dropping millions of leaflets over Germany every week informing the populace of the wickedness of their Führer, at the same time ensuring that no damage occurred to German citizens' private property in case it upset them.

'The Germans aren't stupid,' Wilbert insisted several times a day to anyone who would listen. 'They'll realise they can't possibly win this war and rid themselves of Hitler.' James would be home for the best of the summer, he assured Abby more than once. He could guarantee it. Her father said much the same thing on one of his brief sojourns home at the beginning of April, and in the meantime Abby lived for the postman calling and slept with James's letters under her pillow.

Then, on 10 May, the same day Chamberlain left office and Winston Churhill was asked to form a government by the King, it became clear the days of the 'phoney war' were gone for ever. Germany invaded Holland, Belgium and France with breathtaking swiftness, outmanoeuvring the Allies at every turn.

114

For days afterwards Abby devoured every single piece of news she could find in the newspapers and on the radio, but none of it boded well. And, more frighteningly still, the letterbox had ceased to rattle every other morning.

At the end of May the attempt began to evacuate the British army and as many French soldiers as possible from the trap into which they'd been lured by the Germans. Over a thousand boats took part, varying in size from a Royal Navy anti-aircraft cruiser down to dinghies which were sailed across the Channel to the beach at Dunkirk by their owners from a hundred tiny slips along the south coast and along the reaches of the Thames.

'James will be one of them who comes home, lass,' Winnie said comfortingly, when reports of the pleasure boats, river ferries and fishing smacks full of weary and battered soldiers made news. 'Don't you fret. He's a canny lad.'

Winnie was only trying to be nice, Abby knew that, but she found herself biting her tongue to prevent the sharp reply which had sprung to mind. What did being a canny lad have to do with anything? Did guns and tanks and the bombers of the Luftwaffe take into account that someone was a canny lad? Her Aunty Audrey was shrinking before their eyes with worry for Don and Len who had been sent to France just a couple of weeks before the invasion, and there was barely a family round here who didn't have someone they were waiting news of. They were all canny lads, the lot of them.

By 5 June the last soldier to be rescued in Operation Dynamo was back on British soil, every man with a story to tell, according to the newspapers. A day or two later Abby returned from the office to find Nora waiting for her in the kitchen. 'Audrey's heard today that Don and Len are all right,' her mother said before she'd barely stepped

115

into the room. 'And Mrs Riley and Bertha Longhurst have both heard from their husbands. Seems they're letting folk know immediately if the men are safe. There's been telegrams galore apparently.'

Abby stared into her mother's eyes. Very quietly she said, 'What are you saying, Mam?'

'Saying? Nowt.' Nora tossed her head and reached for the teacup in front of her. 'Dr Benson was going to let you know if they heard owt, wasn't he?'

Abby did not answer her mother but as they stared at each other in silence she was aware of a terrible emptiness creeping over her. The fears she had tried to keep under lock and key since the invasion of France were causing her heart to race and her hands to sweat, but she didn't intend to give her mother the satisfaction of seeing her crumple. She felt a sudden darting pain in the scar at her temple and funnily enough it acted like a shot of adrenalin, enabling her to say quite coolly, 'Where's Clara?'

'Upstairs, and before you ask, you needn't call her down to dinner 'cos she's not having any. I had a load of cheek from that little madam the minute she came in from school and I'm not having her turn out as lippy as you. All right?'

Clara giving their mother cheek? Never, never in a hundred years.

Abby turned and went straight upstairs to the room she shared with her sister. The small girl was huddled on the bed, weeping copiously. Abby took her into her arms.

'She . . . she said . . .' Clara hung on to her and Abby's mouth tightened when she saw the raised weals on the child's legs. 'She said James isn't coming back. He is, isn't he, Abby? She's lying, isn't she?'

'Oh, Clara.' Abby hugged her sister to her.

'She was smiling when she said it. She doesn't want him to come back. She was all long-faced in front of Mrs Riley

116

and Mrs Longhurst when they were talking about it when I came in from school, but the minute they'd gone she started laughing. Horrible laughing. And then she said the rides in James's car were over and . . . and I shouted at her. James *is* coming back, isn't he?'

'I don't know, hinny,' said Abby dully, lifting her feet onto the bed and settling back, still with her sister cradled in her arms. 'We'll just have to wait and see.'

They said nothing more after that, Clara's sobs reducing to sniffs and splutters before dying away completely. Abby heard Wilbert come in from work and the sound of voices from the kitchen but she didn't rouse herself; a leaden heaviness blanketed her mind and body.

Somewhere outside in the distance a dog was barking, and the shouts of bairns playing some game or other drifted into the room through the partly open window. After a few minutes she heard Wilbert in the hall saying, 'I don't care what you say, Mam, I'm just going to check the pair of them are all right,' but as his footsteps sounded on the bare treads of the stairs, Abby shut her eyes and feigned sleep. She didn't want to talk, not even to Wilbert, kind as he was.

When the bedroom door was shut ever so quietly and she heard her brother go downstairs again, Abby didn't open her eyes. Clara was asleep now, twitching once or twice as she lay snuggled into her side. She must have slept herself because when she next opened her eyes the light had all but faded and the June evening was quiet. She lifted her hand slowly, careful not to disturb Clara, and gazed at her ring which still glittered in the shadowed room. She *had* to hear soon. She stared straight ahead, her eyes dry and burning. Whatever had happened, however bad it was, she needed to *know*.

Chapter Nine

Over the next days all road signs were removed as the
threat of invasion became more and more likely, and
in the middle of June the ringing of church bells was banned
except as a signal the Germans had landed. Shortly after
this the *Echo* reported ARP manpower shortages in
Sunderland and Wilbert immediately volunteered his services as a warden. Men in Ivor's position felt the comfort of
vindication as public opinion did a radical turnabout and
proclaimed the wardens to be heroic after the first bombs
were dropped on the town in the latter half of the month.
But as Ivor pointed out to Audrey, the acclaim was bitter-
sweet.

Dr Benson used all his influence and badgered the
authorities daily for news of his son, and at the beginning
of July came the news Abby had dreaded. James's father
was waiting for her when she left the office one sunny
evening, and immediately she looked into his face she knew,
even before he took her gently into his arms and said, 'I'm
sorry, Abby. I'm so, so sorry. I had hoped to bring you
better news one day.'

They went to a little cafe close to the engineering works
and sat over two cups of weak tea which neither of them
touched.

'I had a call this morning,' Dr Benson said painfully,
his face white and strained. 'The telegram came shortly
after. Killed in action. It was that carnage at Dunkirk.' He

stopped abruptly, unable to continue, and Abby put her hand over his. Strangely, she found she couldn't cry; the dead weight of her heart seemed to be anchoring all her feelings under it.

'How is Mrs Benson?' she asked after a moment or two in which James's father struggled to pull himself together.

'I've had to sedate her. She collapsed and went hysterical.' He rubbed a hand over his face. 'My nurse from the surgery is sitting with her and I've called her sister. The way she is, I dare not leave her alone.'

Abby nodded. James's mother had had two miscarriages before she'd carried James full term and he was the apple of her eye. Abby had never really got on with her, certainly not like she did with James's father anyway, and she'd always known Mrs Benson didn't consider her good enough for her son, but now her heart went out to her. She swallowed hard, gazing into the face which was an older version of James's. 'Give her my condolences, won't you.'

Even in the midst of his own grief, James's father was still very much a doctor and he recognised shock when he saw it. He reached out and took the hands of the girl he had hoped would be his daughter-in-law, shaking them slightly as he said, 'I'm going to give you some pills and I want you to take two tonight, however you think you feel. Is that clear? And don't forget you can call me at any time, Abby. Any time at all, day or night, if you need to.'

Even as she thanked him Abby knew she wouldn't call James's father. He was going to have his work cut out dealing with Mrs Benson as well as handling his own loss; she wouldn't add to that. If things had been different between herself and James's mother, she might have called to see them in a few days. As it was, she felt this was goodbye.

'I'll run you home in the car.' As they left the cafe

119

James's father took her arm, but she shook her head at him. She and James had had some wonderful times driving in the country in that car, and even more wonderful times parked in the seclusion of leafy lanes on the way home. She couldn't bear to sit in it now.

'I'd rather walk, if you don't mind. It's just a short way and I need to be by myself for a while.'

'As you like, dear.' They stood together on the pavement and as Abby looked into his face she thought James's father had aged twenty years.

Impulsively she reached up and kissed him on the cheek, her voice shaking as she said, 'If James had had the chance to grow older I'm sure he would have aged just like you, and I would have been very proud to be at his side. I shall miss you.'

'And I you, my dear.'

Tears were running down his cheeks now but still Abby couldn't cry, even though the sight of his grief seemed to be working at the knot around her heart.

Abby couldn't face going straight home to her mother. Instead she made her way through the warm streets lit with sunshine and full of bairns playing their games to the sanctuary of Mowbray Park, walking briskly with her face set and not looking to left or right. Everything was paining her – the sight of little tots sitting in the gutter playing marbles or nursing their rag dolls, two housewives chatting on their doorsteps, a woman cradling a baby in her arms as she chivvied two older bairns in for their tea. It was all so normal, so ordinary. The world was going on about its business and all the time James had fought and died and they hadn't even known. Even the sunshine and the blue sky mocked her. It ought to be raining and cold and miserable, that's how she felt.

She sat for a long time on a park bench, feeling a sense

of panic at some point when she couldn't picture James's face. She hadn't even got a photograph. How stupid that she hadn't thought to ask for a photograph before he'd left. But she could ask his father for one. The thought brought a measure of calm. She would do that, she thought numbly, but not for a little while. She shut her eyes tightly, trying to block out the images the newspapers had created with their graphic reports of the horror of waves of German bombs and machine-gun fire raking the Dunkirk beaches and harbour.

Please don't let him have suffered, she prayed silently, and then wondered why she was praying about something after the event. But God didn't look at time like they did, according to the Bible. Past, present and future, it was all the same to God so He could take this prayer and make it work. She opened her eyes abruptly. But why should He listen to this prayer when He hadn't bothered with the other ones, when she'd pleaded with Him for James's safety? she asked herself bitterly. Maybe some of those women at the pickle factory had been right and there was no God, or if there was He displayed little interest in the beings He had created. Perhaps Betsy McCabe's view of life – that it was a kind of giant lottery where you got good and bad tickets and when you died that was the end of everything – wasn't far wrong. Oh James, James . . . She felt her head would explode.

She stood up abruptly, smoothing her light summer coat with trembling hands and taking a deep breath of the evening air. She couldn't think of all this now. She had to remain strong while she told her mother and she needed to stay in this strange sort of vacuum that had taken her over since she'd first set eyes on Dr Benson. She didn't know why she wasn't crying and collapsing like James's mother but she was grateful nonetheless.

It was nearly seven o'clock by the time she reached Rose Street and she knew she was going to get it in the neck from her mother but this didn't touch her in the slightest.

When she opened the front door she was met in the hall by her aunt, and Clara ran to her and wrapped her arms round her hips in the next instant. 'What is it?' She looked down at Clara's blonde head before raising her eyes to Audrey again. 'Where's Mam?'

'At the hospital.' Audrey swallowed. 'It's your da, pet. He was leaving the docks after his boat had docked and there was an accident. He's all right,' she added quickly as Abby leaned against the wall, one hand going out to steady herself. 'I mean he's not all right, he's injured, but he's not . . . It's his legs. Some crates fell on him and crushed his legs.'

Her da. Her da and James. She felt hot and sick, and as she stared at her aunt the plump face receded and she went into the blackness, murmuring both their names.

When it became clear Raymond was never going to sea again the effect of this on the members of the family varied. For Raymond himself, relief that he wasn't going to lose his legs as he had feared overrode any other feeling. True, the doctors had told him he would only walk with a stick for the rest of his life, but with his limbs still whole and the dock foreman promising him a sitdown job checking invoices and advice notes, at least he would be out of the house all day, which was all that mattered.

Nora, on the other hand, was beside herself. After demanding to see her husband's doctors some days before he was discharged from the hospital, she returned home and wouldn't speak to anyone for forty-eight hours, taking to her bed and declining food and drink. Even when she eventually came downstairs she refused to visit the infirmary, and consequently it was Wilbert and Abby who fetched their father home.

Wilbert, working all day at the shipyard and occupied with his warden duties at night – August had seen an escalation in air raids and casualties – was too tired to think much at all, but little Clara was utterly delighted to have her father home every evening. Raymond had had even less to do with Clara's upbringing than he had with his eldest two children, mainly because by the time Clara was born things had worsened between him and Nora to the point where he was barely home at all. Now the child monopolised him whenever she could and he did not discourage this, finding solace in the little girl's unconditional affection.

But Raymond's sudden change of circumstances influenced Abby's immediate future most of all. Once her father was home, and a few weeks after he had taken up office work, she went to see Winnie one night. 'I'm going to join the Land Army,' she stated flatly.

'The Land Army?' Winnie stared at her as though she had said she was going to join the man in the moon.

'I need to *do* something, Winnie, something specific, and now Clara has Da with her every night I can leave home knowing she'll be . . .' she had been about to say 'safe' but changed it to, 'looked after. You know when Winston Churchill made that speech after Dunkirk, when he said we'll fight the Germans on the beaches, on the landing grounds, in the fields and the streets and the hills? Well, it's never left me. And now James . . .' She shook her head, unable to continue for a moment.

'Oh, lass.' Winnie put her hand over Abby's. She wished her friend would let go and break down or something; this iron control she'd shown ever since James had been killed and her da injured was unnatural somehow.

Abby raised her head almost immediately, continuing, 'It's not just the war effort. I need to get away from my mam before I do something I'll regret, that's the long and short of it.'

Winnie nodded. She could understand that. She had met Abby's mother just once and had reported to her own mother that Mrs Vickers only needed a broomstick to complete the picture. 'You've made up your mind then?' she asked quietly.

'Aye, I have.'

'Then I'm coming with you. I've been thinking of a change from that typing pool for months. What do you say?'

'I'd love that, you know I would, but are you sure? The pay's not brilliant, about twenty-three shillings after deductions for board and lodging, according to one of the neighbours whose daughter joined at the beginning of the war. And they work you from dawn to dusk for that, added to which we could be sent somewhere where there's no town for miles.'

'No blokes, you mean.'

'Well, yes.'

Winnie grinned at her. 'Believe me, lass, if there's just one I'll winkle him out, and anyway I'm not letting you go alone and that's that.'

'Don't be so silly, I'm fine.'

'You're not.' There was deep concern evident in the flatness of Winnie's voice.

Abby stared at her friend. Winnie had been a rock the last weeks since the news about James, and now there was an additional pain tearing through her because of Winnie's loyalty. It was causing her breath to constrict and a lump to rise in her throat. To combat the feeling she tried to tell Winnie she needed to think about joining

124

up, but her voice was strangled and all that emerged was a low moan.

When the floodgates opened she was aware of Mrs Todd poking an anxious face round Winnie's bedroom door and being hastily waved away by her daughter, but she couldn't stop crying. It was only after two or three minutes that she felt able to pull away and straighten up, taking the handkerchief which Winnie silently handed her and mopping her face with it. 'I'm sorry,' she said thickly. 'Whatever will your mam think?'

'That it's a darn sight better out than in,' Winnie said smartly, adding one of her favourite lines, 'as the actress said to the Bishop,' almost without thinking.

Abby gave a hiccup of a laugh. She felt empty and desolate and completely drained, and she had never thought she would smile again in the whole of her life. But then she hadn't reckoned with Winnie. 'What am I going to do without him?' she whispered. 'How am I going to get through the rest of my life?'

'You will, lass.' Winnie patted her arm. 'You're a fighter, same as me. But for now you're going to come down to the kitchen and let me mam fuss over you a bit. You'll have to have a piece of her sly cake and a couple of drop scones along with a cup of tea or she'll give me gyp when you're gone, I can tell you.' And when Abby hesitated, Winnie added gently, 'Me mam's been worried to death about you, lass. We all have.'

Abby nodded. She was unable to speak for the moment at the kindness of these folk.

'And once me mam's got a cup of tea in front of her we'll break the news about the Land Army,' Winnie added, her tone indicating how she thought her mother would respond. 'With you being all upset she won't go too mad, with a bit of luck, although you never know. She won't like me moving away from home, that's for sure. You said anything about this to your lot yet?'

Abby shook her head. She knew full well she'd need more than a bit of luck to divert her own mother's wrath. Her mam wouldn't take kindly to losing her chief skivvy. But whatever her mam said or did, she was going. She was nineteen years old, a grown woman and lately the situation at home had grown intolerable. It was time to spread her wings.

In spite of Clara's tears, her mother's fury and her father's grim face, Abby didn't weaken in the days before she left for the month's training required by the Land Army. She and Winnie were being sent to an agricultural college some distance from Thirsk in North Yorkshire, after which there was no guarantee they would remain together. Farmers had first call on Land Army members, the recruitment lady told them, but they were also employed on food production in large private gardens, commercial nurseries and the bigger market gardens. They had to go where the need was greatest and no quibbling. Abby had glanced at Winnie at this point, and the glint in her friend's eye indicated it would be an exceptionally brave soul who tried to separate them.

Their uniform, they were told, would be supplied at the college once they arrived. It would consist of brown corduroy breeches, short-sleeved biscuit-coloured blouse, green tie and pullover, short khaki overcoat, hat, mackintosh, black leather boots and brown walking shoes with canvas leggings for winter, supplemented by a pair of fawn bib-and-brace dungarees for the summer. An extra item of uniform was rubber boots, but because rubber was scarce, these were generally allocated only to girls who were on milking. Winnie winced visibly at this point.

If, after training, they felt unable to carry on, the officer

126

had continued, her eyes moving over Abby's slim, delicate frame, they were not obliged to remain in the Land Army, but as training involved expense and time, applicants were not encouraged to join lightly. Abby's chin had lifted at this point, and as Winnie had remarked afterwards, 'By, she didn't have your number, did she, lass? If anyone can see it out, you can.'

All of Abby's work colleagues, including Mr Wynford, thought she was mad marooning herself out in the country miles from anywhere. 'What will you do in the evenings?' Felicity Cook asked wide-eyed, fluffing her newly permed blonde curls. 'What if you're not near a cinema or any shops?'

'I dare say I'll survive,' Abby said drily.

'But what do you know about cows and sheep and chickens?'

'Not much.'

'And animals bite, don't they? And kick. And I read in the paper that girls are being asked to fork manure and dig ditches.'

'Good. Plenty of new challenges then.'

Felicity fluttered her mascaraed eyelashes and raised her thin plucked eyebrows in polite disgust and conceded defeat.

Only her aunt was supportive. 'Lass, if I was twenty years younger I'd be coming with you,' Audrey declared, frowning at Ivor, who had shaken his head and clucked his tongue at Abby's news. 'It'll do you good to get away and try your hand at something different,' Audrey went on. 'Don't worry about your da, he's just concerned it'll be too much for you but he'll come round. Me and Ivor'll keep an eye on him. Now he's home for good, him and Ivor can have a jar together in the evenings. Isn't that right, Ivor?'

127

Ivor smiled weakly. 'Aye, I don't see why not, love.'

'So you go and get stuck in, hinny. And don't forget to keep us posted on how you're doing.'

And now they were on their way to get 'stuck in'. Abby glanced at Winnie beside her in the train carriage. Her friend was fast asleep and snoring slightly, her straw hat askew and her brown hair wafting about her perspiring face in the breeze from the open window. The hot dry summer showed no signs of abating but no one was complaining, even though the heat was excessive. The newspapers were predicting a bumper harvest and it couldn't have come at a better time, what with the war and all.

Abby sighed, turning to look out of the window and doing her best to ignore the interested stare of the good-looking RAF officer sitting opposite. He had been giving her the eye ever since he had entered the carriage some minutes before. She didn't want to talk to anyone, least of all a perky young officer who looked full of himself, even if he did have one arm in a sling.

And then she caught at her thoughts, ashamed of herself. The newspapers and the wireless reports were full of the fact that the RAF were giving the Luftwaffe a pasting. The Battle of Britain, the Air Ministry in London were calling it, and the prediction was that it would be a good many days before they were out of the woods. The fresh-faced young man could well have been injured in the dogfights in the skies whilst defending his country, and everywhere wives and mothers were receiving the dreaded black-edged telegrams.

But still, she really did not want to engage in conversation with the RAF officer, she decided. However, she knew someone who would be only too pleased to oblige. On the pretext of asking Winnie for one of the sandwiches Mrs Todd had insisted on packing up for both of them, Abby nudged her friend in the ribs, and from that moment the problem was taken care of. By the time they left the train, Winnie had the young man's name and the address of the base where he was stationed, and he was looking positively glassy-eyed. Abby actually had it in her to feel sorry for him.

They were in the heart of the country. All the signs had been painted out because of the war and they'd had to rely on the conductor to put them off at the correct station. As the train moved off in a burst of steam, Abby became aware of several other women standing around somewhat forlornly, much as she and Winnie were, she supposed. They all gazed at each other in open curiosity, kitbags on their shoulders and suitcases and gas masks in their hands. It was Abby who spoke first, saying, 'Are you all going where we are? Hill Farm?'

'That's right.' A tall slim girl with thin fair hair cut in a short bob and an expensive leather suitcase in one hand frowned at her. 'I thought there would be someone to meet us, didn't you? Poor show, this.' The accent was undeniably upper class. 'I do hope that conductor chap knew what he was doing.'

Another girl, who was as round as she was tall and who was perspiring heavily, stared at them in alarm. 'Hey, you don't think he's put us all off at the wrong stop, do you?' she said. 'I ate all me sandwiches miles back an' I could kill for a cup of char.'

A Cockney for sure. They were certainly a mixed bunch. Abby thrust out a hand to the first girl, smiling as she said, 'Abby Vickers, and this is Winnie Todd. I suppose we'd better see about finding someone who can tell us where we are.'

'Rowena Hetherton-Smith.' Hands were shaken all round and introductions made before, as a group now, they moved off the deserted platform and into the station yard, whereupon a small bespectacled station master appeared. He eyed Rowena's three-inch heels and make-up with world-weary eyes before he said, 'You're the latest crop for Hill Farm, I take it.'

'Indeed we are.' It was clear to Abby that Rowena had noticed the direction of the station master's gaze and taken exception to it, along with the note of thinly veiled scorn in his voice. 'Will transport be provided for us or do we need to call for a taxi?' she asked icily.

'Taxi?' The old man gave a wheeze of a laugh. 'There's no taxi, not since Nathaniel Weatherburn got his call-up papers. Besides, the farm's only five miles or so down yon road.' He indicated what appeared to be a lane leading away into the distance.

'You mean we are expected to *walk* it?'

'Just so.' The station master wasn't even trying to hide his delight at their predicament. 'Course, you could wait here for the next train to take you back whence you've come, if you've a mind, that is.'

Rowena fixed the man with the sort of look which would have caused a lesser being to curl up and admit defeat. 'I don't think so,' she said frostily. And then, clearly distrusting this hostile individual, she added, 'You *do* know where Hill Farm is situated?'

The superior smile slid from the station master's weaselly face. 'I was born an' bred here,' he bit back, 'an' I'll tell you somethin' else. Folk round here don't hold with the government sending bits of girls like you lot to do men's work. Women can look after chickens but they can't ditch. They can feed the pigs but they can't look after the boar. They can mebbe drive a tractor but they can't pitch hay.'

'Really?' Rowena's voice dripped ice. 'That's your expert opinion, is it?'

'Aye, it is, an' you'll find I speak for plenty round here an' all.'

'I see. So if I told you I've had experience in laying

130

drains and spreading chalk and dung, as well as loading it and pulling swedes and mangolds, you'd be surprised?'

It was clear the station master was taken aback. His expression stated as clearly as any words could have done that this highfalutin slip of a girl had no business knowing the terms she had used.

Rowena allowed him a moment. Then she said coolly, 'Perhaps you would be kind enough to direct us to Hill Farm without further delay.'

Once they were outside the station and walking in twos and threes along the dusty lane, Abby tapped Rowena on the shoulder. 'You've done all that? Laying drains and spreading dung and the rest of it?'

'Of course not, darling.' Rowena smiled at her, her somewhat horsey features mellowing. 'But Daddy got me a book which explained all about such things when I said I was going to join up. I think he thought reading it would put me off.'

'But it didn't.'

'Not really.' Rowena glanced down at her fine kid court shoes and then stopped, slipped them off and tucked them into the top of her matching handbag before walking on in bare feet. 'And I only asked that nasty old man if he would be surprised if I'd had experience in those things. I never said I actually had.'

'You certainly cooked his goose,' Winnie chimed in, her voice full of approval.

'Yes, I did rather, didn't I?' Rowena giggled. 'Some cheek he'd got when we're here to do our bit for King and country. I do hope we're sent somewhere near a town when our training is over, though. I've brought a couple of dance dresses with me just in case.'

'Have you?' Winnie smiled brightly. 'I've brought mine an' all.'

131

Abby was walking between the two girls and she found herself inwardly smiling as she listened to their conversation. Rowena and Winnie might be from opposite ends of the social scale, but she rather thought they had plenty in common.

By the time they reached Hill Farm every one of the ten girls knew how it had got its name. Situated on the top of a low hill which had meant walking up a steady incline for the last three miles, the training institute sprawled in front of them. The large farmhouse was surrounded by barns and pigsties and paddocks, all enclosed within drystone walls and appearing well cared for.

It was probably the bleakest of places in winter, Abby thought, but today with the air heavy with the sweetness of warm grass and the summer breeze carrying the fragrance of wild flowers and every growing thing, it was magnificent. Some of the group had been complaining their feet ached during the walk, but Abby had enjoyed the march. It was hard to believe a war was going on and men, women and children were dying every day when you were in peaceful surroundings like this.

She touched her engagement ring which she now wore on a chain round her neck, her eyes darkening. It felt wrong to be appreciating the scented air and the lovely hot summer's day when James would never experience such things again.

As they all walked into the farmyard in front of the house they were met by a tall handsome woman who came striding out of a barn to their right. 'You found us then?' she said briskly. 'Good, good. The rest of the girls are already here. There'll be about thirty of you altogether. I'm Phoebe Taylor and your personal representative of the Land Army. It's my job, along with others, to train you to be tough and resilient in what has technically been a man's world, although over the years I've been involved in

132

farming, farmer's wives and daughters do just as good a job in my opinion. As you can imagine, this is not a popular sentiment with the men,' she added, smiling. 'You will be subjected to what you might feel is a somewhat harsh regime here but, believe me, it's for your own good. Not every prospective land girl is chosen to come here; you've all been hand-picked by your recruiting officer for your mental as well as physical capability.'

'The crème de la crème?' drawled Rowena languidly.

'Possibly.' Mrs Taylor eyed her stolidly. 'Time will tell. But you've passed your first test, you've made it to the farm by shanks's pony. Of course you're all unsuitably shod, unsuitably clad, and make-up and high heels finish from this day on, as does any finickiness about food or sleeping quarters. So . . .' Again she smiled, this time drily, 'enjoy your stay at Hill Farm, girls.'

'Flippin' heck.' As they trailed after the tall manly figure, Winnie nudged Abby in the ribs. 'Whatever have we come to, lass?'

The ground floor of the farmhouse was divided into a sitting room, an enormous kitchen and a scullery beyond, all with stone-flagged floors, gaunt black ceiling beams and heavy, ill-fitting doors. After placing their luggage and gas masks in a corner of the sitting room where several girls were sitting, the group were ushered through to the kitchen and told to seat themselves at a great scrubbed pine table flanked by long oak forms. Along with two high-backed, angular settles on each side of the fireplace which sheltered fireside sitters from the fierce draughts drawn in by the wide chimney, the only other large item of furniture was a massive, dark old dresser bearing a load of crockery.

The hearth was commanded by a big, cast-iron range and on its ample top stood saucepans and frying pans. A side boiler provided hot water.

133

'We eat breakfast and dinner in three shifts,' Mrs Taylor said once they were all seated. 'Lunch is taken out as a packed meal and consumed in the fields or wherever you are working at the time. Once you've eaten you will be shown upstairs where you'll see the two rooms have been converted into dormitories, with three-tiered bunk beds and shelves on the far walls for your belongings. Space is at a premium so tidiness is the order of the day. You will make your beds before you come downstairs in the morning and everyone pulls their weight from the smallest job to the biggest. No slackers. Understood?'

They all nodded and Abby felt she was back at school. That Winnie felt the same was evident when her friend whispered, 'I reckon we've met Miss Ramsbottom's sister, lass, and of the two I prefer Miss Ramsbottom, cane an' all.'

The meal dished up by three red-faced middle-aged women was excellent. Huge wedges of steak and kidney pie with roast potatoes and carrots, followed by apple crumble with gallons of creamy custard, all washed down by as much milk or cider as they could drink.

'The cider is a welcome to Hill Farm, girls,' Phoebe Taylor said at the beginning of the meal. 'You won't get that every night so make the most of it. You will be well fed though, and despite the rigours of your new life you'll all gain weight, I can guarantee it. It's a healthy working environment.'

Winnie made a face. 'I was hoping to end up as a sylph-like little scrap of a thing,' she said with comic forlorn-ness, causing laughter all round.

By the time Abby was tucked up in her narrow bunk bed, Rowena in the bunk above and Winnie in the one below, she was too tired to do more than say a quick prayer for the safety of those at home before she went to sleep.

This in itself was surprising. Ever since she had heard the news about James she had found the night hours long and tedious, often lying awake half the night and desperately trying to dismiss the pictures in her mind of how James had died. But this night she was asleep almost as her head touched the pillow.

The next morning she fully appreciated Mrs Taylor's groundwork the previous day. Up at 5.30 a.m., they all washed in cold water before donning the uniforms handed out the night before and making their way to the cow byres for their first lesson in milking cows. Breakfast was at eight, by which time everyone was starving. Then they were off to the fields at eight thirty until four o'clock, with half an hour's break for a midday meal which they ate wherever they were, careless of filthy hands and dirt-encrusted clothes. After the evening milking they sat down to dinner, and then the cattle sheds and the dairy had to be cleaned. By nine o'clock the girls were quite literally falling asleep on their feet.

'I can't believe I'm getting into bed without cleaning my teeth,' Rowena yawned, flinging her clothes to the bottom of her bunk and pulling on red silk pyjamas. 'I mean, that's absolutely the pits, isn't it?'

'The start of a downward spiral,' Abby agreed solemnly from the bunk below.

'But there was such a queue in the scullery and after washing in freezing cold water before dinner I'd had enough.' Rowena yawned loudly again. 'And it all starts again tomorrow. Do you think we can stand it, girls?'

'Think of the station master.'

'We can stand it,' Rowena decided immediately. 'Anyway, it's not as bad as what Mrs Taylor had to do in the First World War. She was telling me she was detailed to do rat-catching at a farm in Devon apparently, and on her first day had to stand in a smelly dyke and put her arm down a rat hole to see which way the hole ran. I mean, can you *imagine*? They killed rabbits, crows, moles and tons of mice besides rats, using all sorts of poisons – arsenic, red squill, cymag gas and others. I'd hate that.' Her head appeared over the side of the bunk. 'Wouldn't you?'

'I don't think I could do it,' Abby said truthfully.

'What about you, Winnie?' Rowena said, still leaning over the bunk at a precarious angle. A loud snore from the bottom bunk answered her, and both girls grinned before saying their goodnights.

By the middle of September when their training was finished, Abby had ploughed and weeded, hoed and spread dung, sawn logs, stacked hay, milked cows, lifted potatoes and turned crops, and a thousand other jobs as well. She had also made some good friends, and now she, Winnie and Rowena were a trio who stuck together whenever they could. Rowena described the Aertex blouses they had to wear as dishcloths and the wavy felt hats as reminiscent of boarding school, and insisted on milking with bright crimson nail varnish and plenty of rouge, but she was tougher than she looked. She was also a party girl who had a knack of finding out about village dances miles away and then bribing one of the lads who drove the farm lorries to take them there. In civilian life one of the idle rich, she had more than shown she was capable of anything she put her hand to, as were the others. Their group included a die stamper, a wine bottler, a comptometer operator, a chocolate-box maker, two factory workers and office girls, all of whom had proved they had the makings of capable agricultural workers. Of the original thirty girls, four had left within the first week but the rest had been determined to win through. And they had.

Abby leaned back in her chair in the crowded sitting

room. They were due to leave the farm the next day and had all received their official Land Army cards with their name and number printed on them, and as they waited for Phoebe to come and talk to them she glanced again at hers.

'You are now a member of the Women's Land Army. You are pledged to hold yourself available for service on the land for the period of the war. You have promised to abide by the conditions of training and employment of the Women's Land Army; its good name is in your hands. You have made the home fields your battlefield. Your country relies on your loyalty and welcomes your help.'

There followed the official signatures of the Honorary Director and Chairman of the Committee of the Land Army, after which and above her own signature were the words, 'I realise the national importance of the work which I have undertaken and I will serve well and faithfully.'

'We did it, lass.' Winnie grinned at her, her good-natured face rosy with the sun and the wind. 'I just hope we're sent to the same place now, that's all.'

'I asked Phoebe to keep the three of us together if she could but she couldn't promise anything,' Abby said quietly.

'I offered her a bribe,' Rowena whispered from her seat at the side of Winnie, 'but she's made of strong stuff, our Phoebe.' The cider had flowed again, it being the last night, and Rowena gave a loud hiccup. 'But it might do the trick. I said she could have the last of my face cream – I've got a little bottle of glycerine and rosewater which holds powder marvellously – and the curlers I made out of copper wire. They're just as good as the shop ones that broke.'

'How could she say no to an offer like that?' Winnie said with thinly veiled sarcasm.

'Exactly.' Rowena was in the happy state of being more than a little intoxicated and was oblivious to any irony.

In the event the three girls were detailed to a farm not very far away, between Pickering and Scarborough. 'It's not a huge place,' Phoebe told them, 'a five-man job normally, I understand, but they're in something of a pickle. One of the farmer's two sons and his two farm labourers have been called up within a week of each other. Apparently he thought he was being clever employing young lads of nineteen or so, less to pay out on wages at the end of the week than if he'd got older men with families, but of course not being over twenty-one and thus exempt from conscription, the inevitable happened, ironically just a couple of weeks before the government lowered the age at which farming becomes a reserved occupation to eighteen. They've struggled on but he hasn't been able to find men to take the places of the lads who have gone, hence his call to us.'

'Do I take it we're his last resort?' Rowena asked wryly.

'I rather think it might be a little like that,' Phoebe admitted. 'But don't stand any nonsense when you get there, girls. He's very lucky to have you, bear that in mind.'

'Oh, we will.' Winnie grinned at her. 'I'm just the person to remind him if he forgets.'

They stayed up late chatting and drinking with the other girls, eventually falling into bed in the early hours, but for the first time in four weeks Abby found herself unable to sleep. Thoughts of James kept her wide awake, and after she had stared at the photograph Dr Benson had given her for some minutes her mind turned to her family. The week before, Wilbert had written that an enemy bomber had dropped a number of bombs around the railway station and town centre in the middle of the night, just a couple of hours after a German aircraft had been shot down over Hendon with tragic consequences for some of the folk living there. The town was bracing itself for more attacks by the

Luftwaffe, Wilbert had written, although they were getting off lightly compared to London and Coventry.

Abby wished Clara had stayed in the country with Jed, far away from the bombing. She turned over, cracking her elbow on the hard edge of the bunk-bed rail. The ship-yards were a target for the bombers, everyone knew that, but then if Wilbert wasn't working in the yards he would be away at war and that was even worse. He would be eighteen in a couple of weeks' time, and there was talk of the call-up age being lowered from nineteen, although as yet nothing had happened. This terrible war . . .

The minutes ticked on and turned into hours, and by the time a delicate mother-of-pearl dawn heralded another fine September day, Abby still hadn't slept a wink.

PART THREE

Goings on Down on the Farm
1942

Chapter Ten

'Can you believe this'll be our third Christmas here?' Winnie stopped fiddling with her hair and turned to look at Abby and Rowena who were changing into their dance dresses. 'Two years and three months, and we've the muscles to prove it.'

Abby smiled. 'I can believe it when I'm pulling frozen sprouts with no gloves on,' she said ruefully, glancing down at her red chapped hands sticking out of the sleeves of her dance dress. Gloves were useless in the fields because they got wet through and froze solid.

'Or when I'm up to my ears digging out sludge from the sewage settling tank,' Rowena put in drily.

'Or when we're dumping lime, or sending in the terriers to search for rats in the bottom of the corn stacks, or driving the manure cart,' said Abby, warming to the theme.

'Or turning and collecting potatoes in the pouring rain for hours on end.' On the suggestion of the Ministry of Agriculture, potatoes had been left longer than usual this year to grow large, and November had been a month of constant icy driving rain. Rowena hated nothing more than being wet and cold, and the oilskins the Land Army had dished out as part of their uniform were next to useless, leaking like sieves.

'All right, all right.' Winnie was laughing now. 'Anyway, you know what Vincent always says, you're not really wet till the rain's running out of the arse of your trousers.'

Abby and Rowena both smiled but it was forced. Neither of them liked the farmer's youngest son and the comment and language he'd used was just typical of him, but Winnie was sweet on Vincent and wouldn't hear a word against him. The two had been courting in a fashion for some time, although Vincent talked to Winnie as though she was less than the muck under his boots on occasion.

When they had first come to Bleak Farm over two years ago, the three girls had thought a place had never had such an apt name, and that had been on a mild September day with the sun shining. After the first snow had fallen like a thick white blanket, concealing the drystone walls bordering the fields and lapping over the roofs of outbuildings and pigsties, accompanied by an Arctic blast from the east which whipped its way into bones and sinews, they had known they'd need every bit of resolve to get through the winter. For Abby and Winnie, born in the north-east and used to raw biting winds and snow which lingered for months, it was just about bearable, but Rowena was an Exeter girl and moreover one used to living in the lap of luxury. It was then that Abby and Winnie had seen what Rowena was really made of, and their admiration for their friend had increased as the weeks had gone on. Even Mr Tollett, Vincent's father, had been forced to admit that the three girls surprised him.

The farmhouse itself bore little resemblance to Hill Farm where they had trained, having a definite Victorian feel to it and being considerably smaller. The whitewashed kitchen had a huge open hearth with black iron firedogs supporting a big wood fire, and wall ovens flanking the fireplace. Across the mouth of the chimney was fixed a stout iron bar which held several large crook-hung pots, along with skillets on the fringe of the fire. The kitchen served as the only sitting room, the other room downstairs – besides the scullery – being Mr Tollett's office. All main foodstuffs were under strict government control and the farmer bemoaned the paper nightmare the war had caused; his returns of pre-war days were nothing compared to the pile of clerical work required by declarations of output and applications for supplies.

Abby had rapidly come to the conclusion after arriving at the farm that Vincent's father was only happy when he had something to complain about, although Mrs Tollett was cheerful enough. Most evenings the girls retired to their bedroom fairly early to escape the monologue of grievances and grumbles in the kitchen. They shared one of the two bedrooms the farmhouse boasted – Vincent had been turned out of the room he had shared with his brother for what was little more than a long cupboard under the stairs – and read and talked a little by candlelight before they went to sleep, ready to rise at five o'clock the next morning. In the last eighteen months or so, however, Abby had awoken more than once to the sound of their bedroom door quietly clicking to and Winnie's bed being empty. She disliked and distrusted Vincent and she hated the thought that her friend was besotted with him but she could do nothing about it, Winnie having made it plain she wasn't prepared to discuss her relationship with the farmer's son.

Abby walked across to where Winnie stood in front of the old speckled mirror in one corner of the room. 'You look lovely,' she said softly. 'Right bonny.'

Winnie flashed her a quick smile, pulling at her dress where it creased round her middle. 'I reckon I've gained a pound or two since I wore this last. Too many apple dumplings! Why does Vincent's mam have to be such a good cook?'

Abby smiled but said nothing. Her friend had always bemoaned her ample figure but since she had met the

145

farmer's son, Winnie's self-confidence seemed to have plummeted to an all-time low. And Abby did not like that. Neither did she feel at ease about the bruises which had appeared with increasing regularity on Winnie's arms and legs lately, or the fact that her friend seemed to have developed the habit of walking into barn doors. The last marks had only just faded.

'Well, I'm ready to knock them dead, how about you, Abby?' Rowena swayed across to them, holding a dark brown eyebrow pencil in her hand. 'Just draw me in a couple of seams, would you, darling?' she added, hoisting her frock up to her thighs. With silk stockings having disappeared from the shops a year or so after the war had begun, an ingenious substitute had been devised by way of a little gravy browning and the pencil. 'Let's just hope it doesn't snow tonight.' She wrinkled her nose as Abby marked a seam on both legs. 'The other Saturday I had half the dogs in Yorkshire sniffing round my legs.'

She peered into the mirror over Winnie's shoulder, pouting her lips as she turned her head this way and that to admire the effect the burnt cork for mascara and soot for eyeshadow had on her eyes. 'I don't think I'll bother with bona fide make-up after the war,' she announced after a moment or two. 'This is much more fun.'

They were going to a Christmas dance at the local church hall some ten miles away courtesy of Vincent and the farm lorry. For the first few months at the farm Abby hadn't accompanied her friends on the rare occasions they had gone to a dance at the little market town on a Saturday night, but since Winnie had been courting Vincent it made it awkward for Rowena if she didn't go along. At first she had felt every time she was asked to dance that it was a betrayal of James, despite what Winnie and Rowena said to the contrary, but lately she had begun to relax and enjoy

146

the evenings. The farm had no wireless or any means of obtaining news from the outside world and it was good to escape the claustrophobic confines for a few hours and hear the latest songs which the town band played. A few caused her problems, like 'A Nightingale Sang in Berkeley Square' and 'Lili Marlene', but she gritted her teeth and smiled through the dreamier songs of longing and romance, knowing 'Boogie-Woogie Bugle Boy' and 'This Is the Army, Mr Jones' would soon be belted out. She hadn't expected the yearning for James to get worse as the years went by, but it had, and despite all Rowena and Winnie's determined manoeuvring to get her interested in one of the many young RAF men from the base at Scarborough who often called in at the local dances, or one of the local lads, there was no spark with any of them.

Abby liked the Saturdays when they went to the cinema in Scarborough best. Winnie and Vincent would disappear to the back row and she and Rowena would find two places nearer the front. For a shilling or two they entered a dream world where the exhaustion of their days and the worry about loved ones at the front or dodging bombs at home could be forgotton. It didn't matter whether it was the magnificence and splendour of *Gone With the Wind*, Greer Garson's rose-tinted portrayal of an English mother who rallies the loyal villagers in *Mrs Miniver*, Hollywood's *Casablanca*, or stirring war films like *In Which We Serve*, it was enough to be taken out of oneself. Once the film was over and the lorry was bumping and rattling through dark streets back to the open countryside, Abby's concern returned for Wilbert fighting in the North African campaign, Leonard and Bruce – Audrey's oldest son had been killed in the second year of the war – somewhere in Europe, and Clara and the rest of them at home, but she always felt the break had done her good.

'Ready, girls?' Rowena swished to the door in a swirl of parachute silk which her mother had acquired from somewhere and had made up into a stylish dance dress for her daughter. She handed Winnie and Abby a section of the long red liquorice sweets her mother also sent her which stood in for lipstick when chewed and held against the lips. 'Let's boogie.'

They had been at the dance for over an hour when Abby noticed the woman draped all over Vincent on the dance floor. She was no spring chicken, her peroxide curls and heavy make-up unable to disguise the fact that she would never see thirty-five again, but she was attractive enough in rather a coarse way. Abby looked round for Winnie but she was nowhere to be seen. After extricating herself from her dance partner, a young man with two left feet and a proclivity to hold her just a little too close, Abby made her way over to Rowena who was chatting to an RAF officer. She inclined her head at Vincent and the blonde, her voice low as she said, 'Have you seen Winnie recently?'

Rowena shook her head, moving away from the officer and taking Abby's arm. 'Who's the clinging violet?'

'I've no idea.'

'Well, Vincent seems to know her pretty well.' Rowena's thin aristocratic nose wrinkled. 'What a ghastly woman. She's all but falling out of that dress.'

Abby didn't care about the blonde's dress. 'I must find Winnie.'

Their friend wasn't in the lavatory or the small anteroom where curling Spam sandwiches and sad-looking slices of sponge cake were being zealously watched over by the vicar's wife. After declining refreshments at sixpence a portion the two girls made their way to the cloakroom, where too few pegs meant most of the coats were piled high on top of each other on the floor.

Abby fished out her coat and Rowena's, along with Winnie's. 'She has to be outside and she's not wearing her coat. She'll freeze to death.'

'I take it we're going to look for her out there?'

'Of course we are.'

Rowena glanced down at the beautifully dyed dance shoes which had accompanied the dress from home, and which had seen her insisting Vincent drop her at the door to the building earlier before he went to park the lorry. She sighed. 'Lead on, Macduff.'

After several minutes of wandering around, they found Winnie sitting shivering in the lorry. It had begun to snow and by the time they climbed into the front seat next to her, Rowena's pale pink dance shoes had brown streaks from the gravy browning and the curls she'd taken ages over hung limply against her cold cheeks.

'Are you all right, lass?'

Winnie glanced at them but immediately looked away again, staring through the windscreen at the swirling white flakes.

Abby tried again. 'How did you get in here? Didn't Vincent lock it?'

Winnie lifted a hand and keys jangled. 'I took them out of his jacket before I left the room,' she said, adding bitterly, 'He was too busy to notice.'

Abby and Rowena looked at each other. Abby rubbed her cold hands together, searching for words of comfort. 'It might not be his fault, lass. She looked like the type of woman who latches on to a man and then makes it difficult for him to get rid of her.'

'Get rid of her!' Winnie gave a broken laugh. 'When she came up to him tonight she made it clear she thought he was her property so I asked him who she was. Apparently they've been seeing each other on and off for years when she was still married, but recently she's been made a widow.'

'A very merry widow,' Rowena murmured.

'I told him I wasn't having him messing about with her when he was supposed to be seeing me, and he said . . .' Winnie paused, gulped, then went on, 'He said she was worth ten of me. In front of her he said that! He said he'd been sick of me for months and I could go to hell for all he cared.'

'Oh, Winnie.' Abby put her arms round her friend and as she did so Winnie began to cry, great tearing sobs that shook her plump frame.

'He . . . he's been horrible lately, you've no idea, but I kept making excuses for him in me mind. And he still wanted, you know, *that*, so I thought he still loved me and that whatever was wrong it'd blow over. Oh Abby, what am I going to do? I love him, I've never felt like this about a bloke in the whole of me life. He said at the beginning that he loved me and we'd be married one day and that I'd make the perfect farmer's wife. How can that have changed?'

Rowena's response to this contained words that Abby had had no idea her genteel friend knew. For herself she couldn't remember feeling so angry before, not even with her mother when she was at her worst. 'It's all right. It's all right, don't agitate yourself. Look, he'd been drinking before we left tonight and you know his mam's homemade beer is enough to knock your socks off. Perhaps it was just the drink talking, eh?' She stroked Winnie's hair back from her damp face. 'How about I go and see what's what while you wait here with Rowena? I won't be long.'

Rowena scrambled out of the lorry with her, closing the door before she said, 'What are you going to say to him?'

150

'I don't know but he at least needs to come and talk to her and apologise, if nothing else. To treat her like that! And I'm sure he's been manhandling her recently, Rowena.'

'What? Striking her, you mean?' Rowena stared at her, aghast.

'Aye. All those bruises and walking into doors! I recognise the signs. There's enough women round the streets where I live who regularly walk into doors every Friday night when their husbands get paid and get mortalious.'

'But *Winnie*?' Careless of her coat, Rowena was leaning against the dirty lorry. 'She wouldn't put up with that sort of treatment, not Winnie.'

'I'd have thought that once,' said Abby flatly, 'but from the first she fell for Vincent like a ton of bricks, you know she did.' And he had always been offhand with Winnie, that was the funny thing, but it seemed to make her friend keener, if anything. In fact his whole attitude had been similar to how Mr Todd treated his daughter, if she thought about it. Was that something to do with why Winnie had been determined to get Vincent's attention and keep it? Because her father hadn't bothered with her?

'I've never understood the attraction. Vincent's good-looking admittedly and he can be quite amusing in a rather crude way, but that other side of him, the nasty side, is all too near the surface. But *striking* a woman . . .' Rowena's voice trailed away.

'Get back in the lorry with Winnie and don't let her follow me, whatever you do,' Abby said. 'I'm going to have a word with Vincent and see what he has to say for himself. After all these months of them having an understanding and Winnie worshipping the ground he walks on, he could have let her down more lightly if he really intends it to be over. She deserves that at least.'

'Be careful, Abby.' Rowena tottered forward as Abby made to walk off, grabbing her arm. 'I ought to come with you.'

'No, stay with Winnie. He might be double my size but he won't get physical with half the town watching. I'm just going to ask him to come and sort it out properly with her, that's all.'

She stepped forward and opened the lorry door as she spoke, shoving Rowena up next to Winnie before she made her way back into the building.

Couples were still dancing but now the hit of the season, 'White Christmas', was playing on the gramophone on the stage, the band obviously having decided to take a break. Abby scanned the dance floor but Vincent and the woman weren't among the remaining dancers, and then she saw them at the back of the room. They were sitting at a table for two, the blonde nestled into the side of him in such a way that one ample breast was pushed against his chest and he was playing with her hair or stroking her neck, Abby couldn't determine which.

As she made her way across to them, she realised Vincent had been aware of her entrance into the room although he hadn't looked straight at her. When he raised his eyes as she reached them, she saw a small smile was playing round his mouth, and it took all of her will not to snap. This man would be the worst possible husband for her friend, even if he still wanted her which he obviously didn't. Winnie was well rid of him. James had always made her feel that she was beautiful and desirable and, more than that, lady-like. Because he had treated her like a lady she had always felt that way and it had been nice. More than nice. But Vincent was the other end of the pendulum.

It was the blonde who spoke first and the suddenness and aggressiveness took Abby aback. 'What do you think you're looking at?' she said, her voice nasal.

'I want a word with Vincent.'

The woman stared at her for a moment and then made a gesture with one hand as though flapping something aside. 'Get out of it, you and your friends with you. Coming here thinking you can lord it over the rest of us.'

Vincent's smile widened and he murmured, 'You tell 'em, Shirl.'

Loathsome man. Ignoring the blonde, Abby stared the farmer's son in the eye. 'There was no need to say what you did to Winnie, certainly not after leading her on the way you have. She thought she was going to marry you but I have to say I'm very pleased you've shown your true colours. And you,' she turned her gaze on the woman who was now sitting very upright, 'you're welcome to him. I've a feeling you've both got exactly what you deserve.'

'Why, you little— She's chased him from the minute she come to the farm, you know that, don't you? And all he's done is brought the lot of you to the dances and such-like as a friend. He wouldn't touch the likes of her with a bargepole.'

'Oh yes? And you're at the farm every day like we are, I suppose. He's been seeing Winnie all right, and if you don't believe me, ask his mam. She knows. And I'll tell you something else.' Abby bent over the enraged woman, her face just as furious. 'What he's done once he'll do again, so think on.'

Vincent's head was forward now in a bull-like attitude but he had clearly decided not to stand up and make things worse. Several people close by were blatantly listening. His voice a low growl, he said, 'I'll sort you out when we get back to the farm.'

'Like you "sort out" Winnie when she does or says some-thing you don't like? Just you try it. I warn you, you'll regret it.'

153

'What's she been saying? I've never laid a finger on her.'

'I don't remember mentioning you had.'

Realising he had given himself away, Vincent glared at her, and the blonde, evidently realising there had been more going on than he had admitted, twisted in her seat, her voice shrill as she said, 'What's she on about? If you've been carrying on with that little huzzy I'll brain you, Vin, so help me.'

Abby left them to it, marching out of the room without looking back. It was only when she climbed into the lorry that she realised she was shaking.

'What happened? What did he say?'

She could only see Winnie and Rowena's faces dimly in the blackness but even as she thought frantically for a way to let Winnie down more lightly, her friend continued, 'He's staying in there with her, isn't he? She must be nearly twice as old as him an' all.'

'She certainly looks it,' said Rowena. 'And she must be sleeping with half the American army to get access to the amount of make-up she's got slapped on her face.'

'But she's got a good body,' Winnie said dully.

'She's awful, Winnie, like one of the dock dollies back home. You know she is. He must be mad.' Abby leaned across Rowena and caught Winnie's hands. 'I know it's easy to say but he's not worth crying about, lass. He's a wrong 'un, and like I said to her in there, what he's done once he'll do again and again and again.'

'Did you? Did you say that?' For a moment there was a spark of animation in Winnie's voice. 'Perhaps she'll finish with him then. She must know she's too old for him and it can't last, and she didn't look the sort of woman who would make a farmer's wife to me.'

Oh Winnie.

'Don't tell me you'd have him back!' Rowena exclaimed.

154

'Not after tonight? Your life would be a misery, you must know that.'

'He can be nice. Lovely.'

'And when he's not being nice and lovely, what then?' When Winnie didn't answer, Rowena unceremoniously scrambled over her and started the engine of the lorry.

'What are you doing?' Winnie was beside herself.

'Driving us home.'

'You can't. Rowena, you can't. What about Vincent?'

'Funnily enough, I couldn't care less about Vincent.'

'He'll go crazy.'

'With me, maybe, but I'm more than a match for him. He knows you can't drive, or Abby, so there'll only be one person to blame.'

'Don't, please don't.' Winnie actually clutched hold of the steering wheel.

'Let's put it this way.' Rowena turned and now her voice was flinty. 'You can either get out of this lorry and wait for him and find your own way back, and given the mood he'll be in when he knows it's gone I wouldn't recommend that, or come back with us in the warm and dry and try and get some sleep. After how he's behaved tonight he's getting off lightly in my opinion.'

'But you don't know what he can be like, he'll go—'

'Crazy. Yes, you said. But he doesn't frighten me.'

'Abby, *tell* her,' Winnie appealed to Abby as Rowena began to pull out into the road, the windscreen wipers working furiously to fight the thick fat snowflakes falling out of a laden sky. 'It's not our lorry.'

'It's not his either, it's his da's,' Abby pointed out softly. The idea of driving away and leaving Vincent hadn't occurred to her but now Rowena was doing it, it felt wonderful. It was extreme and probably illegal, and with the snowstorm gathering force and rapidly becoming a

155

blizzard it might be dangerous as well, but the thought of Vincent's face when he came out of the dance to find the lorry gone put all other considerations into the shade. 'And I agree with Rowena, he's getting off lightly.'

'But what will his mam and da say?'

'I've no idea but I do know Farmer Tollett needs us more than we need him.'

'A darn sight more,' Rowena put in grimly, peering out of the windscreen as the lorry rumbled its way along in the blackness.

'He'll be so mad.' Winnie slumped back in her seat.

'Winnie,' Abby said gently, 'you're frightened of him, aren't you? That's the truth of it.'

'Don't be silly.' Her friend's voice held no conviction.

'You are.' The darkness helped Abby to say what had been on her mind for months. 'You might have loved him at the beginning, you might still for all I know, but you're definitely scared of him too. He's a bully, can't you see that? And controlling and manipulative. He's made you think you can't manage without him when in fact you're ten times stronger and more capable than he is. You know as well as I do he's always had a chip on his shoulder about being the younger son, his mam's insinuated that to all of us more than once when he's been stroppy about something.'

Winnie was silent for some moments and her voice was very small when she repeated the words she'd said to Rowena, 'He can be lovely.'

'Has he ever,' Abby didn't know how to say it and then decided to just come straight out with it in view of the night's happenings, 'hit you?'

There was an infinitesimal pause before Winnie answered, 'No, how could you think such a thing?' and both Abby and Rowena knew their friend was lying. But

Abby couldn't say anything more tonight, Winnie was at the end of her tether. Abby reached out and took her hand, and when she didn't snatch it away, instead closing her fingers round Abby's, Abby swallowed at the lump which rose in her throat. Poor Winnie. Who would ever have thought it?

She stared ahead into the whirling whiteness, conscious her arms were aching from clearing out ditches all day, and for a moment the longing for home rose hot and strong. She wanted to see her da, to confide in him and ask his advice about this. He might not be well read and know everything about anything, but he was wise, her da, and unshockable. But he was in Sunderland and she was in Yorkshire and so she'd just have to try and support Winnie the best she could, however all this turned out.

Chapter Eleven

Raymond stared at his wife, his face expressionless but for his eyes which were burning with loathing; so were Nora's as she hissed, 'Christmas! Who's got time to think of Christmas but you? If you want to do anything for her, you do it by yourself.'

'I was only saying Paddy can get hold of a little tree, that's all, and a few stars and balls cut out of cardboard and covered in silver paper wouldn't take much.'

Raymond was sitting up in bed, a jumper over his pyjamas and a book on the history of building ocean liners in his hands, and now, as Nora joined him under the covers, they both made sure no part of their bodies came into contact. The room was freezing, ice coating the inside as well as the outside of the window, but neither of them would have dreamed of seeking warmth from the other.

'Put out that lamp. I need my sleep even if you don't.'

Once upon a time he would have done what she ordered, but since he had been forced to live at home rather than escaping to sea for months on end, a stubbornness he hadn't known he possessed had come to the fore. Although he wasn't bringing in the wage he once had, it was enough to provide for all their needs, and with Wilbert and Abby still sending a few bob each week, they did all right. But all she ever did was moan and gripe. 'We can afford a few things for her stocking,' he persisted doggedly, 'an' I can't see you haven't got time to do some bits of decorations with

158

her. It's not like you've got a job outside the home, now is it?'

'Oh, now we have it, that again.' Nora sat up in bed and glared at him. 'Any other man wouldn't want his wife to slave away outside the house as well as in, but you! And that with my stomach trouble on and off.'

'You have stomach trouble because you're constantly getting yourself worked up about something or other. A job would take you out of yourself and there's plenty of openings with the war taking men away.'

'So you'd have me in a munitions factory or working on the railways or something, would you?'

For crying out loud! Every night, on and on. Her harping was endless. If ever a man endured hell on earth, he did. He gave thanks daily that Clara was still at home because if it wasn't for her he'd have swung for Nora before this. Drawing on all his patience he said, 'There's other jobs besides the harder physical ones.' It might have been all right if he had left it at this, but he went on. 'If our Abby can be a land girl and her as slim as any I know, you could do something other than clean a house which doesn't need cleaning and cook an evening meal for three each night.'

If he had pressed a button he couldn't have got a more immediate reaction. '*Abby! Don't you dare hold that little madam up in front of me.*'

'Don't shout, the bairn's asleep. You know she's been middling the last day or two.'

'I'll shout if I want to in my own house.'

'Aye, well, you've never considered the bairns since each of 'em have been born so I suppose it's too much to hope you'll start now.'

'And you're a model father, are you? Is that it?' The truth hovered on her lips, the longing to throw it in his

159

face and see him shrivel away to nothing so strong she could taste it.

When Raymond swung his feet out of the bed, growling, 'Oh to hell with you, woman. I've had enough of this,' and grabbed his dressing gown, Nora shot after him.

'Don't you dare turn your back on me, you spineless nowt of a man. I've got something to say about your precious bairns.'

'I don't want to hear it. They're good bairns, all three of them, in spite of having a mam like you.'

How dare he walk away from her like this! And preaching Abby at her, as though the little madam was the be all and end all. Her hands had been clenched into fists at her sides the last few seconds but now they shot out almost of their own volition, her rage needing the expression of physical contact.

Raymond had just reached the top of the stairs and was feeling for the first tread with the tip of one foot when his wife's fists hit him square on his shoulder blades. His hands came out in a wild grab to save himself as he was catapulted forwards but they met thin air, and then he was hurtling downwards with no hope of saving himself.

Nora remained standing still, panting heavily as she stared down into the darkness where her husband had fallen. There was no sound from him. Although the lamp was burning in the bedroom behind her, its meagre light only gave slight illumination to the landing. The hall below was in pitch blackness.

A slight movement to the side of her brought her head swinging, and she saw her daughter standing in the doorway to the other bedroom, her eyes stretched so wide they seemed to be popping out of her head. She stared at Clara for a moment or two before she said, 'Your da's had an accident.'

Clara remained frozen to the spot. Her mother's voice had sounded normal, but she'd pushed Da down the stairs.

The child's utter immobility and the terror in the small white face told Nora her daughter had seen what had happened. Her hand shot out and pulled Clara's head sharply back by her long plait of hair.

'You get back in that bedroom and don't make a sound if you know what's good for you.' Her mother's face was within an inch of hers, and Clara stared full into the narrowed eyes. 'You hear me, girl? Not a sound. And if anyone comes up, you pretend to be asleep, all right?'

It was only when Clara felt her head being shaken so hard she thought her hair was being torn out by its roots that she managed to stutter, 'Y-yes, Mam.' What had happened to her da? Why hadn't he got up and shouted at her mam or something?

She didn't resist when her mother thrust her into the bedroom and shut the door but once inside she remained standing exactly where she was. Her ears straining, she listened to her mother slowly descending the stairs. When a loud creak told her her mother had reached the second step from the bottom, she held her breath, waiting for voices to reach her. Her da would be mad with her mam, so mad. Da, oh Da.

When no sound penetrated the utter blackness that was the bedroom, Clara bit down hard on her fist, a new fear enveloping her, or perhaps the one she had been trying to keep at bay since she had watched her father fall. Her teeth chattered in the icy darkness and she felt the nausea rise in her throat. She just had time to feel her way to the bed and grab the chamber pot beneath before her stomach rose up into her mouth. It was some minutes before the retching subsided, and after pushing the pot back under the bed she wiped her mouth on the handkerchief she kept up the sleeve of her thick flannelette nightdress and crawled under the covers, her thin arms hugging Milly's stiff unyielding body. When her frozen feet found the warmth of the oblong stone hot water bottle her father filled and placed in her bed each night, she began to cry . . .

It was Audrey and Clara who met Abby at the train station the day before Christmas Eve, and the moment Clara saw her sister she ran to her, flinging herself on Abby in a paroxysm of grief.

'She's been this way ever since it happened.' Audrey's voice was soft with worry. 'We can't get her to eat and she's beside herself most of the time. An' I'm sorry, lass, but we've had word Wilbert's been refused leave.'

Abby nodded, closing her eyes for a second and sucking her lips between her teeth in an effort to stop her own tears falling. Clara needed her to be strong and that was what she had to be, regardless of the way she was feeling inside. The funeral was at one o'clock this afternoon and after the service there would be the ordeal of company back at the house and all that that entailed. She couldn't afford to let go now but she wished her brother had been able to be with them. She took a deep breath, composing her face before she said, 'Come on, hinny, I'm here now. Be a brave little lass for me, eh?'

Clara made no answer, merely tightening her grip on Abby's middle and burying her face deeper into her sister's coat. Audrey shook her head. 'He's made a fuss of her over the last couple of years, that's the thing. And with the way your mam is . . .'

Aye, the way her mam was. Abby rubbed her hand over her face and then took hold of Clara's bony shoulders. She knelt down in front of her. 'Clara, look at me,' she said quietly. 'Stop crying and look at me.'

162

After a moment the eyes in the tear-stained face opened.

'I'm staying over Christmas, hinny. I've got special leave and that means we can be together all the time, all right?'

Clara opened her mouth and then closed it before she said, 'You promise?'

'Aye, I promise. Aw, don't cry, hinny. Don't cry. There, there.' She drew Clara into her and hugged her tight, the two of them oblivious to anyone else. 'I know you loved Da all the world. I did too, but he wouldn't want you to take on like this. He really wouldn't. You know that, don't you?'

When it became apparent that Clara was beyond answering her, Abby rose and lifted the thin little figure up into her arms. Clara wrapped herself round her sister like a baby monkey. And it was like that, with Audrey at their side carrying Abby's big cloth bag, that they left the station.

Chapter Twelve

'Well, personally I think it would be the best thing all round if you took Clara back with you, but would these farm folk mind?' It was Boxing Day evening and the Christmas spirit hadn't even poked its nose into 12 and 14 Rose Street. Audrey and Ivor were sitting on two hard-backed chairs in front of the fireplace in Silas's room; the old man was lying quietly in his bed, on the end of which Abby perched.

'No, they wouldn't mind.' Abby answered her aunt's question without a pause. 'I put it to Mrs Tollett before I left, just in case things were bad when I got here. She said she's quite happy for Clara to come as long as I saw to getting her to school and things like that. They had three evacuees at the beginning of the war apparently, a mother and two bairns, but they left within the month to go back to London.'

'You said anything to your mam yet?' Ivor had been gnawing on his thumbnail but now he stuck both hands between his legs as though to keep them out of reach of his mouth.

'No, but she'll be all for it, I should think, what with Clara crying all day and wetting the bed every night. To be truthful I don't think I'd dare leave Clara with her anyway, not the way Clara is. Mam went mad last night when we changed the bed the second time; you'd have thought it was the greatest crime in history.'

'Dear, dear.' Audrey heaved a sigh. 'What a to-do.' She turned to her father who had said nothing for the last few minutes. 'What do you think, Da? Do you think it's best for Abby to take the bairn back with her?'

Silas didn't answer immediately. He was lying back on his pillows but he hitched himself up a little, the movement feeble but enough to make him gasp for breath for a few moments. Then he said, 'There's two ways of lookin' at it, I suppose. One is that if the bairn stays here she's got her pals at school and everythin' she knows, and her an' Jed have always been very close, don't forget. The other is that there's no one like Abby for Clara, never has been, and maybe a change of scene from where it happened could work wonders. But overall,' he directed his rheumy gaze on his granddaughter, 'gettin' away from your mam might be the best medicine for the little 'un.'

'So you're for it, all things considered?'

Silas nodded. 'Aye, I'm for it,' he said flatly. It would mean Nora was alone in the house and if he knew anything about Audrey, his youngest daughter would feel sorry for her sister, in spite of how Nora was. She'd ask her round for meals likely as not and it could get so Nora was never off the doorstep. He glanced at Ivor and knew the same thoughts were running through his mind. But the bairn came first in all of this and she needed to get far away for a time, it was as clear as day.

'I'll have a word with Mam then before I say anything to Clara.' Abby's gaze took in each of them and then she sprang to her feet. 'I'll go now.'

'Aye, all right, lass.' Audrey rose with her but Ivor remained in the room with Silas.

In the kitchen, Audrey said softly, 'I'll keep an eye on your mam so don't fret about her once you've gone.'

Abby stared at her aunt for a moment. Audrey had lost

weight since she had heard her son had died, and worry for the other two still in the thick of it had caused the pounds to continue to drop off. She looked tired and strained, which wasn't surprising when you considered she had recently taken part-time employment in the munitions factory in answer to the government's plea for more women to get involved in war work. She ran the home and the full load of caring for Granda invariably fell on her shoulders, Abby thought, and yet still her aunt put everyone else first.

Abby reached out and patted her aunt's arm. 'I shan't fret about Mam, Aunty,' she said truthfully, 'not for a second.' She could have added here, 'If you could see the way she's been at home since Da died you would understand,' but she did not. How could she describe the look on her mother's face when she wasn't aware she was being watched? She couldn't because she didn't understand it but her mam definitely wasn't grieving. And she'd cleared out all her father's clothes and possessions before he'd even been laid to rest. If anyone called round she was the epitome of the sorrowing widow, but the rest of the time . . .

When Abby walked through the scullery and into the kitchen, her mother was nowhere to be seen, but she had expected that. Since the funeral her mother lit a fire in the front room every evening and went in there to sit. She took a tray of tea with her and one of the magazines she'd taken to buying. Even on Christmas Day when Audrey had invited the three of them to Christmas dinner, her mother had left early and retired here.

Abby went quickly through to the front room. Her mother raised her head briefly from her magazine. 'Been chewing me over with them next door, I suppose,' she said and turned a page.

There was a good fire in the grate. Abby glanced at it, thinking, She doesn't even seem to have considered that without Da's wage coming in she'll have to cut back. With tightening fuel rations, her father had been in the habit of acquiring an extra bag of coke now and again from a pal involved in the black market. Every recipe you read these days aimed at meals which saved fuel, and with talk that the one hundredweight of coal per household per week would soon be cut further, her mam was mad wasting what little they had left on a fire which simply went up the chimney and didn't heat the range.

Putting the extravagance aside for the moment, Abby said, 'I was talking about Clara with Aunty Audrey and Granda actually. I wondered if it'd help if she came back to the farm with me. A change of scene might take her out of herself and stop her brooding about what's happened.'

Nora continued staring down at the magazine on her lap but her mind was racing. What should she say to that? She'd like nothing better than to be rid of the child whose snivelling and carrying on was a constant thorn in her flesh, reminding her every minute of what she'd done. Not that she'd meant to push him, she qualified silently as she always did when she thought of that night. Not a bit of it. Hit him, oh aye, she'd meant to thump him one and he'd deserved it too, but she hadn't expected the big galoot would lose his footing and fall. And that's what had happened: he'd lost his footing, so it was his fault in the final analysis. Rising in the middle of the night and padding about in the dark, he'd brought it on himself. She wasn't to blame.

'Mam? Did you hear what I said?'

'Aye, I heard.' Nora raised her head to stare at her daughter.

Goosepimples pricked Abby's skin as she looked into her mother's expressionless face. 'Well? What do you think?'

167

'It might be the answer, but if I agree to her going with you, I tell her myself. Just the two of us. I don't want her persuaded into something she doesn't really want. There's no way I'm coming out to fetch her if she plays up once she's there.'

Abby's brow wrinkled. They both knew there was no possibility of that, but if her mother wanted to tell Clara herself, it was fine by her. All she wanted to do was to get her sister far away from Sunderland as soon as she could.

She shrugged. 'Whatever you want.'

'Huh! That'll be the day.'

Abby ignored this. 'I have to leave the day after tomorrow so you'll need to tell her in the morning.'

'I'll tell her when it suits me and I'll thank you to keep your orders to yourself.'

Abby didn't bother to say anything more before she left the room. Her mind was still in a jumble and full of pain knowing she would never see her father again, and the sadness excluded the normal rise of anger or irritation with her mother. She hadn't been able to tell him one last time what he meant to her, that she loved him. She hadn't been able to say goodbye. Somehow it wouldn't have seemed so unfair if a bomb had fallen because the same thing was happening to thousands of people all over the country, but for an accident at home to have taken her da didn't seem right.

She hunched her shoulders, lowering her head as she fought back the tears. But then nothing was fair or right in these times. James and Donald and her da dying when people like her mother seemed to go from strength to strength.

Her eyes unseeing, she stood in the gloom of the hall for a moment. After sighing deeply she began to climb the stairs. Her mind was struggling with the way the world had

168

gone all topsy turvy. Families and loved ones were being torn apart everywhere and there were many folk who were feeling like her, but with James and her da gone and the knowledge that she would never see them again burning in her heart, tonight it was more than she could bear.

Two days later on a cold Monday morning which had the smell of snow in the air, Abby felt a different person to the despondent creature of Boxing Day.

She was standing on the platform of the train station with Clara holding tightly to her hand, her sister's clothes and belongings crammed into their father's old rucksack again. Audrey and Ivor were at work and her mother had still been in bed when they'd left the house so there was no one to see them off, but that didn't matter.

Abby glanced at Clara and her sister smiled up at her. Clara was coming back with her and that was all that counted. Suddenly the world was a brighter and more positive place again.

For the first time since their father had died Clara had not wet the bed the night before, and, small thing though it was, Abby felt it boded well for the future. It might be a bit of a squash in the farm bedroom – it already held the three-quarter-size bed which she and Rowena shared and Winnie's single, along with a rickety wardrobe and chest of drawers – but when she had put the possibility of bringing her sister back with her to the farmer's wife before she'd left, Mrs Tollett had assured her they could squeeze a little pallet bed in somewhere.

'Looking forward to seeing the farm, hinny?' Abby said softly, and Clara, hugging the doll Abby had given her two years before and from which she was rarely separated, nodded earnestly.

But it wasn't the farm. Clara's grip on Abby's hand

tightened. She didn't care where she went as long as she was with Abby. There had been a story in *Sunshine Weekly* which she had read a few weeks ago, and in it the little girl had been sleeping in barns and under hedges with her big sister and little brother because their parents had died. When it had been decided they would have to be split up and sent to different relatives, the three of them had run away. It had ended nice, Clara reflected, but it had left her with a funny feeling because she'd so wanted the little girl to be her and the big sister Abby. But the longing for Abby hadn't been so bad then because she'd still had Da with her.

The sickening feeling stirred again in her stomach at the thought of her father, and what her mother had said to her yesterday morning burned in her mind. 'You say nothing about the night your da had his accident to anyone, under-stand me, girl? Nothing. It's no one's business, no one's. Not Abby's or anyone else's. Well? Do you understand what I'm saying?'

'Y-yes, Mam.'

'You were asleep the whole time and didn't know anything until your Aunty Audrey came to fetch you after I'd been next door for help.'

'But I wasn't. I mean—'

'Saints alive!' Her mother had yanked her up from her seat and shaken her like a dog with a rabbit. 'Listen to me, will you? How many times did we go over this before Abby got here? You had a dream, that was all. A dream, girl, brought on by having something that upset your stomach and made you sick.'

She hadn't been able to answer, such was her fear, but then her mother's voice had grown softer and even more terrifying. 'You ever say anything else than what I've told you and I promise you I'll see you're taken away and put

170

in a home for bad girls and boys for telling wicked lies. You'll never see Abby again, you'll never see no one but mice and rats and spiders. They won't ever let you out, not ever. *Do you understand me?*'

'Here's the train, hinny.' Abby's voice cut into the terror, and as Clara looked up and saw the steam and heard the toot, toot, toot of the engine, she felt weak with relief. All yesterday and this morning she had been scared something would happen to stop her going with Abby. She hadn't slept at all last night, lying awake and pinching herself when she felt sleepy in case she wet the bed again and her mam refused to let her go. But now the train was here and they were going to get on and nothing could stop them. For a moment the platform seemed to narrow down and she felt a ringing in her ears.

'You all right, pet?' Clara's face had been devoid of colour for days but as Abby felt her sister clutch her tighter, she looked down to see the little face had a positively grey tinge. 'Look, only a minute or two and we'll be on the train and you can have one of the sandwiches I've brought. You didn't have any breakfast, did you, and you haven't eaten enough to keep a sparrow alive over Christmas.'

Clara managed a wan smile.

'I've got an orange too.' Abby grinned at her, her voice low. 'Aunty Audrey got it for you but she couldn't get one for Jed so don't tell him when you write to him.'

'An orange?' The distraction worked. Clara couldn't remember the last time she had tasted an orange.

'A nice big juicy one.' Abby was trying to jolly the child along until she could get her seated on the train. She had been shocked by how thin and white Clara had looked when she had first come home, but over the last days she'd swear her sister had got even thinner. She had taken all

171

this so hard, bless her, but once on the train she would get a sandwich or two down Clara and the child could have a little sleep. 'And at the farm there's all sorts of things – fresh eggs, milk, butter, cheese and lovely home-cured bacon, and Mrs Tollett makes wonderful puddings.'

'But what about rationing?' Clara asked, the faintness forgotten.

'Well, there's big differences between town and country eating,' Abby whispered confidingly as they waited for the incoming passengers to alight now the train had pulled to a halt. 'And I think farmers do the best of all. Mr Tollett is allowed to kill a calf every three months and two pigs a year to supplement the official ration town folk have to manage on, and they've got lots of chicken and ducks and geese. Did I tell you Mrs Tollett has some beehives . . .'

By the time they climbed aboard, Clara seemed quite recovered, chatting animatedly about the farm, but the child's brief dizzy spell worried Abby considerably. If she didn't see a significant improvement in her sister's health and general wellbeing over the next few weeks she would take her to a doctor, she decided.

Once the train had left the station, Clara forced down a sandwich and went to sleep with her head on Abby's lap. Abby stroked the small forehead lovingly. Clara had always been a thin little thing, admittedly, but now she looked as though a breath of wind would blow her away, and although losing their father had been a terrible shock for the little girl, her subsequent emotional state was surely extreme for a child of nine. Abby turned to gaze out of the train window, her mind buzzing. And there was the Winnie and Vincent thing to deal with at the farm too. How had it all panned out after she'd had to leave so hurriedly? As far as they knew, Vincent had got back to the farm at some time during Saturday night because he had been at work in the yard

172

the next morning when they had gone down to breakfast. The farmer and his wife had still been up when the three of them had walked into the kitchen after driving the lorry back, and during the subsequent explanation had said very little, neither defending nor denouncing their younger son's behaviour. Sunday had been very strained for everyone and Monday hadn't been much better. Vincent had refused to talk to the three girls at all and Winnie's red eyes were ignored by Mr and Mrs Tollett. Then had come word about her da and everything and everyone else had faded into insignificance.

Clara stirred, muttering something unintelligible and making a flapping movement with her hand before sinking back into sleep. Abby gazed down at her sister as she brushed a strand of hair from Clara's cheek. Thank goodness she'd got Clara away from their mam for the time being. That, at least, was one thing less to worry about. Now Clara was with her she intended to keep her in Yorkshire for the duration of the war, however long it was, and in this she knew she definitely had the backing of her Aunt Audrey and Granda.

It was later that afternoon that Audrey popped her head round the front room door and said to Silas, 'Mrs Ingram's just tipped me the wink there's some rabbits to be had at the butchers on the corner so I'm going to see what's what. Nora's in the kitchen if you want anything. All right, Da? I shan't be long.'

Silas nodded, motioning with his hand that he understood. It had started already, like he'd known it would. As soon as she'd got back from the factory Audrey had been round next door inviting Nora for dinner. He watched his daughter leave the room, affection vying with irritation at her good-heartedness. And what was the betting

173

Nora would play her sister like a violin, not resting until her feet were firmly under the table every night and she practically lived round here? She was still after Ivor if he knew anything about it and he, for one, wouldn't put anything past her. Not Nora.

He heard the sound of voices in the kitchen and then the back door banged and all was quiet.

His mind returned to the question he'd been asking himself for days, ever since Raymond's accident. What should he do? What *could* he do? Would it make Nora less bold if she knew he had tumbled her little game and knew what had gone on in the past? He really didn't know, he admitted for the umpteenth time. His eldest was a law unto herself.

He shut his eyes for a second, and then, decision made, raised himself on his pillows, waiting for the pain in his chest to subside before he called, 'Nora? You there?' A full minute passed with no response from the kitchen, so again he drew on all his reserves of strength, taking as deep a breath as the pain would allow and yelling, 'Nora? You hear me?' before falling back and gasping for air as his heart laboured.

This time he heard the chair being pushed back on the flagstones, and a moment or two later his eldest daughter was standing in the doorway to the room, surveying him with cold eyes. 'What's the matter?' she said flatly. 'You having a bad turn?'

It was a few moments before he could say, 'Didn't you hear me afore?'

'What if I did?'

Let it pass, let it pass. 'I want a word with you, that's all.'

Nora looked down at the old man, her face stretching slightly and her eyes widening before she wiped her face

174

clear of all expression. He couldn't know. No one knew, no one except Clara and she was out of it now. 'What about?'

'Now Clara's out of your hair, you thinkin' about gettin' a job somewhere? You're going to have time on your hands with the house empty.'

She stared at him. 'What's that to do with you?'

'Plenty.' Silas's gaze didn't falter. 'It'll do no one no good you broodin' all day, and likely you'll find company if you get a job, company for the evenings, I mean. Audrey and Ivor have got their own lives to lead.'

Nora wanted to slap her father from here to kingdom come. Audrey! Always, *always* Audrey. 'It might have escaped your notice but my husband has just died. Likely Audrey thought she was doing the Christian thing in asking me round for a bite.'

'Don't come the grieving widow, lass, not with me. You couldn't stand the sight of Raymond, now then.'

'You know nowt about it.'

'Oh aye I do. And I tell you this, you spoil things for Audrey and I'll swing for you. Ivor don't want you, get that through your head. Whatever went on, it's finished with.'

Nora was speechless for a moment and then, her voice trembling with bitterness, she said, 'What's he said to you?'

'That don't matter.'

'*It does to me.*' Her voice had risen and she swallowed hard as she walked into the room, warning herself to keep control of her tongue. Whatever Ivor had said she knew her father well enough to know that shouting at him wouldn't get her anywhere. 'You tell me what he said to you, and every word, mind.'

'I don't have to tell you nowt, woman.' His voice was defiant but as she approached the bed he drew back, his face skeletal against the pillows.

175

'Maybe.' Her voice was low but distinct. 'But I dare bet he made out he was all innocent and light, didn't he? You men, you're all the same.'

'Whatever he said and whatever went on, Ivor's your sister's husband and nothing can change that. How you could do that to Audrey I just don't know.'

'Oh you.' Her lips were pressed tightly together and she stared at him with loathing for a moment. 'You've always thought the sun shines out of her backside. Audrey this and Audrey that until I was as sick of her name as I was of the pair of you. But you might like to know you're wrong about one thing. I don't want Ivor any more, in fact the sight of him makes me sick to my stomach, if you want to know, but every time I'm round here he's squirming with fear and that's good enough to keep me coming. And who knows, it might be today or tomorrow or a year from now I tell your precious Audrey the truth about her wonderful husband, or then again perhaps never. It's all up to me, isn't it?'

Nora was too incensed to notice Silas's gaze had become transfixed over her shoulder. As the old man went to speak, she poked her finger in his bony chest and said, 'Whatever he's told you, know this, Da. He wanted me all right. He wanted me so bad there were times we didn't make it to the bedroom. I didn't have to do much persuading, believe me.'

When she paused for breath her father's utter stillness registered for the first time, along with the look on his face which was like a mesmerised rabbit. Nora knew instantly who was standing behind her but she stepped away from the bed before she turned, and then very slowly.

Audrey had obviously met Ivor on the way back from the shops and the two of them were standing just inside the room. It was Ivor who recovered first, thrusting his way

176

past his wife who was standing in white-faced silence. 'You liar!' he cried. 'You dirty little liar.'

'I'm not lying and you know it.' Nora didn't raise her voice but stared him full in the face until he turned to look at his wife.

His voice trembling, he said, 'Audrey, lass, she's gone barmy. All this with Raymond has turned her brain.'

'She seems rational enough to me.' The words were thin and painful.

'You can't believe—'

She stopped him with a raised hand. 'Just tell me the truth, Ivor. Have you ever touched my sister?'

'Lass, how can you ask? I swear—'

'Don't, Ivor. Don't swear if it's not true.'

'For crying out loud, Audrey, what do you want me to say?' He was blustering and everyone knew it. 'I've told you, she's lying. You're not going to take her word against mine, are you?'

'When, Nora? When did it start?' Audrey walked further into the room but she did not look at her husband, she looked at her sister. 'Tell me when it started.'

Ivor swallowed deeply. 'Now hang on a minute—'

'Years ago.' Nora's chin rose defiantly. 'And it went on for years an' all, whatever he says now.'

This couldn't be happening. Audrey stared into the eyes of her sister. And yet she knew it was Nora and not Ivor who was telling the truth. How did she know? Her head was buzzing. The answer came instantly. Because it explained so many things she had dismissed in the past but which she now knew had been stored in some chamber in her head. Ivor's unease round her sister, the excuses he'd made if she'd ever suggested getting together with Nora and Raymond in the early days, his changed behaviour at Christmas and other holidays when they got together as a family – oh, countless things. 'Why?' Again it was to Nora she spoke.

Audrey's quietness had taken Nora aback. Whenever she had imagined this day – and she had, many times – it had always featured her sister's raised angry voice, floods of tears and maybe the sound of breaking crockery. But here she was as cool as a cucumber. She stared at Audrey, her gaze flicking briefly to Ivor and then Silas before it came to rest again on her sister's frozen countenance.

'Well?' Audrey's eyes hadn't left Nora's face. Her voice still level, her words still spoken in the peculiar undertone which so unnerved her sister, she said, 'I think I deserve to know why you saw fit to take my husband. You, my own flesh and blood.'

'Don't come the martyr, not you who's always had everything. I might as well not have existed after you were born, do you know that? Oh, Mam wasn't so bad, I think she still loved me in her way, but him.' Nora's eyes flashed to the old man in the bed. 'He didn't even see me any more, that's how bad it was. Audrey this and Audrey that, wishing me dead because of you. Oh aye, he did that,' she said as Audrey made a sound of denial in her throat. 'I heard him one night. Bargaining with God he was or, as Mam said, the other side more like. I only married Raymond to get out of the house, anyone would have done, and straightaway I knew I'd made the biggest mistake of my life. And all because of you, you and him. But still I couldn't get away from you. You had to come and live next door when you got wed, didn't you, always rubbing it in how happy you were and how much Ivor loved you. Your precious Ivor! Well, I proved how much he loved you.'

Audrey had taken a couple of steps backwards during this. 'I never did anything to you,' she said. 'Nothing except love you as my sister and make excuses for you all the

178

time.' And then as Nora went to say more, she said, 'Get out of my house and don't come back. I never want to see you again.' Her voice had risen slightly on the last word and although Nora's mouth had opened, something in her sister's face must have warned her to say nothing, because her lips shut with a little pop. The two stared at each other for a moment which seemed to stretch and tighten, and then Nora stalked out of the room, brushing past Ivor as though he didn't exist. They heard her go into the kitchen and then the back door banged and a quivering silence descended.

Ivor was the first to break it. 'Audrey lass,' he said, but even as he spoke Audrey turned to look at her father.

'Did you do what she said? Bargain with God?'

Silas didn't try to prevaricate. In truth he had been cut to the quick, not just because Nora had heard what he'd said all those years ago and the damage it had done to her, but because his Audrey was being made to suffer now. He made a slow obeisance with his head. 'Don't look at me like that, lass,' he said brokenly. 'I couldn't feel worse than I'm feeling now.'

'And you knew about her and him?' She couldn't bring herself to say Ivor's name. 'You knew and you didn't tell me?'

'I didn't know till it'd been over for years and what was the point in saying anything then? And he didn't want her, lass. He—'

'No, don't.' Audrey stopped her father. 'He can lie for himself. He's had lots of practice.' She felt numb, queer, odd. She had never felt like this in all her life, not even when they'd had the telegram about Donald.

'Audrey, you have to listen to me, lass.'

Ivor had tears rolling down his face when she turned her gaze from her father, but the sight of them didn't pierce the numbness in the slightest. 'No, I don't have to listen to you,' she said very clearly. 'You can listen to me for once.'

'Please, lass—'

'You went with her. You touched her and you let her touch you and not once but many times. I don't know who you are. Everything, our marriage, *everything* has been a lie.'

'Lass—'

As he made a move towards her, Audrey stiffened, her voice rising as she said, 'You lay one finger on me and I'll kill you.'

It wasn't the threat, which was ludicrous, but her manner and the way she was looking at him that froze Ivor.

'All the time, for years and years, you an' her have been laughing at me behind my back. Audrey, big, fat, stupid Audrey who'll put up with anything and who can't see beyond the nose on her face.'

'No, no, it was never like that. God in heaven, I didn't—'

'Don't call on God, Ivor.' The numbness was going and she had to get out of the room before she started shouting and pummelling him to a pulp. 'He doesn't approve of adultery, didn't you know?' And again, as he raised his hand, she said, 'Don't touch me. Don't you dare touch me.'

Drawing in a deep breath she forced her legs to move her out into the hall and through the kitchen, one hand clutching at the skin of her throat and the other round her middle. It was only when she reached the privy in the back-yard and the door was bolted behind her that she let out her breath. She sat down on the edge of the seat, bent forward and stared blankly at the floor.

When she heard footsteps outside she didn't alter her position, not even when Ivor's voice came soft and low.

180

'Audrey? Audrey lass, please listen to me. Open the door and let's talk. Look, this thing with Nora was madness but it wasn't like you think. I swear to you I never loved her. From the first it was just of the flesh and even then it sickened me. I was the biggest fool on earth and I know it, but I never stopped loving or wanting you. You're me sun, moon and stars, lass, you always have been. Please come out so we can talk.'

It was some minutes before he gave up and she heard him go back into the house. She hadn't said a word.

Ivor and Nora. Ivor and Nora. The refrain was pulsing in her head. And her da had known. How could he have known and not told her? There was nothing left. Nothing.

She began to sway a little as the hot tears ran down her face but there was no relief in their coming, just a grinding pain that had her gasping. She turned her head and leaned her brow against the brick wall and it was a long time before she moved again.

Chapter Thirteen

Clara had been at the farm for just six weeks when the sisters received word their grandfather had passed away in his sleep one night. He had gone peacefully, Audrey wrote in her large, childish hand, and she didn't expect they would be able to come home for the funeral but she wanted them to know, since she wasn't sure if their mother would write to them. She would be working fulltime at the munitions factory now that she didn't have their granda to see to, so likely her letters would be fewer. She hoped Abby understood.

Abby stared at the letter for some while, reading it over a few times. Her aunt had never been a long letter writer but the weekly news from home had been welcome the last years, her mother never having put pen to paper once since she'd been at the farm. But this letter . . . It wasn't just the sad news it held but there was something else, something strange. It just didn't seem as though it had been penned by her aunt at all, although it was definitely her handwriting. But then Aunt Audrey had cared for Granda for years, she told herself after a time of weeping for the old man she had loved so much, and she would feel his loss badly. That was probably what she was sensing. And her aunt was right, she couldn't request yet more leave on compassionate grounds as she'd done for her father's funeral. It was too soon, for one thing, and she was needed at the farm, and also with Clara settling in so well she didn't want to do anything to upset the child, and taking her back to Sunderland might well do that.

She broke the news to Clara very gently that evening, but although her sister cried for a while she was not too upset. In truth Clara had had little to do with her grandfather and the two had not been close.

With this extra sorrow on top of all that had happened over the Christmas period, Abby was thankful Clara's second stay in the country was proving so much more successful than her first. She attended the small local school and was doing well, and had made lots of friends. She was also gaining weight for the first time in years and had completely won over the farmer's wife whom she was allowed to call Mrs Gladys. The two of them collected the eggs together, churned the butter and did other jobs about the farm at the weekends and in the evenings.

Winnie, on the other hand, had become steadily more and more withdrawn of late, and she was beginning to look drawn and pasty in the mornings, the weight having fallen off her. It was the second morning after Abby had caught her friend retching in one of the cow byres that she finally confronted her with what she'd suspected for a couple of weeks. 'You're expecting, aren't you?' she said softly. 'And no saying it's something you've eaten again, not you with the cast-iron stomach. How far gone are you?'

Winnie didn't look at her as she said, 'I missed me second monthly over two weeks ago.'

'Oh, lass.' Abby put her arm round her friend. 'Have you said anything to Vincent?'

'Oh aye, I told him,' Winnie said bitterly, 'and he told me to go to hell. He says it isn't his and he's not copping for someone else's bit of fun. He called me a stupid fat lump and said I was trying to trap him.' Her voice broke.

'How dare he say it isn't his?' For a moment the pain

of her father's accident followed so closely by her beloved grandfather's demise was put to one side and Abby was hopping mad. 'He knows full well you've never looked at another man since you've been seeing him.'

Winnie was sobbing so hard she couldn't say anything for a while. Then she raised her head, sniffed and wiped the tears from the end of her nose with the back of a none too clean hand. 'That's what I said to him and I asked him who on earth this other bloke is supposed to be.'

'What did he say?'

Winnie shrugged. 'He just repeated it wasn't his and that I couldn't prove he was the father. He . . . he told me to get rid of it and that he knew someone.' Winnie drew in a deep, shuddering breath. 'That was when *I* told *him* to go to hell,' she said more strongly. 'I'm not killing my bairn just because its father is a gutless so-an'-so.' She looked at Abby, her face streaked with tears and dirt. 'But I'm scared, lass. I'm scared stiff. Me da'll go barmy. He's a grand man, me da, but he's not easy to talk to an' he's got set ideas on things. He'll look on this as me dragging his name through the mud, I know he will.'

'Oh, lass.' Abby didn't know what to say.

'What am I going to do, Abby?' Winnie stared at her, still sniffing. 'How can I go home and tell them I'm back because me belly's full and the bloke's washed his hands of me. How can I?'

'You're not going to.' Abby gripped Winnie's forearms with some strength. 'Vincent must marry you and what can your da say then?' One part of her hated the idea of her friend marrying such a swine but the other, the more practical side, realised that this new development had changed everything. Even with people carrying on all over since the war had started, there were still some things which remained the same, and in the sort of streets where she and Winnie came from, an illegitimate child just wasn't an option. A hasty marriage and a bairn arriving two or three months 'early' was a different kettle of fish. Jumped the gun a bit, did they? Couldn't wait for the benediction, eh? Still, these things happen. When the sap's running high and love is in the air it can make fools of us all, and a bairn is a gift from God when all's said and done. That would be the most that was said if Winnie turned up with a husband in tow, that and a few snide remarks from some of the old wives as they gossiped over their backyards.

But a baby born on the wrong side of the blanket? Those selfsame 'understanding' folk would let Winnie know what they thought of that in a hundred and one ways, branding the whole family. And it would be those with their own skeletons in the cupboard who would be the worst. She remembered a family a few doors down in Rose Street who had hounded a lass in Winnie's position to the point where the girl had hanged herself down by Thornhill Farm, and not twelve months later it had transpired that the man and wife were in fact father and daughter, and that he had more grown-up children and his wife still living in Blyth.

'He won't marry me, lass. You don't know him like I do.' Winnie shook her head wearily. 'He'll swear black is white if he has to.'

'Will he indeed? Well, we'll see about that.' Abby's mind was working rapidly. 'His mam and da know he was courting you, whatever he says now, and Mrs Tollett likes you, you know she does. She likes all of us.'

'What, tell them, you mean?'

'Why not? You've nothing to lose the way things are.'

Winnie didn't shake or nod her head, she just continued to stare at Abby. Then she leaned against the aged wood of the byre, her head down again as she said, 'I couldn't, lass. I'm . . . I'm too ashamed.'

185

'Don't be daft.' Now Abby almost slapped at her friend's arm. 'It should be him that's saying that. You loved him, lass, and, right or wrong, worshipped the ground he walked on. And he knew that. Oh aye, he knew all right and took full advantage of it, so for him to take the stand he's taking now makes him the lowest of the low in my book.'

'It takes two to tango.'

'And it takes two to bring up a bairn an' all,' Abby said grimly, 'so don't stick up for him, Winnie. Not now.'

'I wasn't, not really.'

'Good, because much as I care about you I'd have to give you a clip round the ear if you did.' Abby grinned at her and Winnie grinned weakly back. 'Now it's worked out well we're having lunch indoors for once because with Clara at school it's the best time to speak out.' With most of the fields and farm buried in a good few inches of snow, Farmer Tollett had found them work in the barns and outhouses, and his wife had insisted they all come in for something hot at twelve. Unfortunately they wouldn't be able to have a word with Rowena in private before this as she was helping the farmer's wife cut and salt a pig which had been slaughtered the day before, as well as turning its innards into faggots, sausages, savouries and lard. Even its trotters and tail needed pickling and boiling, and the head made excellent brawn. It always amazed Abby that Rowena happily plumped for this grisly task; she herself hated it, especially as the three girls fed the animals their swill every morning and got to know individual animals by their different personalities.

'Oh, I don't know, I don't know, lass.' Winnie gazed at her mournfully.

'Well, I do. He's not going to get away with this, Winnie, and you've got to stick up for yourself. All right?'

At five to twelve when Abby and Winnie walked into the

186

kitchen after sluicing off in the scullery, Winnie was still umming and ahhing. Rowena and Farmer Tollett were already seated at the kitchen table, and Mrs Tollett was busy removing a pan of beef stew from the haybox she used for the occasional hot lunchtime meal. The haybox cooker was nothing more than a packing case lined with newspapers and packed with sweet, dry hay at the bottom and a hay-filled mattress at the top, with a pan nestling deep in the middle packed round by yet more hay. When the pan was put into the haybox piping hot, the food continued to slowly cook and tenderise, thus saving fuel and producing meat which melted in the mouth.

Abby and Winnie sat down silently and moments later they heard Vincent enter the scullery and start washing his hands in the tin bowl. They glanced at each other and their faces must have given something away, because Rowena nudged Abby with her foot and mouthed, 'What's up?'

Abby shook her head in silent warning. She reached across and took a slice of the big farmhouse loaf of bread in the middle of the table as Mrs Tollett bustled across with bowls of fragrant, steaming stew.

'We've had a good morning,' she said to her husband as she placed a bowl in front of him. 'There's only the bits like the sausages and faggots to do later, and starting off the chitterlings. I should be able to have a good hour or two in the dairy this afternoon. You only have to show this lass something once,' she nodded at Rowena, 'and she's got it.'

This was high praise indeed, and for a moment Abby felt a pang of conscience that she was going to ruin the rest of the day for the farmer's wife.

Vincent sullenly took his place at the table and once everyone was tucking into the meal, Abby nudged Winnie with her elbow. Winnie cleared her throat once, then again and remained absolutely silent. After a second or two she took another slice of bread and bit into it as though she was famished.

This couldn't go on. Abby glanced at her friend and for the first time the extent of Winnie's weight loss hit her. Winnie was desperately unhappy and worried to death and she was going to be really ill if something wasn't done. The spoon in Abby's hand wobbled and she placed it in the bowl before she said, 'Farmer Tollett? Winnie has something to say to you and Mrs Tollett.'

The farmer said nothing, merely moving his grizzled head to stare at Winnie enquiringly, as did Mrs Tollett and Rowena. Vincent, Abby noticed, continued to spoon the stew into his mouth, his eyes on his bowl.

To Abby's surprise, Winnie didn't prevaricate any longer. 'I'm expecting a bairn,' she said, not looking at anyone. 'Vincent's bairn.'

If a bomb had exploded in their midst the announcement couldn't have had more effect, but it was Vincent's sudden move towards Winnie which brought both Farmer Tollett and Abby to their feet, the farmer to restrain his son and Abby to stand protectively in front of her friend. The words spewing out of Vincent's mouth would have been worthy of any dockside labourer. Then Mrs Tollett entered the arena. 'Stop it, boy!' she cried. 'Do you hear me? Stop it this instant.'

It was a few moments more before Vincent allowed his father to push him into his seat, but then, his face red and his eyes glaring, he said, 'She's trying to trap me, can't you see? And all three of them are in on it. Loose trollops, the lot of 'em.'

'Vincent *is* the father, Mrs Tollett.' Winnie was as white as a sheet but her voice was steady. 'And whatever he may

188

call me, neither Abby nor Rowena are trollops, far from it.'

Mrs Tollett didn't answer but stared back at her, her eyes stretched wide. Her husband, his hand still on his son's shoulder, said, 'A bairn, you say? Are you sure?'

'Aye.' From being as pale as alabaster, Winnie's skin was now flushed a deep pink. 'I'm quite sure, Mr Tollett.'

'It's not mine, I tell you.' Vincent shrugged off his father's hand, his voice a growl. 'She goes to the dances in town and the pictures, doesn't she? They all do. And I've seen 'em with the RAF blokes and the local lads, making eyes at anything in trousers.'

'That's a lie and you know it.' Rowena came into the fray for the first time and suddenly she was very much the lady of the manor. 'And if you don't want an action against you I would think very carefully about such accusations. Neither myself nor my friends are prepared to tolerate our good names being soiled by someone like you.'

'Someone like me?'

'Yes, someone like you. You ought to be thankful a girl like Winnie would look your way in the first place, especially having seen the type of woman you associate with normally. To call that woman at the dance at Christmas a dog would be giving all canines a bad name.'

This time the farmer had his work cut out to prevent his son reaching Rowena. 'Sit down, the lot of you,' he shouted, 'and shut up! Do you hear? And you,' he turned to his son, staring down into the livid countenance as he held Vincent on his chair, 'you'll do the right thing by the girl. It's high time you learned that everything in life has to be paid for sooner or later.'

'You'd believe her against me? Your own son?'

'Aye, I reckon I would, lad.' The farmer was under no illusions about his younger son, neither was he blind to the fact that Winnie would make an excellent farmer's wife and be a welcome addition to the labour force of the farm. If he'd had to pick one of the three it would have been this big, broad, buxom lass who worked as well as any farm hand and who would produce fine, strong grandsons. 'And that being the case I'll be taking the pair of you along to the parson come Sunday to see about getting the banns read.'

'Well, now I know where I stand.' Vincent was sitting straight now, his breathing sharp and his enmity directed against his father. 'If it'd been Nicholas sitting here you wouldn't have taken this tack.'

Farmer Tollett did not deny this. Instead he said, 'Nicholas is Nicholas and you're you.'

'I know that only too well.'

It was deep and bitter, and the older man's eyes narrowed before he said slowly, 'Your mother and I have never made meat of one and fish of the other, now then, lad. That's all in your mind and always has been. But I don't deny Nicholas is a good lad. That wouldn't be fair.'

'And of course you're always so fair.'

'I try to be.'

'And you think leaving the farm to Nicholas is fair?'

'He's the firstborn, it'd have been the same if it was you.'

'But it's not me, is it?'

'This isn't about the farm.' Farmer Tollett had clearly had enough. His voice rough now, he said, 'This is about you and this young lass here, and like I said, you'll do the right thing by her.'

When Vincent lowered his head without saying anything more, it could have been taken for defeat, but Abby was sitting closest to him and she saw the look on his face. Her stomach turned over, and she asked herself if marrying the farmer's son was the right thing for Winnie to do, even taking into account the forthcoming child. But Winnie would have the backing of Mr and Mrs Tollett, that much was clear, and they would see Vincent treated her well, she assured herself in the next moment. This way Winnie would have the respectability which was so important to her, and her baby would have its father's name, rather than the stigma that being born out of wedlock would undoubtedly bring. It had to be the best thing . . . didn't it?

When the occupants of the farm awoke the next morning to the knowledge that Vincent had crept away in the middle of the night, leaving a note for his mother to say he'd gone to join up, Abby had to admit her immediate reaction was one of relief. She had tossed and turned all night, skimming in and out of nightmarish dreams which embodied Winnie sinking in a sea of mud, drowning, or on one occasion being suffocated by a huge snake, and each time she had been unable to help her because Vincent had prevented it.

He was the worst possible type of man for a prospective husband, she told herself between the snatches of sleep, but there was no other option for her friend.

Now, as she stood with Winnie and Rowena in the kitchen staring at Mrs Tollett who was sitting at the kitchen table, the letter still clutched in her hand and the tears streaming down her face, Abby felt that despite all outward appearances this was the best thing for Winnie.

She listened to the farmer who was ranting and raving that he was going to find Vincent and bring him back, looked at Mrs Tollett who was clearly beside herself at the thought of both sons going to war, and then glanced at Winnie who was standing still and silent beside her. It was a shock for everyone in different ways but she still couldn't bring herself to be sorry Vincent had gone. She was very surprised when Winnie said more or less the same thing a moment later, though.

'Don't try and look for him, Mr Tollett.' Winnie's voice was quiet. 'He'll only go again if that's what he's decided, and he'll make life thoroughly unpleasant for everyone in the meantime. I – I think it's best he's nailed his colours to the mast. And we'll manage here. We'll all work a bit harder until you can get someone to replace him.'

'Right at this minute I'm not so bothered about the work-load, girl,' the farmer said heavily, 'much as we'll struggle. But for a lad of mine to take a lass down and then skedaddle, it sticks in me craw.'

Winnie lowered her head. In truth she was amazed at the stance the farmer had taken. She had expected to find herself out on her ear the minute they learned of her condition and Vincent's attitude. It only went to show you never could be sure how someone else would react.

Mrs Tollett pulled herself together and stood up, her voice low as she patted Winnie's arm and said, 'I don't agree with what he's done but he's my own and I think a bit of him, lass. The thought of him at the front somewhere . . .' She gulped. 'But there's a place here for you as long as you want it, you and the little one when it comes. And as one of the family, you understand?'

'Thank you, Mrs Tollett.'

'Gladys, dear.' Mrs Tollett turned and looked at Abby and Rowena. 'I think it's high time you called us by our Christian names, don't you, girls? Josiah and I couldn't have got harder workers, that's for sure, and with all that's happened I don't think we'll stand on ceremony any longer.'

They all smiled, and Winnie looked as though a huge weight had been lifted from her shoulders. Mrs Tollett bustled over to the haybox which had been cooking the morning porridge all night. 'I think we could all do with a bowl of porridge before we go out this morning,' she said briskly. 'And then I'll get breakfast as normal once you've done the milking and so on. And Winnie?' She turned, her voice low as they heard Clara clattering down the stairs. 'You make sure you have plenty of cream on it, lass. All right? That little 'un needs to be fat and healthy when it's born, living up here.'

As they all sat down at the kitchen table, Abby caught her friend's eye and they grinned weakly at each other, relief on both their faces. This result was better than they could have imagined. They could sort out how they were going to break the news to Winnie's mam and da later; they didn't need to say anything at all for the time being.

Clara joined them, still in her nightie and her face flushed with sleep, and Abby felt her whole body relax. Clara was safe and it looked as though Winnie was going to be set up here. After all the horrible events of the last few months, things were looking up.

PART FOUR

Gum, Nylons and GIs
1943

Chapter Fourteen

The wind was whipping over the docks from an icy North Sea and whistling down the streets of Sunderland, losing none of its power as it negotiated houses and factories. To anyone other than a northerner it would have been hard to believe this was the beginning of May, but a harsh winter followed by a cold spring wasn't anything unusual to the tall man preparing to knock on the door of 12 Rose Street. Besides, with bombed-out buildings everywhere, so many ships and men lost in March and the war seeming to get worse and not better, who cared about the weather? It had been hoped that the Americans coming in would turn things around but there was no sign of it yet.

James Benson took a deep breath, clearing his mind of everything but what he was about to do. He lifted the brass knocker in the shape of a grinning elf and knocked firmly on the door three times. He was not wearing his uniform; he had not worn it since returning to England, although some men who were invalided out of the forces had continued to wear theirs. He couldn't understand that. He had been glad to be done with the army and everything connected with it. He felt no satisfaction, no pride in having fought in a war where mass slaughter seemed the order of the day.

The door opened and Nora Vickers stood staring at him. He knew Abby's mother was alone in the house, his father had ascertained that when he had come to the house immediately

197

after hearing that his son was alive two weeks ago. His father had tried to get her to give him an address or contact number for Abby but although she had asked him in and even made him a cup of tea, he had been unable to get anything out of her.

'Mrs Vickers? I don't know if you remember me.' He had decided to play it cool and calm at first, but he was determined he would get nasty if he had to.

'Of course I remember you.' In truth Nora had to admit that, but for the visit of his father preparing her, she would not have recognised the man in front of her as James Benson. He looked years older for one thing, his hair liberally streaked with grey and his skin patchy and a funny colour. But she had been grateful Dr Benson had called, even though it had been a shock to learn James had been a prisoner of war these last years when they had believed him to be dead. It had given her time to think and decide on the best tack to take. Now she took him aback as she had known she would when she said, 'Come in, lad. It's fair bitter out there. I wouldn't be surprised if we had more snow even now.' She stepped back into the house and he joined her in the hall. 'Take your coat off and hang it there, that's right, and come through to the kitchen where it's warm. You don't mind sitting in the kitchen? The front room is like an icebox with fuel being rationed so tight. They don't give enough to keep body and soul together.'

He struggled a little as he slipped off his overcoat. He still found his useless left arm something of a trial but he had learned to walk in such a way that the limp caused by the injuries to his left leg was no longer noticeable. Not that he was complaining, he thought, as he followed Abby's mother into the kitchen where the range was giving off a comforting glow. He was only too grateful he'd survived with both arms and both legs, and wasn't reliant on a hook where his hand should be like some of the poor devils in the hospital he'd been sent to on arriving in England.

Nora pulled out a chair for him and didn't speak until he had sat down at the table. Then she turned to the hob.

'I'd just made a brew, so that was lucky, wasn't it? You timed it just right.' Her voice was almost gay.

His brow wrinkled. Whatever he had expected it wasn't this friendliness. 'That's very kind of you, Mrs Vickers.' He cleared his throat. 'I suppose you know why I've come.'

'Your father asked me for Abby's address.' Nora swung round with two mugs of tea and brought them across to the table, placing the milk and a small bowl containing a white powdery substance in front of him. 'It's sugar substitute, I'm afraid,' she said with another smile. 'I've no sugar but then who has these days? It's not very nice but better than nothing.'

'Just milk is fine.'

Before he could say anything more, she fetched a tin containing rice cake to the table, talking all the time. 'This is where the last of my ration of sugar went this week so you must have a slice. Dried eggs of course but I've found if I sieve it in with the dry ingredients before water's added it makes a fairly good cake. Anyway, we can't complain in these times, can we? Not about eggs, at least.'

'No, no, I suppose not,' he said, a trifle dazed, as Nora put a piece of cake on a plate and placed it next to his mug of tea.

'Of course some of the bairns hereabouts go guleging. You know, collecting gulls' eggs. They're as big as duck's eggs and very nice, so I'm told, but without any bairns at home and me working fulltime now I have to rely on the dried egg ration.'

He had to stop her talking, it was driving him mad. 'Mrs Vickers, I need to know Abby's address,' he said very

199

quickly when she paused for breath. 'I have to write to her or go and see her as soon as possible.'

Nora stared at him before lowering her eyes. Thousands, tens of thousands of lads and men killed in the war and this one had to survive. She'd hardly been able to believe it when his father had told her that a mistake had been made. He had been badly injured, Dr Benson had said, and with his identification gone and James being in a coma for weeks, he'd been shipped off to one of the German camps and that had been that. When his identification had been found amid the carnage of what had been men before the shells had hit, the obvious had been assumed. She had wanted to knock the smile off his father's face but she'd restrained herself, knowing what she said or did could influence the way this thing went. And it would go the way she determined – by, it would, or she'd die in the attempt. She didn't intend her upstart of a daughter to come up smelling of roses.

'I have something to tell you, James,' she said very softly, wondering if she should reach out and put her hand on his but deciding that was taking things too far.

'Tell me?' She saw his skin turn a shade greyer. 'About Abby? Is she all right?'

'Oh, she's well enough, don't fret about that.' She chose a tone in which sorrow blended with embarrassment. 'It's just that – oh, I don't know how to tell you! She wrote to say she's getting wed this very week.'

'Married?' He put his head forward as if he hadn't heard her clearly. He couldn't take it in.

'Yes, in fact it's probably done and dusted by now. You know she went to Yorkshire as a land girl, to a farm? Your father told you about that?'

He nodded, just the slightest inclination of his head.

'Well, the son of the farmer and Abby . . . She thought

you were dead, of course, you understand that. I'm so sorry, James.'

'I – It can't be.'

'It's a beautiful farm, I understand, although I've never been, but she's got Clara there with her. I can't remember if I told your da that, but Abby took her after Raymond went. You know my husband passed away?' She didn't wait for an answer but continued, 'And they took to Clara right away. But of course she's so much like Abby that's not surprising. So the pair of them are safe and happy, which is everything in these terrible times, isn't it, and of course Abby marrying into wealthy farming stock means Clara will be set up when she's old enough to think about settling down.' She hesitated for the merest moment. 'I thought it would be best to explain things face to face rather than tell your father. I hope you think that was the right decision.'

'What? Oh yes. Yes.'

'And of course it has been, what, three years? You can't blame her for making a new life.'

He ran his tongue round the inside of his lips. This was his worst nightmare come true. How often had he tortured himself, wondering if she was with someone before he'd reminded himself it was Abby he was talking about. His Abby. She loved him and he loved her and it was a lifetime thing for both of them. But she'd thought he was dead. He hadn't known he'd been given up for dead until recently. Suddenly it made everything worthless – the escape from the camp and the beatings and brutality he'd endured in that hellhole, even when he'd been struggling with injuries which should have killed him, the weeks of endless walking in the dead of night when two in their party of five escapees had died of hypothermia and starvation.

He had to make an enormous effort to speak. 'Could

. . . could I still have her address, please? I'd like to write, for old times' sake.' He didn't know if he would write, he admitted silently. He needed to think things through somewhere quiet. But if he got the address now, at least it was an option if he felt he wanted to. He wouldn't be able to face coming back here again.

Nora's voice was very gentle when she said, 'I don't think that's a good idea, James, and I don't think you will when you've had time to think about it. I know this must be a terrible shock for you, but you are not the man you were and she's not the girl she was. Three years is a long time, even without the war and everything you've endured. And she is a farmer's wife now. Everything is different. If you contact her or go to see her, her husband might not like it; in fact he's bound to resent it, knowing you were engaged once.'

'He knows about me?'

Nora inclined her head. 'And men can be very jealous,' she said softly, 'even though there would be no reason, not now. It wouldn't be fair to Abby. You must see that. Far better to leave things as they are. She's made a new life and you will too, I'm sure of that.' She had interjected a bracing note and now stood up, her mug in her hand. 'Would you like more tea?'

He felt a roaring in his ears, the same sensation that overcame him when his mind went dizzying away from him. Sometimes he went back into a past which was much more real to him than his present world, losing an hour at a time as he relived horrors. The doctors had said he had to apply mind over matter and that it would pass, he had to keep employing his will to keep his mind in the present and only the present. There would be a time, he'd been assured, when he could think of everything that had happened without bitterness and hatred. He had almost laughed in their faces when they had said that. But they were right about one thing, he had to exercise control and never more than now in front of Abby's mother. But she had been kind, he had to give her that. Unease stirred. Too kind?

Nora saw the change in his face, the flicker of disbelief. She kept her voice easy when she said, 'Of course it's no secret Abby and I never got on, and I have to say that lonely though I feel here since poor Raymond died, I wouldn't want her back. We'd only argue.' She smiled a sad smile. 'But the war does bring one's values into perspective. She is my daughter after all, flesh of my flesh, and with Wilbert away fighting I'm so glad two of my bairns are out of harm's way.' She stared at him. Had she said enough? Dare she play her trump card or would he take her up on it? If he did, she'd just have to brazen it out somehow, say she couldn't find the address or something similar.

She took a deep breath. 'Look, lad, I can't tell you what to do. If you really want to risk upsetting her marriage and everything that'd entail, I'll give you the address but, like I said, three years changes people.'

She loved someone else. She'd *married* someone else. Had she ever really loved him like he'd loved her? James knew he was being unfair but the disappointment and sense of loss was so acute he didn't know how he could bear it. He stood up, thrusting his mug towards Nora instead of placing it on the table.

'Thank you for the tea, Mrs Vickers.' He had to get out before he started to cry. That would be the ultimate indignity, to bawl in front of this woman. 'Perhaps you'd remember me to Abby sometime.'

'Aye, I'll do that, lad.' Nora felt a surge of joy and triumph which made her turn her back and put the mugs on the hob, frightened he'd read what was in her face.

She followed James out of the room, and he didn't stop to put his coat on before he opened the front door. 'Goodbye, Mrs Vickers,' he said flatly, barely conscious of a woman entering the house next door as he stepped onto the pavement.

'Goodbye, lad.' Nora held her breath as she watched James walk away, head bowed. When no figure suddenly re-emerged from next door, she breathed a sigh of relief. Who would have thought her dear sister would have chosen that precise moment to come home? But even if Audrey had glanced at him, she doubted her sister would have equated the gaunt, middle-aged-looking scarecrow of a man with the young handsome suitor James had once been. She herself would never have recognised him if she'd passed him in the street, that was for sure.

She shut the door quietly and then leaned against it for a few moments, smiling widely. She had done it, and it had all been much easier than she had anticipated.

Still smiling, she walked through into the kitchen and made a fresh pot of tea, allowing herself two slices of cake to celebrate.

Audrey hadn't even glanced sideways as the door to Nora's house opened. Since Christmas she hadn't seen hide nor hair of her sister and that was the way she wanted it.

She walked straight through to the kitchen, past the now empty front room, and as always when she entered the house, she thought, I'm glad I made it up with Da before he went. She hadn't been able to talk to the old man for a few days after the revelation about Nora and Ivor, but then one day she had broken down when she was handing him his tea and he had held out his arms and cuddled her as if she was a bairn again. And after that everything had been all right, between them at least.

Her mouth hardening, Audrey slung her coat on a chair and set about bringing the glowing embers in the range to a decent blaze. Once that was accomplished she put the kettle on the hob and stuck two jacket potatoes into the ashes of the fire where they would bake slowly. She would eat hers before Ivor got home, leaving his and a tin of Spam ready for him when he got in. And he was lucky to get that, she told herself bitterly.

Working fulltime at the munitions factory had proved very tiring in comparison to the four hours she'd done before her father had died, but overall she liked the company and the lack of time to think. The foul language and blue jokes which were commonplace among certain of the women as well as the men she'd more or less got used to now, along with having to wear mannish dungarees and a headsquare turban all day.

When she had told them at the factory she could do fulltime, the manager had asked if she'd consider the job of putting the caps on the detonators of bullets. It was classed as highly dangerous and the eight pounds per week she would earn reflected this, but that wasn't what had persuaded her to agree. It was that the management advised such workers to wear no jewellery, not even wedding rings, and that suited Audrey's state of mind exactly.

She mashed the tea, drinking two large cups without milk or sugar. She'd lost nearly three stone since Christmas, and she liked her new figure. She had let herself go when she had got married, she realised that now. Perhaps it was what happiness and contentment did to you.

The thought brought hot tears stinging to the back of her eyes and she stood up sharply. 'None of that, Audrey lass,' she said out loud. 'He's not worth it.' She squared her shoulders before walking through to the hall and up the stairs to the bedroom in which she now slept alone.

The night it had all come out she had bolted the bedroom door against Ivor, and the next evening he'd come home from work to find all his things moved into the boys' room.

Audrey opened the wardrobe which now held only her clothes and stared at the contents. Some of the women she worked with complained constantly about getting by on sixty-six clothing coupons a year, but considering she'd done without all her life to make sure Ivor and the lads were clothed decently, she had never had it so good as the last months. With a previously undreamed of amount of money in her hand each week the black market had become easily accessible to her, and dress materials or actual clothes could always be had for a price.

She selected a dress she had bought the week before and threw it on the bed. She took off her working clothes, a short-sleeved jumper and dungarees, and in her bra and knickers reached up to the top shelf of the wardrobe and brought down a bottle of Scotch and a small glass. She poured herself a measure, then sat down at her dressing table and surveyed herself in the old spotted mirror. She had never tasted strong liquor until the last few months and at first, when the other women from work had introduced her to it on one of their nights out, she hadn't been sure if she liked the taste.

Just her luck she'd developed a liking for it when it cost the earth, she thought now, staring at the bottle which had trebled in price to one pound and six shillings since the war. Still, she hadn't bought this particular bottle. It had come via Hank, a GI she knew, along with two packets of nylon stockings and some bars of chocolate. She found the alcohol perked her up before Jed came home from his pal's house – the mother looked after Jed once school finished and gave him his dinner for a small fee.

She reached for a slip and pulled it over her head, followed by the dress. She didn't bother with stockings; she would change again later before she went to meet the girls once Jed was in bed, and that's when she'd make up her face and fiddle with her hair.

She finished the whisky in one gulp and squared her shoulders as though preparing to do battle, even though Ivor wasn't home yet. But that was how she felt immediately she set foot in this house, that it was a battleground.

When Ivor came in from the late shift at the shipyard, Audrey was dressed and ready to leave. She stood up from where she'd been sitting waiting for him at the kitchen table but didn't look directly at him as she said, 'I've eaten and Jed's in bed. Your meal's on the hotplate.'

He did not reply to this, saying instead, 'You out again? This is the second time this week and it's only Wednesday.'

'I wasn't aware I had to answer to you.'

'I didn't say you had.'

'It sounded like that to me.'

'Don't start as soon as I get in.'

'Don't shout, Ivor.' It was cold. 'You'll wake the bairn.'

She looked bonny. Ivor stared at his wife and the sickly odd feeling he always got when she went out with the crew from work, most of whom were no better than they should be, hit him. For a moment he felt as weak as a kitten. He had lost her, he knew he'd lost her even though she hadn't physically removed herself from the house, but that was for Jed's sake and all part of the act they put up in front of the child. Mind, he didn't think Audrey's explanation that his snoring had been keeping her awake and that was why he'd moved bedrooms had fooled their son.

He raked back his hair with his hand and said, 'It's been months now. Won't you at least let me try and explain how it was? Please?'

Audrey looked fully at her husband for the first time. 'You could talk until you're blue in the face and I would never understand how you could do such a thing. You must have thought yourself such a canny lad, having your cake and eating it.'

'It wasn't like that. The first time she took me by surprise and . . . and after, I swore to meself I'd never go near her again.'

'But you did,' she said with flat control.

She had been about to turn and walk out into the hall when he suddenly flung himself at her, going down on his knees, his head bowed. She froze, looking down on the rich thickness of his hair as he sobbed that he couldn't go on without her. 'I love you, lass. I've never loved another woman in the whole of me life and I never will. Forgive me. Forgive me.'

Forgive him? Her hands had moved away from her sides as from something repellent but her face was pained as the sobs racked his body.

She had never felt quite good enough for him. Deep, deep down in herself she had always been grateful he had loved and married her, and because of that theirs had been an unequal marriage. She had given too much, and she realised now that he had come to accept her adoration as his right. Perhaps there was an element of blame attached to her in all of this. But that didn't lessen what he'd done. The sheer agony of it cut off her breath for a second. She hated him for it and would go on hating him until the day she died.

Her complete stillness finally got through to him and as he raised his head and drew back a little to look up into her face, Audrey seized the moment. She spun round and

208

out into the hall. He called her name but she flung open the front door and ran down the street as if the devil himself was on her heels.

By the time she reached the Londonderry in High Street West where they'd all agreed to meet up, she was sweating and hot in spite of the cold night. She stood for a moment to compose herself before she went inside. Her hand was still clutching her heaving bosom when she noticed Hank and a few other GIs making their way towards her. Hank smiled when he caught sight of her. He looked as immaculate as always in one of the stylishly tailored uniforms all the American servicemen wore.

'Hey, honey, you OK?' He took her arm as he reached her in the easy friendly way all the GIs had, and for once she let herself relax against him, shaking her head. He must have motioned for the others to go in the pub because within moments it was just the two of them, and his voice was very soft when he said, 'Trouble at home?'

'How did you know?' She was surprised into looking at him.

He shrugged. 'I asked about you. One of the other girls said you were married but that you never talked about your husband. He works in a shipyard, right? So . . . I guess I put two and two together.'

She stared at him. He had asked about her. He had cared enough to ask about her. It felt good. She dropped her gaze from his. 'I still don't want to talk about him,' she said in a small voice, looking at the ribbons on his uniform. But she didn't move away from him.

One hand came round her waist and the other tilted her chin up to meet his eyes. He had nice eyes, brown and heavily lashed. She had noticed his eyes before. 'That's OK by me, honey,' he said softly. 'But does it mean you don't want to come dancing later?'

'Not necessarily.' She had always refused to accompany the other women and the GIs once they left the pubs, even though she knew the Americans took them to the best local clubs and restaurants. But then with an American private receiving nearly three pounds and ten shillings a week compared to a British soldier's fourteen shillings, the GIs could afford to splash out a bit, she reminded herself silently.

'Great.' He drew her closer with the hand at her waist. 'I'll give you your first lesson in jitterbugging if you're good.'

She smiled at him, his accent making the word even more quirky. The American dance craze had spread with such enthusiasm in the last year that many ballrooms and dance halls had had to ban it to protect their sprung floors. The jitterbug was for the uninhibited, like the GIs themselves. 'And if I'm not good?' she said lightly, hearing herself flirt with faint disbelief. From the age of fifteen when she had met Ivor she had never looked at another man, let alone played the coquette.

'I'll think of something else to do,' he said just as lightly. She stared at him, the smiles fading from both their faces as their eyes held, and then he said, 'Come on, you're getting cold out here,' as the shiver she gave transferred itself to him through their now joined hands. And it was like that, with her hand in his, that they entered the warmth and colour of the pub to join the others.

Audrey had had more drinks than she should have by the time they left. She was drunk, she knew she was drunk because she was singing 'This Is the Army, Mr Jones' along with the other girls while hanging on to Hank's arm with one hand and waving to all and sundry with the other. As they neared the three jeeps the GIs had come into town in,

Hank put his arm round her shoulders, drawing her over to his vehicle and then opening the door for her. 'Hop in.'

When he came and sat in the driver's seat she brought her gaze to bear on him with a penetrating stare before she said, 'Well, what now? Where do you want to go?'

Her directness obviously took him aback because he swallowed before smiling uncertainly. 'You're a different gal when you've had a few, aren't you?' he said, still smiling, and touching her hand to let her know he wasn't complaining.

'I don't know. This is the first time I've had a few, as you put it. And,' she gave a shaky laugh, 'it'll be the first time for anything else, besides with me husband, of course.'

There was a short silence before Hank said, 'I know where we can get a room if you like.'

A room? Somehow she had never expected that. A quiet spot on the outskirts of the town maybe, but a room seemed to take the whole thing into a different sphere.

Whether her face showed what she was thinking she didn't know, but the next moment he'd taken her hands in his, his voice soft with the easy American drawl which was so attractive. 'You know I like you, honey. I like you very much.'

She wet her lips and swallowed before answering, 'I like you too.'

It was done. She sat very still as he started the Jeep and swung the vehicle round. They drove off in the opposite direction to the others.

When they came to Queen Alexandra Road, she realised he had cut through the town and into Hendon, and found herself marvelling that the Jeep had taken such little time about it. He stopped the vehicle on the corner of one of the streets bordering Ryhope Road and the Sunderland cemetery. He jumped out and then helped her out with the old-fashioned charm all the GIs had and which made every girl they were with feel like a queen.

Instead of the hotel or inn she was expecting, Audrey found herself looking at a perfectly ordinary house, and when she turned enquiring eyes on Hank, he said, 'One of the guys at the base has an uncle or a cousin, something like that, living here. He's away fighting and his wife and child are in the country somewhere, but he gave a set of keys to Abe for him to use if he needed a bit of peace and quiet, you know? Home from home.'

He reached over and extracted a bottle from under one of the seats of the Jeep and then pulled her across the pavement and into the tiny front garden, which once would have had railings separating it from the pavement until they had been required for the war effort. After retrieving a key from under a pot, Hank opened the front door and ushered her through the hall into a very pleasant front room.

'Drink?' He raised the bottle of whisky in his hand and without waiting for her reply walked across to a small cabinet, on top of which was a tray with some assorted glasses. He poured two decent measures and handed her one, downing his in one swallow before he noticed she was still standing in exactly the same place, the glass clutched tightly in her hand. 'Relax, sugar,' he said softly.

'I don't think I can.'

'Sure you can.' He guided the glass to her lips and when she had taken a sip, he smiled. 'See? That's great. We'll have another in a minute but first . . .' He walked over to the hefty sofa at the end of the room under the window and closed the thick velvet curtains. Then he bent down and slung the large cushions onto the square of carpet in the middle of the room. That done, he pulled the sofa up and then out, to reveal a bed covered by a thin mattress.

'Come here.' When she didn't answer or move, he walked across and again tilted the glass to her lips, taking it from her once it was empty and putting it on the cabinet before leading her to the side of the sofa bed.

When his arms went round her they were gentle, his whole embrace was gentle and his kiss was sweet and non-threatening. She stiffened at first but then, as he coaxed and soothed her with little kisses all over her face, she relaxed, she closed her eyes and put her arms round his neck. He eased her down onto the bed, their arms still wrapped round each other and their faces close. Why that moment should be the one that told Audrey she couldn't go through with this, she didn't know, but she found herself pushing him away as she struggled to sit up.

She adjusted her clothing with shaking hands, her cheeks flaming but her head remarkably clear. 'I'm sorry.' She nerved herself to look at him. 'Hank, I'm really sorry but I shouldn't be here.' She bit hard on the inside of her lower lip to stop herself bursting into tears.

'You still love your husband.' It was a statement, not a question. He swung his legs over the side of the bed and sat with his hands hanging loosely between his knees.

This was awful, terrible. If he had shouted she would have felt better. She opened her mouth to deny the charge but instead she said, 'Yes,' as the truth hit her. And she wasn't going to let Nora completely ruin their lives.

'Does he know what a lucky son of a gun he is?'

'No, I shouldn't think so.' And then she corrected herself in the next instant. 'At least not till recently anyway.'

His glance flashed to her then and he said, 'You're sure he's not giving you the runaround?'

The runaround? She thought of the scene earlier that night, of Ivor sobbing on his knees as he clutched her as

213

though he was drowning. Suddenly all she wanted was to be with him. 'I'm sure,' she said, very softly.

The house was in darkness when she let herself in and for a moment she stood in the hall, uncertain what to do next. Ivor would be fast asleep by now. And then some instinct she hadn't known she possessed kicked in. He was not asleep. Right at this moment he was very much awake. What was she going to do? It was the same thought she'd had on the drive back to Rose Street, Hank's reasonableness pouring coals of fire on her head.

Even when she mounted the stairs she couldn't have said what her next action would be, but when she reached the landing she walked to the door of the boys' room without hesitation. The door was slightly ajar, and it creaked as she pushed it open. Ivor was sitting up in bed, his eyes tight on her.

'I want a word with you,' she said quietly.

He followed her into what had been their bedroom without saying a word. She faced him and said without any preamble, 'I nearly went with another man tonight.'

He reached out and grasped the door frame. 'Nearly?'

'I couldn't do it. I wanted to but for all the wrong reasons, the main one being a desire to get back at you. Can you understand that?'

He nodded.

She stared at him sadly for a moment. 'I hate you, Ivor. I hate you and I love you.' Her voice broke and her eyes filled with tears. 'What are we going to do?'

His shoulders were hunched and her name was wrenched up from the depths of him as he said, 'Audrey, Audrey lass, I'll spend the rest of me life begging your forgiveness if that's what you want. I love you. Believe me, I do. I can't go on without you.'

'Nor me without you.'

He became very still, staring at her in a silence which stretched. When she said, 'I think it's high time you moved back in here, don't you?' he didn't stir for a full ten seconds.

Chapter Fifteen

Mussolini had been deposed, the Germans routed south of Moscow in the greatest tank battle in history, and Hamburg virtually wiped off the map by RAF night bombers and the US Air Force, but none of these momentous events really touched the lives of the folk at Bleak Farm. The outside world with all its horrors seemed a million miles away as each member of the farm worked from dawn to dusk to meet the government's quotas.

When Farmer Tollett had requested another couple of land girls to replace Vincent, he'd been told he had to take Italian prisoners of war. This had sent his wife into such a spin he had refused, saying they would manage as they were. Even Clara had been rising at five o'clock in the morning and working before she left for school, and when she was home again in the evening the child pitched in until bedtime.

Winnie was still working hard, in spite of looking like a balloon ready to pop, but inevitably she had slowed down as she'd grown more ponderous. The farmer and his wife were kindness itself to her, and it was clear they thought of her as part of the family and her child as their grandchild, the more so since they'd received a telegram in May with the news that their eldest son had been killed in action. Their acceptance of Winnie and her unborn child was in stark contrast to her father's reaction. She'd written to him about her situation and his reply had been to the effect that the family would be informing neighbours and friends that she had married whilst in Yorkshire, and until this was indeed the case he didn't expect her to show her face at home again. Winnie had cried for days.

But now it was the middle of what was turning out to be a very wet August; Clara was home all day for the long summer holiday and for once there was sunshine instead of pouring rain. In fact the sun was hot and the sky as blue as cornflowers.

Since Winnie had become too big to work outside, she had taken over Mrs Tollett's duties in the house and dairy, leaving the farmer's wife free to work alongside her husband and Abby and Rowena. They'd just begun gathering in the harvest and the three women were working at the bottom of one of the cornfields when they heard the drone of planes high overhead. This was not unusual with the RAF base at Scarborough, but there had been the occasional dogfight between Spitfires and the Luftwaffe throughout the war in the skies above Yorkshire, and the sound always made Abby feel slightly uneasy. Lately the enemy had begun to use pilotless flying bombs, the V-I. If one of these escaped a direct hit from anti-aircraft fire or fighter planes and was only deflected from its intended target, it could swoop to earth anywhere.

Shading her eyes, Abby looked upwards, and she could just see the shape of a Spitfire high in the sky before the sound of guns rattling and a subsequent explosion rent the still air. 'That's one of Jerry's doodlebugs which won't get to Scarborough,' Gladys said complacently to the others. Abby returned her smile out of politeness. In truth the nature of such indiscriminate bombing made her feel sick. She glanced back at the farmhouse in the distance where Clara was busy helping Winnie, and for a moment had a strong urge to turn and run back there and bring Clara into the fields at her side.

It was only seconds later when more explosions were heard, and then, coming straight towards them in the distance, all three distinctly saw a V-1 rocket. They didn't have time to speak or react before it seemed to stop and dive into a barn in a field of cattle next to where Farmer Tollett was working. The explosion made Gladys scream shrilly while Abby and Rowena clapped their hands over their mouths in horror.

'*Josiah!*' Mrs Tollett took off at a run, fairly flying over the ground which separated her from her husband, with Abby and Rowena close on her heels. The farmer had been close to the dividing wall and the carnage which greeted them was beyond belief. The bomb had flattened the barn and surrounding area, leaving a mountain of chopped-up cattle and debris. It had also brought down a huge oak tree some yards from the barn under whose shade a number of cows had been standing. The topmost branches of the tree had landed on what was left of the farmer and the tractor. The smell, mangled metal, bits of cattle and human flesh was a sight from hell itself.

By the time Abby and Rowena managed to get Gladys back to the farm, all three women had been sick a number of times and Gladys was incoherent. Winnie and Clara joined them at the top of the fields and they had just got Gladys into the kitchen when Winnie gave a groan and clutched the edge of the table.

Oh no, not now. Please, not now. Abby pushed Gladys into a chair and said to Rowena, 'Make some tea, strong and sweet. Use all the sugar ration if you have to. Clara,' she turned to her sister who was wide-eyed and white-faced, 'go into Mr Tollett's study and fetch the bottle of brandy he keeps in the sideboard.'

'No one's allowed to touch that but him,' her sister said. 'We'll get wrong.'

'Don't worry about that.' When Clara still didn't move and Winnie began to gasp, Abby gripped the child by her shoulders, her voice uncharacteristically harsh as she said, 'Go and do what you're told and quick. Do you hear me?'

Clara disappeared, and Abby turned to Winnie. She slid a chair under her and took hold of her hands. 'Is this the first contraction?'

Winnie shook her head. 'No, they started first thing but only mild, like the belly ache we all had after those plums. I was going to say something later or send Clara to get Gladys if they got too bad.'

Oh Winnie. Abby could have shaken her. She had promised she'd say as soon as she had the first pains so someone could go to the village and fetch Mrs Potts, the midwife.

Winnie, sensing what she was thinking, said, 'You're all needed in the fields, that's the thing, with the harvest and all, so I thought if I could manage until it was dark—' She stopped as another pain hit.

Abby glanced at Rowena who had just mashed the tea and was spooning liberal amounts of sugar into mugs, and then at Gladys who was sitting back in her chair with her eyes shut and looking like death. What was she going to do? They had to get the midwife for Winnie and someone had to tell the authorities about Farmer Tollett so they could get help with everything down in the bottom field, but she couldn't leave Winnie. Rowena could go but then who would see to Gladys? She couldn't look after the pair of them, not if the baby decided to put in an appearance.

Clara's arrival with the brandy helped. After telling Rowena to half fill the mugs with tea, Abby poured a generous amount of the spirit into three of them, handing one to Gladys, one to Rowena and drinking one herself. The strong liquor burned its way down her throat and into her stomach, where it created a fireball which ate up the nausea and shakiness and cleared her head. It had a similar effect on Gladys. When she had finished her tea, the farmer's wife raised her head and said to Winnie, 'How far apart are the pains, lass?'

It was a moment or two before Winnie could answer, and then she said, 'Every . . . every couple of minutes now, I think.'

Abby took Gladys's lucidity as a good sign. Her voice brisk, she said, 'Right, Rowena, you take the lorry and go and fetch the midwife, and tell someone what's happened with the bomb. We need help, all right?'

'The lorry's got a flat battery. Don't you remember someone was coming to fix it tomorrow?'

'Then go on Vincent's old bicycle.'

'All right.' Rowena stopped her scramble for the door to say, 'Are you sure you can cope here?'

'I've got Clara.' Abby smiled encouragingly at her sister who had just finished her own milky tea and had tears running down her face. 'We'll be fine.'

Once Rowena had left, Abby called Clara over to her. 'I'm sorry I shouted,' she said softly, 'but I'm upset. It's not you, hinny. Now I want you to be a good girl and do everything I tell you. First, fill the kettle and a couple of pans and put them on to boil. We need hot water, lots of it. And then I want you to find all the towels you can and bring them here.' It was clear they were never going to get Winnie up the narrow staircase and onto her bed.

'There's some clean sacks in a pile in the scullery too.' Gladys entered the conversation; her voice was stronger and some colour had returned to her cheeks. 'I washed them the other day ready for the baby. Bring them an' all, Clara.'

'Abby?' Clara's voice was small and she hadn't moved. 'Where's Farmer Tollett?'

220

How did she tell her sister the truth? The farmer had made something of a pet of Clara since the child had joined them, and Abby knew his kindness had gone some way to help Clara over the loss of their father. Abby took a deep breath. 'You know the big bang you heard earlier? It was a bomb down in the fields and I'm afraid Farmer Tollett was hurt.'

Big eyes stared directly into Abby's. 'Is he dead?'

Oh, the bluntness of children. Gladys gave a small sound, between a sigh and a moan.

Abby said gently, 'Aye, he is, hinny, but it would have been over in a moment and he wouldn't have felt a thing.' This was more for Gladys than her sister. 'Now Winnie's baby is coming and we've got to think about that. I want you to be very brave and help me. Farmer Tollett would have wanted that.'

Clara stared at her sister. Farmer Tollett was dead, like her da, but it had been a German bomb that had killed him. Mrs Gladys loved Farmer Tollett, she wasn't like their mam. She pushed her fist into her mouth and bit down on her knuckles as tears ran from her eyes. Abby went to take her sister in her arms but Winnie gave another groan and it was Gladys who picked Clara up and sat her on her lap, the two of them crying together.

Perhaps it was the best thing to let it all come out now, Abby thought, as she helped Winnie across to the big cushioned settle on the far side of the kitchen. After propping two cushions behind Winnie's back, Abby saw to the kettle and pans herself, but at this point Gladys wiped her own eyes and those of Clara's, saying, 'Come on, child, we've got to help your sister. She can't do this by herself.' From that point all three of them worked together.

Winnie's baby was born just an hour later at half past one in the afternoon. It was a girl, with a mass of black

221

hair, button eyes and a sweet little nose. The cord still attached, Abby, who had delivered the infant, wrapped the tiny morsel in a towel as best she could, laying her across Winnie's stomach. 'She's a beauty, lass, a real beauty,' Abby said softly, and she was.

'She's mine, Abby, my own little person.' Winnie's tone was such that it brought a lump to everyone's throats. She touched the baby's head wonderingly. 'I'm her mother.'

Abby hugged her friend, but she knew they weren't out of the woods yet. Thankfully the birth had gone well with no complications but neither she nor Gladys felt confident to cut the umbilical cord, and Gladys had murmured something about the placenta needing to come away. They couldn't expect Rowena back with the midwife for at least another hour or so, and that was if Mrs Potts was able to come straightaway.

Abby was just deciding she had to take the bull by the horns and do the necessary when the door burst open and Rowena flew into the room. Her eyes widened. 'You've had it?' she said. 'Oh, Winnie.' And then she added, looking at Abby, 'I've had some wonderful luck. I met some GIs on the way and I flagged them down. I was going to ask them to run me into the village but it turns out one of them is a doctor and he's offered to come and help.' She turned her head to the door, saying, 'Yes, come in, come in. She's had the baby.'

Rowena was inviting an *American* into the farmhouse? For a second Abby reacted as though Farmer Tollett was still alive. Next to the Germans and the Italians Gladys's husband had hated the Americans, declaring no English woman was safe within ten miles of a GI, and nothing his long-suffering wife or any of them could say would convince the farmer otherwise. The American base some miles away was never mentioned, neither were the parties the friendly

GIs threw for all the local children, where ice cream, choco-late, bananas, oranges and other wartime rarities were apparently freely available. Farmer Tollett had demanded that the three girls give their word that they wouldn't fraternise with the GIs in any way, and because they liked as well as respected the man, and knew that in his misguided way he had their best interests at heart, they had agreed. But all that was null and void now.

Abby got to her feet as an American officer, his uniform immaculate, appeared behind Rowena.

'Good afternoon.' A pair of very dark eyes set in a craggy face swept the room. 'Is the little lady OK?'

His manner wasn't at all presumptuous or loud as she had been half expecting, in fact it verged on the diffident, and Abby immediately warmed to him. 'I think so,' she said when it became clear Winnie was too astonished to say a word. 'The baby's only just been born though and there's the cord and everything . . .' She flapped her hand helplessly. 'We're not sure what to do.'

'May I come in, ma'am?' He spoke directly to Winnie now.

Her face coloured up before she said, 'Aye, yes, of course.'

Rowena, Gladys and Clara disappeared into the scullery, ostensibly to soak the stained towels and sacking, leaving Abby to assist the doctor. By the time the cord had been cut and other necessities dealt with and the doctor had carried Winnie up the stairs to the bedroom – as if her friend was as light as a feather, Abby noticed with some admiration – they'd discovered their knight in shining armour was Captain Ike Wilmot, widower of some five years, no children and only recently landed in Britain.

'You don't look old enough to have been married,' said Winnie as the captain deposited her on her bed. This was a lie because he most certainly did. Winnie had found her tongue, however, and was determined to ferret out everything she could about this softly spoken, craggily handsome American.

He stepped back from the bed, straightened his uniform and grinned. 'I'm thirty-six, ma'am.'

'Really?' Winnie grinned back, quite unabashed. And then Abby placed the baby in her arms again and Winnie forgot everyone and everything else. 'Isn't she bonny?' she breathed. The captain and Abby exchanged a smile. 'I'm going to call her Joy because that's what I want her life to be full of. Joy Abigail.' She raised eyes glistening with sudden tears to look at Abby who had come to sit beside her. 'She won't look at me and see a stupid fat lump, she'll just see her mam who loves her all the world.'

'Oh, lass. No one looks at you and sees that. Put that lie out of your head,' whispered Abby, swallowing hard. Neither of them noticed the captain's silent and discreet exit.

Winnie put Joy to the breast and soon afterwards mother and child were both asleep, Joy tucked up in the old crib Farmer Tollett had made for his sons. When Abby went downstairs, she found the captain and another GI, who had presumably been waiting outside, just finishing a cup of tea. Gladys had obviously been crying again. The men's faces were sober, and as they rose to leave, the captain placed his hand on Gladys's arm and said softly, 'Don't you worry about a thing, ma'am. There'll be some men along shortly to take care of what needs to be done. I'll see to it immediately we get back. And I'll return with them, if I may. I can check on mother and child again, but I'd like to bring you some medication which you should take for the next couple of weeks before you retire. It'll help you sleep. Will you do that, ma'am?'

Gladys sniffed and nodded. 'Thank you, lad,' she said brokenly, the tears flowing.

Abby saw the Americans out, leaving Clara and Rowena with Gladys, and as they stepped outside into the warm air, the familiar smells of the farm carried the tinge of what was in the field below and she shivered.

'How are you feeling?' The captain's voice was low. 'You've had one heck of a day.'

She looked up into his tanned face. He was a tall man, very tall, broad-shouldered and with an authoritative air about him, but for all that he had a manner which was immensely reassuring. She supposed it was due to his being a doctor.

'I don't really know,' she said truthfully. 'I feel a bit odd.'

'You're doing just fine.'

'Now that Winnie's had the baby, now I know she's all right, I keep remembering Farmer Tollett and how—' She stopped, gulping, before carrying on, 'And poor Gladys, to have seen it all.'

He nodded. He could have said here that there were more terrible sights than seeing someone blown away in a moment of time, even if it was a loved one. Some people left the earth screaming in an agony which had possessed them for months and months; cancer had done that to his Eleanor, and he had been unable to do anything for her. Him, a doctor. He forced his mind to the young woman at his side. 'Mrs Tollett will be all right,' he said quietly. 'She's the sort of person who will be able to grieve and that's very important. Let her cry when she wants to, don't think it's bad for her. She's fortunate to have you all here with her at a time like this. I presume you'll try and keep the farm going?'

'Oh yes, of course.' She hadn't considered anything

else. 'It'll mean we'll have to accept some prisoners of war working here, though. I can't see anything else for it.'

He nodded. 'I think you'll find most of them are just lonely men who are a long way from home and missing their own wives and children. It's the machinery of war which draws them into the arena, not any wish of theirs to be part of it.'

'You think so?' James had wanted to go to war, to fight the Germans.

She was unaware of the shadow in her eyes as she'd spoken, but the captain's voice was even more gentle when he said, 'Any idealistic notions are soon dealt with, believe me. Very quickly even the most staunch patriot realises they've been forced into a mayhem caused by just a very few evil men at the top. Hitler and his minions have to be stopped, of course, along with the Japanese, but there's nothing fine about the procedure to accomplish it.'

'Don't get him started on this.' The other American, a blond, blue-eyed, fair-skinned man, dug his compatriot in the ribs and the captain acknowledged the friendly reproof with one of the slow easy smiles Abby rather thought might be habitual to him.

The two men made their goodbyes and climbed into the jeep. As they drove away, Abby stood staring after them for a while, until the vehicle disappeared from sight.

He hadn't looked back or waved, she mused, but he would be returning soon with the medication for Gladys. And then she caught at the thought, startled by it. What did it matter if Captain Ike Wilmot returned or not? And she hadn't got time to dilly-dally out here. There were a hundred and one things needing attention, and with all that had happened today the last thing she needed was to stand daydreaming. But it was another few moments before she turned and went back inside the farmhouse.

Gladys wouldn't hear of going to lie down or even sitting with her feet up when Abby and Rowena tried to persuade her to take it easy for the rest of the day. 'I'd rather be working as usual,' she said stoutly, 'but thanks all the same. I've never sat and twiddled me thumbs in me life and I don't intend to start now. I'll be all right. Anyway, with Winnie having had the babbie, someone's got to see to things in the house and dairy, and Clara will help me. We'll collect the eggs in a minute and a bit later, Clara, you can take a tray up to Winnie and see the baby.'

Clara nodded. She felt frightened. She wasn't sure if it was more the fear that another bomb would fall, or that after what had happened to Farmer Tollett, Abby might not think it was safe to keep her here any more. She didn't want to go back to her mam. As Abby put an arm round her and gave her a hug before she and Rowena left to sort and bag a recent crop of potatoes, she wanted to cling tightly to her sister and not let go. Instead she watched the two women disappear, her small white teeth worrying the quick of one finger.

She would run away if Abby sent her back to Sunderland, she *would*. She wished her aunty hadn't written to say that there had been no more bombs dropped on the town since May and that they reckoned they'd seen the last of the air raids in the north-east. She'd rather face a hundred bombs here with Abby than go back.

By the time a platoon of Americans arrived, together with the local constable and parson from the village, Clara had worked herself up into a silent state of terror, convinced she was going to be despatched home forthwith. She watched the captain talk to Abby in the yard for a while after he had given Gladys some little blue pills, but immediately his Jeep pulled away her sister disappeared to help

Rowena again and the chance to talk to her alone was lost.

The rest of the GIs left just as it was getting dark after seeing to everything. They even took Farmer Tollett to the undertakers after the parson had had a little talk with Gladys, telling her it was the best thing in the circumstances. The soldiers had stacked the remains of the barn in a pile in the corner of the field, repaired the stone wall as best they could and buried the cattle in a massive pit which they'd then filled in.

They'd been marvellous, Gladys kept repeating throughout the long afternoon and evening, tears rolling down her face as she went about her household duties and fussed round Winnie and the baby. Just marvellous. And they'd even said they'd come and help with the harvest when they were off duty, bless them.

Abby and Rowena only came into the house when it was too dark to see any more, and after they had eaten the meal Gladys had kept hot for them they sat in a stupor, too exhausted to get ready for bed. It was only when Gladys nearly fell off her chair that they realised she had already taken the little blue pill with her cocoa. They took her up to bed and helped her to undress. She was fast asleep when they left her. Winnie and the baby were sleeping soundly too when they checked on mother and child, but Clara was sitting bolt upright in her pallet bed, her staring eyes and white face giving Abby something of a shock.

'I thought you were asleep.' Abby spoke in a whisper as she walked over to her sister. 'Come on now, snuggle down and close your eyes, hinny.'

'I . . . I can't sleep.' Clara started crying again. 'I told Mrs Gladys that but she still sent me to bed.'

Abby glanced over at Rowena who was standing in the doorway of the bedroom looking towards them. Rowena motioned with her hands to say she was going downstairs to have a wash, and Abby nodded. When she had gone and there was only the sleeping Winnie and the baby in her crib, Abby whispered, 'I know it's terrible about Farmer Tollett but try not to be too frightened. It wasn't as if the bomb was actually meant for the farm, you do understand that? It was an accident in a way. Look, your aunty reckons it's gone very quiet at home. Would you like to go and see Jed for a while?'

It was what Clara had dreaded. Her mind was still in turmoil from the events of the day and from the fear which had gripped her to the point where she had been sick twice in the privy, and she spoke with a touch of hysteria. 'Don't send me back, Abby, not to Mam. You don't know what she's like. She—' She stopped as the sobs she was trying to stifle threatened to choke her.

'Course I know what she's like, dear,' Abby said after a second of hesitation when an alarm bell somewhere in her head began to ring. Was there something Clara wasn't telling her? Had their mam done something to her she hadn't let on about?

'No, you don't, you don't.' Clara clutched hold of her, burying her face in Abby's shoulder. 'She knows I saw, and she said if I ever told anybody . . .'

Abby sat very still. What on earth was all this about? Whatever it was had happened before Clara came to the farm.

'What did you see, hinny?' she said very softly, taking the child's shoulders and moving her back so she could look into her face. 'Whatever it was, you can tell me and I promise you won't get wrong from Mam, all right? I promise.'

'You can't.' Clara buried into Abby again, holding on to her with a vice-like grip. 'She'll have me put away, she said so.' And then, after a great intake of breath, the words came tumbling out. 'She said no one would believe me if I said she pushed Da, that they would say I was wicked and making it up. But she did push him, I saw her. I did, Abby. I did.'

Oh no, *no. Not that. No!* Not even her mother . . . Abby's lower jaw began to tremble and it transferred itself to her voice. 'You're sure? You're absolutely sure?' She didn't try to persuade the child she was wrong because suddenly lots of things made sense. Clara's grief and terror when their father had died, the bed-wetting, the little girl's fear of being left alone with their mother. She had put it all down to the shock of their da dying, but it had been more than that. Much more. Abby felt limp and the room began to swim, and it was only with a great effort that she forced the faintness away and took a grip on herself. 'Clara?' Her sister hadn't answered and now she gave the child a gentle shake. 'You definitely saw it? You couldn't have been mistaken?'

'She . . . she said I dreamed it, that I'd had a nightmare but I didn't. I was on the landing and she pushed him right down the stairs. They'd been arguing and it woke me up and I was going to go downstairs for a drink of water . . .'

'All right, all right.' As Clara's voice rose and Winnie stirred and then murmured something, Abby's arms tightened round her sister. 'I believe you, hinny, but be quiet now.'

'I . . . I don't want to go back.'

'You're not going back. You're never going back.'

'Not ever?'

'Not to live with Mam, no. You'll be with me always, wherever I go.'

The relief took the last shred of Clara's control and had her sobbing noisily and without restraint. Abby heard Winnie stir again, and when her friend sat up in bed and

230

said softly, 'Is she all right, lass?' Abby shook her head but didn't elaborate. After a while Clara began to sniff and snuffle. Abby gave her the handkerchief from her dungaree pocket and her sister wiped her face and blew her nose, then allowed Abby to tuck her back into bed.

'Go to sleep now,' Abby whispered softly, 'and try not to think about all this. You did right to tell me and I'll deal with it, all right?'

'Don't tell Mam I told you.'

'You don't have to see Mam again if you don't want to so it doesn't matter if she knows or not.'

'I *don't* want to see her.' It was unequivocal.

'There you are then, you've nothing to worry about. Now with the baby and all, you're going to have to work even harder round the farm so you must go to sleep now. Mrs Gladys is going to need lots of help from us because she'll be very upset for a little while.' Abby was aware she was saying all the right things but it was as if someone else was speaking; a different part of her mind was screaming denunciations against her mother as her spirit called out to her father afresh. Da, oh Da. My lovely da. How could she? How *could* she?

Once Clara had turned on her side and put her thumb in her mouth – a habit which had proved unbreakable – Abby picked up the oil lamp she'd placed on the floor and walked across to Winnie's bed. Her friend was feeding the baby, and when Winnie looked up at her and said, 'I thought she'd take it hard, about Farmer Tollett. He made a fuss of her, didn't he?' Abby merely nodded. 'It's better she lets it all out now than keeping it in,' Winnie continued, echoing the captain's earlier sentiments. 'By, what a day, lass, eh?'

'A day and a half.' She had to force herself to speak. The sight of Winnie doing what was so natural was extra poignant after the conversation with Clara. Why couldn't her mother have loved her father and the rest of them like women the world over?

'Gladys said the GIs are coming to help with the harvest in their off-duty time so that'll perhaps tide us over till we can get some prisoners of war,' Winnie chuntered on contentedly, her hand stroking Joy's tiny downy head. 'All things considered, it could've been a lot worse, couldn't it?'

No, it could not. Nothing could be worse than this day.

Abby nodded again.

'Look, you're all in, lass.' Winnie mistook Abby's silence for exhaustion. 'Go and have your wash or whatever, and get to bed. I'll try and make sure she doesn't wake any of you before you've got to get up,' she added, with another doting glance at the baby.

'Don't worry about that.' There were far worse things than being woken in the night by the sound of new life crying. Abby traced the infant's minute cheek with one finger and said, 'She's the most beautiful baby I've ever seen, lass. Bonny as a summer's day.'

Winnie was still grinning her pleasure at the compliment as Abby left the room.

On the landing, Abby paused before going downstairs to the scullery. What was she going to do? There was no question but that she had to face her mother with this, but with all hands needed so desperately here she couldn't go yet. And to think how her mother had been at Christmas when she'd got home; settling herself in her front room every night as contented as a pig in muck, and all the time she'd had a man's death on her conscience. But that was the thing, her mam didn't have a conscience. Abby shivered although the night was not cold. And then she slowly began to walk downstairs, her shoulders bowed as if the weight of the world was on them. Which was how she felt.

Chapter Sixteen

If it hadn't been for Abby's new knowledge of the real circumstances surrounding her father's death, the next couple of months wouldn't have been as hard as she'd initially expected them to be.

Poor Gladys was in tears much of the time at first but over the ensuing weeks she became almost philosophical about the loss of her husband, which enabled her to get on with life even in the midst of her grief. The weather wasn't inclined to do them any favours, the rain which had proved such a problem throughout August continuing to fall with monotonous regularity in September and the first week of October. Nevertheless, with help from the off-duty GIs and then the hard work of three Italian prisoners of war, the production of wheat, barley and potatoes was good.

Farmers were being exhorted, as they had been the previous year, to 'take the plough around the farm' to find new land that could be taken into cultivation, while worn-out arable land was put to grazing. All this was now Abby's responsibility because Gladys had declared she couldn't cope with the mechanics of running the farm. Consequently Abby found herself in the scary position of manager as well as worker, and it took all of the learning and experience of the last three years to keep her head above water. But Farmer Tollett had taught her well, and much to her surprise Abby found she knew far more than she'd imagined.

Stoic Winnie was up and working as hard as ever within two weeks of Joy's birth, the infant secured in a harness attached to Winnie's back. Joy was a supremely contented baby, adored by her doting mother, grandmother, Abby and Rowena, and not least by Clara who thought of the baby as a live Milly.

It had been decided that the Italian prisoners of war would sleep in the loft of the hay barn, an arrangement the three men seemed perfectly happy with. The loft was warm and sweet-smelling, and the men joined the women in the kitchen for breakfast and their evening meal; lunch was eaten out in the fields. All three men were thoroughly nice and appeared grateful to be at Bleak Farm; one of them had his own farm back in Italy. The youngest, Mario, who couldn't have been more than twenty-five, was single and spoke very good English. He acted as mediator in the first few somewhat awkward days after they'd arrived. They had no supervision apart from Abby: the authorities had decided all over the country that there was little prospect of escape from an island, and most prisoners became resigned to staying where they were for the duration of the war.

Clara, having offloaded the burden of the secret she had carried for so long and thrilled with Winnie's baby, was coping with the farmer's death very well. She had taken it upon herself to stick like glue to Gladys to make sure the older woman didn't brood unduly, and there was no doubt the two of them had a special relationship. They were like granddaughter and grandmother and that this was proving to be a great comfort to Gladys in her hour of need was obvious to everyone.

There had been one or two times lately when Abby had thought she might be able to steal a couple of days away and dash up to Sunderland to confront her mother, but on each occasion some minor emergency or other had prevented her. But she was determined to go as soon as ever she could.

And so the month of October came to a close. One piece of heartening news came from home: Wilbert wrote to say he was out of the war due to injuries sustained to his legs which, although not severe, were bad enough to invalid him out of the army for good. Knowing Wilbert was safe was wonderful, but only forty-eight hours later Rowena received a telegram from her father informing her that her brother, her only sibling, and her brother's best friend had been killed in action.

It was after this that the faint unease Abby had been experiencing for some time concerning Rowena and Mario's relationship blossomed into real worry. The handsome young Italian and Rowena had struck up a friendship almost as soon as the prisoners of war had arrived at the farm, and the morning Rowena heard about her brother, Abby walked into one of the storage barns to find Mario holding a weeping Rowena in his arms.

It could have been no more than a friend comforting a friend, but the tender emotion on Mario's face as he gently stroked Rowena's hair, and the way she nestled into his broad chest suggested otherwise, as did the way they sprang apart at her entrance. Rowena was clearly embarrassed but not Mario, who simply looked at her in silence, as if challenging her to say something. Rowena's family were top-brass military folk and consorting with the enemy would bring fierce condemnation from that quarter alone; Abby couldn't rid herself of the fear that Rowena was storing up a whole load of trouble.

It was therefore more with the intention of getting Rowena away from Mario for the night that Abby agreed to accompany Rowena to the village barn dance on Guy

235

Fawkes Day. Abby initially took it as a good sign that the suggestion had come from Rowena, although over the next day or so she had a sneaking suspicion that it might be something of a smokescreen. Nevertheless, with Rowena still terribly upset about her brother and her own mind preoccupied with the thought of the coming confrontation with her mother, Abby thought an evening out would be good for both of them.

'The GIs are donating a whole heap of fireworks apparently,' Rowena enthused, 'along with food and drink, so it should be a great evening. They offered to hold the dance at their base but a few of the diehard locals objected.' She wrinkled her nose in disgust. 'Not that they'll refuse the whisky and everything else. Why can't people just accept other people for what they are, regardless of nationality?'

Abby looked hard at her friend. Rowena had made a number of similar observations since Abby had caught her and Mario in the barn.

On the Friday night when they were getting ready for the dance, Abby found herself thinking about Rowena's comments. She'd just heated the stub of a candle end and rubbed it over the soles of their dance shoes to make the leather waterproof, and now she sat back on her heels, gazing into space. She hadn't seen Ike since the week Farmer Tollett had died. He'd come back to help with the harvest with some of the other GIs and she had got the impression then that he'd sought her out. She had half expected him to drop by in the following weeks but he hadn't appeared.

According to Rowena, who had a knack of ferreting out local gossip, one of the young married women in the village whose husband was overseas had been consorting with the Americans and was now visibly pregnant. This had caused outrage, to the point where the woman's father-in-law had gone ranting and raving to the commanding officer at the camp, and now the woman was a social outcast and the stout fathers of the district were virtually locking up their daughters.

This hadn't dimmed the local women's fascination with the smart and snazzy strangers in their midst one bit, according to Rowena, and the children worshipped the GIs who always seemed to have a Hershey Bar or a stick of gum to hand.

Abby frowned to herself, gathered up the shoes and marched upstairs. She definitely didn't intend to throw herself at any man, American or otherwise, and the fact that Ike hadn't followed through on his initial interest didn't bother her in the least.

Rowena was splashing about in the tin bath in the scullery, and the others were all in front of the roaring log fire in the kitchen. Finding herself in the unusual position of being alone in the bedroom for once, Abby reached underneath her bed and drew out the big cloth bag lying on top of her kitbag. She had packed her personal toiletries and odds and ends in this when she had first left home, and now she lifted out the chocolate box James had given her on their first evening together. All his letters were in it, tied with a silk ribbon, along with the photograph she'd obtained from Dr Benson before leaving Sunderland, the watch and brooch James had bought her, and her engagement ring.

She sat down on the bed with the photograph in her hand, staring at the youthful face smiling up at her. 'James, oh, James,' she whispered, stroking the photograph with the tip of one finger. If only she could go back in time for one day, one hour even and see him again, tell him she loved him and that he was the best thing that had ever happened to her. They should have had years together. He should have been able to see his first child born and then his grandchildren. This awful war. 'Oh my darling, I still love you,' she murmured, her heart aching as it always did when she looked into his dear face. 'I'll remember you for ever, whatever happens. I promise.'

She sat for a few minutes more, and then when she heard Rowena bounding up the stairs she did what she always did when she got the box out. She wiped her eyes, blew her nose and squared her shoulders, before placing the photograph tenderly back between its two layers of tissue paper and returning the box to its place under the bed.

When they walked into the village hall an hour later, Abby saw immediately that Rowena had been right. The solid, righteous citizens who were busy making the young wife's life hell hadn't felt so outraged that they had refused the Americans' food and drink. The aroma of fresh coffee pervaded the air, and on a separate table there were bottles of spirit along with the usual homemade wine and beer. Another table was laden with cakes and sandwiches.

'There, told you.' Rowena frowned. 'Such hypocrisy!' And then she grinned at Abby. 'Still, as good old Winnie would say, it's not worth getting your knickers in a twist about.'

Abby smiled back. It was always amusing to hear Rowena say such things in her upper-crust accent. 'Let's forget all our troubles and have a dance or two,' she suggested, slipping her arm through Rowena's.

'And a drink or two, or three! We haven't anything else to spend our wages on. I can't believe I've actually saved money since I've been in the Land Army. The allowance Daddy used to give me at home slipped through my fingers in no time.'

It was moments like this that reminded Abby that

238

Rowena came from a different world, which made it all the more amazing her friend had taken to farm work the way she had. Until Clara had joined her at the farm, Abby had sent most of her wage home to her mother, but since then she had decided Nora had no excuse not to work and support herself. Consequently she now had a considerable amount of money stacked under James's chocolate box in the cloth bag, but as Rowena had pointed out, there was rarely anything to spend it on. Unlike Rowena, however, she would need every penny she could save now for after the war when she would have to support Clara and herself, because there was no way she was letting her sister go back to live with their mother.

'I think you'd better make it two drinks,' she said to Rowena as they skirted the dance floor. 'You've got to drive us home, don't forget.'

'Believe me, the speed that old lorry goes I could drive it blindfolded with one hand tied behind my back.'

'Possibly.' Abby's voice was dry. The sporty little number Rowena had apparently driven before the war was one thing, the lumbering lorry another, but Rowena's driving didn't account for any differences and sometimes it could be hair-raising. 'But I'd prefer not to spend the night in a ditch, if it's all the same to you.'

'No appetite for danger, that's your trouble.' They were giggling as they reached the drinks table. The current barn dance finished and the band took a break. One of the musicians put a record on the gramophone in one corner of the stage.

Having bought a glass of wine each they found two seats at the edge of the dance floor and sat down, surveying the couples presently dancing to 'The Last Time I Saw Paris'. Rowena was just saying that the farm's lack of electricity was the thing she missed the most when a group of GIs

239

came through the door and the record was whipped off the turntable and replaced with 'Don't Sit Under the Apple Tree With Anyone Else But Me'.

'They've done that on purpose.' Rowena was instantly up in arms. Everyone knew the popular Andrews Sisters song expressed fighting men's real concern that their wives or girlfriends might be tempted into affairs in their absence. Rowena glared her disgust across the room to the band member who had put the record on. 'That is a definite dig at the Yanks and I think it's absolutely disgraceful.'

'I don't think the GIs are so sensitive they'll go home in tears.' Abby looked across to where more Americans were entering the room. 'In fact I should imagine it'll make them more determined to find a girl and dance all night.'

'I should hope so.' And then Rowena's eyes narrowed. 'Your doctor's just walked in, Abby.'

It took all of her willpower not to turn her head again. Instead she said casually, 'If you mean Ike Wilmot he's not my doctor.'

'Your doctor or no, he's spotted us and he's coming over.' Rowena raised a hand, smiling.

The next few seconds were the longest of Abby's life, but then he was standing looking down at them, his dark eyes warm as he said, 'Hi there, I was hoping you might be here tonight. No Winnie?'

'I'm afraid a dance can't compare to Joy,' Abby said, her tone light. 'Which is just as it should be, I suppose.'

'Sure thing.' He smiled, his eyes crinkling at the corners.

'We haven't seen anything of you all over the last weeks,' Rowena cut in when it became clear Abby wasn't going to say anything else. 'We thought you'd forgotten about us.'

'No way.' He glanced at the empty seat next to Abby. 'Mind if I sit down?'

'Go ahead.' Rowena said.

'There's been a bit of trouble with one of our guys and a local woman, I don't know if you've heard about it?'

Both girls nodded.

'So we got read the riot act and reminded about the official booklet of advice we all got before we came over.'

'Official booklet?' Abby asked, trying to seem relaxed although she felt far from relaxed so close to him. He smelled wonderful, a fresh and lemony scent coming off his skin, and she'd forgotten how big and broad and altogether masculine he was.

'Yeah.' He grinned. 'A little thing about stopping and thinking before we sound off about lukewarm beer or cold boiled potatoes, or the way English cigarettes taste. That kind of thing. And of course we were told to never make fun of British speech or accents, never to criticise the King or Queen and, most important of all, not to brag or bluster or "swank", as you British say.'

Abby smiled. 'A tall order.'

'I guess.' He stretched his long legs, moving one arm casually along the back of her seat. 'But can we help it if the kids have taken to our comic-book heroes such as Superman, or if your women are clicking their fingers to the rhythms of swing and jazz gods like Artie Shaw and Fats Waller? It's a free country. That's what we're all fighting for.'

'So you don't think your man was at fault then?'

'Hey, I didn't say that. I can understand why some of your guys are spitting bricks. We swan over here into their territory while they're away fighting, we earn five times as much and we wow the ladies with nylon stockings and perfume and the rest of it. I can see why they're mad.'

'You plead a good cause for being irresistible though,' Abby said, half laughing. And then she blushed. Was she flirting? He might think so. But she did like him. She didn't

241

think he could ever make her heart threaten to jump out of her chest like James had, but there was definitely something about Ike Wilmot that was terribly attractive. It wasn't just his craggy good looks, it was the man himself. A woman would always feel protected, safe, feminine with a man like him.

'Irresistible?' He leaned towards her and there was a wry smile on his lips as he said, 'I don't think so, do you?'

Well, she had got herself into this and she had no one to blame but herself. Aware her cheeks were burning, she forced a laugh. 'Let's just say there are still women who look beyond nylon stockings and nail varnish.'

'Not this one.' Rowena grinned at them both, finishing her drink in one swallow. 'Not if the alternative is gravy powder and a friend with a steady hand. It took Abby five minutes to get the lines straight at the back of my legs.'

'She kept wriggling.' Abby blessed Rowena for getting her over a sticky moment.

'She tickled.' The record finished and the band returned to the stage with a lively dance number. 'I'm off to find myself a dance partner as I presume you two are going to cut a rug.' Rowena stood up and moved away before Abby could restrain her.

'Cut a rug?' Ike said. 'That's another of your cute English sayings, right?'

'It means have a dance,' said Abby, flustered and taking her blessing back. How could Rowena more or less order Ike to dance with her? It was so embarrassing. He'd probably been about to get up and go.

He disabused her of that idea when he said, very softly, 'Would you dance with me, Abby? It's why I turned out tonight, the idea you might be here and that I could hold you in my arms.'

She stared at him, totally taken aback. The few times

242

when he had been at the farm he had been very circumspect. Friendly, admittedly, but nothing like this.

'I understand from something Rowena said the last time I was at the farm that you were engaged to be married but he was killed at the beginning of the war,' Ike went on quietly. 'That it was three years ago?'

She nodded, and when he put out his hand and took hers she didn't draw away.

Abby hadn't spoken but was just looking at him, and his face was serious when he said, 'When my wife died I thought it was the end of the world, and it was for a time. Not that I would have wished her to continue the way it was, not with the cancer.' He swallowed, moving his head a little. 'But that was five years ago and since then I haven't dated.' He looked straight into her eyes. 'Does that surprise you?'

Did it? No, not with a man like Ike. He would feel things deeply, there wasn't a shallow bone in his body. Quite how she knew this about him Abby wasn't sure, but she was certain she was right. 'No, that doesn't surprise me,' she said softly.

There was silence between them, the noise and laughter and people whirling around a few feet away hardly registering on either of them. Then he said quietly, 'I like you, Abby, and I would appreciate the chance to get to know you better. I'd like us to . . .' He paused, half smiling as he continued, 'What is the English word for dating?'

'Walk out?' She smiled back. 'At least that's what we say where I come from.'

'Walk out it is then. Will you? Will you begin to walk out with me? I'm older than you, I know, some fourteen years older, so if you feel that's too much of an age gap—'

'Of course it isn't.' She saw his shoulders relax and realised he had been holding himself very tensely, despite

243

his apparent equanimity. The sudden rush of tenderness she felt surprised her. 'It isn't at all,' she repeated, and then, more shyly, she added, 'And I'd like to walk out with you, Ike.'

'You would?' He grinned and squeezed her hand. 'That's swell, just swell.'

Suddenly he appeared much younger, almost boyish, and again Abby felt an emotion stirring she hadn't expected to feel again, at least not for a long, long time. It was quite scary, the more so because there was still a war going on and no guarantees that if she let herself fall for him he wouldn't be sent into the thick of things.

'What is it?' She had dropped her head. 'Not regretting it already, are you?' he said, his voice jocular enough but a seriousness underlining the words which brought her face up to meet his gaze.

She did not give him a direct answer. Instead she said, 'I didn't know how to bear it when James was killed.'

He nodded in understanding. 'I felt the same when Eleanor went and I shut myself away in here,' he touched his temple, 'for years. I don't want to remain like that for the rest of my life, Abby, shut away and going through the motions of living, not when it's possible I've found something I thought had gone from me for ever. Do you?'

Her eyes were misty as she shook her head.

'So we'll brave it together and see what happens, OK? Because the thing is,' he paused, his voice becoming even softer, 'I've found life is a beautiful, crazy roller-coaster of a ride again and I don't want this feeling to leave me. Does that make sense?'

She couldn't reply for a moment or two, and then her voice was as low as his and he had to bend nearer to hear her. 'It does to me.' She loved James, she would always love him but he had been destined to forever remain a poignantly handsome young man on the screen of her mind. He wouldn't grow old, he wouldn't get wrinkles or grey hair. He would just always be her darling, her first love. Her James.

PART FIVE

Grasping the Nettle

1944

Chapter Seventeen

'Cheer up. This is supposed to be a wedding not a funeral.' James was smiling as he glanced at his father standing next to him at the front of the church, but there was no answering smile on Horace Benson's face. 'It's not too late, you know,' his father said, 'not till the ceremony is over. Are you sure about what you're doing?'

'Don't, Dad, not now. I've no other choice and you know it.'

'Course you have, lad.' His father's voice was low but urgent. 'We'll all do our part in seeing that Phyllis is looked after financially and that the child has a decent education.'

'*Dad.*' James's voice had a cracked sound and he cleared his throat twice. 'This is not about me or even Phyllis. I got her pregnant and that's an end of it. I'm not having a child of mine born a bastard.'

'But do you love her?'

'Love her?' The look James bestowed upon his father could have come from a man three times his age. It carried a wealth of cynicism. 'What has that got to do with anything?'

'Oh, James.'

He could hear the quick intake of breath his father made and then the sound of it being expelled. Irritation rose hot and strong and he had to remind himself that whatever his father said or did, his motive was governed by love. But he had spoken the truth when he'd said he had no choice. Phyllis was the daughter of his mother's best friend and he'd always known she carried a torch for him. He and his father had laughed about it in times past when his mother had insisted on trying to pair him off with the daughter of her dear friend Cecilia. Her matchmaking endeavours had finally borne fruit. His mother had inveigled Phyllis back into his life at a time when he was feeling suicidal, and, grateful for her unstinting adoration, they had ended up in bed together.

The organ started up and a rustle at the back of the church announced the bride had arrived. James kept his eyes on the priest smiling benevolently in front of him. He had no one to blame but himself for this.

As Phyllis reached him he forced himself to turn his head and smile at her. Her white gown was a triumph in the present circumstances when most brides were marrying in a smart serviceable suit, but it emphasised the mockery of what they were doing – at least to him. But she did love him. Whatever else, he believed she loved him.

'Dearly beloved, we are gathered here . . .'

He would feel better once it was over. The last four weeks since Christmas when she had told him she was expecting a child had been sheer murder, with both mothers insisting on a grand white wedding and all that that entailed. He didn't know if they were fooling anyone, but his mother and Phyllis's seemed to think so. He just thanked his lucky stars he'd had his father to talk to or he would have gone mad. He glanced at him now. He had asked his father to be his best man, needing the older man's unconditional support and understanding, and he hadn't let him down.

'And who giveth this woman to be married to this man?'

Phyllis's father was all smiles as he made the appropriate response, but then he had five unmarried daughters, of whom Phyllis was the eldest; an orang-utan could have asked for her hand and he would have obliged.

For a moment as he looked at his bride James saw a monkey's head superimposed on the small, tight features of Phyllis's face, and he had to remind himself to concentrate on the present and not slip away into that other universe which came under the heading of shell shock, according to the doctors.

Phyllis smiled at him, her pale blue eyes bright, and he tried to smile back. This wasn't her fault. She had always wanted him and he'd known it; it had been up to him to call a halt before things went too far. His father insisted it was a psychological thing, that as a result of the rejection and hurt he'd felt over Abby's desertion he had subconsciously grasped a love which had stood the test of time. James knew his father and mother had had the bitterest of rows over him and Phyllis once her pregnancy had become known, his father blaming his mother for it all. They were still hardly speaking.

'I now pronounce you man and wife.'

It was over. James blinked; more than twenty minutes had gone by without him really being aware of it. He was a married man. Oh, Abby. *Abby*. Why didn't you wait? Why didn't you love me like I loved you?

'All right?' Phyllis's voice was soft, her expression faintly anxious when he looked at her. He knew that look. She was frightened he was going to have one of his 'turns' and spoil her big day. But no, that wasn't fair. She had never belittled how he felt or been offhand about the nervous breakdown he had suffered shortly after visiting Abby's old home. That her understanding took the form of virtually smothering him was just the way she was and he would have to learn to live with it. It and her.

'I'm fine and you look beautiful.' It was the best he could do but it seemed to satisfy her, and as they walked into the vestry at the front of the church to sign the register, there was a happy tilt to her blonde head under its frothy veil. When he sat down to sign the book himself, she immediately put her hand on his shoulder, her slim body turned towards him and her voice soft and encouraging as she said, 'That's it, write clearly and take your time,' as though he was five years old like the children she taught. He didn't acknowledge she had spoken, merely finishing what he had to do and then standing up again, but as he did so he caught his father's eye and the older man's expression was one of commiseration.

It was as they were leaving Phyllis's parish church on the outskirts of Hendon close to Ryhope that a familiar face in the small crowd outside caught his attention. Was that Abby's mother? He turned sharply, almost stumbling and treading on the hem of Phyllis's dress as he did so.

'Sorry.' He looked down at his bride and she smiled back at him, holding his arm tightly. By the time he scanned the crowd again he could see no sign of Nora Vickers and he told himself he must be mistaken. Why on earth would Abby's mother be here now, today? He hadn't heard a thing from her since the day she had told him Abby was a married woman, or as good as. She wouldn't know he was getting married today and she certainly wouldn't have come to the church if she did. He was imagining things. He brushed his hand over his face as they reached the bottom of the path leading from the church door. It was time for one of his tablets and then he would feel better.

The day was bitterly cold as he climbed into the back of his father's car with Phyllis. His parents took the seats in front and they all set off to the little reception which had been arranged at the Grand Hotel in Bishopwearmouth. Sleety flakes of snow began to fall from a heavily laden sky. It seemed fitting somehow.

It was done then, thank the heavens for that. Nora Vickers's mouth was set in the normal grim line it assumed these days, but inside she was elated. It had paid off, her keeping tabs on James Benson, because now she could relax knowing he was beyond Abby's clutches should her daughter decide to come back to Sunderland after the war.

Nora was walking swiftly along Ryhope Road, her head down as the weather worsened and the snow became more like a blizzard.

James Benson's bride came from a good family and the father-in-law had given the lad a job in his own accountancy firm, so there was no reason at all why James and Abby would ever meet again, not with the newlyweds settling in Hendon close to the wife's folks. It had worked out very well, all things considered.

As she passed the trees and open grass of Hendon Burn on her left, the wind hit the side of her face with such force it almost whipped her hat off. What a day to get wed! The euphoria she'd felt on seeing Abby's old beau leave the church with his bride on his arm heightened. She couldn't have wished James Benson a nicer one. But although she felt this was the end of the story, she'd keep popping along to the family butcher who supplied the Bensons now and again to hear the latest. His daughter cleaned for Dr Benson and the butcher liked to think he was in with the doctor and his wife. Amazing what you could pick up from folk if they were trying to impress you; the man was all strut and swagger. Her lips curled with contempt.

Drops of water were trickling down her neck and she knew she would be soaked to the skin before she got home.

But it had been worth it. Wilbert was now living at home once more, and the foreman at the yard had just taken him on as a welder in one of the fitting-out quays, so they were sitting pretty: Wilbert was clear of the more dangerous work he'd done before the war, and with a bit of luck she'd be able to cut down her hours at the hospital laundry. By, she hated that place and the smell was enough to knock you off your feet most days. Still, the work was safer than some, she had to admit that. The munitions factories were lethal, from what she could make out, although her dear sister seemed to be doing all right. But that was Audrey all over. Drop her in a cesspit and she'd come up smelling of roses.

Nora had only caught the odd glimpse of her sister over the last months, and Audrey's increasingly slim shape and new hairdo and clothes had been enough to make her seethe with frustration. Her mind continued to worry and chew at the past, especially the events just after Christmas which had signalled the end of any further contact between her sister and herself. So wrapped up was she in her thoughts that she hardly noticed the mile and a half walk from the church to Rose Street. It was only when she let herself into the house that she realised how cold she was. Her hands and feet were numb.

She didn't pause in the hall to hang up her coat and hat, intending to put them on the clothes horse in front of the fire in the kitchen to start drying out. At the kitchen door, she stopped dead and stared. Abby was standing by the range.

'Hello, Mam,' she said, her tone and face expressionless.

In a moment, Nora recovered herself. 'Well, this is a surprise.' She divested herself of her hat and coat and hung them on the clothes horse. 'What's brought you home?'

'I wanted to talk to you about something.'

254

'That's a first if ever I heard one, you wanting to talk to me.' Could Abby know about James getting married? Is that why she was back? But no, it was impossible. She knew for a fact her daughter didn't correspond with the family. 'How long are you back for and where's Clara?' She kept her voice flat; she had no real interest in her youngest daughter's whereabouts.

'I left Clara at the farm.' Abby didn't elaborate. 'It's about Clara I've come actually, or rather something she told me.'

It caught Nora unawares and her eyes shot to meet her daughter's steady gaze. They exchanged a look that held for a moment and then Nora pulled herself together, her voice deliberately airy as she said, 'Oh aye? And what's that then? Some tale or other, I'll be bound.'

'How can you say that when you don't know what it is she's said?'

'I don't have to know. The child's a born mischief maker, always has been, although you've never seen it.'

Abby ignored this. 'It's something to do with the night Da—'

'Where's Wilbert?'Nora interrupted abruptly. 'Is he home yet?'

'No.'

'Any tea in the pot?'

It took all of Abby's patience to answer quietly, 'I only made enough for one and that was over an hour ago.' Then she continued, 'Clara said she saw you push Da down the stairs and that you told her you'd send her away if she said anything to anyone.' This was blunter than she'd intended but the way her mother was behaving they could go on for ages fencing with each other.

'*What?* The little madam! You wait till I get my hands on her.'

255

The apparent outrage and shock would have been believable in anyone else, but Abby had seen what was in her mother's eyes in that first unguarded moment. 'You're saying it's not true?'

Nora tossed her head. 'I surely don't have to, do I? You can't believe her.'

'Aye, yes, I believe her.'

'I've heard everything now.' Nora pulled in her chin and narrowed her eyes. 'My own daughters to turn against me like this. Well, I'm not wasting my breath on you, girl.'

'Look me in the face and say you didn't push him.'

'I shouldn't have to, like I said.'

'You can't, can you, Mam?' Abby's voice was still quiet but it was taking all her self-control to remain outwardly calm. On the journey to her mother's house she had felt sick with nerves but she'd promised herself she wouldn't shout or lose her temper. 'You can't because you did it. Did you mean to do it? Was it an accident? What?'

For the briefest of moments her mother seemed to hesitate and an expression flitted across her face that Abby couldn't pin down. Then it had gone, and Nora said, 'How you can take the word of a bairn against that of your own mother I don't know.'

Abby glanced about her. There was no trace of her father remaining in this house, her mother had seen to it that every last item, every belonging had gone. 'Da was a good man,' she said painfully, 'and he never hurt a living soul, but you made his life hell when he was home from the sea. No wonder he couldn't wait to get back to the ships all the time.'

'You'll go too far, girl, so be careful.'

Abby's chin went up a notch. 'Everyone loved him, do you know that?'

'You know nothing about it. No one knows what I had to put up with.'

'Don't come that. You lived like Lady Muck compared to some round these parts. Da provided for us and well too, but more than that he loved us. He'd have done anything for any one of us, me and Clara and Wilbert, and we all knew it.'

'You stupid little fool.' Abby's idolisation of Raymond was too much for Nora. Over the last weeks and months she had assuaged the guilt which attacked her now and again by exaggerating the direness of her life with her husband until now she believed the excuses she'd given herself. 'Your da was a great lump of nowt, that's what he was. He hadn't got the gumption he was born with half the time.'

'He was the best father in the world,' Abby shot back, 'and he only stayed with you because of us.'

'Oh aye?' Nora was red-faced with temper. 'Then he was the biggest fool in the world because not one of you has a drop of his blood in your veins. Father the three of you? Don't make me laugh. He was useless. Years he tried with no result.'

'What?' Abby stared at her mother. 'What are you on about? He was our da.'

'I'm telling you he wasn't. Haven't you ever wondered why none of you look like him or how it is that Wilbert doesn't like the water? And not just being a bit windy about it but scared into a cold sweat at the thought of going to sea. I'm your mother whether you like it or not, but as for him, he was nowt to you, your precious da.'

Abby felt faint, but she held her ground rather than sit down as she wanted to. She scrubbed at her mouth before she managed to say, but weakly now, 'I don't believe you.' But she did. Somehow she didn't doubt her mother was telling the truth. 'Who?' she said at last. 'Who was it?'

Nora's eyes hadn't left Abby's white, stricken face. Grimly, she said, 'Ivor, who else?'

'No.' Abby moved her head slowly from side to side. She put her hands to her cheeks, her eyes wide with shock. 'No, Mam.'

'Ivor's your da and Wilbert and Clara's an' all.'

The only sound in the room now was the ticking of the clock on the shelf above the range, and as it started to get louder and louder Abby knew she had to get out of here before she did something terrible. She had never wanted to hurt anyone in her life the way she did right now. She picked up her handbag and walked past her mother and out into the hall, taking her hat and coat from the peg but not stopping to put them on. She had already opened the front door when her mother's voice called behind her, 'And you'll get what's coming to you afore too long, girl. You hear me? Don't think you can come here playing the big I am because it don't wash with me, madam. It never has.'

Abby almost fell out into the street, shutting the door behind her and cutting off the torrent of words from the kitchen but still hearing them in her head. She slipped on the snow on the step and ended up sitting on the pavement. She didn't immediately scramble to her feet but sat motionless for a moment or two, her heart pounding fit to burst. Then slowly she pulled herself to her feet, her glance sliding from her own front door to the one next door.

Ivor and her mother. She swallowed against the rising nausea. It was horrible, dirty. All the years he'd pretended he didn't like her mam, they had been . . . She swallowed again, harder. And her Aunty Audrey. She had seen her aunt and uncle carry on like a pair of bairns at times and she could have sworn they were happy together. Did her aunt know? And then she answered herself immediately. Of course she didn't. Easy-going though her aunt was she would never have put up with that, not in a million years.

The snow was settling on her hair and shoulders but

Abby was unaware of it as she stood staring at her uncle's front door. How could he have gone with her mother, his wife's *sister*? And to betray her father like that, all the time pretending to be his friend. It was wicked. She did so hope the priests were right and there was an afterlife, because she wanted him to rot in hell for all eternity. Her mam had said her da wasn't her da, but he was. In everything that counted he was. Oh, Da, *Da*. How could they?

When the nausea was too strong to ignore, she forced herself to run to the end of the street, diving into the narrow back lane bordering Rose Street and Violet Street. She only just managed to reach it before her stomach came up into her mouth. Afterwards, although she felt shaky and weak, her head seemed to have cleared a little. The initial compulsion to confront Ivor and tell Audrey everything had gone. She just wanted to get away as fast as she could from these streets and the people in them, and she never wanted to come back.

She straightened and wiped her mouth on her handkerchief. She was shivering as she pulled her hat and coat on. They were damp from being thrown onto the ground along with her bag before she was sick but it didn't matter. Nothing mattered except Ike and Clara and her friends and the farm. They were her new life. Everything here was finished, *everything*. But she couldn't go back to Yorkshire just yet.

She reached into her handbag and fished out a small package. Three times Winnie had written to her parents enclosing a photograph of Joy, and three times the thick manilla envelope had come back unopened. Winnie was in no doubt that it was her father's doing. The first two times she had been in a state for days, crying and carrying on. The third time the envelope came back Abby had seen something change in her friend. She couldn't quite put her

259

finger on what had happened but from that day Winnie only talked of her mother and never her father. When Abby had said she was coming to Sunderland to see Wilbert and find out how he was, Winnie had taken her aside and pressed the package into her hand. 'Try and give it to my mam, would you?' she'd pleaded. 'We were all right, me mam and me, and I know she'd like to see her grand-daughter whatever *he* says.' The last words had carried great bitterness.

'Course I will.' Abby had hugged her friend, her heart heavy. She would have loved to have shared the real reason for her trip back home with someone but she couldn't. Clara seemed to have put the circumstances of their father's death out of her mind since the night she had told her the truth, and Abby was glad of that, even though it meant she couldn't talk about it with anyone. Once or twice she had been tempted to tell Ike, and several times she'd found herself on the verge of confiding in Winnie, but she never had. And she knew now she never would. It wasn't something you could share with someone else. No matter who they were.

Tucking the package back into her bag, Abby glanced at her watch. It was exactly two o'clock which meant that, with any luck, Winnie's mother would be home alone.

Mrs Todd was at home, but from her horrified expression Abby understood she wasn't exactly welcome on her doorstep. But then Winnie's mother disabused her of this idea when she reached out her hand and drew her into the house. 'Whatever's wrong, Abby?' she said worriedly. 'You look dreadful, dreadful. Come in, lass.'

The motherly warmth and bustle was almost too much for Abby's overwrought nerves, but this was about Winnie and Joy, not her, and she found herself saying, 'I'm all right, Mrs Todd, just a bit cold, that's all.'

The range was giving off a comforting glow and the air was redolent with the smell of baking bread, but as Mrs Todd pushed her down into a rocking chair in front of the fire, grabbing a poker and stirring the red coals vigorously until they blazed, Abby was barely aware of her surroundings. She needed to say what she had to say before Mr Todd or any of the lads came home and she wasn't sure what shifts they were on.

Winnie's mother made it easy for her to start when she turned, dusting her hands on her pinny, and said, 'I'll get you a hot drink and a bite in a minute, lass, but first I must ask. There's nowt wrong with Winnie or the bairn?'

'No, no, Mrs Todd. They're well, bonny.'

'Thank the Lord.' Mrs Todd crossed herself, her eyes filling up. 'Was it a boy or a girl?'

'A little girl. Here.' Abby passed over the package. 'There's a letter and a photograph in there for you. Winnie had it specially done at a posh photographers in Scarborough,' she added, aiming to lighten the moment a little as slow, painful tears were now coursing down Mrs Todd's face.

'Oh me bairn, me bairn.'

Abby didn't know if Mrs Todd was referring to her daughter or her granddaughter as she stared at the photograph.

'How was it for my lass? Did she have a bad time?'

'Not at all, Mrs Todd. In fact, the phrase "easy as shelling peas" was bandied about, if I remember. And the baby is doing so well now, putting on weight and laughing all the time. You would love her.' She stopped abruptly, aware this wasn't particularly tactful.

'She looks just like Winnie when she was born.' Mrs Todd raised tear-filled eyes from the picture of Winnie sitting with the baby on her lap. 'Happiest day of my life, that was, although I wouldn't say it in front of any of the lads, of course. But I was longing for a little lassie. Mr Todd,' she shook her head, glancing down at the photograph again, 'he's not a man who's any good with bairns, never has been, and he had even less time for Winnie than he did the lads when they were little. It's just the way he is,' she added, her eyes pleading as they met Abby's again. 'He's not a bad man at heart, just . . .'

Her voice trailed away and Abby made no effort to finish the sentence because she didn't think Winnie's mother would like to hear what she thought Mr Todd was. Instead she said, 'The photograph is for you, to keep. Read the letter now.'

'I will, lass, I will, but first let me make you a cup of tea.'

Mrs Todd wouldn't be deflected from putting a plate of freshly baked girdle scones in front of Abby, with a small saucer of jam, and although Abby was sure these had been meant for the men's tea and had used up precious rations, Winnie's mother insisted she ate two with her cup of tea.

There were more tears when she read Winnie's letter, and for a little while afterwards Mrs Todd sat staring at the photograph, her finger tracing the outline of Winnie's face and that of the baby's.

'Winnie would love you to see her in the flesh.' Abby's voice was gentle. 'She could bring her here or you could come to the farm.'

'Oh no, lass. No.' Winnie's mother looked anxious. 'Her da would never allow it. There were ructions here when she wrote and told us she was expecting and that the lad wouldn't marry her.'

'He's a horrible man, Mrs Todd, and Winnie is better off without him.'

Winnie's mother stared at her as though she was mad.

262

'But she's had a bairn,' she said, as though that outweighed any other consideration.

Abby tried a different tack. 'Winnie could come here on a day when Mr Todd and the lads wouldn't be around, or you could meet her somewhere. She could pay for you to meet her at a point between the farm and Sunderland if that would make you feel better. It's not too far by train. Hartlepool maybe, or even Whitby. You could see Joy and spend a bit of time with Winnie before you went home.'

'I couldn't, lass.'

'You could, Mrs Todd. You want to, don't you?'

Winnie's mother's face crumpled. 'Oh aye, lass, I want to. I can't tell you . . .'

'Well then.'

'But her da would go fair barmy. He . . . he's washed his hands of her, that's the truth of the matter.'

'Does he have to know?'

'Not tell him, you mean?' For a moment a ray of hope seemed to shine, and then Mrs Todd's face fell and she shook her head. 'He'd find out, somehow he'd find out. I couldn't take the risk, I wouldn't dare. He's been like a madman over it all, banning me and the lads from mentioning her name and saying he's never had a daughter.'

'But she's your daughter too.'

Mrs Todd said nothing to this. She poured them both another cup of tea. Her hands were shaking slightly and she spilled tea into the saucers, clucking at herself as she did so. 'You have to understand how things are, lass, for us,' she said suddenly, passing Abby her cup and sitting down on one of the hard-backed chairs at the table. 'Mr Todd is well thought of down the mine, looked up to, and if word of this got out . . . Well, he wouldn't be able to stand it, that's the thing. He's a proud man, in fact there's

263

none prouder and before you say anything,' she held up her hand as Abby went to speak, 'he's a good man an' all. When we got wed I couldn't read an' write. With me being the eldest in a family of fifteen bairns there wasn't time for any schooling, but he taught me himself and never was there a man so patient. She . . . she shouldn't have done it.'

'She knows that, Mrs Todd.'

'There's no chance this man will marry her?' It was piteous.

'I don't think so.'

Mrs Todd began to cry again and after a few awkward moments, Abby said, 'Would you like to write to Winnie, Mrs Todd, and I'll take it back to her?'

Winnie's mother nodded, wiping her eyes with her pinny before she said, 'Aye, thanks, lass. Winnie's got a good friend in you so that's something to be thankful for. You'll stick by her, won't you?'

'Of course I will and it works both ways. Winnie's always been a good friend to me.' She had been thinking as she'd spoken, and now she said, 'Mrs Todd, is there anyone you could trust to receive letters for you, someone you know wouldn't tell your husband? I was just thinking if you could write to Winnie and she to you, you'd still be able to keep in touch with her and know all about Joy and everything.'

A light spread over the older woman's face. 'Aye, lass, there's one of me sisters who lives in Southwick,' she said eagerly. 'I was always like a mam to her and we're still close, Martha an' me. She's the only one I've told about Winnie. She'd do that for me and be glad to help.'

'When you write to Winnie, put your sister's address down then.' Abby glanced at her watch. Four o'clock. She was going to have to leave for the train station soon.

Mrs Todd wrote slowly, her tongue sticking out of the

side of her mouth as she concentrated on her letters, but eventually it was done and with the letter safely tucked in her bag, Abby made her goodbyes.

'Tell my lass, tell her me arms are fair aching to hold the babbie.' Mrs Todd's face was awash again and she was wringing her hands over and over as she stood on the doorstep. 'And tell her it don't make no difference to me, what's happened. She's still my precious bairn and always will be.'

'I'll tell her, Mrs Todd.' Abby just wanted to be gone now. It was already dark and it would be hours before she got back to the farm. She felt exhausted in mind and body and she was longing to be by herself, to be alone so that she could think. It wouldn't alter anything but she had to work out how she felt. Until she was able to do that she didn't know how to handle all this. All the time she had sat and talked with Mrs Todd there had been a pressure in her throat as though something was stuck there. It had been a huge effort to swallow and it still was.

'Goodbye then, lass.'

Abby realised Winnie's mother was peering at her a little anxiously and too late she became aware she'd been staring at her without really seeing her. 'Goodbye, Mrs Todd.' She forced a smile before turning and walking swiftly away, the snow beneath her feet already two or three inches thick.

Mrs Todd continued to stand on her doorstep, her work-worn hands clutching at her neck and pulling at the loose, lined skin there. When she could no longer see Abby she took a deep gasp of air, as though she had been running, before she stepped back into the house and slowly shut the door.

Chapter Eighteen

The early morning fields were glistening with thousands of single spider-silk threads; their gossamer beauty made Abby pause and drink in the delicate tranquillity surrounding her before she made her way into the farm kitchen for breakfast. Later on they would rise and float away in the rising air currents as the dew evaporated with the warmth of the sun, but for now they added to the charm of a perfect May morning.

She was glad the farm didn't have a wireless. Abby flicked a wisp of hair from her eyes as a distant echo signalled the arrival of the first cuckoo of summer. The war was dragging on and the end seemed as far away as it had after James was killed in 1940. She had long since lost the ability to discern if news was good, bad or indifferent; the only thing it always seemed to be was depressing.

When the newspapers had extolled the fact that American forces had launched a Pacific assault earlier in the year with great success, they'd also had to admit to considerable losses. It was only by the grace of God Ike hadn't been sent abroad yet and her worry that this might soon change made her doubly aware that every item of news, every incident and report, meant death and heartache for someone.

And now there was all this trouble at the farm too. Abby looked up into a silver-blue sky which heralded another sunny day, but now she was frowning. The roof had nearly gone off the farmhouse some days ago when Rowena had finally admitted that she and Mario were in love. Mrs Todd had got herself into such a state she'd had to go and lie down, and Winnie and Rowena had had such a bitter exchange Abby didn't know if their friendship would ever recover. For herself, she had suspected the truth for so long it was just a relief when Rowena finally admitted it. Besides – Clara called her name and she turned and began walking to the farmhouse – she liked Mario. She liked him very much. He might have fought on the wrong side and therefore be out of bounds as far as social convention went, but he was a genuinely nice man with a big heart who was clearly head over heels in love with her friend.

'Winnie and Rowena are going at it hammer and tongs again.' Clara ran to her, clutching Milly against her thin chest as she always did in moments of stress. 'Mrs Gladys has dropped the frying pan 'cos they made her jump when they started, and Joy's crying and—'

'Slow down, slow down.' Abby took her sister's hand, shaking it slightly as she said, 'It'll all come out in the wash eventually, hinny, just you see, and things will go back to normal. Now don't you get yourself in a tizz-wazz about it.'

She didn't actually believe this and maybe her voice wasn't convincing enough, because Clara wailed, 'It's like they hate each other, Abby. You ought to hear them. It's horrible.'

'All right, but don't you get upset, now then. That won't help anyone.' They had reached the back of the farmhouse and as they walked through the yard and into the scullery, Abby could hear Winnie shouting, 'You're stark staring barmy, that's what you are! All the offers you've had and you take up with him! You'll get us all hounded out of here.'

'Oh, don't be so melodramatic.' Rowena was on her high horse and nothing was guaranteed to wind Winnie up more.

'Melodramatic? He's the *enemy*, you silly blighter, or did that little fact escape your notice?'

'He's no more our enemy than . . . than that little baby is.'

As Abby and Clara entered the kitchen, Rowena was pointing at Joy who was now being nursed at Winnie's breast.

'Don't be so daft! He fought against our lads, probably killed a few, for all we know.'

'What are you so concerned about? Correct me if I'm wrong, but it's me who's lost a brother and Abby who lost her fiancé and cousin. All your menfolk are still alive and well, aren't they?'

'And her granda?' Winnie nodded her chin at Joy. 'You've forgotten about him already, have you?'

'Oh, I'm sorry, Gladys.' Rowena turned to the farmer's wife who was now sitting on a chair fanning herself with her pinny, the bacon scattered at her feet and fat congealing on the flagstones. 'I didn't mean anything, you know I didn't. But it was a German bomb that killed Josiah.' She swung round to Winnie again. 'The Italian people were never enthusiastic about the war, Mario's told me. They were forced to fight with inadequate weapons against an enemy they didn't hate, yoked to an ally for whom they felt no allegiance. That's the truth of it whether you accept it or not. Why do you think so many Italians changed sides at the end of last year?'

'They didn't change sides, they surrendered,' Winnie said grimly. 'There's a big difference there. They knew they were beaten and they valued their hides.'

'You just don't want to see, do you? Mussolini was Hitler's puppet, everyone knows that. It's always a few men

268

at the top who force ordinary people to fight in wars they don't understand and for which they've got no real heart. Mario's lost two brothers that he knows of, and his aunt and uncle and their little children were all killed by our bombs, but he doesn't blame the whole English race.'

Abby walked further into the kitchen. 'Ike was saying just the same sort of thing,' she said calmly as though the two women weren't red in the face and glaring at each other. 'The little people fight and suffer and have their lives ripped apart because a few fat cats at the top decide so.'

'You're not saying you agree with her, are you? You're not happy about Mario and her.' Winnie hitched Joy from one breast to the other.

'Lots of folk will see it as a betrayal, on Mario's side as well as Rowena's, but . . .' She paused, looking Winnie straight in the face. 'They just fell in love,' she said after a moment or two. 'They haven't committed a terrible crime.'

Winnie stared back at her, her plump face expressing her shock and disapproval. 'You've changed your tune,' she said tightly.

'No, I haven't.' Abby didn't want to argue with Winnie, she didn't want to argue with anyone. She had more than enough to contend with as it was. 'When all this came out I said I wished Rowena had fallen for someone else and I do. There was that awful case a couple of weeks ago where a poor girl was tarred and feathered because people found out she was sweet on a prisoner of war, so how can I be glad Rowena's done the same thing? It puts her in danger, if nothing else.'

'I can look after myself,' Rowena said stiffly.

'And the rest of us? We'll all be tarred with the same brush,' said Winnie, unaware of the pun.

'Well, excuse me, but I hardly think you're the person to cast the first stone.' Rowena was ramrod straight now, her head back and her tone icy as she glanced meaningfully at the baby nestled in Winnie's arms. 'As reputations go, yours was shot some time ago.'

'Why, you—'

'Stop it, the pair of you.' Abby found herself shouting and she hadn't intended to. 'The war's supposed to be going on outside these doors, not inside. This isn't doing anyone any good.' Joy was whimpering again, and Abby moderated her voice. 'Clara, clear up that mess on the floor while I make a fresh pot of tea. We could all do with one.'

'Not for me, thank you.' There were tears in Rowena's eyes but her voice was still haughty when she said, gathering up some buttered bread from the table, 'Mario and I will eat in the barn, we wouldn't want to soil you all by our presence.' And with that she marched out of the kitchen.

'Don't look at me like that.' Winnie scowled at Abby now. 'I only said what everyone else will say when they know. And she'll get worse in some quarters, believe me.'

'I do believe you,' Abby said flatly. 'But isn't that all the more reason for us to support her? We all like Mario, don't we?' She glanced at Gladys but she merely looked down into her lap. 'We like all three of them if it comes to it. They're nice men, just like our brothers and fathers and sweethearts. They're not monsters.'

'Huh!' Tears were dripping off the end of Winnie's nose now and she got abruptly to her feet. 'I'm going upstairs to change Joy and I don't want any breakfast.'

'Neither do I but I'll get you something if you want it,' Gladys said stiffly to Abby as Winnie left the room.

For crying out loud! For a moment a burning sense of

270

injustice swept over Abby. She was getting it in the neck from everyone. Even Clara was huddled against Gladys's legs and staring at her as though she'd said something awful. She ground her teeth, self-pity rearing its head for a second. Here she was coping with the knowledge that her mother had pushed her father to his death, that Ivor was her real da, that Ike could be sent into the firing line at any time, and they were all squabbling like a bunch of bairns. She was sick of the lot of them.

She swung round in a sharp movement which said more than words could have done and strode out of the kitchen. She did not stop until she was some distance from the farmhouse. Taking a deep breath, she said out loud, 'When is it going to end, God?' It wasn't only the war she was referring to. She was tired of being the strong one, tired of managing the farm and all the paperwork and everybody telling her their troubles and the rest of it. She wanted—

She bowed her head to the thought which had just come.

She wanted Ike. She wanted them to be in a world where there was no war and no separations, where they could be together properly, marry, have bairns. She loved him. Her eyes opened wide. Why hadn't she realised it before? But she did, she loved Ike Wilmot. She hadn't wanted to love him, not with the war still on and everything so uncertain, but she did, she couldn't help herself. It wasn't the feeling she'd had for James, not even the wild roller-coaster ride Ike had talked about the first night they had started seeing each other, but it was good. He was a special man, a precious man, and if God spared them both to the end of the war and he asked her to marry him, she would follow him to the United States like a shot. He would take Clara too, wouldn't he? And then she shook her head at herself, faintly embarrassed. She was running away with herself here. What would Ike say if he knew she'd got them married and settled in America with a ready-made family in the shape of her sister? Daft she was.

Nevertheless, she felt herself again, the momentary resentment against the others gone.

She'd try and get Winnie and Rowena on a level footing again, she promised herself, walking towards the tractor some distance away. Get them to talk to each other without shouting and flinging insults right, left and centre. They had to stick together; if they didn't do that, what was life all about? Winnie had to understand that Rowena falling for Mario wasn't the end of the world and that no one in the immediate vicinity had to know about it anyway, and Rowena had to accept something like this was hard for people to take, certainly initially. Rowena had written to her parents about Mario the same day she'd taken the bull by the horns and told them all in the farmhouse, and she was bound to get plenty of stick from that direction. That should appeal to Winnie's natural inclination to defend the underdog. Not that Rowena would appreciate being referred to as a dog! She smiled wryly.

When she climbed into the tractor she didn't immediately start the engine, her growling stomach reminding her she'd walked out on breakfast. It was going to seem a long time till lunch. Thank goodness she was seeing Ike tonight; they were going dancing in Scarborough. But before she left she'd make sure she put it to her two friends that nothing and no one was worth coming between the three of them. And if they couldn't see that, she would bang their heads together!

In the event, she didn't have to.

Abby was tightening nuts under her tractor, having just drained the sump, when Gladys called the three women in for lunch from various parts of the farm. She had already taken the three Italians their food and drink – they were

272

drilling mangold seed with the two shire horses, Bessie and Bunty, in the far field, a pleasant job on such a beautiful day. Winnie had been planting potatoes all morning and Rowena had been occupied carting dung and sawing logs. Both women were closer to the farmhouse than Abby and were already indoors when she made her way across the farmyard, rubbing her oily hands on a piece of rough sacking.

So she was the first to see the slate-blue, state-of-the-art Bentley making its way with imperious smoothness along the rough track which led to the house. As it got nearer she saw a small Union Jack waving merrily on the front of the car, a uniformed chauffeur in the driving seat and what looked like a man and another person – she couldn't quite make out if it was a man or a woman – in the back seat. It wasn't until the car had come to a standstill that Abby thought she should have run to tell the others, but in truth she had been so amazed it hadn't occurred to her.

The chauffeur exited the car, ignoring her, and opened the rear door. For a moment nothing happened, and she was just wondering if she was expected to go to the vehicle when a tall, well-dressed man levered himself out of the car, leaving the chauffeur to help the equally well-dressed woman who followed. *Rowena's parents.* As the penny dropped, Abby said, 'Can I help you?'

The man was standing very straight and he surveyed her through his narrowed eyes in much the same way she imagined a scientist would examine an unpleasant bug under a microscope. He smoothed his neat moustache with the thumb and index finger of one hand, before saying, 'And you are?' His tone was insulting.

Abby waited a second or two, looking hard at him. Then she said, 'My name is Abigail Vickers, Mr . . . ?'

273

'Hetherton-Smith. *Colonel* Hetherton-Smith.' The tall fair woman who looked remarkably like Rowena was now standing at his side, but the colonel made no effort to introduce his wife. 'I have come to see my daughter, Miss Vickers, and I haven't much time. Please get her for me.'

Abby's mind was racing. These two certainly hadn't come to give Rowena a pat on the back. All things considered, it was probably better for her friend if others were present when she had to confront her father. 'She has just been called in to lunch,' she said as if Rowena was dining at the Ritz. 'Won't you join us?'

'I would like to talk privately to my daughter. Tell her I'm here.'

This time there was no pretence at courtesy. Abby stared at him. What a horrible man. And to think he was Rowena's father. 'Just a minute, please,' she said stiffly, glancing at the woman at his side and receiving a cool, steady look in return.

When she entered the kitchen the others were already seated and Gladys was placing bowls of steaming beef and vegetable soup in front of them, a large freshly baked wholemeal loaf cut into inch-thick shives on a plate in the centre of the table. With no preamble, Abby said, 'Rowena, your parents are outside.'

Rowena's head, which hadn't lifted at her entrance, now shot up, her eyes wide. 'They're here?'

Abby nodded. 'Your father says he wants to speak to you. I asked them to come in but he wouldn't.'

Rowena's eyes stretched a little wider and her face was pale. She glanced at Gladys who had paused at Abby's words and was now standing with a bowl of soup in her hand, midway between the hearth and the table. 'I don't want to see them alone,' she said in a low voice. 'Do you mind if they come in, Gladys? My father . . . Well, he can

274

be difficult. I don't know what he's likely to do.'

'The Lord preserve us.' Gladys, who wasn't a great churchgoer but regularly called on the Almighty in any crisis, big or small, placed the bowl on the table and flapped at her red face with her pinny. 'And with me halfway through the ironing and bits everywhere.' She glanced at the flat iron resting on an ancient ironing board and the pile of clothes beside it, some of which had spilled out of their basket and had been placed on one of the kitchen chairs. 'Well, they'll have to take us how they find us. They should have let us know they were coming if they wanted a tidy kitchen.'

'I'll go and tell them to come in.'

As Abby made to turn, Rowena said urgently, 'Tell them if they want to see me it's in here or nothing, Abby. He won't like it but tell him.'

She was scared stiff of him. Confident, strong Rowena, who could shrivel any man with one of her disdainful, contemptuous glances, was petrified. Abby happened to catch Winnie's eye as she turned and she read the same thought in her friend's lifted eyebrows.

The two visitors were standing exactly where Abby had left them but the chauffeur was back in the car with the doors and windows shut. It didn't look as though they had spoken to each other either. There was an almost tangible air of aloofness between the two.

This time it was the woman who said lazily, 'Where is she?' with a note of what could almost have been amusement in her languid voice.

Abby didn't reply to this directly; looking at Rowena's father as she said, 'She wants you to go inside. She's not coming out but you're welcome to see her inside.'

'I told you, Algernon. She's never responded well to autocratic decrees but you would—'

'*Shut up*.' The colonel didn't look at his wife, he kept his eyes fixed on Abby. 'Tell her if she's not out here in sixty seconds there will be hell to pay.'

There was no way she was trotting backwards and forwards at the demand of this little tyrant. Abby said steadily, 'I thought I'd made myself plain, Colonel. If you want to see Rowena you are welcome to see her inside. Otherwise . . .' She shrugged. 'It would appear your journey has been wasted.'

She had never seen anyone swell before but she was seeing it now.

There was a moment or two of screaming silence and then the colonel bit out, 'Lead the way.'

She turned quickly away from him, aware of the sharp clip of Rowena's mother's high heels as they followed her into the scullery and then through to the kitchen. Rowena was still sitting at the table and she didn't rise as they entered.

'Hello, Father. Mother.'

'Go and get your things together. You're leaving.' The colonel had his eyes fixed on his daughter but his wife was glancing around her, her expression neutral.

'What? Don't be ridiculous.' The colour had surged back into Rowena's face. 'I'm not going anywhere.'

'You are returning home with your mother and me today and she will then be responsible for seeing you are kept confined to the house until you learn how to conduct yourself. Have I made myself clear?'

Rowena had stiffened but her voice was still defiant. 'This is because I told you about Mario, right? Well, I'm sorry, Father, but we love each other and—'

He moved a step or two towards her. 'I said get your things together.'

Rowena made them all jump by springing to her feet,

276

her voice loud. 'I'm not going anywhere and the days are gone when you can control my life,' she cried. 'You can't bully me any more, Father, don't you see? I've escaped you, and so has Richard. He never wanted to join the army and you knew that, you knew he hadn't got the stomach for it but as soon as he was eighteen he was in. Well, he's gone and I hope you're satisfied he made the ultimate sacrifice in the name of King and country in this terrible, horrible, *crazy* war!'

'Control yourself.' It was razor sharp.

Joy, upset by the angry atmosphere, began to bawl.

'Like Mother always does?' Rowena glanced at the beautifully coiffured woman who was surveying her daughter with more interest than she had displayed thus far. 'You've always held her up as the pinnacle to which I should strive, but I don't want to be like her. I'm sorry, Mother, but I want more than a beautiful home and social acclaim and the rest of it. I want what I've found with Mario and I'm not letting him go.'

'No daughter of mine is marrying a damn Eyetie.' The colonel was apoplectic. 'I'll cut you off without a penny, do you hear me? Without a penny.'

'I don't care.' Rowena was visibly shaking. 'I've discovered I can manage quite well on my own.'

'You would turn your back your inheritance? And don't forget it's all yours now, the lot. Town house, country estate, the shares, the—'

'I don't want it,' Rowena almost barked at him. 'I don't want anything from you! When I have children they won't be sent to prep school and boarding school and have nannies and maids. *My* children will know what it is to have a real mother and father.'

'And what do you mean by that?'

'I mean they'll have a mother who is interested in *them*,

277

not the next social engagement and what hat to wear for Ascot. And their father will actually communicate with them, even,' Rowena waved her hand wildly, '*listen* to them.'

'You've lost your reason.'

'No, no, I haven't lost my reason, in fact I've come to realise it's only in the last four years I've *had* my reason. I am nearly thirty years old and yet I've only been grown up, *really* grown up since I left you and Mother.'

'You are not marrying him.' The colonel's voice was not loud now; it was soft, almost gentle, but it carried a quality which was more menacing than all his blustering. 'I'll see you dead first.'

'I wouldn't talk like that if I were you, Colonel, not in front of so many witnesses.' Winnie had been cradling Joy, trying to comfort her, but now she handed the baby to Gladys and rose to her feet. 'My father is a bully. Oh, not like you, he hasn't got as much clout where it matters as you, but he's a man who feels he can rule everyone and everything just because he thinks a certain way. Mario is a good man and he will make your daughter very happy but that doesn't matter, does it, not to you. So why don't you just clear off back to where you came from and leave Rowena alone from now on? It's not likely your paths will ever cross again because she sure as gummings won't be calling on you for help. She doesn't need to. She's got friends who will stand by her and a man who will love her for exactly what she is. Warts and pimples and all.'

There was dead silence in the room after this until Rowena's mother broke it, her voice a cool trickle in the red-hot atmosphere. 'I think you've had your answer, Algernon, don't you? Shall we beat an ignominious retreat and go and lick our wounds in that perfectly heavenly little inn we noticed on the way up here? I'm starving.'

Abby wasn't sure whether this little speech was meant

to inflame the situation or calm it. She stared at the woman and Rowena's mother's gaze caught hers, the pale blue eyes faintly condescending and a small smile playing at the edge of the perfectly made-up mouth.

'From this day on I have no daughter. Do you understand me?' The colonel's voice was low, the words drawn out.

For a second Rowena didn't reply. Then she said, 'Only too well, considering I have never had a father.'

'You ungrateful little chit! I ought to horsewhip you—'

The colonel came to an abrupt halt as Abby stepped in front of him, cutting off his advance on Rowena. 'You'd have to take us all on, I'm afraid, Colonel,' she said very clearly.

He glowered down at her, his hands clenched fists by his sides. Then he turned abruptly, jerked his head at his wife and said, 'Back to the car,' before stalking out of the room.

'Goodbye, Rowena.' Mrs Hetherton-Smith's face had lost all semblance of amusement as she moved to stand directly in front of her daughter. 'May I wish you happiness for the future?'

Rowena swallowed. 'If you mean it.'

'I mean it.' The older woman bent and kissed the stiff face. 'We've never understood each other, have we, and I'd be the first to say I've never got the hang of this mother thing, but . . . you are my child. I would like you to be happy.'

'Thank you.' They all saw Rowena relax slightly but she said nothing more as her mother left the room.

There was a stillness in the kitchen which no one broke until the sound of the car drawing away came to their ears. Tears were running from Rowena's eyes and she sank back down into her seat, but then a wan smile surfaced when

Winnie said, 'By, lass, and I thought my da was a rum 'un.'

'His life's the army, it always has been. He eats, drinks and sleeps it. And Mother, well, you saw how she is. As a little girl I used to wonder why she wasn't like some of the other mothers I knew. Why she never cuddled Richard or me, and why we were only allowed out of the nursery to kiss her goodnight at a specific time. I thought it was us, that there was something wrong with my brother and me, until I learned she just has very little feeling.'

'That's putting it kindly,' Winnie said bluntly. 'So, poor little rich girl, eh, lass?'

'Don't say that. It's what I've dreaded you all saying since we met, that's why I never explained what it was like at home. I know I had it easy and compared to you it was all a doddle, but—'

'We're not saying you had it easy.' Abby took one of Rowena's hands and Winnie clasped the other. 'There are lots of different ways of being miserable.'

'Aye, that's the truth,' Winnie agreed softly. 'Me, I've always eaten for comfort. Fat old Winnie, always good for a laugh.'

'You're not fat,' Rowena lied stoutly. 'Plump, maybe, but fetchingly so.'

'Oh, lass.' Winnie was laughing now. 'Only you could say I'm fetching.'

Thank goodness they were all right again. Abby smiled at Gladys who was still holding the baby and received a smile back.

'We'd better finish our lunch,' Abby said practically, 'and when we've finished perhaps you'd like to go and get the men's water bottles, Rowena, so Gladys can take them a drink a bit later. And tell them we expect them in for dinner. All right?'

This last was directed at Winnie and Gladys, who both nodded. Everyone knew she was really saying Mario was welcome in the kitchen again.

'All right, boss.' Rowena was now grinning from ear to ear and looking happier than she had in weeks.

Abby and Rowena left the kitchen together a short time later, while Winnie stayed behind to feed Joy, and as Abby watched her friend fly across the fields to where Mario was as though she had wings on her feet her expression was pensive. The two of them wouldn't have it easy. Italian prisoners of war throughout the country were no longer kept in camps and hostels and sent out to work in gangs under the control of armed soldiers like they had been to begin with, they were allowed to live on farms with relative freedom, but there was still a good deal of resentment against them. And certainly the shilling a day the farm paid them, as laid down by the Geneva Convention, wouldn't provide much of a nest egg for when the war ended. In the *Farmers Weekly* there had been a report only the other week which had labelled all Italians excitable and born lazy, finishing with the bitter comment that to see them cycling around the countryside in their time off was little short of offensive. This was obviously written by someone with a real grudge but that didn't help the ordinary working man's perception of the prisoners of war. Abby had had the foresight to rip the offending article out of the magazine before Rowena had had a chance to read it, but she had thought about it often since. It reflected the current mood and it wasn't pretty. She just hoped the two of them would have the sense to keep their heads down and say little until the war ended and things began to get sorted.

Abby watched Rowena talk urgently to Mario for a moment or two before he lifted her up right off the ground

281

into his arms and swung her round and round. She smiled to herself. Maybe they would be all right.

Suddenly she wanted the warmth of Ike's kindly voice, the strength of tender arms about her and the feel of his hard body holding her close. She was longing to see him tonight. This love which had crept up on her had become very precious.

Chapter Nineteen

A s with James years before, Abby knew immediately she looked into Ike's face what he was about to say. 'You're going to be sent abroad.' She stared at him, her hand going to her mouth as he jumped out of the Jeep and took her into his arms.

'Hey, honey, come on.' He pulled her into him, his voice deep and soft. 'We knew it would happen sooner or later, didn't we?'

When she could speak, she said, 'When?'

'Tomorrow morning.' And as she gave a little gasp, he added, 'Early.'

'Where?'

'Not sure exactly. The US War Department's announced the Japanese homeland must be invaded soon; it's going to be an all-out push against them now. That's all we've been told for the present. Then again the long-awaited invasion of Europe is well overdue and there's been noises about that too. The fact is no one knows for sure and maybe it's best that way.'

It wasn't best. How could he say it was best? She wanted to know where he was going.

Her face must have spoken for her because as she drew away from him and looked up into his eyes, he smiled, saying, 'Don't fight it, honey. Go with the flow. It's the only way.'

Go with the flow! The American saying grated like never

before. She didn't want to go with the flow. She wanted to scream and yell and hang on to him for dear life. 'I don't think I can be very grown up about this,' she said in a small voice.

In spite of the gravity of the situation and her tragic face, Ike found himself chuckling out loud. 'You're priceless.' He hugged her to him again, smelling her freshly washed hair which carried the scent of apple blossom and summer days. His voice husky now, he said, 'Can we get out of here to somewhere private? Somewhere we can talk a while?'

Abby nodded. She climbed into the Jeep without another word and drew her cardigan more closely round her shoulders. The evening had turned quite chilly, but she knew the shivery feeling which had taken hold had nothing to do with the weather. He was going away.

After a minute or two of silence as the Jeep bumped and jolted its way along the farm track and out into the rough road beyond, Ike said, 'Do you mind if we don't go dancing tonight? I'm not in the mood.'

'Me neither.' She felt as if the world had fallen about her ears.

They went to a little pub they knew some way between the farm and the village which had a garden bordering the river. After Ike had bought two beers and handed over half a crown to the barmaid, they made their way out of the bar and into the grounds outside, finding a quiet bench close to the water. The air was heavy with the sweetness of freshly mown grass, the water as clear as crystal as it lapped and gurgled its way over stones made smooth by age. There were one or two other couples dotted about the garden, all the men in uniform and each couple talking very quietly. The rear of the pub was covered in wisteria and the perfume from its fragrant blooms carried on the breeze. It was too beautiful. Too poignant. Abby felt as though her heart would break.

'I'll come back for you. However long it takes, I'll come back for you. You know that, don't you?'

The velvet brown of his eyes was almost black as he put his hand over hers, but Abby found she couldn't reply. She had the urge to let the tears flow but she told herself she couldn't let go now. Every minute, every second of this evening was precious and not to be squandered on self-pity. She had to show him she could be strong; he had enough to think about without worrying about her.

It took a few moments but then she was able to say, 'I'll be waiting. *You* know *that*, don't you?'

She felt his fingers tighten on hers. 'I hoped so. Abby, I never thought I would fall in love again, not the way I felt after Eleanor had gone. It was too painful, too . . .' He waved his free hand, unable to express himself further.

'I know, I know,' she said.

'And I certainly never expected to ask anyone to marry me.'

'No, don't.' Her hand lifted to his lips. 'Don't say it. Please don't, Ike. When . . . when you come back. Say it then.' James had asked her and then he had gone away and never come back. It would be history repeating itself. But if he didn't ask her now, if he waited, it might be all right.

She knew she had disconcerted him and for a moment it looked as though he was going to protest, then his face cleared. His voice soft, he said, 'When I come back? It's a date, my love. Because I'm coming back for you and nothing will stop me.'

He had understood. Her hand moved to his chin which was freshly shaven and her fingers stroked the little cleft there. 'I love you,' she said. And she meant it with all her heart.

PART SIX

Changes
1945

Chapter Twenty

When the alarm jangled her awake, Abby lay for some moments in the semi-gloom before she remembered. It was VE Day. Churchill was going to announce the war in Europe was over at three o'clock that afternoon. Everyone was going to a special thanksgiving service at the parish church at noon, followed by a tea party in the village hall after the Prime Minister's broadcast. *It was finished.*

She glanced across the room to where Joy was lying snuggled into Winnie's side like a puppy. The child was teething, and although she started off each night in the small bed Mario had made for the little girl, which had been squeezed in next to her mother's, she invariably ended up in Winnie's. Joy was fast asleep, rosy cheeks flushed and silken brown curls drooping over her fore-head. She was a beautiful little tot with the sunniest nature imaginable, and, pray God, Abby thought, she would never have to go through another war. This *had* to be the war that ended all wars.

Abby's gaze moved to Rowena. Today's announcement would have little effect on them here at the farm, espe-cially for her friend. How long it would be before Rowena and Mario could or would dare marry she didn't know. Certainly for the foreseeable future the government had decided prisoners of war would continue working on the land where applicable, and there were no plans to disband the Land Army for the present. Gladys had heard nothing from Vincent from the day he'd left the farm so they didn't know if he was dead or alive, or whether he would ever come home even if he had survived the war.

Abby turned onto her back, staring up at the white-washed ceiling. She'd have to try and enter into the spirit of things today, but with Japan still needing to be subdued and Ike in the thick of it she didn't feel like letting her hair down. Twelve months. Twelve months of missing him and worrying about him and feeling now and again something terrible had happened, only to receive a letter which would put her mind at rest. For a while. She'd learned her presentiments weren't to be trusted because she'd had Ike dead and buried at least half a dozen times.

'Stupid,' she muttered to herself, swinging her legs out of bed. But she didn't seem able to apply any logic or reason to how she felt. And she missed him so.

She padded across the room and drew back the thin curtains. The morning was wet and thundery. The black-out restrictions had been lifted a couple of weeks ago and it had been wonderful to take down the thick black material which had blocked even a chink of light, although since then a wet spell had meant the skies had been dull and grey. But the summer was coming and soon sunshine would herald the start of a new day. It would be wonderful to wake up to sunbeams dancing across the room.

No daydreaming. She turned to face the room and its sleeping occupants. The animals had to be seen to and jobs had to be done, VE Day or no VE Day. When they went to the celebrations in the village, Mario, Roberto and Luigi would take care of the farm, but before that there was the usual hard day's work in front of them all.

Later that morning, just after half past eleven, the four women, Clara and little Joy were dressed in their Sunday best and ready to leave. The preceding week three stout members of the WI in the village had made it their business to collect money for food and decorations and organise the purchase and cooking of the feast. There were going to be jellies, custards, blancmanges, sandwiches, tarts, cakes large and small, ice cream and even a victory cake, iced in red, white and blue. Clara had been sick twice with excitement already.

It was drizzling as they left the farmhouse and climbed into the lorry. Gladys sat beside Rowena in the front seat, and Abby, Clara and Winnie, with Joy perched on her mother's lap, made themselves comfortable in the back on temporary seats made of straw bales.

Mario and his two comrades had come to receive their instructions for the rest of the day from Abby some minutes earlier, and now the three men waved and smiled as the lorry drew away. The women knew the men's smiles hid a certain amount of pain and sadness. In the atrocities which had occurred shortly after Italy's surrender eighteen months ago, Luigi had lost his immediate family. Not through any act of aggression by the Allies, but at the hands of retreating German soldiers taking revenge on their Italian 'betrayers'. Everyone at the farm had been upset when Luigi had received word from one of his sisters describing how his wife and children, his parents and one of his brothers and his family, along with nearly eighty other citizens, had been herded into a church planted with landmines which had then been detonated.

'What a day, eh, lass?' Winnie said. 'We've been waiting for this for a long time.' She settled Joy more securely on her ample lap as the lorry trundled along, then, realising she had been a mite tactless, she added hastily, 'And it'll be another celebration day when Ike comes home.'

'It's all right, Winnie.' Winnie's face was so transparent Abby knew exactly what her friend had been thinking.

'This *is* a great day and we're going to make the most of it.' Peace had come to a battered Europe after years of senseless bloodshed and whatever the private pain and sorrow, Britain was going to rejoice.

There was some weeping during the church service as individuals remembered loved ones whose ultimate sacrifice had made this day possible, but later in the afternoon as Big Ben chimed out three o'clock, everyone was holding their breath as they listened to the Prime Minister's broadcast over loudspeakers in the village square. Although Japan remained to be subdued, he said, the war in Europe would end at midnight. 'Advance Britannia!' he proclaimed. 'Long live the cause of freedom! God save the King!'

It was the signal for the release of years of pent-up feelings. Abby kissed and hugged Clara, Winnie and the others and was in turn kissed and hugged, and then everyone in the square found themselves doing the same to neighbours, friends and strangers; dancing, blowing whistles, throwing confetti and rose petals and generally going wild with an infectious joy which gathered pace as the afternoon progressed. Church bells pealed as Abby and the others sat down to tea in the village hall. Afterwards, all the adults listened to exuberant reports on the wireless about the impromptu parades and massive hokey-cokey dances snaking round Queen Victoria's statue in the capital, and the way the King, Queen and two princesses had made countless appearances on the palace balcony to the delight of the ever-swelling throng of jubilant folk below.

In the lull before the evening events, which included dancing and fireworks and a huge bonfire with an effigy of Hitler on the top, Abby sat having a quiet cup of tea with Gladys. Rowena was cheering Clara on in some game or other the children were playing, and Winnie had taken

Joy into a side room where the younger children were all having a nap, so it was just the two of them. Abby reached across and took the older woman's hand, her voice soft as she said, 'You've been wonderful, Gladys. Wonderful.'

'Me?'

'Aye, you. Not just today but all through this war.' Gladys had lost her husband and firstborn, maybe even Vincent too for all they knew, and yet she had put her personal feelings aside and had entered into the day's celebrations with gusto. 'It can't be easy at times like this.'

'Well, you know me. I get on with what I have to get on with and that's an end of it.' Gladys smiled through the tears Abby's kind words had brought on. She hesitated before saying, 'I can't help praying my Vincent's safe, Abby. Oh, I know he treated Winnie shamefully and I don't excuse that, I really don't, but if he came back now and saw Joy . . . He'd have to marry the lass, wouldn't he, seeing what a bonny little thing his daughter is?'

Abby squeezed Gladys's hand but said nothing. Where Vincent was concerned, she certainly wouldn't be holding her breath he would do the right thing.

'He was a handsome little lad, my Vincent. Everyone used to say so. But Josiah and him never got on, you know, not from when Vincent was knee high to a grasshopper. Vincent always had it in his head that his father favoured Nicholas, although he didn't really. It was just that Nicholas was more like Josiah, that's all, and with being the eldest and the farm going to him, Josiah spent more time teaching him about the paperwork side and all.'

Abby nodded but again made no comment. This wasn't the first time she had thought how ironic it was that a nice warm woman like Gladys could love and forgive a son like Vincent anything, whereas her own mother, who had had three decent children, hadn't got an iota of maternal affection in her.

'Do you think he's still alive, Abby?' Gladys had withdrawn her hand and now her fingers were working against each other as she stared into Abby's deep brown eyes. 'Tell me the truth, do you?'

It was some seconds before Abby replied. She drew in a long breath, trying to find the right words. 'I think if anyone could survive, Vincent could. I don't want to rake up old history but he's a master at looking out for number one.'

Gladys looked at her for a moment more and then the corners of her mouth lifted. 'You're right there,' she said wryly. 'By gum, you are. Well, bad as he's been I hope his luck has held out. He's my own flesh and blood, my boy, and I love him.'

This last was said somewhat defiantly and now it was Abby who smiled. 'He's lucky to have a mother like you, and I mean that.'

'Go on with you! You can't soft-soap an old biddy like me, Abby Vickers.'

As darkness fell, the street lights were switched on all over the country for the first time since the outbreak of war. For Clara and some of the other children who could barely remember a time before the blackout, it was like a fairyland. The ruddy glow of the huge bonfire and the fireworks were enjoyed all the more by lots of the villagers who had brought out drinks they had been saving for the peace celebrations, which was just as well as the pub had had to close early because it had run out of supplies.

The night was cold and damp but it wasn't raining any more. As everyone gathered round the bonfire for baked potatoes in their jackets and hot roasted chestnuts, the big loudspeakers continued to report the news from London where it was said Winston Churchill, wearing his famous siren suit and homburg hat, had appeared on the Ministry of Health balcony as the Guards' Band struck up 'For He's a Jolly Good Fellow'. The Prime Minister had sung and conducted the crowd below in 'Land of Hope and Glory', and they expected the celebrations and scenes of unrestrained joy to go on all night.

'Not here though.' Abby motioned with her head at Clara who had gone to sleep clutching a bag of roasted chestnuts in one hand and a Union Jack in the other. She smiled at Winnie and the others as she said, 'I'm ready to go home. How about you?'

'More than ready.' Gladys eased her aching feet back into her boots, wincing as she did so. Abby gently woke Clara and they all walked back to the lorry parked behind the parish church.

They didn't say much on the way back to the farm. Abby knew Rowena was anxious to see Mario and her driving reflected this as the lorry skidded and raced through the night. Clara, now thoroughly wide awake, had trouble staying on the straw bale, and Winnie was hanging on to Joy like grim death. The baby, however, thought it was great fun, clapping her dimpled hands and gurgling with laughter.

They all felt relieved when they reached the farm in one piece. They could see the faint glow of an oil lamp from the barn where the three men were ensconced, and as Rowena scooted across to see Mario, Abby, Winnie and Gladys made for the house. On entering the kitchen they all came to an abrupt stop, Gladys actually bumping into Winnie who was in front of her.

'The wanderers return.' Vincent was sitting on one of the kitchen chairs with his slippered feet propped on the table, a steaming mug of cocoa at the side of him and a plate of Gladys's ham and egg pie on his lap. He took a bite and wiped his mouth with the back of his hand. Gladys, after her initial shock, rushed forward to hug him. He didn't rise or respond to his mother's garbled, tearful greeting.

'I'll get you something hot to eat, lad,' she said. 'Leave that pie.'

He stared at them all for a full ten seconds before saying, 'The pie is fine. Sit down, all of you.'

'Oh, lad, lad, to know you're safe. I've prayed for this day.' Gladys was dabbing at her eyes with her handkerchief. 'Every night I've prayed you'll come home.'

'Then you're the only one who has.'

'No, no, lad,' Gladys said awkwardly when there was no response from the others. And then she added, 'Look, Vincent, you have a daughter, a little lassie and as pretty as a picture. What do you say about that then?'

'The same as I said before I went.' His eyes shifted to the baby who, young as she was, sensed the atmosphere and began to whimper in her mother's arms. 'She's nothing to do with me and I'm not being stuck with another man's flyblow.'

'You rotten liar!' Winnie stepped forward, her eyes blazing, but Abby caught her friend's arm, pulling her back. There was something more here, something she didn't quite understand. It was as if Vincent had planned this moment for maximum effect, his being here when they all got home.

She stared at him. 'When did you get back?'

'Back? Back in England? Back in Yorkshire, or back here in *my* home?'

The emphasis on the word 'my' told her she was right. Vincent was playing some nasty little game of his own as only he could. She said nothing, and after a second or two he drawled, 'I've been back in England a month or two. Caught a few pieces of shrapnel in the last assault we were engaged in, as luck would have it, although you'll be relieved to know I'm fit now.' After raising mocking eyebrows, he continued, 'As to Yorkshire, I've been in the vicinity long enough, shall we say.'

'Long enough?' It was his mother who spoke. 'What do you mean, lad? You've been here and you've not come to see me, to put my mind at rest? You must have known I've been worried to death about you. You . . . you know your father and Nicholas have gone?'

'I know.'

For the first time since coming into the house Gladys raised her voice. 'Is that all you can say? Your father and brother are dead—'

'Don't upset yourself, Mother.' He didn't look at Gladys but kept his eyes on Abby. 'I didn't want to come here until I knew where I stood, that's all. And now I do. I own the farm, the land, every stick of furniture . . . Need I go on? The solicitor was very clear. My dear *father* had been very clear. The farm has been in the family for generations and that is the most important thing, did you know that? Of course it was meant to go to Nicholas, in which case I was to inherit nothing, a big zero. But if anything happened to big brother then second best would do, namely me. You,' he turned to Gladys who was standing with her hand pressed against her lips, 'get nothing.' His lips curled. 'Caring, wasn't he, your wonderful husband.'

'Don't you speak about him like that,' Gladys said shakily, and then, as Abby put her arms round her and led her to a chair, she added, 'Whatever he did, he'd have done it for the best.'

'Whose best? Mine? Yours? I don't think so.' He pressed

his lips tightly together but his eyes betrayed his resentment. 'The only thing that mattered to him was the farm. You, me, even Nicolas were expendable.' He took another bite of pie which he chewed and swallowed. 'But it's worked out very well. For me, that is. For you too, if you want to stay. As for you,' his eyes came to rest on Abby again, 'you can get out this minute.'

'What are you saying? Abby and the others have worked their fingers to the bone for this place, and Winnie . . .' Gladys choked to a stop. 'Winnie and your child—'

'I have no child,' he cut in before she could say more. 'And as for her,' he glanced at Abby, 'she's always been working for her own ends. Oh, I had her number long ago. Do you think that one,' he gestured at Winnie, 'would have had the gumption to say the child was mine if this one hadn't put her up to it?'

'You *are* the father of Winnie's bairn but, praise God, Joy only takes after her mother.' Abby's voice had risen and no one heard the scullery door open, but then Rowena hurried into the kitchen.

'Mario said Vincent was here,' she said breathlessly.

'Mario?' Vincent's eyes narrowed. 'Cosy, aren't we?'

'I asked Rowena to check that the men had carried out the duties I left them,' Abby said quickly. She sensed it wouldn't be a good idea for Vincent to know of the relationship between the youngest Italian prisoner of war and her friend at this point. 'And it's not a question of being cosy. It would have been ridiculous for us to call the men by their surnames. A farm doesn't work like that.'

'Now you're preaching to *me* about how to run a farm?'

'You would have had nothing to come back to if we weren't as capable as any man.'

'You want thanks?' He stared at her, unblinking. 'Thanks. Now get out. As for you two,' his cold eyes flicked over Winnie and Rowena, 'you can stay if you toe the line or else you can get out right now with her.' He smiled. 'VE Day means more for some than others, doesn't it?'

She was right, he *had* planned this to happen on this particular day. He'd probably been thinking about it and plotting for weeks, envisaging how his little moment of victory would turn out.

Abby stepped right up to him. 'You might own this farm and be nicely set up,' she said grimly, 'but under the skin you're just a bit of scum. Your father was a good, hard-working man and there's not a nicer woman than your mam, but *you*. I can understand perfectly why your father didn't want you to have any part in the handling of this farm. He knew you through and through, didn't he? And even without meeting your brother I can see why he was the apple of your father's eye.'

She had scratched the sore place which had stung from his boyhood. Vincent moved suddenly, shooting to his feet, his face as black as thunder. Whether he would have actually tried to hit her, Abby wasn't sure, but immediately Winnie and Rowena were at her side.

For a long moment things remained still and tense, and then Vincent ground out, 'I want you off my land within ten minutes or I'll treat you like the vermin you are and take a gun to you.'

'And go to prison for the rest of your life? I think not,' Abby said scornfully. 'Everyone knows we've kept this farm going when you skedaddled. You wouldn't have a leg to stand on. But don't worry, I'm leaving, but not now, not in the middle of the night. I shall go when it suits me, in the morning.'

'Aye, and I'm going with her,' Winnie growled, ignoring Gladys's little gasp and cry of, 'No, Winnie, no. You can't take Joy away.'

'Make sure it's early.'

'It will be. I don't want to breathe the same air as you.'

'Thought you'd fallen on your feet here, didn't you?' Vincent said bitterly. 'Toadying round my father, making sure you knew all the ins and outs. I know, I know. Thought you were sitting pretty, with her,' he nodded his head at his mother, 'eating out of your hand. But you've caught your toe. It wasn't her everything came to, but me.'

'It takes a nasty mind like yours to think like that.' Abby saw his cheek jerk with a movement like a tic at her tone of contempt, but neither of them said anything more as Rowena took one of the oil lamps and they all left the kitchen and its two occupants. They climbed the stairs to their room without a word being spoken.

In the bedroom Winnie deposited Joy in her bed just as she was, and the baby was asleep in seconds. They all plumped down on their beds in various stages of numbness. There was a short period of silence before Abby said, 'You don't have to leave too, Winnie. Gladys would make sure you were all right, what with Joy and everything, at least until you've decided what you want to do.'

'I know what I want to do, lass,' said Winnie fiercely, 'but I'd be had up for it and I'm not going down the line for that callous blighter. No, I'm leaving with you and I hope it lands him in a mess because he won't manage with just four workers.'

'Three.' Rowena managed a watery smile. 'I'm coming with you. How could I stay after the way he's talked to you tonight?'

'But what about Mario?' Abby said at once. 'And it would mean Gladys is here by herself. Think it over, Rowena. I don't expect either of you to cut off your noses to spite your face.'

'Sorry, but it's all for one and one for all.' Rowena

300

turned to Winnie, and she nodded agreement. 'I couldn't work for that little worm anyway, disgusting individual. Once everyone's asleep I'll creep down and have a word with Mario. I'll find a job somewhere round here so we can still see each other, even if we have to meet after dark in the lane or somewhere. What are you two going to do?'

'For now I suggest we all try and get some sleep.' Abby knew she'd evaded the question but the truth was she didn't know where to go from here. She had Clara to support, and now there was Winnie and the baby because Winnie couldn't go home to her father's house. She had thought her friend was set up here but that clearly wasn't going to be the case. And even Rowena was weighing on her. It was all very well for Rowena to say she would pick up work, but with the men coming home from war it might not be that easy. She rubbed at her aching forehead and then said again, when the others didn't move, 'Come on, let's get some sleep. Rowena, set the alarm for a couple of hours away so you can be sure Vincent's asleep before you go to see Mario. When you come back, set it for five, OK?'

So saying she shooed the others into changing into their nightclothes and within minutes silence reigned, apart from the small grunts and snuffles Joy always made in her sleep.

Abby must have gone to sleep straightaway because when she awoke in the dead of night she had no recollection of lying awake. She sat bolt upright, the idea which had blossomed whilst she'd been asleep causing trickles of excitement up and down her spine. Rowena was back and fast asleep, and after feeling her way cautiously across the room Abby reached the little chest of drawers on top of which the oil lamp was placed each night. After lighting it, she peered at the alarm clock. Three o'clock. And it was freezing.

Shivering, she left the lamp burning and padded across

to where she'd left her work clothes in a heap after changing into her best ones for the VE Day celebrations. She dressed swiftly, looped her hair into a ponytail and then sat down on the bed, her mind examining and dissecting the idea. It could work. It really could. But she had to get things straight in her mind before she woke the others.

Half an hour later she shook Winnie and Rowena awake, leaving Clara asleep. When the other two were sitting bleary-eyed and shivering on the bigger bed with Abby, she whispered, 'Listen, I've got an idea what we could do when we leave here. All of us, together.'

'It's half-past three!' Winnie's voice was too loud and she moderated it when she added, 'Couldn't it have waited till morning?'

'No. I want to tell Gladys before we leave.'

'Let's hear it then.' Winnie gave a yawn wide enough to swallow her tonsils. 'We're all ears.'

'The *Farmers Weekly* has been saying for ages that even when the war finishes there's going to be a massive world food shortage, right? The market's going to take years to recover, but according to the government they're committed to growth and self-sufficiency for British agriculture. The Minister of Agriculture himself has said that allotment holders and gardeners and nurserymen can't afford to slack, and that it's likely even flour and potatoes are going to be rationed in the coming months and years. People have got to think home grown.'

'So?' Rowena's yawn was more delicate than Winnie's.

'So what's to stop us starting our own business? A kind of nursery? I know seeds and plants are hard to come by but we'll beg, borrow and steal what we can't buy. The government's saying the next few years are going to be even tougher than during the war because once Japan's taken, America's likely to stop its supply of Lend-Lease goods so

302

we'll lose all sorts of things we've had previously. If we get a big enough place we could grow cereals and potatoes and sugar beet too, and have a covered part where we'd sell seeds and plants and give advice to the ordinary house-holder with a garden.'

Winnie and Rowena were sitting up straighter now. 'You don't mean a farm then?' Winnie said.

'No, not really.' Abby paused. 'You know the small-holding that's for sale on the edge of Fylingdales Moor that Gladys was on about, the one where the lady's husband died and their sons were killed in the war? That's got some fields attached to it and a great big greenhouse, Gladys said.'

'But how could we get it?' Winnie asked. 'I mean, they're not going to give it to us, are they?'

'We'll buy it.' Abby grinned into their astonished faces. 'We've all got a bit put by. Being stuck out here with nothing to spend our wages on, we didn't have any option, did we? If we put everything together it might be enough for a down payment and then,' she shrugged, 'we'll borrow the rest.'

'Borrow it?'

'From a bank or a building society or something. They lend money to people for houses, why not this?'

Winnie stared at her friend. Abby came from the same neck of the woods as she did and folk didn't buy houses there. They rented them. They worked their fingers to the bone most of their lives and ended up with nowt to show for it whilst the landlords got rich. 'How long have you been thinking of this?' she asked faintly.

Abby paused. She had to be honest. She couldn't pretend this was something she had thought through for some time. 'It was Vincent who gave me the idea actually,' she said, a gurgle of laughter in her voice. 'Although he'd

303

be heartbroken if he knew! It was when he said about me knowing all the ins and outs. I do, we all do. We know as much as any man and we can work as hard as any man too. We can. And with me doing all the forms and letters and reports since Farmer Tollett died, I know about that side of things too.'

'But putting all our money into it.' Winnie swallowed deeply. 'If it failed . . .'

'It won't fail. I won't let it.' There was a glint in Abby's eye that Winnie recognised of old. 'Look, you can't go home the way your da is about Joy. Rowena's become another black sheep, and I . . .' She paused. 'I don't want to go back. This way we can all stay together. The four of us. Sorry, five counting Joy. Maybe even six if Gladys wanted to come in with us rather than stay here with Vincent.' And at Winnie's snort of disbelief, Abby added, 'She might, you know. She worships Joy. I've lost count of how many times she's said she always wanted a little girl.'

'She wouldn't leave here, her home.'

'It's not though, it it?' Rowena put in soberly. 'It's Vincent's now.'

'That's right.' Abby nodded. And Vincent wasn't the sort of man to be content with just his mother for female companionship. Now he owned the farm he would be after getting himself a wife, maybe even the blonde he'd been seeing before he left the area.

'What do you think?' she said. 'We could make enquiries today while we find some rooms to rent until we know what we're doing. Do I mention it to Gladys? Are you with me?'

Winnie glanced at Joy in the flickering lamplight. The baby was lying with one dimpled hand cupping her cheek, her long lashes resting on smooth cheeks. She took a deep breath. 'Aye, we'll give it a go.'

'Rowena?' Abby said.

She nodded. 'Brilliant idea,' she said, grinning. 'Anything that keeps me in this area close to Mario has got to be good.'

'It'll mean hard work, even harder than we've done here, at least to start with,' Abby warned.

They both nodded, smiling.

'I'll go and tell Gladys.' Abby stood up. 'And you two start packing. If we can get our things ready and into the lorry before Vincent wakes up, I've a mind to borrow it again like we did once before. We'll leave a note and tell him he can collect it in Scarborough behind the Empire.'

On the landing, Abby paused in the darkness. She had known before she said anything to the other two that she was committing to something big here. If Ike came back, if he asked her to marry him, if he hadn't changed his mind – she shook her head at all the ifs. But if he did, she wouldn't be able to up sticks and go to America, not for years and years anyway. So why had she followed through and put her idea to Winnie and Rowena?

She knew why. She sighed in the darkness. It was partly because it *was* a brilliant idea, like Rowena had said, and she could see it working in the present climate, but also because her friends needed this. Winnie was an unmarried mother who couldn't rely on her family and Rowena was going to marry a prisoner of war. Both situations took them out of the normal. But she wasn't being altogether noble here. She was doing this for herself too. Her mother had always called her an upstart and maybe she was, but she knew she could get her teeth into this and make it work and it excited her. She didn't want to lose Ike – she bowed her head and bit hard on her lip as her heart twisted – but if he really loved her he would wait until she could leave England. Wouldn't he?

Her head remained bowed a moment longer before it

305

lifted, her chin thrusting forward. She would go and see what Gladys wanted to do now, and that was how she had to approach the next few months. One step at a time. She would deal with what needed to be dealt with, like Gladys. It was the only way. She didn't feel her brain could cope with anything else.

Chapter Twenty-one

By the time VJ Day dawned in the middle of a hot August the price of victory and defeat could be counted in fifty-five million men, women and children having lost their lives. The nuclear bombs that fell on Hiroshima and Nagasaki ended the war, but although the government declared a two-day holiday and the street parties and bonfires again covered England, Abby was not celebrating. She hadn't heard from Ike in weeks and she was terribly afraid something had happened to him. Or – and here her stomach always turned right over – he'd decided it was not going to work out between them after she'd written about the proposed venture with Winnie and Rowena.

She looked up into the clear blue sky as she finished her second slice of toast standing at the back door of her new home. They had been with their kind landlady in Scarborough for eight weeks, during which time they had worked picking crops and helping with the harvest in neighbouring farms, before moving into the smallholding. After receiving one scribbled note from Ike there, obviously written in extreme haste and basically saying she must think things over very carefully and make sure of all her facts before she parted with hard cash, there had been nothing. She knew Mrs Fraser would pass on any letters for her and she'd written to tell Ike her new address immediately they'd moved in July, but still there was no news. And with the bloodiest land fighting of the war in the battle for Okinawa, and fierce attacks on Tokyo and other key Japanese cities in the weeks before the atomic bombs fell, she knew casualties on both sides had been heavy.

'Come and sit down and have another slice of toast. You're going to be on your feet all day so at least sit down when you can.'

Gladys's gently chiding voice brought Abby out of her black thoughts. She turned, glancing at the three women and Clara sitting at the kitchen table and Joy engrossed in crumbling a piece of toast in her high chair, and smiled. 'I'm all right, Gladys. And two pieces of toast is enough.'

'Hmph.' Gladys's snort said it all. Each of them knew Abby was far from all right but they could do nothing to influence things one way or the other. They were all praying Ike was safe and well and that the lack of news was a breakdown in communications due to the chaos and mayhem over the ocean. 'Well, have another cuppa then,' Gladys persisted. 'You're getting like a lath.'

Abby's smile widened. Dear Gladys. She had already forced a hearty cooked breakfast down her by the simple expedient of placing a heaped plate in front of her and standing over her till she'd finished. 'I haven't lost a pound, Gladys. How could I with you feeding us so well?'

The 'hmph' wasn't so loud this time, which indicated Gladys was mollified. When Abby had first told her of their plans, Gladys had been torn between staying in her home with the son she'd secretly been mourning as lost for some time, and leaving with the granddaughter who was her sun, moon and stars. A week after Abby and the others had moved into the smallholding, Gladys's mind had been made up for her once and for all. Vincent had brought his blonde home, stating that the woman was going to live with them from that point on and that his mother would give her the respect he demanded. Gladys had packed her bags the same day.

Wielding the teapot, she now said, 'You wouldn't join in the merrymaking yesterday so I don't suppose you will today. Am I right?'

Abby nodded. The others had spent just a couple of hours in Whitby the previous day but had soon returned home, declaring it wasn't the same without her, besides which they'd already done this once before.

Abby took a sip of her tea before she said, 'We've got two seed-firm reps calling this afternoon and one of them said he'd put us in touch with some gardeners who are willing to barter the stock they have now in return for our next season's potatoes.'

Gladys's eyes were soft as she looked at the young woman she had a great deal of love and respect for. Nevertheless her voice carried a note of reproach as she said, 'When are you ever going to relax? That's what I want to know. You're the first one up and the last to bed and in between you tear about like a blue-arsed fly.'

Winnie added her two penn'orth to the proceedings, chiming in with, 'She's right, lass, and you know it. You're wearing yourself out and, whatever you say, you *have* lost a few pounds.'

Abby shrugged. She could have said she needed to keep going and fill each minute of every hour or she would probably go mad with worry about Ike, but she didn't. She guessed the others knew anyway and to voice her concern wouldn't help anyone. They all had enough on their plates without dwelling on the negative.

The smallholding had come with four large fields, an old crumbling barn and a couple of dilapidated byres and pigsties, although all the animals had long since been sold. The house itself was a ramshackle affair and they would be working to get it round for ages because they had no spare cash for such frivolities, but it was the massive greenhouse

309

which came with the property which was the main focus and that was in the best condition of all. The fact that they were sleeping with buckets stationed at various points to catch the water trickling through the ceilings when it rained, and that every window in the place was rotten and falling apart didn't matter.

'We all agreed this was going to take some blood, sweat and tears. Right?' she said, letting her gaze rest on each face in turn. 'And it's these early days that count. The bank didn't think it was doing us any favours when they offered the loan for this place. They saw a return for their investment and I intend to prove them right.'

'Aye, yes, Mam.' Winnie's voice was that of a cowering child.

'Aw, you. Go on with you!' said Abby, laughing in spite of herself as Winnie grinned at her.

That afternoon, just when Abby had come into the house for a cold drink of water – the greenhouse where she had been busy planting up some seeds was like a Turkish bath – there came a knock at the front door. She watched Gladys bustle away to answer it without any real interest. One seed representative had already come and gone, this was doubtless the other. The first man had been desperate for their custom which was why he was working when most of the country was celebrating; likely this one would be the same. She had done some business with the first and she would do some with this man too, but her heart wasn't in it today. The smallholding had come complete with decrepit furniture and a hackneyed wireless which nevertheless had given them news all day of the riotous jollification across the country. Abby didn't like to acknowledge she was resentful of the merrymaking, but she knew it to be the truth. Ike might have lost his life for this day and it wasn't worth it.

Oh, stop it! The words were so loud in her head she thought for a moment she'd spoken them. If she carried on like this she'd turn into a bitter old hag and no one would want to have anything to do with her. And he was alive. She wouldn't let herself believe anything but that.

She rinsed the glass in the deep white sink and turned to face the door into the hall. Gladys was standing there, her face working as she tried to speak. Then she just held out the telegram in her hand. Abby found her feet were glued to the flagstones. They stared at each other. Joy, who was having an afternoon nap on the old high-backed settle in a corner of the kitchen, stirred briefly, whimpering, before becoming quiet again, but still neither woman moved. Then Abby held out her hand and Gladys walked across to her. She placed the brown envelope in Abby's fingers and then stood and looked at her, her hands clasped into fists at her mouth.

Abby's whole body seemed to be shrinking. It was a long time now since she had experienced this feeling; it was a weird sensation. Before this day only her mother had been able to produce the shrivelling sense of cold dread. Numbly she opened the envelope and stared at the message it held. Then, shaking from head to foot, she blindly reached out a hand and felt her way into one of the rickety kitchen chairs. 'He's coming home, Gladys,' she whispered through the constriction in her throat. 'He's safe.'

'Praise be to the Lord, lass!' Gladys found she had to sit down too. 'When I saw that messenger boy standing there . . .' She didn't have to finish. They had both thought the same thing. Rousing herself, Gladys said, 'I'll put the kettle on and we'll have a cuppa to celebrate. Shall I go and fetch the others?'

'If you wouldn't mind.' Abby smiled. Her legs had turned to jelly and she couldn't have stood to save her life.

He was coming back to her. *He was safe.* He'd survived the carnage and they could be together for the rest of their lives.

After Gladys left, Abby sat quietly staring at a shaft of sunlight slanting through the kitchen window, dust motes dancing in its golden beam. It was only now she could admit to herself that she hadn't dared believe he would come through. Always at the back of her mind she'd been preparing for the worst. But now, now the future was open to her. Marriage, children, grandchildren. She smoothed a lock of hair back from her brow with trembling fingers. She could embrace all the things she'd thought had for ever died with James.

'Be happy for me, James,' she whispered into the sunlit room. And then, although it might be fanciful, she felt she needed to say, 'You're my love, you know that, don't you? You will always be my love. I do love this man but in a different way. He's not you, my darling, no one could ever be you, but I think we can make a good life together and be content.' And that had to count for something. After all the butchery and loss, she would settle for contentment.

And then there came the sound of running footsteps and Winnie and Rowena calling her name, their voices full of excitement, and Abby stood up to meet her friends, her legs steady again.

Chapter Twenty-two

James stared at his wife and he found he was battling with the desire to smile, such was the irony of the situation. After a few moments, he said, 'You're telling me you want a divorce?' He'd hardly been able to believe his ears.

'Yes.' Phyllis returned his gaze, her pale eyes steady although her bottom lip was trembling.

He reached for his coffee cup and drained the contents before he carefully returned the bone china cup to its saucer. Settling back in his chair, he said, 'Are you sure?' His heart began to beat harder against his ribcage. She meant it. It was the last thing he'd ever imagined, but she meant it.

'Yes, I'm sure.' She was twisting her hands together in her lap and she must have become aware of this because she suddenly placed them on the fine linen tablecloth, looking down at her manicured nails. 'I've . . . met someone.'

'You've *met* someone?' She had amazed him twice in as many minutes.

She nodded without raising her head.

'Where?' She never went anywhere unless he accompanied her, she wasn't like that.

'He . . . Simon is a teacher. He was invalided out of the army twelve months ago and decided to return to teaching then. His wife was killed when he was fighting in France at the beginning of the war.'

James found he didn't want the man's life history. 'And he came to your school?'

Again the pale head nodded.

She had floored him. He hadn't thought it possible but she had actually floored him. He glanced at the table in front of him which still bore the remains of the excellent dinner Phyllis had served an hour before. How like her to wait until he had dined before she said anything, thoughtful and considerate to the last. But then it had been that intense drive to mother and look after him which had caused him to feel he was suffocating every day of his married life. Maybe if she hadn't had the miscarriage a month after they had married, maybe if she had become pregnant again in those early days when he had felt so sorry for her and had tried to be the husband she needed, maybe then they might have had a chance. But he doubted it.

'I'm sorry.' Her voice was soft, pleading.

His eyes rose to meet hers. 'Don't be, we both know this isn't your fault.' A ridiculous thing to say in the circumstances, he thought, and anyone listening to their conversation would wonder what on earth he was on about, but it was the truth nonetheless. No one could have tried harder than Phyllis to be a good wife, but when after a year or so he had found himself unable to perform his husbandly duty, even she had taken exception. He had understood but had been at a loss to remedy the situation. He'd gone to their family doctor who had referred him to a specialist, talked to the priest, even bared his soul to his father but still he had been unable to make love to her.

Impotency, the specialist had declared. A powerlessness to achieve sexual erection or orgasm. Common enough in men who'd been through what he had; the mind and body could be adversely affected for years, often with delayed problems like this one. But James had known it wasn't

314

that. The longer he had lived with Phyllis, the more he had struggled to keep his head clear of the stifling blanket she had persisted in trying to wrap round him every minute of every day.

Her love took the form of smothering, and to such a degree he had found himself working longer and longer hours just to delay the moment when he would have to walk through his own front door. It couldn't have gone on. He had been telling himself that for the last few months, wondering how he could broach the fact that they must separate when he knew it would break her heart. But apparently he couldn't have been more wrong there. The last thought prompted him to say quietly, 'I had no idea, Phyllis. Why didn't you speak to me before about this?'

Colour flooded her face. He saw her hesitate, and then she said, 'I was hoping things would work out between us, I suppose.'

'But if you love this man—'

'I don't love him.' She cut into what he was saying in a most un-Phyllis-like way, and now she said quickly, 'At least not like I've always cared for you, but . . .' She shook her head. 'I've had to accept you've never loved me like that. I thought when we got married I could make you love me but instead it's driven you away.'

James didn't know what to say. She wasn't the type of woman to bare her soul and it was as painful for him as it was for her.

'Simon wants me,' she went on after gulping a couple of times, 'even though he knows how I feel about you. It's . . . it's my chance to have a family, children, to be a mother.'

'I understand,' he said very softly.

The look she now fastened on him carried sadness and a certain resentment in its depths. 'I knew you would.

315

Simon wanted to be here when I told you, he was worried you might react badly or get violent, but I told him he couldn't be more wrong. You don't care enough to get angry, do you?'

In truth he was feeling nothing but relief at this moment but he couldn't very well say so. James cleared his throat. 'I value your friendship very highly, I always have, and I do care about you.'

'As a friend.'

There was nothing he could say.

She stared at him for a moment more before dropping her head, and now slow tears began to drip down her face. They sat in silence for a minute or two and then Phyllis wiped her face on her napkin and sniffed. 'The parents will be horrified, of course. There has never been a divorce in our family.'

There hadn't been one in his either, not to his knowledge. 'The war's changed all that sort of thing,' he said, knowing this wasn't quite true. Not in the staunch Roman Catholic families they came from.

'It won't matter that they know we've only attended Mass at Christmas and Easter since we've been married, they'll still expect us to abide by the Church's teachings. I'll . . . I'll be branded a scarlet woman.'

'That won't happen.' He sat up straighter. 'Do you hear me, Phyllis? I won't let that happen. I shall make it clear this is my fault, I promise. Look, I'll move out, all right? You can tell your parents and my mother I walked out; only my father will know the truth and he won't say anything. You needn't say anything at all about Simon until you want to, even until the divorce is through if you like. No one will point the finger at you.'

She was sobbing in earnest now, and when, thinking to comfort her, he got up and put his hand on her shoulder, she turned into him, holding him tight round his waist and burying her head in the folds of his jumper.

As always her overwhelming need of him created a feeling exactly the opposite to what it should. He forced himself to pat her shoulder while he murmured what he hoped were soothing words.

It seemed like an age before she drew away.

'Silly,' she whispered, 'but I was hoping even now that when I told you, you'd realise you want me.'

'Phyllis—'

'No, don't say anything.' She stood up. 'You would never have asked me to marry you if it wasn't for the baby, and I have always known that in . . . in my head. I just couldn't make my heart believe there was no hope, not even when you couldn't bear to make love to me.'

'It wasn't like that.' He stared at her. 'Truly, it wasn't like that. I looked on you more as a sister, I suppose, that was the trouble.'

'Oh, James.' The shadow of a smile touched her mouth. 'That's probably the worst thing you could say right now.'

'I didn't mean—'

'Would you mind terribly if you moved out tomorrow?'

His eyes widened with surprise for a second but he said, 'No, of course not, whatever you want.'

'Thank you.' She gestured to the glass of brandy she had served with his coffee, which remained untouched. 'Drink your brandy. I'm going to bed.'

He nodded. They had had separate rooms for the last nine months, ostensibly because he hadn't been sleeping well and had insisted he didn't want to keep her awake with his tossing and turning. 'Goodnight,' he said softly.

He didn't go into the office the next morning. Once Phyllis had left for school, he began sorting papers and books and

317

other miscellaneous items. By mid-morning two big cardboard boxes were installed in the boot of his car along with most of his clothes on the back seat, and a waste-paper basket full of torn-up papers had been disposed of in the dustbin.

Just before midday he shut the front door and walked past the sitting room en route to the garage, his heart thudding as he told himself it was the last time he would ever do that here. He felt little except a sense of urgency to get away, which had been with him since he'd woken that morning.

It wasn't until he had driven down the drive and out into the spacious tree-lined avenue beyond that the breath left his body in a great whoosh of relief. It was over. His hands were gripping the steering wheel so tightly the knuckles showed white.

Whatever furore came from their families he would deflect from Phyllis as far as he could, and he would pay her whatever she wanted in the way of maintenance, but he would never go back to the house again. This was a new start and it had to be a clean break, for Phyllis as well as for himself. She had her Simon and if the fellow was prepared to take her on knowing how she felt, he must love her deeply. It would work out for her. He shook his head at himself, ashamed at the relief again flooding through his mind.

He must book into a hotel, and then he had to go into the office and face Phyllis's father. He would leave the practice, of course. Today, if her father wished it.

He was driving quite slowly and carefully, aware he had to concentrate in view of the circumstances, but as he passed a young woman pushing a pram, something in her bearing reminded him of Abby. A feeling like a tiny electrical shock ran through him, as it always did if someone or something brought her to mind.

The knowledge that Abby was living and loving somewhere else, with someone else, had nearly sent him mad in the early days. He'd had to school his mind to face the fact that she was alive in the world, breathing the same air and looking at the same sky, but not thinking of him. One of the psychiatrists at the hospital, the only one there who had seen any military action, had told him that trying to understand anything was pointless because mostly there were no answers.

'Acceptance, old boy,' Dr Owen had said. 'That's the secret. Acceptance. Once you acknowledge that the whole damn world is as mad as a hatter and you're the only sane one, you'll do all right. Simple really.'

He hadn't known then if it was that simple, he still didn't, but what he did know was that Mortimer Owen had brought him back from the brink of lunacy. For that he'd always be grateful to the small Welshman.

Warning himself to go even slower, he continued along the main road. Although his mind rarely jumped back into the dark dungeon it had taken refuge in after he had been invalided out of the army, high excitement or stress could bring on a funny spell if he wasn't careful. He had learned, again with Dr Owen's help, to combat this by concentrating very hard on the immediate task to hand. It didn't matter what it was – a book he was reading, some work, a car journey – the trick was in refusing to let his mind swing off course for an instant. He had perfected this now, even in sleep he had control of his thought process and he could actually wake himself up if a nightmare took hold.

As James drew nearer to the town centre he noticed many of the shops and businesses were still covered in bunting and the flags of the victorious countries, even though the VJ celebrations had been over for some days. Brass bands, street parties and dancing in Mowbray Park had been the least of it, and even though large areas of the town had been flattened by enemy bombs, folk everywhere had declared it was the start of better things.

Better things. He repeated this to himself. He hadn't believed that at the time, not with things so bad between him and Phyllis, but now . . . Now maybe it was possible. One thing was for sure, he had survived the war and, God willing, he had another forty or fifty years before he was put six foot under. He didn't intend to waste them.

Chapter Twenty-three

During the weeks following the euphoria of the victory celebrations the lives of the women at the smallholding were underlaid by a curious feeling of mental exhaustion. If they'd but known it, Abby and her friends were not alone in experiencing this.

The years of worry and separation had caused many couples to grow apart but, more than that, women in general had learned to live independently. Most of Britain's women had been out to work in a 'man's world'; others had brought up their children single-handedly; some had managed to do both. Sometimes the sudden return of a war hero meant more than mere domestic inconvenience though. The newspapers regularly reported cases where a soldier came back to discover his wife had been unfaithful and ended up in court for attacking his rival, or worse. Gladys, in common with most of her generation, clicked her tongue, shook her head and declared she didn't know what the world was coming to. Abby and others of her age knew the world had changed for ever. Everyone was having to adjust and it was strangely tiring.

Abby was now corresponding regularly with Ike again but it wasn't the same as seeing him face to face, and she ached for the moment they would be reunited. She'd sensed from his letters that the last months of the war had been harrowing, and as the media reported more and more unspeakable horrors, she wondered how he would be when they met. Men all over the world had had their faces, bodies and personalities redrawn by the experience of war, and Ike was such a gentle, caring soul. She felt he would be troubled more than most by the cruelty and depravity they were hearing about.

The government didn't seem to be in any hurry to rush through the necessary legislation and documentation to enable the thousands of British GI brides to join their husbands across the Atlantic – not that that really affected her, Abby kept reminding herself. She knew from the tone of Ike's letters that he hadn't changed his mind about asking her to marry him when they met again, but with the fledgling business and all her new responsibilities, he was going to have to wait for some time. Would he be happy with that? It was a question she asked herself often but to which she received no answer.

Rowena, too, was in a state of turmoil. She and Mario only managed to meet under cover of darkness now, and that was proving more and more difficult. The women had invested in a stout bicycle for her but still it was a long haul up hill and down dale to the farm, and the light summer evenings meant she couldn't leave for her rendezvous until gone ten o'clock. Added to this was the worry that Vincent would find out about their love affair and make things difficult, although to date this had not happened. Mario had reported that Vincent was treating them well but then it was in his own interests to do so. After his cavalier dismissal of the three women, the authorities had refused him more prisoners of war or land girls.

With the retention by the new Labour government of wartime disciplinary powers of enforced supervision and ultimately dispossession for farmers who did not meet their quotas, Vincent must be a worried man. Everyone who knew him, with maybe the exception of Gladys, thought he deserved whatever he got. It wasn't often payback time came so swiftly.

As autumn slipped past, the wartime slogan 'Dig For Victory' became 'Dig For Victory Over Want' as more and more food restrictions began to bite. With German and Italian prisoners of war working on farms and Polish servicemen being recruited as coal miners, Britain was doing what it could to survive, and by the beginning of December Abby and the others could already see signs that their venture was going to be successful. Large gardens, family estates and even allotments had suffered during the war. The enemy's bombs had played their part in this, but even more importantly, lack of labour had meant that glasshouse repairs had been neglected, paths became over-grown, plants had been left to run wild or were lost alto-gether, and private stocks of seed were dissipated. With the prediction that bread, cakes, flour and oatmeal would be rationed in the New Year, every household was desperate to make the most of any land they had, however small.

Yes, everything had changed, one way or another, and there was no going back.

The first day of December found Abby alone in the house for the first time since moving into her new home. She had been laid low with influenza over the last few days and was still feeling awful but had struggled out of bed that morning, anxious about all the work to be done. On reaching the kitchen and finding she didn't have the strength of a kitten, she hadn't protested too hard when Gladys had scolded her roundly and sat her in the ancient rocking chair in front of the fire. Even Clara had ticked her off. Her face solemn, she'd stood by the chair and said, 'You're being very silly, Abby. You'll make yourself much worse if you try and get up before you're ready, now then. I'll help as soon as I get back from school and all the jobs will get done, I promise.'

Abby had smiled but it had dawned on her that Clara was growing up fast. She was twelve years old now and was as pretty as a picture, as Gladys often said.

After Clara had left for school, the others all went about their various jobs, Gladys declaring she would help out in the greenhouse for a while before returning to see about the dinner.

Abby sat staring into the red glow of the fire. She ought to put some more wood on but her limbs felt like lead and it was too much effort to move, swathed as she was in an old blanket which Gladys had insisted on tucking round her as if she was an old woman in a bathchair. There was a muffled hush over the house which she attributed to the snow which had begun to fall early that morning. Already it was inches thick outside and the forecast was not encouraging, predicting more of the same over the next few weeks.

When would she hear from Ike? She shut her eyes, leaning back in the rocking chair which creaked violently at any movement. His last letter had stated he had things to see to at home before he could come and see her, and she didn't understand this. She'd expected he would come immediately he was demobbed. She pushed the old fear that he would rethink their situation and decide she wasn't worth waiting for to the back of her mind with some effort, telling herself sternly she didn't intend to go down that route again. She had to trust him, had to believe that what they had was real and would stand the test of time and anything else thrown at it.

She wasn't aware of drifting into sleep but she must have done because when she next opened her eyes, Ike was sitting in the old stuffed armchair opposite her. She blinked once,

324

then again but the apparition didn't dissolve. 'Ike?' Then he was kneeling by her chair, his arms round her as he murmured, 'My love, my love, I didn't want to wake you.' He took her lips in a long, hungry kiss that left no doubt he was very real.

Abby clung to him, responding so fiercely that they were both gasping when their mouths reluctantly drew apart and even then Ike's lips couldn't leave her face and nose and ears, covering her skin in quick burning kisses while he muttered incoherent words of love.

It was minutes later before he rose to his feet and then he gathered Abby up in his arms before sitting down with her on his lap in the armchair. She was feeling light-headed, dizzy. 'When? How? I mean, what . . . what are you doing here?'

'Loving you,' he said very softly, kissing her again. He gazed at the lovely face he had pictured so often in his mind in the worst of the mayhem. It had been thoughts of Abby and the dream of a future spent with her that had got him through and he knew it, otherwise he'd have gone mad like so many poor devils had done.

'I . . . I look awful.' Abby raised a shaky hand to her hair which hadn't been washed for a week. When she'd imagined herself welcoming him into her arms it had never been with lank hair and a shiny nose.

'You're beautiful.' He kissed the tip of her nose. 'Just beautiful.' He kissed her eyelids. 'And kissable, so, so kissable.' He kissed her mouth. 'Delicious in fact.'

'But you're in America.' She sat up a bit straighter.

'Clever ole me.'

'You know what I mean.'

'I had things to sort out. They're sorted.' He pulled her into him again. Her cheek rested against his and her arms were round his neck. She drank in the clean fresh smell of him; the aftershave he always wore had never smelled so heavenly. 'So now I'm with my girl, for good if she'll have me.'

'Ike—'

'Marry me, Abby.' He turned her round on his lap, reaching into his pocket with one hand and drawing out a tiny box. 'Be my wife. Soon. And before you say anything,' he put his finger to her mouth as she went to speak, 'I understand how things are here which is why I've sold up back home and have got my tail across the Atlantic. Hell, if you can't beat 'em, join 'em, eh, honey? We've thousands of GI brides trying to get into the States so one American doctor moving country for love isn't too big a deal. I think I knew the day I met you this relationship was never going to follow traditional lines.'

She stared at him through misty eyes and when he opened the box and took out a ring, she couldn't see it clearly for a moment or two. She blinked rapidly. He slid the ring onto the third finger of her left hand and for a second, just a second, she remembered that other occasion and the smiling, confident young man who had thought he was invincible and would be coming home for her. And then she ruthlessly put the memory from her. This was Ike's moment, and hers, and it didn't belong to anyone else, not even her darling boy.

She looked down at the ring and an enormous solitaire diamond glittered back at her, its magnificence making her hand look tiny and fragile.

'I love you, Abby.' His voice was thick and throaty and now there was no lightness in his tone. 'I'll love you till the day I die. I want to cherish you, adore you, protect you and worship you. Will you have me?'

She looked into the craggily handsome face, lifted the hand with the ring and ran her fingers through his hair, which was much greyer than when he'd left. 'Yes please,' she said.

Over the next few days Ike was heard to laughingly remark that he thought he'd found a cure for influenza, and certainly from the moment she had seen him Abby had felt much better. They'd decided on a Christmas wedding, and since Ike was staying at a hotel in Whitby, all the legal niceties and preparations were left to him. At first Abby had wanted the quietest of weddings, just Ike and herself, Clara, her three friends and little Joy, but when Ike had gently informed her his parents and brother and sister and their families would expect to be present, she had to face the fact that she must inform her own relations in Sunderland. But not her mother. On that she was resolute. If her mother caught wind of her wedding she'd spoil it. Somehow she'd ruin the day, besides which she never wanted to set eyes on her again.

Abby pondered the matter for some days. She'd all but lost touch with Audrey and she knew this was partly her fault, but not altogether. When she'd discovered the truth about her parenthood she'd felt unable to correspond with her aunt as she had been doing, but Audrey had never written to enquire what was wrong or whether everything was all right, which was strange. It wasn't like her aunt. It was almost as if Audrey herself had been relieved their contact had waned. Nevertheless, Abby did feel her aunt would be upset if she married without at least giving her the chance to be present. Wilbert was no letter writer but they had written to each other once or twice and she loved her brother dearly. She would ask him to give her away. He could tell their mother he was coming to visit her for Christmas. Her mother wouldn't like it but she could hardly stop him.

And Ivor? She no longer thought of him as Uncle Ivor. If her aunt came, he'd no doubt accompany her. Well, she'd cross that bridge when she came to it. But just let him try and act the benevolent uncle and devoted husband and she'd give him what for! Not in front of her aunt though; her aunt was the last person she wanted to hurt and it was possible Audrey would never recover if she found out her beloved husband had had an affair with her own sister.

And so the arrangements continued. If Ike or any of the others thought her attitude regarding her mother a little hard, they didn't say so. Abby felt she couldn't explain the true facts to anyone, not even her future husband, and so she simply stated they'd had a falling out and that reconciliation was not an option. It was only Clara who mentioned Nora, and then to say, 'I'm glad you're not telling Mam about you getting wed, Abby.' The two of them were standing in the greenhouse planting seeds before Clara had to leave for the village school.

It came out of the blue and the two sisters stared at each other before Abby said, 'She'd try and spoil things, wouldn't she?' and Clara nodded. Their eyes held some moments longer, both thinking of their father and the way he had died, and then Abby said, 'I want you to be my bridesmaid. Would you like that?' and the moment passed and Clara whooped and hugged her. They had never discussed the manner of their father's passing since the night Clara had blurted it all out, but that morning Abby realised Clara thought about it as often as she did, which was a comfort of sorts.

Abby had decided not to get married in the Catholic church at Whitby. Ike was not of the faith, in fact he declared himself to be an agnostic. She'd looked this up in the dictionary and found it to mean a person who believes that nothing is known of the existence or nature of God or of anything beyond material phenomena. Immediately she'd read it she knew the term was not right for Ike. In the past he'd admitted that when his wife was dying he had railed against God constantly, one moment begging Him to heal her and then asking Him to take her quickly to end her suffering. He'd wrestled long and hard with the manner of Eleanor's death and the distress and pain he'd seen in others since, and the result was a bitter resentment towards the Almighty for allowing such agony. Abby could understand this. She felt confused and angry herself that a lovely man like her father who had never hurt a living soul had been treated the way he had by people who were alive and well and had got off scot-free. It was monstrously unjust. And there was her mother acting all holy and toadying round the priest, her reputation as a good Catholic unblemished. It made Abby feel sick. Which was maybe why the decision to marry at Whitby's register office was set in concrete as far as she was concerned.

The wedding was due to take place the morning of Christmas Eve, which was a Monday. On the Saturday afternoon Wilbert, along with Audrey, Ivor, Leonard, Bruce and Jed, were due to arrive at the smallholding and Abby was beside herself. She knew the others were surprised she was so het up, especially as she had managed to meet all Ike's relations, who had arrived the previous day, with complete poise and calm, but the thought of seeing Ivor, of having to look into his face, made her feel ill. But she'd get through, she told herself, staring into the speckled mirror on the dressing table in the bedroom she shared with Rowena. On Monday Rowena would move into the room Gladys had previously had to herself. Winnie, Clara and Joy occupied the third bedroom in the smallholding. All three bedrooms were large and spacious, which was fortunate.

It was also fortunate, Abby thought, that there were no spare rooms in the property because this meant all the guests had to stay in town. Ike had insisted on treating everyone to a top-notch hotel, both his relations and Abby's, and when she'd protested about her side he'd cupped her face in his large hands and smiled at her. 'I can afford it,' he said softly, 'and there's no your side and my side, at least not from Monday anyway. They'll all be ours, like everything else. OK, honey?'

Abby sank back on the stool, reflecting how very lucky she was to have found Ike. Not just because of his generosity, which knew no bounds, but because he was the dearest man on earth. She smiled slowly, thoughts of Ivor retreating. Ike was bringing what Abby considered a small fortune into the marriage, and he'd already made it clear he wanted to be a fourth partner in the smallholding and their business, albeit a sleeping one. Suddenly the four women had a wealth of funds at their disposal for all the repairs to the existing house and barn, plus another big greenhouse they'd had in mind for the future. On top of that he had suggested a large extension for the house which would effectively give himself and Abby a home of their own, whilst still being close to the others.

They had plenty of land, so the three-bedroom extension, complete with sitting room, dining room and kitchen, would present no problem, and he proposed it should have its own front door, but also an interconnecting door. He was intending to return to the medical profession in due course, and Abby knew he was thinking of the times he might be called out for long periods and she would be alone. 'You don't want to be scampering out in the cold when it's snowing a blizzard or raining cats and dogs,' he'd said. 'Better if you can just open a door and stay in the warm.'

Abby patted the shining coil of her hair and smoothed

330

the collar of her dress. She went to look out of the window for a moment or two. It had snowed on and off all through December and the wind had carved the deep drifts into curves of exquisite beauty. The smallholding's shovels had become the most important items they possessed. Abby had found herself praying the snow would continue to fall and prove a deterrent to Ivor and the others, but instead they'd had a partial thaw followed by days of cold frosty sunshine. And now they'd all be here any moment. Ike had met their train earlier and taken them to the hotel so they could freshen up before he brought them to the house.

As though on cue she heard the engine of the big car Ike had acquired. Her legs trembled as she turned from the window. They continued to tremble as she walked down the stairs and into the square hall. Off it on one side were the kitchen, scullery and dairy, and on the other side their comfortable but shabby sitting room and a small storeroom. Clara hurtled out of the sitting room just as Abby reached its doorway, her voice high with excitement as she cried, 'They're here, Abby! Aunty Audrey and Jed and the others!'

'I know.' Abby forced a smile. 'Have you finished decorating the tree?'

Clara nodded. 'Joy fell asleep after a little while but I laid her on the sofa.'

The night before, the four women and Clara had stayed up to the early hours cutting out cardboard circles, tiny Christmas trees, stars and other shapes and covering them in silver paper for the fir tree Ike had brought to the house. He had also arrived with a big bag of sugar mice and tiny candy shepherd hooks which he'd bought in America with Christmas in mind, and when he'd presented these to Clara her excitement had known no bounds.

But then, Abby thought now as she looked into her

sister's bright eyes, Clara had never really decorated a tree with the unthinkable luxury of dozens of pink and white sugar mice and gaily coloured candy sticks before. The war had made such a thing impossible. When they had finished cutting and sticking at two in the morning, Clara had declared that she and Joy would trim the tree once the toddler was awake. She had received no argument from the bleary-eyed women.

'How does the tree look?' Abby asked.

'Smashing!' Clara declared, and then the door opened and Ike was ushering folk in.

Audrey was the first to enter and for a moment Abby didn't recognise her. Gone was the big, dowdily dressed housewife she remembered and in her place was a smart, attractive woman with carefully styled hair and discreet make-up. The voice was the same though when Audrey let out a screech of delight, clasping Abby and Clara to her as she cried, 'Eee, me bairns, me bairns,' before bursting into tears.

In the ensuing few minutes of bedlam Abby found herself lifted right off her feet in a bruising bear hug from Wilbert and kissed soundly by a grinning Leonard and Bruce – the latter with an empty left sleeve to his jacket which told its own story. And then she was smiling down at a reserved and shy Jed who held out his hand to be shaken, clearly horrified by all the kissing and endearments flying around. 'You remember Clara, don't you, Jed?' Abby said to the young lad after she'd decorously shaken the proffered hand. 'You used to be inseparable at one time.' She glanced at her sister and was amazed to see Clara was beetroot red, her voice a mumble when she muttered a quick hello.

In the moment it took for Abby to take in how very alike the two youngsters were – same blond hair, straight fine noses and wide full mouths – she became aware of a bulky

332

figure standing half hidden by the side of the open front door. She felt herself stiffen but the trembling had vanished. As Ivor walked fully into the house, a big smile on his face, Abby stared at him. She did not return the smile but her voice was level when she said, 'Hello, Ivor.'

Whether it was her tone or the lack of 'Uncle' before his name, he stopped about a yard away instead of taking her in his arms and hugging her as he'd obviously intended. His eyes narrowed fractionally. 'Hello, Abby.' Almost immediately his gaze dropped to Clara and his voice was jolly as he said, 'This can't be Clara! Not this grown-up young lady in front of me. I don't believe it.'

Clara wriggled with embarrassment. Abby stared at the man she now knew to be her father. He hadn't changed much. A little older, a little plumper and there was a heavy smattering of grey in his hair, otherwise he seemed the same relaxed individual she remembered from her childhood and youth. She'd loved this man as her Uncle Ivor, trusted him, run to him with little problems when her da was at sea. How could he have done what he had?

'I couldn't believe it when we got your letter, hinny.' Audrey took her arm. 'You getting married an' taking on this place an' all. By, lass, you're one on your own and no mistake. An' I like your American,' she added in a loud stage whisper as they all walked through into the sitting room where a crackling log fire was burning in the stone fireplace, the flames reflected in the steel-topped and brass-tailed fender. 'An' him a doctor too,' she murmured with a touch of reverence.

Abby couldn't help but smile. Ike was clearly one step down from the Pope himself in her aunty's opinion. 'You didn't say anything to Mam?' she whispered. 'She hasn't caught wind of anything?'

'Your mam?' For a moment her aunt's voice held an

inflection Abby couldn't put her finger on. Then it was gone as Audrey said quietly, 'We're not on speaking terms any more, lass. Haven't been for years and I have to say I prefer it that way. Your Wilbert comes round now and again; brings his young lady in to see us. You know he's courting strong the last little while with a Southwick lass?'

Abby shook her head. She was lucky if she got a letter from Wilbert every six months and then it always followed the same pattern. A few scrawled words enquiring if she was well, if Clara was well, and stating the health of them back home. This was followed by a commentary on the present state of the weather and that was about it. When she had written telling him about the wedding she'd received a two-liner back stating he'd be pleased to give her away and telling her the time of his arrival, and that he would be travelling down with their aunt and uncle.

'Aye, well, he is,' Audrey carried on, 'an' she's a right bonny lass an' all. I understand your mam can't stand the sight of her.'

'Why aren't I surprised?'

They looked at each other and neither was smiling. It was Audrey who changed the subject, pointing to Joy who was curled up like a small puppy on the sofa and still fast asleep. 'Is that Winnie's bairn?' she said softly.

Abby nodded. She had gone to some lengths in her letter to her aunt to explain the circumstances of each of the women in the household, thinking it better things were straight before the visitors arrived.

'Poor little mite.'

Abby looked at her aunt. 'Joy is very much loved and she'll be brought up in a family where she'll want for nothing. There are worse starts in life. Most important of all, Winnie dotes on her.'

'Oh aye, lass, aye. I wasn't meaning . . .' Audrey's voice

trailed away. They both knew what she had meant. Then the slightly awkward moment passed as she said warmly, 'I'm glad you wrote, Abby. I've been meaning to put pen to paper so many times but then something would come up, you know how it is. I was working full-time when the war was on but with the men coming out of the forces that's all changed. I've got a nice little part-time job in the laundry in St Marks Road now though, nine till two. The money's not brilliant but it's enough for what I want. I couldn't go back to being stuck at home all day and I like me own pay packet, you know? Little bit of independence.'

Abby stared, she couldn't help it. This was her aunt and yet not her aunt and it was weird. But the war had changed everyone, she reminded herself as Gladys bustled in with a trolley containing tea and cakes. No one had come through unscathed. And Audrey's transformation was not a bad thing, far from it, except – Abby blinked as she tried to marshall her whirling thoughts – there was something behind the soft brown of her aunt's eyes. Sadness? Melancholy? Grief? But then she would be mourning Donald, wouldn't she? He was her firstborn, her boy. It was only natural.

Winnie and Rowena followed close on Gladys's heels and as Joy chose that second to wake, the moment was lost. It wasn't until much later, when she was lying in bed and sleep seemed a million miles away, that the haunted look in her aunt's eyes returned to Abby's mind. And she wondered . . .

Chapter Twenty-four

'All I'm saying is, she doesn't seem like the same lass who left Sunderland five years ago. That's all. It wasn't meant as a criticism.'

Audrey's sceptical gaze spoke volumes, as did her 'Huh!'

Ivor looked somewhat sheepishly at his wife as he struggled with the top button of the new gleaming white shirt purchased especially for the wedding with precious clothing coupons. He had wanted to wear his Sunday one but Audrey wouldn't hear of it. The button finally fastened, he felt as if he was choking. 'Does she seem the same to you then? Now tell me, does she?'

'Aye, she does. More beautiful than ever but just the same old Abby under the skin.' Audrey smoothed the lapels of her tweed suit after turning to check her appearance in the full-length mirror in the hotel room. Twelve pounds this suit had cost her, double what it should, but you had to be prepared for that if you bought on the black market. With the only new things in the shops being utility clothes that looked as drab as dishwater, it'd been worth it, and even Ivor had said it was a grand bit of material. That had been before he'd known it had cost her three weeks' wages mind. But never again would she stint on herself. She might not be earning what she had during the war, but what she earned was *her* money and would remain so. It was one of the terms she'd laid down when she'd taken him back.

'The same old Abby?' Ivor was now fighting with his tie,

and after clicking her tongue Audrey walked across to him and took over. 'I don't think so. I really don't, lass. Not with me anyway.'

'You're imagining things.' The tie in a perfect knot, Audrey handed him the jacket of his Sunday suit. 'Now hurry up, I bet we'll be the last ones downstairs and we don't want to keep them all waiting.'

Ivor caught his wife's arm as she went to turn away. 'You look bonny, lass,' he said softly. 'Right bonny.'

Audrey smiled but did not say anything. He was always complimenting her about her appearance these days. He also praised her dinners, the way she kept the house, even the way she ironed his shirts. And she wished he wouldn't. He'd never understand, but it was a constant reminder of the affair which had blighted their lives. And he was so grateful for any little show of affection from her, and this had the effect of restraining her somehow. The old Ivor had taken her completely for granted, mind you, and she wouldn't want to return to that. Of course she wouldn't. But . . .

Here Audrey's reasoning ran out and she mentally shrugged. Life was funny, and not in a ha-ha sense either. But she was glad things were back on a level footing between herself and Abby. When the chance had come to cut off contact with her niece, she had taken it because anything connected to Nora was a reminder, but when she'd begun to feel a bit better about things she had regretted it. It had seemed too late, then, to suddenly start writing again.

Ivor looked at Audrey as she walked across the room. The cut of the expensive suit, the classy high heels which emphasised the slim firmness of her legs made her look like a million dollars, he thought worriedly.

He'd gone through hell on earth when he had thought he'd lost her, but since she had taken him back he had

337

found it was hell of a different kind. He was terrified he might lose her again and this time permanently, that some bloke, younger or richer or more intelligent and amusing than him, would steal her away and that would be that. It could happen, oh aye, because Audrey's feelings for him were not what they once had been. She was still kind and warm, and in the privacy of their big bed as generous with her loving, but now something was held back. Some part of her which once had been his was no longer given. Or was it more that an armour was in place now? A barrier he knew he could not penetrate?

When she stood in the doorway and said, 'Well? Are you coming?' Ivor nodded, telling himself as he did a hundred times a day that it would be all right. She was his wife, wasn't she? And underneath this perfectly groomed, attractive veneer, the essence of the old Audrey remained. But it was hollow comfort. And now there was this wedding to get through and, whatever Audrey might say, he knew Abby wasn't the same with him.

Did it matter? he thought as he followed Audrey into the corridor. No, not at all, he answered himself. He hadn't seen his niece for years and it wouldn't bother him if he never saw her again, if he was being truthful. Just so long as her coolness wasn't anything to do with what had happened between himself and her mother, that was the thing. Then it might have the potential to explode in their faces and cause trouble between himself and Audrey if everything got raked up again. But Abby couldn't know. Nora wouldn't have told her, surely; she'd gain nothing by doing so. No, he was being daft, but all things considered he'd be glad when this day was over.

Some miles away Abby was thinking exactly the same thing. At first light everyone in the house had been rudely awakened by the sound of fierce banging on the front door which had seemed to shake the rafters. Abby and Rowena had met the others on the landing, and after Abby had told Winnie to stay upstairs with Clara and little Joy, she had gone downstairs followed by Rowena and Gladys.

Vincent was on the doorstep and it was clear he was in the grip of a furious rage. 'You knew, didn't you? You knew about that one,' he indicated Rowena with a vicious stab of his hand, 'and that dirty little Eyetie.'

'*I beg your pardon!*' Before Abby could answer, Rowena shoved her out of the way, her eyes sparking. 'Mario is ten times the man you'll ever be and don't you dare refer to him in that way.'

Abby pulled her friend back when it looked as if she was going to strike Vincent but it took both her and Gladys to hold the angry woman. 'Get off this property.' She glared at Vincent whilst trying to restrain Rowena. 'You're not welcome here.'

'Been spying on me all this time, haven't you?' He was beside himself. 'Telling them to do the least work they can so I get deeper into the mire. I know, I know.'

'You heard what Abby said, get off our land.' None of them had heard Winnie come up behind them but suddenly she was there, and she was holding the shotgun they'd found buried under a pile of junk in the barn. They had cleaned off the cobwebs and dirt and given it a bit of a polish but had had no intention of getting any cartridges for it, deciding to stick it in the cupboard under the stairs in case some day they needed to warn off any undesirables. None of them had imagined that day would come so quickly though.

Vincent stared at Winnie for a moment and then he folded his arms, his voice a touch calmer as he said, 'You wouldn't use that on me, not you.'

'Try me.'

'Don't be stupid.'

'I'm not stupid, Vincent, but that's something you've never really understood. Mind, going with you could have been termed stupid, but everyone's allowed one mistake in life.'

They all saw he was taken aback, but none of them expected what came next. 'Shirley's gone, Winnie. I threw her out. If you and the child want to come back I'm prepared to take you both on, all right? Marriage too if you want it. I can't say fairer than that. And Mam?' His glance went to Gladys who was still holding tight to Rowena. 'You're welcome back an' all. No hard feelings.'

The sheer arrogance of the man! To come here ranting and raving one minute and the next to act as though he was handing out favours. Abby was dumbstruck.

Not so Winnie. She didn't look at Gladys and she kept the shotgun trained on Vincent's chest when she said, 'If your tart has gone it's because she's had enough of having to work for the first time in her life, not because you threw her out. Like I said, I'm not stupid. And I'd rather cut me own throat and the bairn's an' all than ever set foot in your place again.'

His eyes narrowed but he still refused to recognise his power over her had gone. His voice softer, he said, 'Winnie, lass, don't be like that. I admit I made a few mistakes but nothing I can't put right if you'll let me. Remember how it used to be between us, eh? We had some good times, didn't we? And it's all mine now, the farm, everything. Don't forget that.'

'I'm not forgetting a thing; I'm remembering, in fact.' Her tone was icy.

'What about her, the nipper? Don't you want her to have a name?'

If he thought he'd hit her below the belt, Winnie proved him wrong. She hadn't raised her voice throughout the exchange and she didn't raise it now when she said, 'She has a name and it's a good one. She also has a future, as do I, and it's not linked with you. You were right to question whether you're her father. You're not, OK? So you have no right to her at all.'

'You're lying.'

Abby wasn't the only one who thought it ironic how things had turned round.

'Prove it.' Winnie eyed him steadily. 'And now get off my property before I mistake you for a thief and shoot you.'

'Mam?' Vincent hadn't moved an inch. 'Are you in this with them? The farm's going down the drain, everything Dad ever worked for, and they're doing their bit to help it along. I wondered why those bits of scum were dragging their heels and now I know.'

Gladys let go of Rowena's arm, her jaw working. This was her lad and whatever he'd done she still loved him. She stared into his infuriated face and her voice was husky when she said, 'They are good men, Vincent, but you've never been able to distinguish between good and bad company or you would have made an honest woman of Winnie when you had the chance. When you brought your fancy woman into my home you told me I had to toe the line or else. I chose the or else and this is my home now. I'm not leaving. Those men have worked hard for you because Rowena's told us so, and that in spite of how you've behaved, but they can't do double the work, however much you create. You got rid of three of the best workers you're ever likely to have when you threw Abby and the others out and you lost a damn good housekeeper in me, boy.'

'You don't care I might lose Dad's farm if I can't keep up the quotas?'

'It's not Josiah's farm, it's yours. You told me that often enough when I was still there and you fair hammered it home the day you brought your floozy in. I've a stake in this place and this *is* part mine.' Her voice softer, she added, 'Go and see someone in authority, plead your case. Beg if you have to.'

'Don't you think I haven't already done that?'

'Then pay the going rate and hire some men. It doesn't have to be POWs or land girls.'

'Of course it does, you stupid woman.' For a moment his frustration was foremost. 'I can't afford top whack, it's as simple as that.'

'That's enough.' Abby saw that Gladys was close to tears. 'You've had your say, now go.'

'Oh, I'll go all right.' His gaze swung from his mother to Abby, and he actually ground his teeth before saying, 'You lot aren't the only ones who can use a gun. There's been many a night I've shot a fox breaking into the hen cree or skulking round the barns. I just hope I don't mistake her fancy fella,' his eyes fastened on Rowena for a moment, 'for vermin because that'd be a right shame, wouldn't it? With them so lovey dovey, I mean.'

'You try anything like that and we'll all see you go down the line for it,' Abby warned him, now hanging on to Rowena once more, who was swearing like a trooper at Vincent.

'Huh!' He backed away a few steps, his voice thick with bitterness as he growled, 'Like your dear friend said earlier, you'd have to prove it.'

Rowena continued struggling until the farm lorry had disappeared out of the square yard in front of the house, then she collapsed on Abby, crying hysterically.

Between them they got her into the kitchen and sat her down. The level of brandy in one of Ike's bottles went down

342

sharply in the next few minutes as Abby poured them all a measure which would have cost a fortune in a pub. But the neat spirit helped dispel the shock the ugly encounter had caused, and by the time Gladys had made a pot of strong tea and Clara had brought Joy downstairs, some normality had returned.

'You don't think he'd really hurt Mario, do you?' Rowena sat pulling at her nightdress, smoothing it as if it was of vital importance all the creases were flattened.

'No I don't,' Abby said firmly. 'It was an empty threat to frighten you. He values his hide too much and he knows we'd have him up in court before he could blink. Besides which I can't see Roberto and Luigi standing by and letting him shoot Mario without getting involved, can you? It's one thing to make a mistake and shoot one man, quite another to make the same mistake three times. But I tell you what, we'll let Ike go and see him and put the wind up him. Ike might be the gentlest soul on earth but Vincent doesn't know that.'

'Oh Abby, when am I ever going to see him now?' And then Rowena's face suddenly changed and she clapped her hand over her mouth. 'It's your wedding day! Abby, it's your wedding day.'

'I know,' said Abby a touch wryly.

'What a start to it. Oh, I'm sorry, dear, I really am.' Abby found herself engulfed in a big hug. 'You mustn't think of this for a second again today. We can't let Vincent spoil things.'

By the time the taxi Ike had hired brought Wilbert to the house later that morning, Abby was dressed in the wedding finery that sixty clothing coupons and hard cash had bought. The yearly allowance was sixty-six coupons per person and the other three women and even Clara had

343

contributed generously to the occasion. When Abby was ready they all declared their sacrifice had been worth it.

'You look beautiful, lass.' Winnie was wiping her eyes. 'The bonniest bride this side of heaven an' no mistake.'

Abby hugged her, careless of the cream brocade wedding gown and hooded cloak in the same material which was trimmed with imitation fur. She hugged each one of them, clasping Clara to her the longest. She looked remarkably grown up in her bridesmaid's dress of blue velvet, again with a matching cloak. Clara's dress had been made by a local dressmaker and Abby had bought enough material to have a miniature version made for Joy as a surprise for Winnie on the day. The presentation of this an hour earlier had started Winnie's tears and they hadn't really stopped since.

Outside, the day was bitterly cold; desultory flakes of thin snow whirled haphazardly in a north-east wind which cut to the bone. But Abby was warm, and it was nothing to do with the fire blazing in the hearth in the sitting room. She was so fortunate to have this family – and it was a family even if their root wasn't genetic – behind her.

She had mourned her father being unable to give her away the night before, shedding a few tears in the privacy of darkness, but this morning she felt at peace. She was marrying a wonderful man who loved her deeply, she had those she loved around her and that was enough. Her mother, Ivor, the whole sorry situation would be put on the back burner today and she wouldn't let it intrude, any more than she would allow the unpleasant start to the morning to sour the occasion. This was her and Ike's day and she was going to enjoy it to the full.

Wilbert's eyes were full of pride as he led her to the waiting taxi, the one behind it designated for the other three women, Clara and Joy. He had been horrified when

Winnie had quickly put him in the picture about Vincent's unwelcome arrival at the house that morning, and deeply indignant. Now, as the car drew away from the house to begin its journey to the register office, he mistook Abby's quiet serenity for worry, thinking she was fretting about the incident. Determined to take her mind off it, he said, 'Who'd have thought it, lass? You marrying a doctor an' an American one at that.' Like most of the folk in the streets where they had been brought up Wilbert considered a doctor only one step down from a priest, and to be greatly revered.

Abby brought her gaze from the snowy fields beyond the car window and smiled a little absently.

'Funny,' Wilbert rattled on, trying to do his best, 'but I could never see you living anywhere else than our parts, but here you are in Yorkshire with your own business an' all.' He shook his head in wonder. 'All I can say, lass, is that whatever went on between you and James you ended up smelling of roses.'

'James?' Wilbert had her full attention now. Her brother was one of the nicest people on earth and she was shocked he could bring James's name up at such a moment. And there had been something in his tone she couldn't put her finger on.

'Aye, James Benson.' Wilbert looked embarrassed at her reaction. 'Oh, I'm not prying, don't think that, I'm just saying that whatever went on between you two, you've done as well as him in the end.'

For a moment Abby didn't speak; then, looking at him, she said, 'I don't understand what you mean, Wilbert.'

Wilbert stretched his neck, easing the starched collar of his shirt. 'I mean him marrying that lass whose da owns the big accountancy firm in the High Street, I forget the name. I saw them at the Palace one night a few months back when I'd just started courting Lucy, and when I said I thought I knew the bloke, she said she'd worked in the firm as a temp in the typing pool for a while and that his name was Benson and the woman was his wife.'

Abby felt weak and faint. She swallowed, knowing she had to say something. But she couldn't.

'Still, like I said, you've done right grand for yourself, lass, and your Ike is a champion fella.'

She managed a mumbled, 'Yes, yes he is.'

'An' I like his folks an' all. I thought they might be a bit stuck up, them being well off and Americans an' all that, but they're salt of the earth. Like him.'

'Yes, they are. Wilbert, I've . . . got a bit of a headache. Could we just sit quiet until we get there?'

'Aye, lass, of course. You should have said.' Wilbert patted her hand and settled back in his seat.

By the time the taxi reached its destination Abby knew she had to have a few more minutes to compose herself. In spite of her request, Wilbert had talked on and off the whole way and her head was whirling. Nearly everyone was waiting inside the building but Audrey had stayed outside, and now she came running to meet them, her face one big smile which faded when she saw the expression on Abby's face. 'What's wrong?' In one of the characteristic gestures Abby remembered, her aunt unceremoniously thrust Wilbert to one side. 'You feeling bad?'

Abby nodded. She was feeling bad but not from nerves as her aunt probably assumed. 'Have they got a lavatory here? I need a couple of minutes . . .'

She didn't have to finish the sentence. Before the taxi bearing the others had even arrived, Audrey had whisked her into the building and into the Ladies which, thankfully, turned out to be one small cubicle which meant her aunt had to wait outside. After closing the door and sliding the bolt, Abby stood with her back to it, her hand covering her eyes, and she whispered to herself, 'James, James, how could you?' He was alive. *Alive.* And married to someone else. All the time she had been grieving and mourning him he had been *alive.*

She stared at the wall sightlessly, dry-eyed, but she was crying through every pore of her body. He had come back from the war and he had married someone else. It seemed ludicrous, impossible, but she didn't question the truth of Wilbert's words; he wouldn't have spoken out like he had if he'd been unsure of his facts. She felt herself shrinking, shrivelling down to nothing.

She was never very sure of how long she stood there but after a while Audrey's voice penetrated the vacuum and she forced herself to come back to the present. She called out that she was nearly ready, opening her eyes which had been tightly shut and staring at herself in the small square mirror. A chalk-white face with eyes so dark they appeared black looked back at her. Automatically she began to pinch her cheeks and bite her lips to give herself some colour, a strange calmness settling on her.

Ike was waiting for her in there and he had all his nearest and dearest watching, along with her family. Whatever she was feeling she had to act the eager bride right now, nothing else would do. And nothing had changed, not really. James was still gone from her as he had been the last few years, it was just the reason for his absence which had altered. She breathed deeply, watching the figure in the mirror with curious detachment. There was a weak sensation churning through her but she would not give in to it, she told herself dully. This was her wedding day and Ike deserved a radiant bride. Well, she would be radiant, she would laugh and glow and shine all day long. For him. For her Ike.

She adjusted the collar of the cloak so it fell more closely round her upswept hair, pinched her cheeks one last time and then, stitching a smile on her face, she opened the door.

Chapter Twenty-five

Ike turned round to look at her when she entered the room and walked with Wilbert between the two sets of waiting families. The love shining out of his eyes carried her through the brief but pleasant ceremony and the reception at the hotel with every appearance of enjoyment.

And she had enjoyed it in a way, she told herself later in the afternoon during a lull in the proceedings. It was the first time she'd had a moment to herself; everyone seemed to be in conversation or watching Ike doing a little impromptu ventriloquist act for his sister's four young children with some puppets the youngsters had brought with them. As long as she didn't let her mind veer off for a second and concentrated wholly on what she could see and hear, she was all right. Thinking, remembering, could come later. Much later.

'He'll be a natural when your bairns come along.'

Abby hadn't noticed Ivor come up behind her but now he sat down at the side of her, his eyes on Ike and the children. It was a full ten seconds before she said, 'Yes, he will make a wonderful father.' Her voice was stiff.

'Meself, I was never much good with ours when they were little, couldn't get on their wavelength I suppose, but he's got 'em in the palm of his hand, hasn't he?'

'Yes he has.'

'Audrey was like that with the lads. They thought the world of their mam, still do, but then she's that sort of woman. Draws folk, always has done.'

Oh, the hypocrisy of him. The hurt and pain she had been battling with all day rose up like a ball into her throat. She turned her head, staring into the face she had been trying to ignore. 'I'm a little surprised you didn't add "like her sister",' she said icily.

'What?'

'You heard.'

Ivor was looking at her but he did not speak again. Abby waited for a moment before she said, 'You don't deny it then?'

'Deny what?'

'That you went with my mother.'

Saints alive! She knew. But then hadn't he suspected it at the bottom of him? She'd been so reserved with him, so distant, and the way he'd caught her looking at him once or twice . . . Damn it, why hadn't he stayed where he was instead of coming to sit beside her? 'It . . .' His voice broke and he had to clear his throat before he could say, 'It isn't like you think, Abby.'

'You have no idea what I think.' Her voice was low and controlled. 'You couldn't or you would have made some excuse to go home before now.'

He straightened in his chair. For this to come out now, at her wedding. But maybe it was the best time at that. At least she was keeping her voice down. He glanced swiftly round the room. Audrey was in a far corner talking to someone or other from Ike's side, with her back partially to them. He breathed in deeply, his voice little more than a whisper when he said, 'Look, lass, let me explain. I got meself in a fix. Your mam, well, she tricked me—'

'Time and time again over a period of years she tricked you?' It was scathing but still quiet. 'You're easily duped then. Or stupid. Or both.'

'Now look—' He caught himself, lowering his voice again

which now held a fawning quality. 'I can understand how you feel and it's only natural—'

'Don't talk to me about natural, not when you've gone with your own wife's sister and given her three bairns into the bargain. But let me tell you something, my da might not have been my flesh-and-blood father but he was my da in every way that counted.'

Ivor's mouth dropped open. 'Who told you that, about me being . . .'

'My father? And Wilbert and Clara's? The same person who told me about your affair. My mam, of course. And before you deny it, I know she wasn't lying so save your breath.'

Ivor wetted his lips, then dug his teeth tight into the flesh of the lower one and bent his head. Staring at his boots, he said, 'I didn't know. I swear to you, lass, I didn't know, not afore this day.'

'Because you didn't want to know.' It was a statement not a question. 'My mam and da had been married years with no sign of a child and then you came along.' It was bitter. 'Don't tell me you didn't wonder.'

'No. Yes. I mean . . .' He shook his head, his shoulders hunched. 'She didn't say. Your mam didn't say.'

'And you didn't ask, but then you wouldn't, would you? Why ruin the novelty of having your cake and eating it?'

'It wasn't like that.'

Silence reigned for a moment, then Ivor said, 'What are you going to do?' When Abby didn't answer, he turned his head slowly towards her. 'Look, your aunt knows about me an' your mam and we've put it behind us, all right? Made a new start like. But if you tell her . . .' His lower jaw worked. 'It'll break her, you see that, don't you? And what good would it do, eh? Tell me that. What good would it do?'

351

'Perhaps I don't care about that.'

'You care about your Aunty Audrey, you always have done.' When she did not deny this, he added, 'You told Wilbert or Clara about this?'

'If I had, Wilbert would have bashed your face in.'

'Please, Abby,' he pleaded. 'Please let sleeping dogs lie. Your da was your da, I'd be the first to say it. Whether he actually . . .' He paused before continuing, 'It don't matter, not that part. It's the rest of it, the bringing up of bairns that counts.'

'I know that.' Her eyes met his for a moment and he saw they were filled with pain. 'I don't need you to tell me that.'

Clara danced up at this point and spent a few moments talking to them before Jed came and tapped her on the arm. The pair of them went to help themselves to the hot mince pies and steaming mugs of coffee and cocoa the hotel staff had just brought in as a conclusion to the proceedings.

'So what are you going to do?' Ivor asked again. 'If it's any consolation, I'll never forgive meself for what I've done, never as long as I live.'

'It's no consolation at all,' Abby said, willing herself not to break down.

Ike caught her eye from across the room. 'You OK, hon?' he mouthed, and she smiled, nodding and mouthing back, 'I'm fine, Dr Wilmot,' whereupon he grinned and continued the puppet show.

Her throat was tight, too tight to swallow. What was it that made some men, men who had once been honourable and good and kind, men like Ivor and – here Abby found herself taking a long painful breath – James Benson, forget the women they were supposed to love and chase after someone else?

'I'm sorry. I can't say more than that, can I? There's

352

nowt I can do to change things now but your aunty knowing this would, well, it'd turn the knife for her. Surely you can see that?'

This elicited no response from Abby, and after a moment Ivor went on, 'There's Wilbert and Clara too. If they don't know, what's the point in upsetting them an' all? It don't make sense.'

'Don't talk to me about sense, not you.' She stood up. 'I won't say anything but only for Aunty Audrey's sake. She's had enough to put up with.'

She left him without another word, meeting Ike halfway across the room.

'That looked like a serious conversation to have with someone on your wedding day, Mrs Wilmot.' His tone was light, even amused, but there was a question in the dark eyes.

Abby chose to ignore it. She answered just as lightly, 'Not jealous already, Dr Wilmot? I've heard of these men who turn into tyrants the minute they're wed.'

'Oh, this is just the start of it,' he agreed solemnly. 'It's downhill all the way from now on.'

'And here was me thinking I'd landed in clover.' This was too near what Wilbert had said and now Abby dropped the bantering tone. 'I love you, Ike, and we're going to have a good marriage, aren't we?'

'The best.' Recognising something had upset her, he drew her closer, holding her against his chest. 'I'm going to make you happy, Abby. More happy than you would have dreamed possible or my name isn't Ike Marshall Wilmot.'

'I believe you.' She put up a hand and tenderly stroked his chin where the stubble was beginning to break through tanned skin. 'And the same goes for me. I'll be – what's the word? – an exemplary wife. How about that?'

His mouth went into a quirk. 'Just one who loves me will do.'

'You have that.'

'Let's say our goodbyes then and go up to our room.' He had reserved the honeymoon suite for several days, and now, at the look in his eyes, Abby found herself turning pink. He lowered his head, whispering into the silk of her hair, 'I love it that you can still blush. The way things are changing it's becoming a lost art.'

'Ike, don't expect – I mean, I'm not experienced or anything and I don't want you to be disappointed—'

She had hinted at this concern of hers several times in the run-up to the wedding, and now he cut off her voice with a kiss that carried a wealth of love in it. When he drew away, she was pinker than ever, and in the moments before he let her go he murmured, 'I'm experienced enough for both of us so don't worry, OK?' He didn't add that from the first moment they had met, when he had felt the pull of her so strongly it had initially astounded and then deeply disturbed him, he had known he had to have her. It wouldn't have mattered if she had had a hundred men before him or, as was the case, none, he had been ensnared and was completely hers. It had not been like that with Eleanor and if he hadn't been able to make Abby love him, if he had been forced to walk away from her, he knew it wouldn't be like it with anyone else. He would tell her all this later, once they had made love in the big four-poster bed the honeymoon suite boasted and were content in each other's arms. For now it was enough that the time he had waited for was upon them, and he intended to make it as special for her as he could.

So this was what marriage was all about, and yet no, no, it couldn't be like this for everyone or else all the married women she knew would walk about with a great big smile stitched on their faces. Abby wriggled closer into Ike's side and even in sleep his arm tightened instinctively around her.

She had been so shy and nervous when the door of the honeymoon suite had closed behind them and they were alone, even though she knew she was being silly. She was a grown woman of twenty-four but suddenly she'd felt like a schoolgirl again. And it wasn't that she was afraid of Ike or even of the act of love itself, it was just . . . the unknown. Winnie had sported with a number of fellows and Rowena had made no secret of the fact that she and Mario were intimate, but for some reason she hadn't felt able to ask either of her friends exactly what the physical side of marriage entailed.

But it had been . . . She couldn't find a word to express how she felt. Not just the lovemaking but the things he'd whispered and the promises he'd made. She had expected it to be a quick thing, this physical union, but once he had undressed her and encouraged her to undress him, the urgency she had sensed in him at the reception had gone. They had touched and tasted and done things which still had her face burning when she thought of them. But it had been wonderful, and even the brief pain when he had finally entered her had changed into something pleasurable.

And then in the rosy afterglow he had held her in his arms and talked of the future, a future rich with children and grandchildren, of travel, new experiences. She hadn't thought of James then, she hadn't thought of him until Ike had fallen asleep and she had lain in the darkness with a sweet warm throbbing between her legs which had reminded her she was a woman in every sense of the word at last.

She didn't understand why James had betrayed her, nor how he could have fallen in love with someone else knowing she was still alive and waiting for him, but that was all part of her old life and she had to let it – and him – go. She had never seen it so clearly. She had been given a second chance of happiness with Ike and he was such a special, dear man. Her da had always said you played life with the cards you'd been dealt, not the ones you would have liked, and it was true; she couldn't honestly have said she would have willingly given up the chance of meeting Ike. Of course if she had still been engaged to James or even known he was still alive things would have been different, but she hadn't and they weren't.

She felt the sting of tears in her eyes and scrubbed at them angrily. She wasn't going to cry, not tonight, not when she had been given the most precious gift in the man lying beside her. He had embraced a new life in a new country for her, and not only that, he had taken on her friends and her sister as though they were his nearest and dearest. Clara was happy and content here and there was no reason for them to ever return to Sunderland and their mother. All ties were cut and they would remain so. Wilbert and his lass would always be welcome and after today she suspected if Audrey visited it would be by herself, which was just fine. This was a new beginning . . .

Within a few minutes Abby was sleeping peacefully, her forehead and Ike's touching and their arms round each other.

When she next awoke it was to the realisation that the nightmare which had gripped her wasn't quite gone, in spite of Ike's arms holding her tight and his calming tone as he said, 'It's all right, it's all right, love. You're safe. You're with me. Open your eyes. It's over.'

'She . . . she won't let up, she'll keep on. She's after me.'

'Who, love? Who's after you?' He clicked on the bedside lamp, drawing her against his bare chest and stroking the hair from her damp face. 'It was a dream, hon, that's all. No one can hurt you now.'

The light banished the last of the horror but the memory of her mother's twisted face as she had come at her with an axe was still vivid. Abby lay stiff and taut, her voice a whisper as she said, 'It was my mam. She was after me.'

'She can't hurt you, honeypie. The only power she has is what you give her.' Even as he spoke the words, Ike wondered what on earth had made her scream out like that. She'd told him her mother had mistreated her when she was young, knocking her about a bit and neglecting her, and that she had been the same with Clara which is why Abby had taken her sister under her wing, but there had been sheer terror in her voice before he had managed to wake her up. 'Do you want to talk about it?' he asked softly.

'No.' She turned in to him, seeking the warmth and strength of his big male frame. 'I don't want to give her that much importance in my life.'

It was bitter and the doctor in him recognised a wound which was still raw. Nevertheless he did not press her, gathering her up and soothing her with gentle words and caresses until her breathing steadied and she relaxed against him. But for a long time after she slept he lay awake and wondered if it was his imagination that made him feel there was much more that Abby didn't feel able to tell him.

She was right, he'd lied to her. She'd *known* there was more to Wilbert's visit than a Christmas reunion. Nora sat on the edge of her son's bed, the letter she had found hidden on top of the wardrobe crumpled in her fingers. So Abby was marrying a GI, was she, and a fancy one at that. A doctor no less. By, she knew when she was on to a good thing, always had. Nora ground her teeth, the sound loud in the silence. And Wilbert going along with it all and fooling his own mam. She'd give him what for when he slunk back in. Leaving her all alone at Christmas and gallivanting off at Abby's beck and call, the sneaky little runt.

She opened the letter and reread the words which had filled her with such fury, pacing the room, her face dark at the thought of a smiling Abby on the arm of a rich GI.

She had the urge to rip the letter to pieces and fling it about the room, but then she stopped herself. No. She had to think this out before she did anything hasty. On second thoughts it might be as well to let Wilbert think he'd fooled her. That way she had one up on him.

She walked over to the wardrobe and replaced the letter exactly where she had found it. Then she began to remove any evidence of her search, systematically going over the room until it was exactly as it had been when she entered it.

Nora stood for a moment at Wilbert's window, looking down into the dark street. Christmas Eve had passed into Christmas Day an hour ago and the rest of the world was asleep, apart from her. Self-pity and resentment pulled her mouth into a thin line. Not a card or a gift in the house, and she'd be eating Christmas dinner alone. She just wished that daughter of hers was a bairn again so she could thrash her within an inch of her life like she'd used to: that'd teach her to turn everyone against her.

A sudden thought brought her eyes narrowing. She knew Audrey and the family had gone away for Christmas to Ivor's brother's widow because Maud Duffy on her sister's other side had taken great pleasure in telling her so, flaunting the fact she knew more about the family's goings-on than she did. But what if all that had been a tale Audrey knew Maud was sure to tell her? Aye, the more she thought about it, the more it all fitted into place. Abby had invited Audrey and her lot as well as Wilbert to the wedding, she would bet her life on it.

She wished she'd done something before Wilbert had gone now; she should have trusted her instincts that there was more to this reunion than met the eye. She'd always been able to smell a rat before it was stinking. And Ivor there with them all, no doubt enjoying himself and acting the cuddy for the benefit of all and sundry. She'd expected a blow-up when she'd told Abby Ivor was her da but as the months had gone on she'd realised it wasn't going to happen. Now it looked as though they were going to be one big happy family. So much for Abby worshipping Raymond. Little hypocrite.

Nora walked across the room, smoothing down the coverlet on Wilbert's bed before going downstairs to the warmth of the kitchen range. It had been icy upstairs, and now she stood holding out her cold hands to the heat before putting the kettle on to boil. She made a cup of tea and added a double measure of whisky to it, drinking it down almost in one go before pouring herself another, again with whisky. She'd go to first Mass and tell Father Finlay the latest. He understood what she had to suffer, did Father Finlay.

After the third whisky-fuelled cup of tea, she sat staring at the half-empty bottle. She was getting through a couple of these a week now, but then what else did she have in life to cheer her?

Maudlin tears began to fall as they did almost every night after she had drunk herself silly.

The little bit she earned was her own after all, she told herself fiercely. If she wanted to treat herself, why shouldn't she? This time she didn't bother adding tea to the cup.

Half an hour later her chin fell to her chest and loud snores began to fill the room, but even in sleep her fingers kept tight hold of the cup in her hand.

PART SEVEN

Completing the Circles

1955

Chapter Twenty-six

The tall slim woman who was standing looking out of her kitchen window at a blue March sky dotted with fluffy white clouds could have been any age between twenty and thirty. Few folk would have guessed she was in fact thirty-four years old. Abby did not have the faintest of lines on her face, her thick hair was still as rich and shiny as when she'd been in her teens, and her beauty – now matured to its full potential – was striking.

But the last ten years had not been easy, far from it. For the first five rationing had bit harder than ever, and the ferocious winter of 1947–8 had devastated the potato crop nationwide. In spite of all Abby's and the other women's efforts, their fledgling business had almost been finished before it had really begun, their losses substantial.

Ike, as one of the local GPs, had been run off his feet with thousands of cases of pneumonia, pleurisy and hypothermia, all of which had culled the old and very young more ruthlessly than ever Hitler's bombs had. Abby had no doubt that the eighteen- and nineteen-hour days Ike had put in at this time had contributed to the first of his three heart attacks some months later. The last one in June 1953 had occurred as they had watched Queen Elizabeth's Coronation in the home of one of Ike's doctor friends in Manchester – London, Birmingham, Cardiff, Manchester and Glasgow were the only cities where programmes could be received – and had been fatal. He had died in her arms; but for their two little boys, Abby would not have wanted to go on.

The children's noisy entrance now into the kitchen brought Abby turning from the window to say quickly, 'Ssh, darlings, you'll wake the baby.' She glanced at the dark-haired infant fast asleep in his pram in a corner of the room.

'I don't like the baby.' Henry, at just two and a half, put his thumb into his mouth and prepared for a sulk. John, from the lofty maturity of six years old, assured their mother, 'He does really, but Aunty Rowena always used to say Henry was her baby before Enrico came.'

Oh dear. Abby scooped Henry up in her arms, smiled at John and said, 'How about some lemonade and iced biscuits? Yes?' And at their delighted cries, she added, 'But only if you are as quiet as mice, all right? John, you get the plates and, Henry, can you get your and John's rabbit mugs?'

'Course I can, Mammy.' His normal sunniness restored, Henry grinned at her. She put him down and for a moment a miniature Ike was standing in front of her. It was amazing how like his father he was, whereas John had her fair hair and features. Abby tousled Henry's hair before he marched importantly away on chubby legs, his brow slightly wrinkled in concentration on the task entrusted to him.

When the boys were busy tucking into the iced biscuits and lemonade she had made that morning, Abby walked across to the window again and picked up the letter she had placed on the window-sill earlier. She had read it through a number of times since the postman had delivered it first thing but was no nearer a decision on the contents. Why had this come now? she asked herself, staring out at the pretty garden surrounded by a six-foot fence. Ike had put the fence up shortly after the extension had been completed a few months into their marriage, with the safety of their future children in mind. Since his untimely death it was only recently she had begun to feel herself again, she mused, her life having fallen into a comfortable and reassuringly predictable pattern.

Rowena had finally married Mario two summers before, the pair of them occupying one of the big double bedrooms in the original part of the smallholding. This left Gladys with her own room, and Winnie and Joy in the other. The week after Ike's heart attack Clara had insisted on moving into the extension to keep Abby company, and Abby hadn't protested too hard, needing her sister's love and support as she'd struggled to come to terms with her loss and look after a young child and nine-month-old baby.

But that had been two years ago. Now, with the business doing very well, her children healthy and happy and Clara still living with her, Abby was finally able to reflect on the sweetness of the eight years she'd spent with Ike and get comfort from them without breaking down. She missed him, and every day she mourned the fact that he wouldn't see his two boys grow up, but over the last few months she'd seen her life settle into a calm, familiar routine which was likely to go on without change into the future.

Her boys had their 'Grandma' Gladys to take care of them if she was occupied with business matters, Winnie was perfectly content being a mother and an active partner in the business, and now that little Enrico had arrived, Rowena and Mario declared themselves ecstatic. Even the niggling worry that had occupied Gladys for years had been settled just before Christmas. Vincent, who had been forced to sell up years ago and had moved away down south, had sent his mother a Christmas card with a letter enclosed in which he'd extended an olive branch which

Gladys had grasped with both hands. Life, it had seemed, was at last flowing in calm waters.

But now, with one letter, everything had changed. Wilbert had written to say Audrey had died suddenly. A brain haemorrhage, Wilbert's scrawl explained. She'd gone with no warning. Uncle Ivor had gone to pieces and Jed wasn't much better, so he and Leonard and Bruce were arranging the funeral. Lucy was going to put on a spread afterwards, and they all hoped she and Clara could come. He and Lucy sent their love as always.

She was a saint, that lass, Abby thought as her eyes scanned the page again. Her mother had done everything she could to split up Wilbert and Lucy, according to her brother, both before and after their marriage, which had been an elopement to prevent Nora spoiling everything at the last moment. How Lucy could stand living in the same house as her mother-in-law Abby didn't know, but her mother's emotional blackmail on Wilbert had been effective and when the pair had returned from Gretna Green, Lucy had moved into 12 Rose Street.

'We're back!'

Abby had been so deep in thought she hadn't heard Clara come in through the interconnecting door in the hall, and now she turned, the letter still in her hand.

'What's wrong?' Clara said immediately, which meant, Abby presumed, her face had given her away. 'What's that?' her sister added, pointing at Wilbert's letter. 'Bad news?'

Three questions in as many seconds. Typical Clara. From being a shy and retiring child she had blossomed into an exuberant and outgoing young woman who was amiable and sociable but did not suffer fools. In reply, Abby handed her the letter, watching her sister's pretty face as she absorbed the contents.

'Oh, poor Aunt Audrey.' Clara's voice expressed mild compassion but no real sorrow. They hadn't seen their aunt since she had visited when John was born, and although Abby had corresponded fairly regularly with Audrey, she was little more than a nice warm fixture of the past to Clara. Nevertheless, her sister now said, 'When are we going then? Are you taking the boys too?'

'I don't know if I'm going yet.' Abby took the letter back and folded it into its envelope.

'Not going?' Clara looked shocked. 'Of course we have to go, Abby. If you're worried about John and Henry, you know you can leave them here. Gladys is in her element when she has them all to herself.'

'Who's taking my name in vain?' Gladys, white-haired now but still as nimble as ever, poked an enquiring face round the door before walking fully into the room, ruffling the boys' hair as she passed them still munching away at the iced biscuits. Mario had driven Rowena into town to buy some new curtains for their room and Clara had gone along for the ride and to do some shopping, leaving Winnie, Joy and Gladys in charge of the nursery and any customers. 'Now you're back, Clara, I've come to tell you Winnie wants some help,' Gladys said meaningfully. She didn't hold with gallivanting off into town when there was no real need, even if it was Saturday.

'All right, all right,' Clara said lightly. 'I'd just come to take Enrico back, that's all, but Abby's had a letter to say our aunt's died and they want us to go to the funeral.'

'They've invited us to the funeral if we want to go,' Abby corrected.

'Same thing.' Clara walked across the room and took hold of the handle of the pram. 'Anyway, I wouldn't mind going back up to Sunderland, to see if things have changed from how I remember them and meeting everyone again,

367

even Mam.' There was a slight touch of defiance in her eyes as she glanced across at Abby. 'I can always go by myself if you don't want to come.' So saying she wheeled the pram out of the room and into the hall, manoeuvring it through the interconnecting door.

'Can we go and play in the garden, Mam?' John was lifting Henry down from the table as he spoke, ignoring his brother's protestations that he could do it himself.

'Put your coats and gloves on then.' Despite the sun there was a nip in the air which said winter hadn't quite relinquished its grip yet. 'And don't kick the ball over the fence because you won't be allowed to go and get it.' This last was for Henry's benefit. He had just discovered if the ball needed to be retrieved he could escape the confines of the garden for a while; the greenhouses and the comings and goings of customers fascinated him.

Once the children had gone outside, Gladys said, 'Got time for a cuppa?'

She hadn't really. By agreeing to take care of Enrico she hadn't managed to tackle the huge pile of ironing which had been mounting steadily for days while she had been tied up with getting the company books ready for their accountant to look at, but she nodded, saying, 'As long as you don't mind me ironing while we talk.'

When the ironing board was up and Gladys had made the tea, they talked of inconsequentials until Gladys suddenly said, 'You can't keep her from seeing your mam, you know. Sooner or later she'll want to put the past to bed.'

There was a long pause. Abby had been thinking of Audrey all morning since she'd got the letter – Audrey and her da who had been the two innocents in the whole miserable dirty tangle – and right at this moment she wanted to confide in someone more than she ever had. The words

368

were there but she couldn't get them out. Instead she shook her head, saying, 'My mam's sheer poison, Gladys, but there are other things I can't go into which make me feel I never want to set eyes on Sunderland again. But you're right, I don't want Clara seeing our mam.'

'She's not the wee child you rescued all those years ago, Abby. She's a young woman of twenty-two with a mind of her own, like her sister.' Gladys smiled wryly. 'Perhaps she needs to see that your mother is as terrible as she remembers, I don't know, but if she's made up her mind she's going, she'll go. What you've got to decide is whether you want her to go alone or not.'

'I don't.' It was sharp and definite. She couldn't do anything about what Clara had seen all those years ago, and that was bad enough for anyone to take on board. But hopefully she could protect her from knowing the rest of it.

'Then it looks like you'll be going to Sunderland.'

Abby put down the iron and the two women exchanged a glance at each other. 'You'll look after John and Henry? I don't want to take them.'

'Course I will. They'll be as happy as two bugs in a rug with me, you know that.'

Yes, she knew that. The original part of the house where the others lived was the boys' second home, and Gladys took care of them so often when she was working they wouldn't turn a hair.

'Thanks, Gladys.'

'Don't thank me, lass. It's what families are all about.'

'Not the family I come from.' There was deep bitterness in her voice.

Gladys finished her tea and rose to her feet. 'It might be good for you to lay a few ghosts too. You thought of that?'

'Nothing good will come out of this visit, Gladys. I can assure you of that.'

Gladys's eyebrows rose at the vehemence in Abby's tone but she didn't comment on it. 'Let me know the arrangements and we'll go from there. If you want to stay overnight that's fine by me.'

'We won't be staying over.' If Clara was determined to attend the funeral then she would accompany her in order to act as a buffer between her sister and their mother because, as sure as spring follows winter, she would need to. Their mother would try to hurt Clara or herself or both of them. Perhaps not physically because that time had gone, but in a more dangerous way – in their hearts and minds.

'See, I told you it would be all right.' Clara's whisper was full of satisfaction. 'And Wilbert and Lucy were so pleased to see us, weren't they?'

'Yes, they were.'

'And Lucy putting on a spread back at Mam's for everyone. She's such a sweetheart. But poor Uncle Ivor, he looks terrible. Ill. Still, they were married a long time, him and Aunty Audrey, and they always seemed so happy, didn't they?'

'Yes, they did.'

'But seeing Leonard and Bruce and their wives and families and Jed is lovely, or it would be if the circumstances were different.' Clara wrinkled her small nose. 'I didn't recognise them, did you? Well, I recognised Jed.' There was a brief pause. 'You didn't mind me saying we'd be happy to go back to the house, did you?'

Abby wanted to scream at Clara to stop talking. They had arrived in Bishopwearmouth just in time for the funeral service and then the burial. At the bleak, windswept cemetery she had glanced across at Ivor, standing gaunt and white-faced as he stared down at the coffin, and for a moment she had thought he was going to fling himself into the hole on top of the wooden box. That Wilbert and Lucy thought the same had been apparent when her brother and his wife had each taken one of Ivor's arms, moving him back a step or two and then continuing to hang on to him until he was safely returned to the funeral car some minutes later. Ivor's utter misery had disturbed Abby greatly. She wanted to hate him for what he had done to her father and her aunty, but faced with such total despair . . .

'Did you mind, Abby? About me saying we'd go back?'

'What? Oh no, I don't suppose so.' Abby drew in a long breath. In fact she minded very much. Her mother was at the house. Was she frightened of her? She considered the question as Clara talked on and the taxi took them towards Rose Street. Not of her mother, she decided, but the lengths to which she might go to hurt Clara. If her mother suspected she hadn't told Clara about Ivor being their father, she was more than capable of revealing it if she thought it would wound her youngest child. But then Wilbert would know. Abby turned and gazed blindly out of the window. Her mother wouldn't want that. She relied on Wilbert for a roof over her head and if he found out she had been lying to him all these years, that he was in effect a bastard, the illegitimate offspring of the man he'd always looked on as an uncle . . . Oh, she didn't know what was going to happen. How could she predict what someone as nasty as her mother might do? But she dreaded seeing her again.

When the taxi pulled up outside the house, Clara became silent for the first time since they had left the cemetery. It was drizzling and the sky hung heavy over the rooftops. This, combined with the ominously drawn curtains of the two houses and those of their neighbours, added to the sense of foreboding as the two women stepped out of the vehicle.

After Abby had paid the driver, she and Clara stood together on the wet pavement, neither of them making a move to their old front door. It was only when Wilbert and Lucy appeared in the first of the two funeral cars with Leonard and his family that the women walked across the pavement and stood outside the house. Ivor, Jed and Bruce and his wife and child were in the second car, and as that drew up Wilbert opened the front door and ushered his sisters into the hall.

'Go on through, you know the way.' Wilbert was trying to make light of the moment as he took Clara's arm and led her to the kitchen, but Lucy hung behind, catching hold of Abby and drawing her aside as first Ivor and his sons, and then friends and neighbours filed into the house.

'I just wanted to tell you that Wilbert's told his mam to behave today if she comes down,' Lucy said in a low voice. 'She didn't want to come to the church, said her legs are playing her up, but my guess is that she feels awkward because her and Aunty Audrey haven't spoken for years. Anyway, she took to her bed yesterday and made noises about feeling ill this morning.'

'Did she know Clara and I were coming?'

Lucy nodded. 'But like I said, Wilbert's given her a talking to so I don't think there'll be any trouble.'

Abby didn't comment on this. She could have said that if her mother wanted to play up, no power on earth would stop her, least of all her own son whom she'd always manipulated since he was a bairn.

Abby could see that the house was different to how she remembered it. Lucy had certainly put her own ideas and stamp on the place. This surprised her. Lucy seemed such a meek and mild little creature and she knew changes wouldn't have been wrought without fierce protest from her mother, but she felt it boded well. Wilbert was paying the rent and had been doing so for the last eight years since her mother had given up her part-time work, so maybe he and Lucy felt they could be more assertive.

The hall was now painted a light cream colour and there was red carpet on the floor and up the stairs, which immediately gave a welcoming feel. The door to the front room was open and it was filled with various people chatting away, but again Abby could see that her mother's holy of holies bore no resemblance to the room she remembered from her childhood. The multi-coloured carpet and pale walls made it look bigger, and her mother's stiff horsehair suite had been replaced with a red velvet one. Lucy obviously liked red but then she'd need its cheerfulness living with her mother, Abby thought wryly.

'Come through to the kitchen.' Lucy ushered her forward and here Abby received her biggest surprise. The old kitchen had been gutted and in its place was a room which boasted wall and floor cupboards with a worktop running along two walls, bright lino on the floor and a smart new kitchen table and chairs. The table was groaning with food and so were the worktops. The draining boards either side of the sink held bottles of sherry, whisky, port and beer.

All this Abby took in with a fleeting glance before she turned to Lucy and said warmly, 'This is lovely, everything is lovely. You've transformed the place.'

Lucy blushed her pleasure at the praise. She whispered confidingly, 'Don't tell your mother because she thinks we still rent it but we're buying it. The landlord wanted to sell a few years ago now and so we decided to take a mortgage. I've been earning good money at Ramshaw and Sons, the accountants I work for, so we said we'd put off having a family for a while and get the house round first. Wilbert's wage only really covers the mortgage and bills and food, you see. But Wilbert didn't want his mam knowing all our ins and outs so we've kept it quiet.'

Abby nodded. That she could understand. She glanced across to where Clara was standing talking to Jed, a glass of sherry in her hand, before her gaze moved to Ivor who was sitting in a corner of the kitchen. He had Bruce, Bruce's wife and their little boy around him, and Leonard was standing at the back of his father's chair, his hand resting protectively on Ivor's shoulder.

Lucy followed the direction of her eyes. 'He's inconsolable,' she said quietly. 'We've had such a time with him. Everyone's been worried to death. I've been taking an evening meal into him and Jed because he won't come in to us, although I know Jed would prefer that. But when they get home from work he just sits in those four walls, won't even go down the pub with Jed for a pint like he used to before Aunt Audrey died. Leonard and Bruce have been good too, trying to get him out of himself a bit. They think the world of their da, like Jed does.'

'Everyone's rallied round then.'

Lucy heard the bitter note in her voice and looked at her in surprise. 'Of course they have, it's only natural, isn't it?'

Abby warned herself to tread carefully. All she needed to do was get through this day and then she could go home.

'I think he'd come in to us if your mam wasn't here,' Lucy continued. 'Wilbert said they've never got on, Uncle Ivor and your mam, not even before your mam and Aunt Audrey had the big falling out. Do you know what that was over?'

The question took Abby aback although she perhaps

374

should have expected it. She was about to murmur something noncommittal when Lucy's gaze went behind her and she said, 'Oh hello, Mam. I wondered if you were going to come down.'

'Did you indeed.'

Her voice was just the same. Abby knew she ought to turn and say something but her blood had frozen.

'Wondered so much you came and asked, eh? I could have been dead up there for all anyone cared and me with my legs so bad. So, how did it go then?'

'All right.' Lucy hesitated. It was clear her mother-in-law had no idea it was Abby's back she was facing and she didn't quite know how to handle the situation.

She was relieved when Abby slowly turned round, her face devoid of expression. 'Hello, Mam.'

Nora's shock was evident. She had seen that Lucy was talking to someone who was dressed exceedingly well, the charcoal and black suit the woman was wearing shouting class and the black hat which came low into the neck a beautiful bit of work. She had assumed it was perhaps Ivor's boss's wife. Now she found herself staring into the face of the daughter she had never liked and in latter years had come to resent with an enmity which outstripped even what she'd felt for Audrey.

Abby, too, was astounded but for a different reason. In her childhood all her friends had envied her because her mother was beautiful, and in her forties and fifties Nora had retained an attractiveness which her sullen expression and harping couldn't diminish. Even on her last visit to this house eleven years ago her mother had still been presentable. But the woman she was staring at now looked at least ten years older than her sixty-four years, and that was being generous, but more shockingly there was no vestige of the handsome woman she had once been in the shrunken figure glaring at her. Her mother was recognisable, but in the way that a cruel caricature is.

No trace of what Abby was thinking showed in her expression, but as Nora stared at her daughter's smooth skin and lovely face, Abby's youth and beauty were like an insult. Her wrath was visible and Abby braced herself for what was going to come, but then she felt someone take her arm and turn her round. Ivor faced her.

'I want a word, lass,' he said, his tone flat. 'In private. We'll take a stroll in the back lane, Lucy,' he added to Wilbert's wife who had been watching the interplay with increasing agitation.

'I don't want to leave Clara in here,' Abby muttered as Ivor walked with her to the back door. 'My mam might go for her, the mood she's in.'

'It's not Clara she's gunning for and the lass is all right with Jed for a minute or two. You'll do better letting your mam calm down for a while.'

Abby could see some sense in this and so she opened the back door and stepped into what was now a pristine backyard, continuing into the back lane before she turned and faced Ivor. 'What do you want to say?' she asked directly.

He stared at her. 'My Audrey died thinking the one thing we had between us which no one else had was our boys,' he said heavily. 'And for that I'm grateful. But you're my daughter. I'm not proud of the way you came into being but I'm proud of the end product, so to speak. Aw,' he shook his head, 'this sounds like a load of blather even to me. Look, your da was a grand man and I wronged him. I'm heart sorry for that.'

'I don't understand why,' said Abby as they began to walk along the dreary back lane, the wind whipping at her legs. 'Why my mother when you had someone like Aunty Audrey?'

376

Ivor, his head deep on his chest, said, 'Because I was a fool, lass. That's it in a nutshell.'

Seconds passed before she said, 'Mam . . . she looks awful.'

'She drinks.'

'Drinks?'

'Aye, when she can get it which isn't so often now. But they've had a time with her, young Wilbert and Lucy. She's a devil, Abby, but then you know that.' He stopped and leaned against the brick wall. 'I'm mourning my Audrey to the point of doing away with meself but there's another part of me that's glad she's gone. Because of your mam, you understand. Because of what she might have said or done.'

Abby couldn't make any comment to this. After a few moments she said, 'We ought to go back.'

'Aye.' And then as though to refute this he suddenly straightened, his eyes tight on her as he said, 'I didn't know, about you and Wilbert and Clara. Do you believe that?'

Did she? She wasn't sure.

'I promise you, lass, I didn't know. If there was some way I could make amends . . .' He wiped each side of his mouth with his fingers, swallowing hard before he repeated, 'I didn't know.'

'It doesn't make any difference now,' said Abby dully, turning as she spoke and beginning to retrace her footsteps. She shouldn't have come. She had known that all along, hadn't she? She didn't want to feel sorry for Ivor, not after what he had done to her da. But this man beside her, he was her da. No, no he wasn't. Not in the things that counted.

Abby had barely stepped into what used to be the scullery but was now part of the kitchen when her mother confronted her. Nora had clearly been waiting for them. Her voice was low but vicious when she said, 'You. You're not back two minutes and you're causing trouble.'

'*Mam.*' Wilbert was near enough to hear and his voice carried a warning but nothing was going to stop Nora now. Her daughter's fine clothes, the air of unconscious affluence and poise and, the final insult, Ivor's championing of Abby had infuriated Nora beyond reason. 'It was always the same but the men can't see it, not where you're concerned. Butter wouldn't melt, would it?'

'This is your sister's funeral.' Abby's voice was icy cold. 'After all you've done, the least you can do is to show her respect.'

'Don't you preach at me, girl. Not you!'

Nora's voice had risen and Abby was aware of the deathly hush which had fallen over the proceedings. She caught sight of Clara's horrified face and knew her main priority now was to stop her mother blurting out the truth about their paternity. With this in mind and in order not to rile their mother any further, she turned, meaning to exit the way she had just come, but Nora caught her arm. 'Think you've been so clever, don't you, with your airs and graces. Think you've got one over on me but I've had the last laugh. You hear me?'

'I think everyone can hear you,' Abby said.

Wilbert was trying to pull his mother out of the room but Nora resisted, her voice all the louder as she said, 'I cooked your goose, girl. I told him you'd married someone else. What do you think about that? You ever think about James Benson? Wonder where he's lying on foreign soil? Well, he's alive an' well and with a high-class wife an' all. Someone of his own sort.'

'What did you say?' Abby motioned to Wilbert to let Nora stay.

'You heard me.'

'He came to see you? James came to the house?'

'Aye, sniffing about as soon as he was back but I sent him away with a flea in his ear.' Nora was triumphant in her fury. 'First his father and then him, and both as thick as two short planks. Nineteen forty-three it was, or forty-two, I don't remember, but I told him.'

Abby stared at her mother. James had come for her. When he had come back from the war he had come for her and her mother had told him she was married. It was unbelievable that someone could do such a thing. But then her mother was capable of anything. She had always known that.

Wilbert was staring aghast at the woman still in his grasp and behind her Abby could hear Ivor cursing. Apart from this the room was utterly silent, all eyes trained on Abby and her mother. Nora was quite still now, her eyes fastened on Abby. Unconsciously Abby drew herself up, her expression carrying scorn and distaste in equal measure and her voice quiet and strangely without a tremor as she said, 'I had eight wonderful years with the kindest, best man in the world and I have two healthy and happy sons. I am content, Mother. Whatever you sought to do, it failed.'

She saw the words register in her mother's change of expression but didn't wait for the outburst she knew would follow. Signalling with her head to Clara she said, 'Come on, we're leaving.'

There was a commotion behind her but she didn't pause, and then she was outside in the street, almost falling down the step in her haste to get away.

She walked a few paces before she leaned against the wall of a neighbour's house and closed her eyes, breathing in deeply in an effort to combat the giddiness in her head. Clara clutched her arm, her voice shaking as she said,

'Abby, oh Abby, I can't believe it. How could she have done such a thing? You were right, we should never have come. I'm sorry, I'm so sorry.'

'It's all right.' She opened her eyes as she spoke and saw Jed was beside them, his young face anxious as he hovered in the way all males do when they don't know how to handle an emotional situation. And then Lucy came running out of the house after them, and again Abby said, 'It's all right.' Wilbert's wife was obviously very upset.

'Abby, I'm so sorry about all of this, she's a dreadful woman.' Lucy glanced back to the open front door as the noise within the house rose. 'Do you think she really saw James Benson and told him you were married?'

Abby nodded. She found she wanted to get as far away from Rose Street as she could. James, oh James. What must he have thought of her? How would he have felt, after all he must have been through? She'd heard of other men wrongly reported killed in action when in fact they had been either badly wounded or captured.

'It's just that . . .' Lucy paused, as if unsure whether she should continue. Then she said all in a rush, 'I work for an accountant, as you know, and there are get-togethers, seminars and things where they all meet up and chat and that. Most of them belong to the Gentlemen's Club . . .' She shook her head at herself. 'You don't want to know about the Gentlemen's Club. What I'm trying to say is that James left his father-in-law's firm at the same time he got divorced. It was something of a major scandal in those circles at the time.'

Abby stared at Wilbert's wife. 'James isn't married any more?'

'No.' Lucy didn't mention here that if half the rumours were true, James Benson was doing very nicely with the ladies without being constrained by the bonds of matrimony.

'Do you know where he works?'

Lucy and Clara both looked taken aback, and it was Clara who said, 'Where he works? What do you want to know that for? You're not planning to go and see him, are you? Not today?'

'I can't go home until I do. I . . . I owe him that at least. We were *engaged*, Clara.' She thought of the little bonfire she had made the day after she and Ike had returned home after their marriage. The chocolate box, photograph and letters had burned to ash in seconds. She hadn't known quite what to do with the brooch and watch he'd given her, and the engagement ring. In the end she had decided that out of sight was out of mind and had put them in a box which she had stuffed under the eaves, telling herself she had to forget about it. And she had. Mostly.

'James has his own business now.' Lucy's voice was hesitant and Abby had the feeling she was regretting saying anything. 'Just a small place in Holmeside, but Mr Ramshaw thinks very highly of him. He's even put one or two clients Mr Benson's way, folk who were more suited to a small practice. I'm not quite sure of the number of the building but I know it's close to the Regal, and it's above Winterspoon, the jewellers.'

'I'll find it, and,' Abby patted Lucy's arm, 'thanks, lass.'

'I don't think this is a very good idea.' Clara was looking anxious.

'Good idea or not, I'm going,' said Abby, forcing a smile to soften her words.

Clara recognised defeat. 'I'm coming in with you then.'

'You are not! This is something I have to do by myself. Anyway, he may not even be in this afternoon.'

'There's another thing, Abby,' Lucy said. 'There was

381

an accident a few years ago, a car accident. Both his parents died.'

Abby stared at her aghast.

Jed broke the silence. 'I'll take you both in my car if you like. Clara can wait with me while you see Mr Benson.'

Abby smiled her thanks as Clara said animatedly, 'You have your own car, Jed?' Clearly he had gone up a notch or two in her estimation.

'Aye, Morris Minor.' Jed tried unsuccessfully to appear offhand about his pride and joy. 'She's one of the first models so she's getting on a bit, but she drives well. Me an' Da did a bit of work to her when I got her last year, and we all used to go for a run in the country on a Sunday afternoon, me, Da and . . . and Mam.' Jed's face changed on the last word and for an awful moment the three women thought he was going to cry, but after swallowing hard he turned away. His voice thick, he said, 'I had to move her up the road a bit this morning with the funeral cars coming but come and have a look if you want.'

'You go, Clara. I'll be with you in a minute.' Abby pushed Clara after Jed and turned back to Lucy. 'Jed will tell you how we get on,' she said quickly, 'but Clara and I won't come back again to the house. Give Wilbert my love and tell him I'll write soon. I'm sorry about all this, lass, with you having worked so hard to put a good spread on and everything.'

'It wasn't your fault, Abby, it was your mam's. She's a perfectly horrible old woman. It just amazes me that you and Clara and Wilbert are so lovely. You must take after your da.'

Abby forced a smile. 'He was a grand man,' she said softly.

'I don't know how much longer I can stand her, to be

truthful, but Wilbert won't see her put in a home. And it's not as if he even likes her.'

'I don't think any of us ever have.'

The two women looked at each other, pity for the other's plight in their faces. After hugging Lucy, Abby turned and walked to where Clara and Jed were waiting by the car.

Chapter Twenty-seven

James Benson leaned back in his comfortable leather chair and stretched his legs. He glanced at his gold wristwatch. It was getting on for four. Damn it, where had most of the afternoon gone? It didn't seem a minute or two since he'd sat down after lunch and started work again. He still had a couple of urgent matters which needed prompt attention; tonight would be another occasion when he wasn't home till eight or nine o'clock. But he couldn't complain, not when the business was doing so well and he was looking to hire another junior accountant within the month.

He'd decided to branch out by himself at just the right time, he thought, his mind flicking back over the last years. The postwar housing crisis had produced a host of enterprising private contractors keen to satisfy the demand for houses, and new homes needed new furniture, which in turn saw fresh modern firms springing up to meet the need. It was all good business for him. He nodded to himself. One thing everyone who was starting out needed was an honest, reliable accountant who wouldn't charge too much but would do a good job. He was building his name with such folk and it was proving lucrative.

He rose to his feet to relieve the touch of cramp his gammy left leg was disposed to, automatically flexing his left arm as he did so. He could manage to hold a fork or other light objects with his left hand now and to all intents and purposes appeared fine to a casual observer, but the arm would take no weight of any consequence and his fingers were still inclined to be stiff and cumbersome first thing every morning. But this was a small price to pay for still being alive.

He walked round the large mahogany desk that dominated the room, the available space made narrow by filing cabinets along one wall. He peered through the glass panel above the four-foot partition wall and looked into the outer office. His young assistant who had yet to take his accountancy examinations had his head down and was working hard, but his secretary was on the telephone. She caught his eye and smiled. 'Time for a cuppa?' she mouthed, to which he replied with a thumbs up before returning to his desk. Instead of immediately taking his seat he stood looking down into the busy street below for a moment or two.

A good part of the view was obscured by the awnings stretching out in front of shop windows, and as always James found himself clucking in irritation. He could understand the need for the sheets of canvas on hot sunny days when they provided welcome shade for shoppers and protection for some of the consumable goods on show, but a drop of rain never hurt anyone and it had only been drizzling all day. Then he caught himself, shaking his head slightly as he continued to stare down into the street. He'd promised himself he wouldn't carp on about such trivialities only yesterday and here he was doing it again. He'd turn into a cranky old man long before he should if he didn't take himself in hand. He refused to acknowledge here that his whole life was an irritation for a good part of the time. To do so would mean digging deep to the cause of his dissatisfaction and that was forbidden territory.

A car stopped just in front of the jewellers above which James rented his three rooms, the third being divided into a tiny kitchen and separate cloakroom with a toilet and washbasin. His gaze idly followed the young man who leaped out of the vehicle and folded his seat forward to allow his passenger in the back to alight. It was a sombrely but well-dressed woman, the sort of client the jewellers were used to. Just before the woman crossed the pavement to the shop, she glanced upwards and he caught a fleeting glimpse of the face the dark hat had been hiding.

He took a sharp step backwards as something like a blow in the solar plexus hit him. The breath left his body in a whoosh of shock and he sat down heavily in his chair. For a moment he was quite still. Then he wiped his hand across his mouth, angry to see it was shaking slightly. Damn it, but the woman had reminded him of Abby so strongly. He stood up again and peered cautiously through the window. The car was still there but the woman was nowhere to be seen.

He raked his hair back from his brow, more shaken than he would care to admit. He wasn't going to start the old trouble again, was he? Seeing her in every woman's face, hearing her voice at odd moments and, at his worst, actually watching her walk towards him and reaching out to her, only to find there was nothing and no one there. The doctors had assured him eleven years ago when he was recovering from his breakdown that his mind wouldn't play such tricks on him again, and he didn't think he could stand it if it did. But no, he was running away with himself here. He forced himself to sit down and pick up his pen. People the whole world over were reminded of other people they knew in strangers' faces. It was natural, normal. It happened. It didn't mean a thing. And he had work to do.

As he ran his eyes over the row of figures in front of him he heard the door to the outer office give its customary loud creak which was better than any bell, and then the

386

sound of voices. Sitting as he was now he couldn't see out through the glass panel, but he had a four o'clock appointment and assumed it was old Fairley arrived early. On his desk were Fairley's company books, tied up and waiting for him. The old man had a tiny locksmith's business involving just him and his son, but as he was barely literate and his son wasn't any better, bookkeeping was beyond them. Fairley was one of what Mrs Howard, his secretary, called his 'wing and a prayer' cases because he charged them only a tiny fee and ended up doing more work than was financially sensible. But he liked the oldtimer and his son very much and had plenty of cases which did bring in the bread and butter, not that Mrs Howard accepted this as a reason to work for next to nothing.

The very able lady in question now knocked on his door and opened it. James waited for her to announce Mr Fairley – she always gave him his full title even though she strongly disapproved of him. Instead she came into the room and closed the door behind her, her voice low as she said, 'I'm sorry, Mr Benson, but there's a lady who wishes to see you. I've explained you have an appointment at four o'clock but she, well, she's most persistent.'

'A lady?'

'A Mrs Wilmot.'

He wrinkled his brow. 'To my knowledge I know no one of that name.' And to the tiny question mark in his mind and his churning stomach he said silently, It's impossible. Quite impossible.

'Do you want me to tell her to come back another time? To make an appointment?'

'No, no.' He checked his watch. 'Tell her I can give her ten minutes but that's all. If that won't do she would be better making an appointment as you've suggested.'

The door hadn't closed behind Mrs Howard above a

second when it opened again, and now, as his secretary stood aside and the woman he had seen in the street came into his office, James remained perfectly still. Even before she raised her head so he could see more than just her lower face, he knew it was Abby. His gaze was riveted. She was even more beautiful than he remembered. And she was another man's wife.

Somehow he managed to rise and say quite normally, 'Hello, Abby. It's been a long time.' And then, before his secretary shut the door, 'I was just going to have a cup of tea. Would you care to join me?'

'Thank you.'

'Two cups then please, Mrs Howard. Come and sit down, Abby.'

She remained standing when the door had closed, her eyes enormous and her face pale. He looked so like his father. Older, more rugged than in his youth but just as handsome. 'I'm . . . I'm sorry about your parents, James.' It wasn't how she had meant to start at all.

'Thank you.' He became aware he was staring and cleared his throat, indicating the seat in front of the desk with a wave of his hand. 'Do sit down and tell me what I can do for you. I presume it wasn't just to offer your condolences about my parents that brought you here?'

'No.' She sat, swallowed, and then found herself unable to continue.

James made a small movement with his head, his eyebrows raised as he prompted her. It was only then that Abby managed to say in little more than a whisper, 'I don't know where to start.'

'Are you in some kind of financial trouble? I'll try to help you if I can.'

He was so distant, so correct. She hadn't known what to expect but this wasn't it. *He didn't love her any more.*

But of course he didn't love her any more, she hadn't expected him to, had she? Not after fifteen years and with him having married and divorced and probably had other women since then. And he thought she'd betrayed him, fallen in love and married someone else long before the war ended. No, of course she hadn't expected he would still care.

But she had. Because she still loved him.

With a quick drooping movement of her head she said, 'I'm not in trouble, not in the way you mean, but this afternoon I found out that my mother had lied to you when you returned from the war. It was my aunty's funeral today and I came back' – here the nerves which had caused a huge lump in her throat overcame her and she had to swallow twice before she could go on – 'I came back to pay my respects. There . . . there was a row and she told me, my mother told me she'd said I was married when you called at the house.'

'You did marry, you're Mrs Wilmot.'

'That was much later.' She hadn't raised her head. 'He was a doctor, an American doctor and we didn't marry till the war was over. I . . . I thought you were dead, you see.'

There was utter silence in the room now and Abby didn't dare look at him, dreading what might be on his face. Disinterest? Puzzlement at why she had bothered to come even if what she said was true? Worse, pity or embarrassment that she thought it might matter to him now? She shouldn't have come, she was such a fool. She should have written, phoned – anything but this. What should she do now? She didn't know.

And then he made a sound, a tiny sound in his throat and she raised her head and saw the look on his face. Suddenly it was the easiest thing in the world to say, 'I'm sorry, James. I'm so, so sorry. I never knew. I never knew.'

389

He bent forward, his elbows on the desk as he held his face in his hands, and when the door opened and Mrs Howard took a step into the room with the tray of tea, Abby turned and said, 'I'm sorry, could you give us a minute or two?' She wiped the tears from her face with the back of her hand as she spoke. For a second she thought the woman was going to protest but then she put the tray down on a table just inside the door and backed out, shutting the door behind her.

Abby didn't realise James was crying until she saw the tears run through his fingers onto the papers beneath, and then it seemed the most natural thing in the world to walk round the desk and gather him against her. He jerked away from her, visibly pulling himself together. He rose and put a few feet between them, standing with his back towards her as he wiped his face with a handkerchief. 'Your husband?' His voice was cracked and thick. 'Does he know you are here today?'

'Ike's dead.' She saw the words register in the stiffening of his back. 'He died two years ago. A heart attack.'

It was a moment before he turned and then he said, 'I'm sorry. And I'm sorry for reacting like this, what must you think of me? It's the shock. All those years . . .'

'I know.' She was looking into his eyes and she knew she was trembling. 'I heard you came home and married someone else. I thought you'd decided we'd made a mistake and you'd fallen in love with this girl—'

'I've only ever loved one woman, Abby.' He made no move towards her. 'And the marriage was a disaster from day one. Hell!' Anger stirred, sharpening his voice. 'I should never have believed your mother, I wouldn't have if I'd been in my right mind but I was ill, how ill I didn't realise till much later. And she was convincing.'

'I'm sorry,' she said again.

'And you found out today she had lied?' His eyes were moving from one feature of her face to another. 'And you came straight here?'

There was a question in the words which had nothing to do with what he'd asked. It was to this she replied when she said, 'Of course I did, what else could I have done?'

'And if your husband had still been alive? Would you have come then?'

Again it was a question within a question and this time Abby paused. Then she said simply, 'I loved Ike.' She watched him blink. 'I wouldn't have married him otherwise. It wasn't the same as with us but it was good.'

He didn't like the jealousy he felt towards a dead man but he managed to cover it when he said, a little tersely, 'You were happy then?'

'Yes, we were happy.'

He should say he was glad but he wasn't. What kind of a man did that make him? Almost certainly less of a man than this husband of hers had been. 'Bairns?'

'Two boys. The youngest was only a few months old when Ike died.'

This time he could say and mean it, 'I'm sorry, that must have been a bitter blow for you but at least he saw them before he went.'

She nodded. 'Aye, yes he did.' She had thought it was going to be all right a minute ago but now, since the talk about Ike, she wasn't sure. But then what did she mean by all right? She heard herself saying, 'I'll get the tray, shall I?'

'No, no, let me.'

She watched him as he walked across the room, noticing the slight limp with a rapid beating of her heart. She hadn't known if he'd survived the war intact but he seemed fine apart from the limp. He was one of the lucky ones. But then he'd spoken of being more ill than he'd realised. What had that been about?

James lifted the tray with his right hand, steadying it with his weak one but the contents weren't equally balanced and as the small plate of biscuits beside the cups, sugar bowl and milk jug began to slide, he made a hasty effort to tilt the tray upwards. The extra weight made his left arm give way completely and the result was disastrous as the whole lot crashed to the floor. Tea and milk mingled with broken biscuits and sugar lumps, along with a few choice words from James. As Abby rushed to help, embarrassment at his inadequacy made his voice a bark as he said, 'Leave it, leave it. It doesn't matter.'

He repeated this when Mrs Howard flung open the door. As she stood hesitating on the threshold, saying, 'The carpet, Mr Benson, the carpet,' he growled something distinctly rude about the carpet which caused Mrs Howard to turn pink and close the door very quickly, deciding it wasn't the moment to announce Mr Fairley had arrived.

'James?' Abby's touch on his arm was tentative. There was a second when she thought he was going to brush her away but then he turned, his arms going round her and his mouth taking hers in a kiss which took her breath away. Even in the emotion of the moment she was conscious that only one arm was really pressing her to him and the rush of feeling this caused was painful.

When eventually his grip lessened they were both trembling, and his voice was gruff as he murmured, 'I'm sorry, I'm sorry. A bull in a china shop, that's me. Abby, you're not going to go out of my life again?'

She looked into his blue, blue eyes, the eyes of her love, and said, 'Not if you don't want me to.'

'What I want—' He stopped, shutting his eyes for a moment before shaking his head, saying, 'I'll tell you what

392

I want but not here. Can we go somewhere? Who is that waiting for you in the car?'

'You saw me?' said Abby, surprised.

'I didn't know it was you then.' His eyes were roaming over her face, drinking in each feature as though he had to memorise them.

'It's my aunt's youngest boy and Clara.' With this came a return to reality.

He must have seen something in her face because now he said, 'What is it? What's wrong?'

'James, I have to get the train back home soon. I only came up for the day for Aunt Audrey's funeral.' This was happening too quickly; she felt light-headed, dizzy.

'Send Clara home,' he said urgently. 'Tell them you'll go back tomorrow.'

'I can't. There's my boys. They'll be waiting for me.'

He didn't make it hard for her. 'Your boys, of course, how silly of me. I wasn't thinking . . . I'm not used to children.' His left hand moved up to stroke the silky skin of her face. 'Can we just go somewhere for a coffee then? You can tell Clara to meet you at the train station, can't you?'

Could she? Of course she could. If they were going to have any chance at all they needed to talk now, to put things right so there were no more misunderstandings between them. She had to make it clear how important the boys were in her life, that she had responsibilities, ties. She was no longer the carefree girl he remembered, any more than he was the fresh young soldier who had left her so confidently all those years ago. But he was still her James. The other part of her. Whatever happened, she was sure about that.

'I'll go down and tell Clara, shall I,' she said softly, 'while you explain to your secretary?'

'No way.' He let go of her just long enough to tuck her arm through his. 'I'm not yet convinced you're not going to vanish in a puff of smoke or that all this isn't a dream.'

She knew exactly how he felt because she felt the same.

Chapter Twenty-eight

From the moment that Abby arrived back in Yorkshire, still with a slightly dazed look in her eyes, things at the smallholding began to change. Some changes were barely perceptible. Only Clara really noticed that Abby was always singing as she went about her work these days, and that her sister was subtly but very definitely delegating more tasks to the others. Abby was encouraging both Winnie and Rowena to cultivate a working knowledge of the way the company books were drawn up, despite the two women's protests that such matters weren't their forte, and she was no longer the one who always dealt with awkward customers or complicated orders.

Other changes were far more apparent. Every other weekend James would arrive at the smallholding late on Friday night and leave first thing Monday morning. On the weekends he didn't come down to Yorkshire, Abby and the boys went to stay in a small hotel in Holmeside, close to where James's flat was situated in a converted house in St George's Square, overlooking Mowbray Park. After some initial shyness, both boys took to James. When a warm spring and short-sleeved shirts laid bare the savage scars on James's left arm, John in particular was deeply affected, asking searching questions about the war. Abby noticed a deepening in John's affection for James from this point on and this was a great relief. Henry had never really known his father but John had been very much Daddy's boy, and she had been worried he would not accept another man into their small family unit. That her fears were totally unfounded was the icing on the cake.

Clara often accompanied her to Sunderland on the weekends she visited James, but although her sister stayed at the same hotel, Abby saw little of her. Clara and Lucy had struck up a strong friendship and the two young women frequently met up to have lunch out together, usually followed by shopping or a visit to the cinema. Clara was a regular visitor to both Leonard and Bruce's family homes too, where she was made a great fuss of, and she called in to see Ivor and Jed regularly.

Abby felt great misgivings about the renewed contact with their family but in the circumstances she felt she could do nothing to stop Clara seeing everyone. Her sister was a grown woman who, having in a sense 'found' her relatives once more, was determined not to let the contact cease again, whatever Abby said.

Abby's one comfort lay in the knowledge that Clara had no wish to see their mother. Her sister never set foot in Wilbert's home, always meeting her brother and Lucy away from the house and its eldest occupant, and for this Abby was grateful. She felt a profound sense of unease whenever her mother came to mind, and it had increased rather than diminished over the last months. Ivor had said her mother was only interested in hurting her, and Abby believed this, but Clara was very dear to her as Nora well knew and therefore she felt her sister was vulnerable.

'Darling, I know she's a dreadful woman, but what can she do now?' James asked when Abby shared her fears for Clara with him. 'Wilbert himself has told you he's warned your mother to toe the line or else she'll find herself without a roof over her head. She's a nasty piece of work, I'll give you that, but she is not stupid and she won't risk losing her home for the sake of an act of spite against Clara. She's done her worst and she can't hurt either of you now. She has lost and she knows it. We're together,' he took her in his arms, kissing her long and hard to prove it, 'and nothing will ever separate us again. That's all that matters.'

Abby smiled, reaching up and stroking back the errant lock of hair which always fell over his brow. For once they were alone in James's flat, Clara and Lucy having taken the children to an afternoon matinee at the Ritz. The boys hadn't been to a cinema before and this one, fitted out as it was with lavish chandeliers and deep-pile carpets, was sure to fill even Henry with awe. 'I love you,' she said softly. 'I can hardly believe three whole months have gone by since that day in your office. I have nightmares sometimes, wondering if we would ever have found each other again if Aunty Audrey hadn't died.'

Tony Bennett's latest hit, 'Stranger in Paradise', was playing on the wireless, and James said, 'Stranger in paradise sums it up, doesn't it? That's just how I feel. But I want more, Abby. I know we've done this before but,' he slid off the sofa onto his knees and took her hand in his, 'will you marry me, darling? I've been patient, I've waited like you asked but I'm fairly sure I've won the boys over as well as their mother.'

'You know you have.' She flung her arms round his neck, overbalancing him so they both rolled onto the carpet, limbs entwined. And like that, with their faces almost touching, she said, 'I'd love to marry you, James, and thank you very much for asking me – again.'

'My pleasure.' He grinned at her, his expression changing as his eyes fell on her lips . . .

Some time later when they were sitting on the sofa again, a celebratory glass of wine in their hands, James said, 'It won't be a long engagement, you know that, don't you? In

397

fact,' he drew a piece of paper out of his pocket, 'this special licence says it can be next week if you like.'

'Next week?' Her eyes were wide. 'But there are a hundred and one things to sort out. Where we're going to live, the boys' schooling, your business, my business—'

'It was simpler last time.' Again he was grinning.

She fell against him and as he removed the glass of wine from her hand and placed it with his on the side table, she thought for a moment that such happiness could only come to few people. And then his lips were on hers and she ceased to think.

They were dishevelled and flushed some minutes later when James pulled away and sat up abruptly.

'What is it, what's wrong?' she asked. He shook his head and rose to his feet.

He looked down at her as she shakily fastened the buttons on her blouse. 'Don't look like that, you know I want to,' he said very quietly. 'But I want it to be different with you. The others,' he pulled a face, 'well, let's just say I didn't have to wait with any of them. With you I've waited eighteen years and I want us to be able to look back and know we've done it all properly. I . . . I want our wedding night to be special.'

'Oh James.' She didn't know quite what to say. Part of her was still slightly offended that he hadn't taken what she'd made clear she was offering, but the expression on his face melted her. She knew he'd had lots of women – he hadn't wanted any secrets between them, any more than she had – but Abby believed him when he said none of them had touched his heart. 'It will be special,' she said, standing up and moving into his arms. 'Very special.'

'Will you . . .' He stopped.

'Yes? Go on.'

He took a deep breath. 'Can I buy you an engagement ring?'

She knew what he was asking. She still had Ike's engagement ring and her wedding ring on her finger. 'There's no need,' she said softly. She reached down and picked up her handbag. She opened it and slid the zip on the little pocket which held her mirror. She took out the tiny box inside and handed it to him without speaking. Then she removed Ike's rings and slipped them on the third finger of her right hand. Ike would have understood this, and James had to understand that her first husband had been a precious part of her life and she wasn't about to deny that by disposing of his rings entirely. 'This has been in my roof at home for years until that day in March,' she said quietly. 'Since then I've had it in my handbag just . . . in case.'

'You kept it?' He had opened the box and was staring down at the ring he'd bought her so many years ago, and the look on his face moved her so deeply she could only nod. As he slid the ring onto her finger, Abby decided the special licence would be used the following week. All that mattered was that they were man and wife as soon as possible. Everything else could be sorted out later.

They were busy preparing dinner in James's immaculate kitchen when the boys returned, and had been larking on like a pair of sixteen year olds. Abby's eyes were bright and her cheeks were flushed when she flung open the front door of the flat, and as Henry leaped into her arms, John began to tell James all about the cartoons and pirate film they had seen, without pausing for breath. So it was a moment or two before Abby realised Clara was not with Lucy.

'We bumped into Jed when we came out of the cinema,'

Lucy said by way of explanation, 'and he offered to buy Clara dinner out. She didn't think you'd mind.' Lucy didn't add that she was sure the 'bumping into' had been carefully orchestrated by the two in question.

A dart of anxiety took the smile from Abby's face but she managed to say, 'No, no, of course not.'

A few minutes later Lucy left.

Jed and Clara? As Abby shut the front door, she leaned against it for a moment, hearing the boys' chatter as they regaled James with the wonder of the cinema. But no, she was imagining things surely. Her sister had never said anything to indicate she thought of Jed in a romantic way, but then she had said very little altogether the last few weeks. Clara couldn't understand why Abby hadn't embraced the renewed contact with their family as enthusiastically as she had, and for the first time in their lives their relationship had been somewhat strained.

Abby sought to throw her apprehension off for the rest of the evening. After dinner, she and James sat the boys down and explained very carefully that they were going to get married and all live together in one house. Not the smallholding, Abby said, and not this flat either, but a new house with a big garden for them to play in. They had decided it had to be a fresh start on neutral ground, but this was more for James's benefit than anything else. Abby knew he still found it hard that she had loved Ike, and to ask him to live in the same house she and Ike had shared would not be fair.

The boys stared at them both solemnly. Little Henry didn't really understand what was being said but as always he took his cue from John and realised something momentous was afoot. 'So you'll be our other daddy?' John asked after a moment or two when he had digested the news in his usual thoughtful way.

'If that's all right with you,' James replied quietly.

John nodded. 'I'd like that,' he stated firmly. 'You'll be able to come and see my teacher with Mam and come to the Christmas concert and things like that, won't you, and help me with my cricket practice. Mam's not very good at cricket,' he added with an apologetic glance at Abby.

'It's my favourite game.' James ruffled John's fair hair.

'Where will the new house be?' John asked next. 'Near our home or near here?'

'Well, your mam and I haven't really decided on that yet,' James said evenly, 'but I think near your home would be best, don't you? Then you can still see all your friends at school and Aunty Winnie and everyone, and your mam can work at the nursery when she wants to.'

'James, you don't have to do that,' said Abby quickly.

He smiled. 'Drag you away from Winnie and Rowena and Gladys? I wouldn't dare. It'd be more than my life was worth. Selling up here and setting up somewhere else won't be the end of the world. I might even work from home for a while and see how that goes. To be truthful, money isn't a consideration. I invested my inheritance from Mother and Dad and if I never did another stroke of work we would still be all right.'

Abby stared at him wide-eyed. 'I'm marrying a rich man?'

He grinned. 'A comfortable man, but then it works both ways. I'm marrying a woman of means.'

John had been listening intently to this. Now he made them aware of little flapping ears when he said, 'If we're rich, can I have a bicycle at the new house, Mam?'

'An' me, an' me.' Henry wasn't going to be left out.

'Time to go, I think.' Abby was laughing as she fetched the boys' coats, but in James's car the feeling of apprehension returned more strongly. She needed to see Clara.

At the hotel they said goodbye to James in the reception area as usual. As the lift took Abby up to her family room on the first floor, she prayed Clara would be back. After hurrying the boys through their bath and into their pyjamas, she left them drawing pictures in bed with some new crayons and colouring books she'd brought with her, and popped next door. She knocked on the door of Clara's room but there was no reply.

Once the boys were asleep she checked every half hour, but at half past eleven decided she would have to speak to Clara in the morning and went to bed.

In the morning it was Clara who knocked on Abby's door to go down to breakfast, and Abby immediately noticed that her sister was particularly bright-eyed and bushy-tailed. 'Come in a minute,' Abby said. 'The boys haven't finished dressing yet and I've got some news for you.'

'Nice news?'

By way of reply Abby held out her hand, and the next moment she was engulfed in a bear hug. 'Oh, I'm so glad, Abby! I knew he'd ask you. And Henry and John? Have you told them?'

Abby nodded. 'Henry doesn't really understand what's going on but John thinks it's great so it's all right by Henry.'

'Oh, I could see James had won John over from the first week. Well, it looks like this is a day for celebrating because I've got some news too.' Clara paused for just a second. 'Jed asked me to marry him last night and I accepted.'

For a moment Abby was unable to think. She heard the words but they weren't real.

The expression on Clara's face altered and her voice was stiff when she said, 'Don't be *too* over the moon for me, will you?'

'Clara—'

'I know you don't like him but it's not fair, Abby. Just because you can't stand Uncle Ivor you don't want anything to do with the rest of them, but don't forget Jed and Bruce and Leonard are Aunty Audrey's sons too.'

'But . . . but you can't marry him. He's family.'

'He's my cousin.' Clara's voice had turned hard. 'Cousins marry all the time. We love each other. We knew the second we met again that we loved each other, if you want to know.' Her voice softened as she said, 'Be pleased for me, Abby. I've wanted to tell you so many times but the way you are about all that side of the family I knew we'd have a row. But Jed and I, what we have is special, like you and James.'

'It's not like me and James.' Abby's voice had risen.

'You're the only one with the right to fall in love then?'

She was doing this all wrong. Oh, what could she say? Abby bent her head, her teeth nipping at her lower lip. 'It's not that I dislike Jed,' she said as she looked at Clara again. 'Far from it. And I like Bruce and Leonard too.'

'But not Uncle Ivor.'

Abby didn't reply to this. 'Does he, Uncle Ivor, know about you and Jed?'

'He will do later today when we tell him.'

'But he hasn't known you've been . . . seeing each other?'

Clara frowned. 'You think he'll object? Well, let me tell you, he likes me. He likes you too for that matter although I don't know why when you won't give him the time of day. But no, as it happens, no one knows we've been seeing each other. With you being the way you are we thought it was best not to cause waves, and if we told the others it could have got back to you. I . . . I didn't want to upset you when you'd just found James again, but considering you couldn't care less about my feelings I don't know why

403

I bothered. You've changed, Abby, and not for the better.'

'There's a very good reason why it's impossible for you to marry Jed.' She had to tell her. Right now.

'Mammy, I can't undo Henry's pyjama buttons because he keeps wriggling and saying he wants you to do it.' John appeared round the corner of the large L-shaped room, red-faced and disgruntled at his brother's lack of co-operation.

'How could you say such a thing?' Clara hissed. 'That it's *impossible*,' and she turned and exited the room in a swirl of outrage, banging the door behind her.

'Is Aunty Clara cross? *Mam?* Is Aunty Clara cross?'

'Yes, John. Yes, she is.'

'So am I, with Henry. He's being very naughty and won't get out of bed, and he says he's the king of the castle and I'm the dirty rascal.'

In spite of the awfulness of the situation a glimmer of a smile touched Abby's lips at her son's indignation. John was the most fastidious of little boys and clearly considered this below the belt, which was exactly why Henry, who loved nothing more than getting thoroughly dirty and messy, had said it.

'That *is* naughty,' Abby agreed gently, 'but thank you for trying to help. I'll come and see to Henry right now.'

When they went down to breakfast, Clara was nowhere to be seen, and she did not answer her door when they went upstairs again after breakfast. Abby couldn't eat a thing, her stomach had twisted into a giant knot and her mind was racing. Before she and James had been reunited she'd thought she could never tell anyone about her mother and Ivor and what their affair had led to, but more than once it had been on the tip of her tongue when she and James were alone. Now she knew she had to tell him and ask his advice. This was too huge with too many repercussions not to face it together.

He arrived to pick them up promptly at ten o'clock for the day out on Roker Sands that they'd planned. Fortunately they hadn't mentioned this to the children in case the weather should prove inclement. James's wide grin of welcome and his, 'It's a fine day for it,' changed immediately he saw the expression on her face. 'Abby, are you all right, darling? Whatever's wrong?'

She had wanted to cry when she saw him come smiling towards her but conscious of the boys she bit back the emotion, saying, 'The plans for the day have changed since last night. Can we walk to Mowbray Park so John and Henry can kick a football about while I talk to you?'

'Of course.'

They didn't say much on the way to the park, the four of them walking hand in hand, with the boys between Abby and James. Once the children were playing with the ball, James said, 'Is this anything to do with us?' He lifted up her hand with his engagement ring and kissed her fingers.

'No. Yes.' She shook her head. 'Indirectly, only in as much as it affects Clara, Wilbert and me. James,' she looked into his eyes now, 'you'll find this shocking.'

'I gave up the ability to be shocked years ago, sweetheart. Go ahead.'

She had thought about what she was going to say so now she was able to tell him the whole story quickly and concisely. She kept her gaze on him as she spoke, and although his face was deadpan throughout, Abby felt that in spite of what he'd said, she had shocked him. When she finished she dropped her eyes to their joined hands, her voice small as she said, 'Do you still want to marry me? Knowing I'm – that my mother and father were not married?'

'What do you think?' Careless of onlookers he drew her to him, kissing her hard. 'And I don't want any more of

405

that talk. You're not a stupid woman so don't act like one.'

She bit on her lip. 'I feel I ought to go and see Ivor and tell him what's happened if Jed and Clara haven't already done so. I would have liked to have seen Clara first but she was in such a tear there's no knowing if she'll be back before we have to get the train home. She's going to be broken-hearted on top of finding out about Mam and Ivor. She's absolutely convinced Jed is the love of her life.'

With little stroking movements James rearranged the smooth sheen of her fringe which their embrace had ruffled. 'We'll go in the car. I'm sure there's someone at the hotel who could take care of the bairns for a while.'

'No.' Now she knew what she had to do she felt better. 'I have to do this by myself and I wouldn't want to leave John and Henry with a stranger. If you'll stay here with them, I can go now. You can take them to the museum for a while, they'd love that, and perhaps buy them an ice cream. I'll be as quick as I can but if I'm more than two hours I'll see you back at the flat.'

'Are you sure?' He looked worried.

'Quite sure.'

When Abby reached Rose Street it had the sleepy air she remembered on Sunday mornings. There was the normal quota of bairns playing their games, but quiet games, no kiss chase or mount-a-kitty, not on the Sabbath. She walked straight past number twelve, hoping she wouldn't be noticed, and knocked on Ivor's door. It was a moment or two before she heard footsteps and then the door opened and he stood looking at her. He didn't seem surprised. He stood aside for her to enter the house and this she did, being very careful not to let her body come into contact with his. Right at this moment she hated him and her

406

mother for what their affair was going to do to Clara more than she would have thought possible.

'Has Clara been here this morning?' she said without preamble after turning to face him in the hall.

Ivor said nothing. He passed her and walked through to the kitchen, leaving her no option but to follow him. The kitchen was a shambles; even Audrey, who had not been the most houseproud of women, would have been itching to set it right. 'Well?' Looking straight into Ivor's face she said again, 'Has she been here?'

'Aye, she's been.'

'And?'

'They told me they're going to get wed.'

Don't lose your temper, keep calm. 'And what did you say to that?'

'I wished 'em well and gave me blessing. Clara's a grand lass.'

Abby stared at him. Was he mad? Had her aunt's passing turned his brain? 'You know as well as I do they can't marry. They're not cousins, they are brother and sister.'

'Half brother and sister.'

'In this situation it's the same thing.' She wondered if he realised what they were discussing here and forced herself to say the word which had haunted her all morning. 'It's incest.'

'I don't see it like that.'

'It doesn't matter how you see it, that's what it is.'

'They're just two bairns who think the world of each other.'

'*Stop it!*' Her voice startled even herself and it silenced Ivor. 'They're not bairns,' she went on more quietly. 'They are a man and a woman who intend to marry and have bairns of their own. What might be the result of such a union? You know full well such children can be born

407

damaged. You can't let them go on thinking they are cousins. And what about my mam anyway? Do you think she would keep quiet? Think again. The world and his wife would know the minute after she does, if not to hurt Clara then to get at me.'

'I'll take care of your mam.'

'No one can take care of my mam,' Abby returned bitterly. 'You of all people should know that.'

'It's her word against mine that you three aren't Raymond's.'

'Mud sticks, you know it does. And if all this comes out publicly, you won't be able to lie convincingly, and what about Jed and Clara? It might break their hearts to be told now, but it would be a million times worse in the glare of publicity.'

Ivor slumped onto a kitchen chair. 'I can't tell our Jed, I just can't. Him and me, well, we're all right together, always have been, an' he was close to his mam an' all. If he knows I went with your mam . . . I can't do it, lass. An' he's set his heart on Clara.'

Abby looked at him, long and steadily. 'Then I'll tell them.'

'No.' He wiped his hand across his face. 'Look, no one has to tell 'em. They think they're cousins, same as everyone does apart from you. And what about your Clara – you love her, don't you? Why do you want to tell her something that'll smash her life, eh? And as to their bairns, who says they'll have bairns anyway? An' if they do, ten to one they'll be all right. By, if I had a bob for all the bairns that've been born round these streets who've been fathered in that way I'd be a rich man.'

They were going round in circles here. Abby forced herself to keep her voice calm and reasonable when she said, 'If they had really been cousins I would have been more than happy for Clara to wed Jed, and I'm not saying I don't believe they are really in love. But the facts are the facts. Not only would this thing be illegal, it's . . . unclean.'

'Two youngsters who think the world of each other are unclean?'

'Not them, you know I don't mean them.' Her voice had risen and she fought to keep control. Nothing would be gained by a shouting match. 'You have to tell them and if you won't, I will. They can't marry and that's the end of it. I'm not standing by and seeing Clara's name dragged through the gutter by all and sundry. And it would come to that, I know it.'

Ivor remained silent for a moment and then he said, 'You mean your mam.' It was a statement, and Abby did not dispute it.

Ivor did not look at her now. He sat staring straight ahead, his face pallid. The ticking of the clock on the mantelpiece above the kitchen range seemed to fill the room, and just when Abby couldn't stand it any more and was about to speak, he said, 'I don't want you to say anything, I want to do it. But not the pair of 'em together. I couldn't cope with that. I . . . I want to tell Jed private like, just the two of us. Will you allow me to do that?'

Abby's body relaxed with relief. 'If that's what you want.' He still did not look at her and she waited a moment before she said, 'When will you tell Jed – because it's cruel to let them go on thinking everything is all right.'

'Tonight. I'll tell him tonight. Likely he'll come down to see you tomorrow morning to break the news to Clara. He's . . . he's a good lad. He'll feel he'll want to do that if I know anything about it.'

He rose as he spoke and the two of them appraised each other in silence for a moment. 'I can trust you to do this?'

said Abby, knowing he wouldn't like her doubting him.

If he minded he showed no sign of it, however. 'Aye, lass, you can trust me to sort it,' he said heavily. 'An' for what it's worth I think you're right about your mam. She wouldn't keep quiet. If ever there was a she-devil walking this earth, it's that woman.'

And yet he had fathered three children by her while being married to a woman who was worth her weight in gold. The words hovered on Abby's lips but she did not say them. Somehow the situation had gone beyond such retorts. She hesitated for a second, then she said, 'I'll be going then.'

'Aye, lass, you get along. I dare say that young man and the bairns are waiting for you.'

She turned and walked to the front door without saying anything more but she was conscious of Ivor following her. After opening the door and stepping down into the street, she turned, her voice flat as she said, 'Goodbye then.'

'I'm sorry, lass. For all of it I'm heart sorry. It don't mean nowt now but I'd give me two legs an' two arms if it would turn back the clock.' He waited for her to say something and when she continued to stare at him, he said gruffly, 'You go then and, like I said, I'll sort it.'

Abby nodded. If it wasn't for the fact that another two lives were going to be ruined by this man she would have found it in her heart at that moment to speak kindly to him. He seemed so lost, pathetic. But Clara was going to receive a blow she might never fully recover from and all because of his weakness. His weakness and her mother's wickedness. 'Goodbye,' she said again, and turned and walked away.

Chapter Twenty-nine

When Ivor re-entered the kitchen he stood for a moment looking about him with the air of a man who was confused, but in fact this was not the case. For the first time since his wife's death his brain was working clearly and without the befuddlement of self-pity and grief, but the thoughts filling it were of such magnitude he wasn't conscious of his surroundings.

He stood where he was for a good ten minutes. Then with a long-drawn-out 'Ahhh' of a sigh he sat down. There were some hours to go and he couldn't rush this. The timing had to be perfect. But that was all right, he had it all sorted in his head now.

He hadn't mentioned to Abby that Jed and Clara had told him they were going out for the day and that Jed was going to drive her home rather than Clara catching the train with her sister. Clara was going to leave a message at the hotel for Abby, and it would make no difference to Abby that Jed would be back here late tonight. She would assume he'd tell Jed then. But he had no intention of telling Jed anything.

He reached for the cup of tea he'd just made for himself when he'd heard the knock at the door and drank it down although it was stone cold. He'd known she'd come. He replaced the cup on its saucer and relaxed back in the chair. Aye, he'd known she'd be in a two and eight about her sister. Abby loved her, that was the thing, which was how sisters were supposed to feel about each other. He glanced towards the wall which divided number twelve and number fourteen, and as though he could see Nora in front of him his eyes narrowed with loathing. He wouldn't let that fiend destroy any more lives. He loved his lad, and if Jed wanted Clara he would have her. With that one taken out of the way, Abby wouldn't say anything, he was sure of it. She loved Clara, she'd want her to be happy.

He cooked himself egg, bacon and tomatoes for his Sunday dinner, ignoring the piece of topside he'd bought for himself and Jed the day before. Egg, bacon and tomatoes was his favourite meal and today he wanted to enjoy it. It would be the last food he would ever taste so it might as well be something to set his taste buds going. In the old days Audrey used to cook it for him after steeping the tomatoes in sugar and that had been right handsome. He didn't let his mind dwell on his wife; the loss of her was still so crucifyingly painful it would sap his energy. Instead he turned the wireless on, listening to *Two-Way Family Favourites*, a programme where families at home kept in touch with servicemen and women abroad by way of record requests. Later in the afternoon there was *Life of Bliss* with George Cole, and he made a fresh pot of tea and opened a packet of chocolate digestives for this.

When the programme had finished he rose from where he'd been sitting with his feet up on another chair and walked through to the front room. Opening what Audrey had grandly called 'the cocktail cabinet' when she'd had the room done up, he extracted a bottle of good whisky. This had been a present from Len and his family at Christmas but he hadn't touched it. With this in his hand he mounted the stairs to his bedroom where his sleeping tablets sat on the cabinet by the bed.

Downstairs again, he placed the whisky and bottle of

tablets on the kitchen table before fetching a bowl and Audrey's rolling pin from the cupboard. The bottle of tablets was full, as luck would have it; he'd only fetched a new prescription Friday morning. He emptied all the tablets into the bowl and then proceeded to grind them to a fine powder with the rolling pin. It didn't take long but he continued for some minutes just to make sure no tiny lumps remained. When he was satisfied with the texture, he fetched the big poppy-patterned water jug from the dresser and emptied the whisky and powdered tablets into it. It took some time to make sure no remnants of the fine powder floated but eventually it was done.

He tipped most of the liquid back into the bottle, leaving just enough to fill one of the two small glasses he fetched from the dresser. He washed the bowl, rolling pin and jug and put them away, and then found some writing paper and a pencil. The note was brief and to the point.

We've both had enough in our own ways and decided this was a comfortable way out once we'd made our peace with each other. Don't grieve because this is what we wanted. Be happy, bairns, and live life to the full.

He did not sign it.

Ivor sat staring at the writing for a while before rising from the table and walking through to the front room. He propped the note beside the clock where it would be seen immediately by anyone entering the room. It was done. He expelled his breath through his nose. Now all he had to do was persuade Nora to come and have a drink with him once Wilbert and Lucy had left for six o'clock Mass.

He stood behind the net curtains in the front room as the minutes ticked by, and when Lucy and Wilbert's front door opened and they stepped out onto the pavement, he heaved a sigh of relief. Lucy never missed Mass on a Sunday evening but he'd been worried this one Sunday might be an exception, and it was essential they weren't around. He knew they had fought tooth and nail to keep Nora off the drink as much as they could the last few years; they wouldn't have appreciated him calling round with a bottle of the hard stuff.

He waited another two minutes and then walked through the house to the backyard with the bottle of whisky in his hand. When he knocked on Wilbert's back door he thought for a minute Nora wasn't going to move her backside and come to see who it was, but eventually he heard her shambling footsteps and then the door was opened. 'Hello, Nora.' Her mouth fell open for a moment, showing the brown teeth in the receding gums. He hadn't stared her in the face since the day of Audrey's funeral and then he had thought she looked like an old, old woman. Now, with her hair unkempt and wearing a stained cardigan, she didn't look as though she'd changed for a week, she looked worse.

'They're out so you can sling your hook.'

She'd recovered quickly but that was Nora. 'Aye, I thought they might be. That's why I popped round with this.' He held up the bottle which he'd been holding behind his back. 'Fancy a glass or two?'

'*You're* asking *me*?' The hard eyes narrowed. 'What's your game?'

He had expected this and decided she wouldn't accept he'd had a massive change of heart. His voice flat, he said, 'I don't want to drink alone and you're better than no company at all. Jed's out like he is most of the time now, ungrateful so an' so. You bring 'em up and sacrifice your own life and what do you get? Sweet nowt, that's what.'

414

'Feelin' sorry for yourself, are you? 'Bout time you got a shot of your own medicine.'

He couldn't appear too eager or she'd smell a rat. 'Oh well, if that's how you feel I'll drink alone.' He had seen the way her eyes had fastened greedily on the bottle in his hand.

He made to turn and had actually stepped away from the door when she said, 'No need to be like that,' and as he watched, her tongue came out and licked her bottom lip. 'Wilbert and her don't keep any drink in the house. Mean as muck, the pair of 'em.'

He shrugged. 'It's been all that's kept me going the last months.' He wondered if she would believe the lie. She might be feeble in her body but her brain was as sharp as it had ever been, from what he could make out. The drink hadn't made any difference there.

It was clear she did believe it. He saw her glance back into the house and now her voice held a touch of conspiracy as she said, her gaze on the bottle, 'They always come straight back after church so if you're coming in you'd better get a move on.'

He stepped into the kitchen. Then he forced a slightly uneasy note into his voice. 'You say they don't keep no drink in the house? Look, I don't want to get on the wrong side of Wilbert. How about you come round to mine and we'll have a drink there? They can't object to that. A man's allowed to have a drop in his own house. When they come back you can nip out and say you just had the one with me.'

Nora looked at him. A leopard doesn't change its spots, she thought, and asked herself the reason for this sudden visit. She had no illusions that any spark of feeling for her remained in Ivor unless it was dislike, and for him she felt resentment and deep bitterness. He had used her and then treated her worse than any dockside dolly, she told herself, and never so much as a word of remorse, but the bottle was full and a right good make. Quality stuff. And she hadn't had a drop in weeks. Likely it was what he'd said, he didn't want to drink alone, the big galoot. Weak as dishwater, he was, always had been. And to think she'd let him walk all over her. Still, she wouldn't cut off her nose to spite her face. Decision made, she said, 'I'll come round for half an hour, no longer. Then I can be here for when they get back and no one's the wiser.'

'Whatever.' Ivor kept his voice offhand as though he didn't care much one way or the other. He turned and made his way back to his own house, and Nora followed.

In the kitchen he watched as she looked about her before plonking herself down at the kitchen table and glancing at the two glasses. 'Sure of yourself, weren't you?' she said, and then, 'How many have you had before you came round to me?'

'A few.' Ivor picked up the glass with the whisky in it and swallowed it, before refilling both to the brim and passing one to her. 'Funny after all that's happened that we should be sitting here like this,' he said quietly, switching on the wireless.

Nora gulped at the whisky as though it was water, and when she put the glass down again it was empty. She smacked her lips. 'Funny aftertaste, isn't there?' she said. 'How long have you had it opened?'

'Nowt wrong with it as far as I can tell.' He picked the bottle up as though to examine the label. 'Good stuff, this is, and that's probably the trouble. You're likely used to rubbish. Still, if you don't want a refill . . .'

'I didn't say that.' She pushed her glass towards him. She took another deep drink when he had filled the glass and then relaxed back in her chair with a sigh. 'By, I

416

needed that. Treat me like a bairn, them two next door, and her, she wouldn't give you the drips off her nose.'

'Lucy? I thought she seemed a nice enough lass.'

'Well, you would, wouldn't you? You're a man. Oh, she knows how to turn on the charm all right but I live with her. She's turned Wilbert against me and it was her who made the house dry. I know, I know. "It's bad for you, Mam".' The mimicry was savage. '"Think of your liver". Me liver. Who the hell cares about their liver when they get to our age, eh? You answer me that.' Again the glass was emptied and when Ivor silently refilled it Nora did not object.

'Never misses Mass of a Sunday,' Nora went on, as though Lucy's attendance at the church was a crime, 'an' Father Finlay thinks the sun shines out of her backside. Fooled him good and proper, she has. He's not the man I thought he was.'

Ivor let her talk and as he listened to the list of complaints and grudges he caught a glimpse of Lucy's life over the last years. Poor little lass, he thought. She won't mourn this one's passing, that's for sure. There were them who had a good word for no one and then there was Nora in a class apart. He must have been stark staring mad all those years ago but then he hadn't been thinking with his head in those days. All his reasoning had come from a lower part of his anatomy altogether. If he agreed with Nora on one thing it was that all men were fools.

When her speech became slurred the venom slowed down, and when Ivor got up and switched off the wireless, she lifted her head to stare at him out of bleary eyes. 'Hey, I was listening to that.' She tried to rise, presumably to turn the wireless on again, but fell back in her chair with a thud. 'I always listen to the Palm Court Orchestra from the Grand on a Sunday.'

417

Should he tell her she was dead? She was still breathing but that was the last music she would ever hear in this world and he doubted there'd be much melody where she was going. But as he stared at the woman who had cursed his life he found the need to have the final word had left him. He was taking her life and his own, he was going to have enough to answer to God for. He would let her die peaceably.

The bottle was almost empty now and as he tipped the last of it into the two glasses, a few particles of white powder floated to the surface. He found he didn't have the energy to lift the glass to his lips, however. Nora's head was resting on her arms on the table now, and as she mumbled something about taking a little nap, he closed his own eyes. Who would have thought all those years ago when he first sported with her that it would come to this? he mused groggily. She had been beautiful then. A witch under the skin, but a beautiful one.

And so at the end his final conscious thought was not of the wife he had loved and adored, or even the children he imagined he was protecting, but of Nora.

Chapter Thirty

It was late on Monday evening when Jed arrived at the house in Yorkshire. Because she'd been expecting his visit Abby had made sure John and Henry were in bed and asleep early. When the knock came at the door, only she and Clara were still up, but within the first few moments Abby was disabused of the idea that Jed had come to say he and Clara couldn't wed. Instead the young man broke down, blurting out in the hall that his father and their mother were dead.

They helped Jed into the sitting room where, sobbing, he told them Ivor and Nora had taken their own lives with an overdose of barbiturates and whisky. They had left a note to the effect that life wasn't worth living for either of them. This was now in the hands of the police but there was no doubt about what they had chosen to do. His da had never really got over his mam going, that was the thing, and Wilbert and Lucy were now blaming themselves, believing that because they had withheld the drink from Nora she had decided to end it along with her brother-in-law.

Through the whirling maelstrom of Abby's thoughts, one dominated. Her mother would never, *never* have killed herself. She knew this as sure as night follows day. While she helped Jed off with his coat and then fetched him a brandy she couldn't think beyond this, but after a minute or two her mind accepted what Ivor had done. Even as she asked the right questions – who had found them? What exactly had the note said? Had the rest of the family been informed? – her mind was working on a different level entirely. Ivor was telling her as distinctly as though he was standing in front of her now that he believed he'd removed the threat to Clara and Jed getting married. He had doctored the whisky and somehow, probably through her mother's enslavement to the alcohol, had persuaded her to drink with him. Rather than face telling his son the truth, Ivor had killed himself and taken her mother with him.

'Both of them, Clara.' Jed had managed to pull himself together but his voice was choked. 'I can't believe Mam and Da have gone within months of each other. I should have known how Da was feeling, I should have done something.'

'There was nothing you could do.' Clara had her arms round him and her own face was wet. 'He was a grown man, darling, and if he'd made up his mind he wanted to be with your mam, you couldn't have stopped him. Sooner or later he would have found a way.'

Dear God, dear God, help me. Abby was silently praying and she hadn't done that in years. They still don't know the truth. What do I do now? Do I have to tell them? She was the only one left who knew the truth besides James, and he'd never tell if she told him not to. The Bible said it was a sin but that was only if the people concerned knew, wasn't it? The sin would be on her shoulders, not theirs, and she could live with that if it meant Clara being happy and Jed not losing the third person in his life who meant the world to him.

But what about their bairns? Her stomach turned over. What if she kept quiet and a child was born who was handicapped in some way? It happened in these cases sometimes.

420

But not always, the argument in her mind went on. Often the children of such unions were perfectly whole and healthy.

But was it fair to let Jed go on thinking there was something he should have noticed which would have prevented his father's death, or to let Wilbert and Lucy blame themselves for her mother's demise?

When Jed broke down once more and Clara turned to her for help with an anguished look on her face, Abby moved to kneel in front of the pair who were sitting closely together on the sofa. She didn't know if she believed in Father Finlay's Catholic God of her childhood and youth, but somehow she felt her prayers had been answered. Their union could affect both their own children and possibly those of their grandchildren, and she didn't have the right to keep such knowledge from them, however much it might wound. She had to speak.

'I have something to tell you both,' she said quietly, her voice trembling a little. 'And, Clara,' she reached out and touched her sister's hand for a moment, 'try not to hate me because I kept it from you. I thought I was doing the right thing and never in a hundred years did I imagine you would fall in love with Jed, and he with you.'

Both young faces were staring at her now and for a second she experienced the pain their separation was going to mean to each of them. She couldn't do it, she couldn't tell them. And then she heard herself saying, 'It's to do with your father, Jed, and our mother.'

'You know something about why they did this?' Jed asked shakily.

She didn't answer this directly, saying instead to Clara, 'Some years ago Mam told me she'd had an affair with Ivor when Donald, Leonard and Bruce were little.' And at Jed's exclamation of disbelief, she added gently, 'I asked him about it and he confirmed it was true. Our mother instigated it and she kept it going. I think he never really wanted her. He did love your mam, Jed, always.'

'No, no, it's not true.' Jed had shot to his feet, his eyes blazing. 'My da wouldn't do that to my mam.'

'I'm sorry. Truly I am, but it's true.'

'Why are you saying this now?' Clara rose to her feet, holding on to Jed's arm. 'Even if it is true, how can you be so cruel when Uncle Ivor's just died?'

'Our da couldn't father his own bairns, Clara.'

'What?' Clara stared at her and it was clear she didn't understand. 'What on earth are you on about? We're here, you, me and Wilbert, aren't we?'

'Aye, we are, but not through Da.'

Clara still couldn't fathom what she meant but Jed's strangled, 'No,' told Abby he understood only too well.

Clara glanced from one to the other. She looked as perplexed as she sounded when she said to Jed, 'What's the ma—' And then she clutched her throat, looking dazedly at Abby. 'You don't – you can't mean . . .'

'Ivor knew Mam would never keep quiet if she thought you and Jed had fallen in love, and I agree with him. She wouldn't have. I think he decided to take her out of the equation for good.'

'No, it's not true. You've never liked Uncle Ivor and now to say this! It's wicked. *You're* wicked, as bad as Mam. Jed,' Clara clutched hold of him again, 'you don't believe her, tell me you don't believe her.'

Abby looked levelly at her sister, pity and understanding in her gaze, before she said softly, 'If I could have made it different I would have but I couldn't keep it from you, not now.'

Jed sat down, closing his eyes and easing himself further back into the sofa as he murmured, 'I'm going mad. That's the only answer to all of this. Things like this don't happen to ordinary people like us.' And then, his head falling into his hands, he said bitterly, 'If they weren't already dead I'd kill the pair of them, I swear it.'

Clara flung herself onto him, crying uncontrollably. 'You can't believe it, Jed. You can't. We're cousins, just cousins.' And when he didn't answer her, merely continuing to sit as though he'd been turned to stone, she gasped, 'I don't care if it is true anyway. We think of ourselves as cousins and that's all that matters. We can't let anything part us.'

Abby took herself out of the room at this point, her head bowed. She went straight to her bedroom where she sat on the edge of the bed, her knees and feet together and her hands clasped in her lap as though she was listening to a sermon in church. She hoped she'd done the right thing. She shut her eyes very tightly. Clara and Jed were suffering for something that had happened years and years ago, something that wasn't their fault. But they *were* brother and sister. Something outside herself hammered the point home. And in the end it all boiled down to the fact that she simply didn't have the right to keep it from them. Or from Wilbert, come to that. He'd have to be told now too.

She rose to her feet and began to pace the room. What a mess, what a terrible muddle of a mess. She felt like Jed. If her mother and Ivor hadn't already been dead she would have wanted to kill them. Even from the grave her mother's power went on; she was still casting a shadow over their lives, perhaps more in death than she ever had done in life. Nevertheless Abby was glad she was dead. At this moment she did so hope there was a hell and that her mother was in it.

She kept her thoughts in this vein for some time because

what she couldn't admit, even to herself, was the pain of thirty-four years of knowing that the one person who was supposed to love you best in all the world had always disliked her.

Two hours later there was a knock on her bedroom door. Abby was in bed but far from asleep. Her heart was racing when she walked across the room, wondering if Clara was going to go for her again. But when she opened the door Clara lifted her head and said, 'I'm sorry, Abby. I'm so, so sorry for what I said to you.' Abby opened her arms and her sister fell against her chest, beginning to cry.

'It's all right, it's all right.' But it wasn't all right. It never could be because Clara and Jed would always be brother and sister.

Clara moved her head to speak. 'I should never have said those things to you. And to say you're like Mam! I'm sorry, I didn't mean it.'

'I know you didn't, and I've been stupid, Clara. I should have told you about Ivor and Mam years ago and then that would have prevented all this.'

'It wouldn't.' There was a break in Clara's voice. 'We've agreed we've always loved each other when we look back, right from bairns. I can't do without him, Abby, and he can't do without me. And I'm not going to let our mam take him away from me. We don't care about anything else but being together. We're going away, far away. Abroad. We'll make a new life there. Legally we're cousins and that's all anyone will ever know.'

'Clara, you haven't thought this through.' She tried to stop the shock from sounding in her voice.

'We have.' Clara looked at her, her eyes seeming to spread and encompass her delicate features. 'And nothing is going to stop us, Abby. None of this is our fault.'

'I know that, darling.'

'I don't regret falling in love with him, not even now.'

Abby swallowed hard. How did she put this without it seeming harsh? 'You . . . you understand about the repercussions? With starting a family?'

'Jed is enough for me and I'm enough for him.'

'Now maybe,' Abby said. 'But loving each other as you do, it's the most natural thing in the world to want bairns.'

'Natural?' Clara gave a croak of a laugh. 'There's not much natural in our family.'

'Don't, darling.' Abby held her tighter. 'Don't torment yourself.'

'But it's true.' Clara drew away slightly, looking at her with eyes bright with tears. 'I hate Mam, and him – Ivor. Did Da know? And Aunty Audrey?'

'I don't think Da knew about any of it. Aunty Audrey knew about the affair but not about . . . us.'

'And she killed him, Abby.' It was the first time they had spoken of it. 'Mam did all that and then she killed him. It should have been the other way round.'

'Clara, you must take time to think about this.'

As though she had said something shocking, Clara jerked away. 'I can't do without him,' she said tonelessly. 'I mean it, Abby. If I can't be with him I'd rather be dead.'

There was a trembling sensation now in Abby's stomach. Her mother had been besotted with Ivor and the result had been devastation. Pray God history wouldn't repeat itself with Clara. But then look at her with James. Much as she had loved Ike – and she had loved him – the feeling she'd had for him couldn't compare with the overwhelming intensity of what she felt for James. Had something been passed on through the genes? Did the women of their family love obsessionally, without rhyme or reason?

No, she wouldn't accept that for herself or for Clara.

Clara believed she'd fallen in love with her cousin, and her own love for James was a healthy thing. Her mother's relationship with Ivor had been quite different. She tried one last time to convince her sister to wait. 'Don't make any immediate decisions now, not when no one knows anything.'

'Have you told James?' And then, when Abby didn't immediately reply, Clara said, 'But of course you've told him. I would have told Jed if the boot had been on the other foot.'

Abby looked into the great sad eyes and her heart felt as if it was breaking. Clara stared back at her, holding her gaze. 'Don't take on, Abby. What's done is done. I want him and he wants me and nothing in the world can change that. Jed's always had a hankering to travel a bit and I wouldn't mind seeing new parts of the world. Every cloud has a silver lining.'

'Will you wait and come to our wedding next week before you go?' Abby asked quietly.

'Of course. It'll take time to sort out all the necessary travel documents and things anyway. We . . . we shan't marry in England though. Neither of us could face a family do. Jed wants me to go back with him so we can see Wilbert and Lucy face to face and put their minds at rest that they had nothing to do with Mam's going. We'll tell them it all but there's no reason for Leonard and Bruce to know anything. I'll come back before the wedding but I'm taking some of my things now.' She raised her head, a touch of the old feisty Clara in her voice as she said, 'I shall stay with Jed and if anyone says anything I'll tell them to mind their own business.'

This last was for her as much as anyone, Abby thought wryly. She wanted Clara to be happy but not this way. Jed was their brother and these things didn't ought to be. But they were two adults and their birth certificates gave them

426

every right to marry. She nodded. 'I won't come down again but tell Jed to drive carefully,' she said shakily. 'You both must be exhausted.' She was losing her; she was losing her but she had to let her go.

They clung to each other for a second and then Clara left, closing the door behind her.

Chapter Thirty-one

It was eight days later and the morning of Abby's wedding. Clara hadn't returned to the house like she'd said she would, and when Abby and James went to 14 Rose Street at the weekend, no one came to the door. They called in on Wilbert and Lucy who said they hadn't seen anything of Clara and Jed since the night they'd called to tell them about Ivor and Nora. It was clear to Abby that Wilbert was confused and upset, both by the sudden knowledge forced upon him about his paternity and by the decision Clara and Jed had made to be together. Abby couldn't blame him for feeling like this, but when Lucy whispered that Wilbert had refused to kiss Clara when she left, Abby was deeply saddened.

Because of the circumstances, Abby and James had decided to marry very quietly at the local register office, with just the children and her three friends present. Mario was staying behind to take care of little Enrico and any customers, and Joy had kindly offered to help him. They had discussed the matter of James's divorce with the priest from the local church and he had been very understanding. Although unable to marry them, he had privately expressed the view that he felt the Church's teaching would have to change to keep pace with the modern world, and that he wished them every blessing.

Abby's worry about Clara and Jed meant she hadn't even thought about a wedding dress, deciding to wear one of her newest frocks instead, but when the household were having breakfast – Abby and the children having joined the others – Winnie and Rowena presented her with several boxes.

The first held a perfectly beautiful pale peach dress and jacket, the second an exquisite little hat complete with a veil of fine netting, and the third a pair of court shoes in cream suede and a bag to match the shoes. Henry and John hadn't been forgotten either. Two small crisp white shirts with little bow ties and two pairs of smart black trousers were produced for the children.

Abby was overcome and burst into tears which promptly set the other three women off. Mario hastily muttered something about one of the greenhouses needing attention and disappeared, Henry and John trotting after him. They liked nothing more than pottering about with their little trowels and spades with Mario, but whereas John always returned as spick and span as when he went, Henry managed to cover himself in dirt.

Winnie, aiming to comfort but in fact making things worse in her own inimitable way, launched into an attack on Clara. 'I don't hold with what she's done and I shall tell her straight when I see her,' she announced, her face red with concern for Abby. 'I'm heart sorry for Jed about his da of course, an' your mam,' she added as an after-thought, 'but it still don't make it right that they haven't been in touch. It's all this talk about teenagers and such, that's what's started the young people of today thinking they're different to the rest of us. Teenagers! A new word to excuse all sorts of goings-on which wouldn't have been allowed in our day.'

Rowena, in her own, equally inimitable style, said, 'I think I sense a slight case of the pot calling the kettle black here.'

Winnie ignored this. 'And these Teddy boys, what's that all about?' she went on. 'They look ridiculous if you ask me, with their drainpipes and brothel creepers. Why can't they just call them trousers and shoes, and get clothes that look as though they fit? And do you know what they call that stupid hairstyle they've all got nowadays?'

'A duck's arse?' supplied Rowena in her upper-crust accent.

'Exactly. I mean it's not a respectable way of going on, is it?' Winnie cast a sidelong glance at Joy who was listening to the conversation with some interest. Winnie's daughter had recently discovered pop music and with the first of the weekly Top Ten charts being published at the beginning of the year, Joy and all her friends were quickly becoming besotted. Abby knew Winnie was worried to death. Joy was now twelve years old and showing all the signs of becoming a beauty.

'Jed's quiff is just a small one,' Abby protested mildly as she wiped her eyes and blew her nose. She had explained her sister's sudden departure by saying Clara had decided to go and keep Jed company for a few days, him being so distraught about his father doing away with himself because he couldn't cope without his wife. She knew the others had been a little shocked to hear that Clara was staying with Jed in the house alone, which was pretty funny, Abby thought, considering both her friends had been free with their favours in their youth.

'If Clara and Jed do turn up at any point I don't want you laying into them, Winnie,' she said. 'Now promise me.' Not that she thought there was any chance of seeing either of them. The most she could expect was a letter from some far-flung place in due course, she told herself, ignoring the ache in her heart at her sister's precipitous exit from her life.

430

'Aye, I promise, lass, course I do.' Winnie scrubbed at her face with a red flannel handkerchief which had seen better days. 'You know me. All wind and water.'

'You never are.' They exchanged a glance which had years of tried and tested friendship as its foundation, before Abby said, forcing a bright note into her voice, 'Gladys, I think I could eat another couple of rashers of bacon if there's any going,' which prompted one or two ribald remarks from Winnie and Rowena along the lines of keeping her strength up for the night ahead. Joy looked askance at the pair of them.

Rowena drove the little wedding party into town. Abby joined in the banter which went on but all the time she was thinking of Clara. She had left messages all over the place for her sister saying what time the wedding was, but if Clara didn't contact Wilbert – which was highly likely after the way they'd parted – or Jed's brothers, or return to Rose Street to find the note she'd pushed through Ivor's letterbox, she wouldn't know.

She wanted to see Clara so much. It had touched her greatly when she'd gone into Clara's room after her sister had left and found that along with a few essentials, Clara had taken Milly. Clara might be twenty-two but she was still her baby sister. She needed to know Clara and Jed were all right, that they hadn't done anything silly . . . And then she brushed the thought aside as she forced herself to do a hundred times a day. They were young, they had their whole future in front of them. They wouldn't take their own lives, not Clara and Jed.

Henry was sitting on her lap and John was cuddled close into her side, both the boys awed by the occasion and their new clothes. Abby pressed her children to her, needing the reassurance.

James and herself and the two boys were going to a hotel in Bournemouth for two weeks after the wedding lunch he had organised for the small wedding party, and while the thought of becoming Mrs Benson at last was so poignant no words could express it, she still couldn't help aching to see Clara.

By the time they drew up outside the town hall she'd prepared herself to expect nothing, so when John said animatedly, 'I can see Aunty Clara and Uncle Jed with James, Mammy. Are they coming to the wedding too?' Abby couldn't take it in for a moment.

'Praise God for that.' Gladys's heartfelt words were echoed in Abby's own heart as she saw the young couple standing either side of James who had a big smile on his face.

James engulfed her in a bear hug and whispered in her ear, 'They arrived a few minutes ago. They've been staying in a hotel in Gateshead. I don't think either of them could face remaining in the house where it happened but Jed went to see his brothers a couple of days ago to find out when we were getting married.'

After kissing her hard on the lips he let her go and then Clara was in front of her, smiling faintly. Abby gathered her sister into her embrace in much the same way she would have done John and Henry, and they clung to each other for a moment, half laughing, half crying.

'You look bonny,' Clara murmured when they drew apart. 'So bonny. Here, I've brought you this instead of a wedding present for the two of you. You've got everything you need between you anyway, in more ways than one.' She pressed a small box into Abby's hand.

Abby opened the box and stared down at the gold locket it held. She couldn't speak.

'Here, open it,' Clara said and clicked open the tiny catch to display two miniature paintings, one of Abby and one of Clara. 'I had yours done from a photograph I took with me,' Clara said softly. 'This is so you don't forget about me.'

Again they were hugging, and then Abby said, 'I want to wear it now. Put it on for me,' and as she felt her sister's hands gently fasten the locket at the back of her neck, it was with equal pain and joy.

It was done, they were man and wife, and outside the town hall the wedding party made up for the lack of numbers by positively deluging the bridal pair in confetti and rice, while Henry screamed with excitement and jumped up and down which added to the general furore.

When James had put the gold band on her finger a stillness had taken possession of Abby's body for a few moments, a stillness born of a feeling almost too wonderful to contain. She was his wife. She had loved this man for nearly half her life and now at last she was his wife. They had come through all the twists and turns, all the devious routes life had led them along, and they had found each other again. They had been given a second chance.

When they had finished the meal at the hotel and Winnie, Rowena and Gladys had already left for home, Clara said softly, 'Abby, I have to tell you something.'

She wasn't going to like this. Immediately Abby looked into her sister's face she knew what Clara was going to say, but still she said, 'What is it?'

'We're leaving – leaving England, I mean. We . . . we're going tomorrow. We sail at six in the evening from Southampton.'

'Where to?' Let it not be too far away.

'Australia. Jed knows a family who moved out there years ago. They had some sort of assisted passage and now they're doing really well.'

To hear her fear put into plain words was hard. Abby's gaze moved from Clara's face to Jed's, and it was to him she said, 'Are you sure you'll be all right? You've thought everything through properly?'

'Don't worry.' Jed's voice was soothing. 'I'll look after her.'

He looked years older than the fresh-faced boy of a couple of weeks ago, the strain of the last days showing in his tired eyes. Abby's heart was flooded with pity and her voice was too emphatic when she said, 'I know you will. Of course I know that.'

An embarrassed silence fell on the four of them and it was a relief when Henry came rushing up, shrieking and laughing, with John right behind him. John had taken his younger brother to the cloakroom, and now he said to Abby, 'Tell him, Mam! Tell him he's naughty. He ran away from me again.'

After James had settled the bill for the meal and drinks, and Abby had had a word with him, she said to Clara, 'Would you mind if we came to see you off? You don't have to say yes and we'll under—'

Clara's hug cut off her words. 'We'd love it but with you supposed to be on honeymoon we didn't like to ask.'

'We'll alter things round a little.'

'Thank you. I can't tell you what it will mean to have you there.'

And then Clara's eyes lost their sadness for a moment as Henry came bounding up to her, calling, 'Huggy buggy, Aunty Clara! Huggy buggy!'

It was a pet saying between the two of them and Clara whisked Henry up into her arms, hugging him tight for a moment. 'I really need a huggy buggy right now, Henry. How did you guess?'

Plump little arms were tight round Clara's neck and

over the top of Henry's curly head, Abby saw her sister close her eyes. The look on Clara's face said everything, and Abby felt a pang of deep concern. They would have children, Clara and Jed. Clara's need to be a mother would override any anxiety about the possible consequences. Pray God things would turn out all right.

The next day she stood with James and the children on the quay at Southampton. Their wedding night had been everything she had known it would be, and such had been their pleasure in each other that they hadn't settled down for sleep until the early hours, curled up in each other's arms. Abby had fallen asleep immediately. She hadn't expected to, knowing the next day she was saying goodbye to Clara and it could be years before she saw her sister again. James had already said a trip to Australia some time in the future was not out of the question, but it wasn't the same as having Clara close, or even a train ride away.

Clara and Jed had been waiting for them when they reached the quay. At the last moment Clara clung to Abby, tears washing her face. 'You don't hate me for what we're doing, do you? You don't think I'm . . . dirty?'

'Oh, Clara, Clara.' Abby held her arms, looking deep into the sad little face. 'I love you all the world, you must know that. Nothing you could do or say would make me love you any the less. And of course you're not dirty. Put that thought out of your mind.' And she had pressed her sister fiercely to her. It wasn't right what Clara and Jed were doing but as God was her witness, she couldn't condemn them.

'Do you think everything will work out for them?' she asked James now, as they waved to the two tiny figures among the throng on the top deck of the huge liner.

'Of course it will, she's your sister,' James said quietly.

'You've brought her up, you encouraged the steel in her backbone to form when your mother would have crushed it out of her. She's her own person today because you made it possible and you've got to accept that, right or wrong, she'll forge her own destiny, lass. You have to let her go, like you'll have to let John and Henry go and, God willing, the bairns we have together.'

'You make it sound so simple.'

'It is.' He put his arm round her, drawing her into his side. 'Simple but hard to do. You gave her everything it was in your power to give and now she's a grown woman who has to take responsibility for her own actions.'

'I'm frightened for her.' She looked up at him for a moment. 'I've got this feeling . . .'

'That's your own anxiety.' He put his hands on her shoulders and made her face him. 'That's all it is, Abby. No one knows the future.'

'I feel my mam's spirit will still strive to mar her life.'

'That's because you're tired.' He stroked her hair gently. 'Emotionally drained. Your mother has no power over any of you any more. She's gone, Abby.'

'Yes, yes, you're right.' She turned from him and looked towards the ship again, drawing in a long, shuddering breath. 'She's gone and we're still here, living, breathing, loving.'

He saw her straighten as though she had thrown a weight off her shoulders and when she glanced at him again she was smiling. 'My husband is a very wise man,' she said, the lilt of laughter in her voice.

'And my wife has a very big heart.'

'I love you.'

'And I love you.'

She would see Clara again. As the massive liner began to move, tears blinded her eyes but her heart was at peace for the first time in weeks. And whatever this new life held for her sister, Clara would stand up to it because that was the way she was made.

They stood there with the two children who were mesmerised by the huge ship until almost everyone else had gone, and then Abby wiped her eyes with the handkerchief James silently gave her and sniffed hard.

'I'm ready to go now,' she said, reaching up and kissing the corner of his mouth. And then the four of them walked away.